Eden's Gate

Angels of the Ages: Book II

Eden's Gate

Angels of the Ages: Book II

Wilma Styles

Grateful Steps
Asheville, North Carolina

Grateful Steps Foundation
Crest Mountain
30 Ben Lippen School Road #107
Asheville, North Carolina 28806

Styles, Wilma

ISBN 978-1-945714-59-7 Paperback
ISBN 978-1-945714-62-7 Ebook

FIRST EDITION

www.gratefulsteps.org

TO MY HARRIS FAMILY. DADDY AND MAMA, JIM
AND WILLIE HARRIS. MY BROTHERS, HAROLD
(JIM), KENNETH, ROY AND DOUG HARRIS.
MY SISTERS, MARGARET, HUNNICUTT, PEGGY
GREGG, SHIRLEY GOUGE AND
BRENDA RODGERS.

Preface

I wrote the *Angels of the Ages* trilogy because of my own search to find God. I went through in my own life many of the things I have penned in the trilogy. The endless war between good and evil I faced daily. The constant challenge of not being sure about what was right or what was wrong kept my mind in chaos. I was in my early 20s when I became serious about wanting God in my life. Desperation pulled me to that place. I urgently needed a sense of balance.

I had heard numerous depictions of God and how to serve Him. I couldn't make up my mind if I believed any of the scenarios presented to me. I prayed God would guide me to the Truth. I learned early in my quest not to believe everything I heard. Therefore, I put my life before God and prayed that He would guide me in my pursuit to know Him. After eight years of prayer, intense study, fasting, watching and listening, I wrote the *Angels of the Ages* trilogy.

I wanted to use this fiction trilogy sprinkled with truth to share parts of my journey—facing forces from the dark kingdom on every hand, there to destroy me. Meeting God's angels from the Crystal Kingdom sent to me in many forms to help me fight and win my battles. Learning about the two trees in the garden was essential. The Tree of Life, where I could go daily and be cleansed in the Holy Fire of God was one option. Or I could be lured by the dark magic to the Tree of the Knowledge of Good and Evil. There a deceptive fire burns that would have destroyed me had I not cried out for God's help. That fire still burns today with a passion that even lured Adam and Eve. What kind of power did the tree hold that could so easily persuade perfect human beings like Adam and Eve to yield to its powerful magic? I heard about an "apple" tree . . . could any fruit tree possess the kind of power it would take to affect a perfect bloodline?

In Book II of the *Angels of the Ages trilogy, Eden's Gate,* Stephen Daniel Harris has also started his journey to find truth. Knowledge empowers Stephen as he faces the realities that God reveals to him. His journey becomes an adventure as he encounters the excitement of the unknown, the horror of masked evil, the reassurance of salvation, the comfort of love and the certainty of the battle as his life unfolds. Is Stephen a special vessel who God has preserved for the end times, or not? His journey is a long difficult challenge. His mission . . . to find Eden's Gate.

List of Characters

Steven Daniel Harris: Son of John and Rachel Harris of Todd's Creek. Owner of Eden's Gate farm at Calvin's Point, Georgia.

Paul, Cordilia and Philip Dawson: Best friends of the Harris family. Former neighbors at Todd's Creek where Stephen grew up. Philip is Stephen's best friend since childhood.

Jason, Jamie and Leann Conner: Neighbors of Stephen Harris. Leann and Stephen are engaged. Leeann's parents, Jason and Jamie, are future in-laws.

Victoria Stanton: A beautiful, rich aristocrat and Stephen's house guest for three months while she writes a story about farm life in the small town of Calvin's Point, Georgia. She is as mysterious and sassy as she is beautiful.

Brenda Stanton: Victoria Stanton's wealthy grandmother. Charles and Liz Driver are housekeepers for Brenda Stanton. Their son, Grant, is a student of University of Georgia.

———

Sheriff Ronnie Bolton: Sheriff of Calvin's Point.
Ian Jackson: Good friend and foreman of Stephen's farm, Eden's Gate.
Ginger Banks: The only attorney in Calvin's Point.
Pastor Don Reynolds: Pastor of Calvin's Point First Baptist Church. His wife is Sandra.
Martha Mitchell: Waitress at Mitchell's Station.
Effie Brown: Neighbor of Harris family at Todd's Creek, owner of the tome *Angels of the Ages*.

WHITE STONE KINGDOM WARRIORS
Soldiers are Armor Bearers

King Rayon: King of White Stone Kingdom, which is the third—and highest—heaven. (Genesis 28:12, Deuteronomy 10:14 and 1 Kings 8:27)

General Rakar: Top-ranking general in the White Stone Kingdom.

Michiah: High-ranking warrior of White Stone Kingdom.

Haleb: High-ranking warrior of White Stone Kingdom.

Mylo: A battlefield healer in the White Stone Kingdom.

Destiny: Victoria's angel guide.

General Raptor: Seven-foot eagle, leader of the Eagle Army.

Hopewell: Angel from the White Stone Kingdom. Elderly, ragged-looking encourager to Stephen.

Jim Lee: One of the Armor Bearers.

Angelique: Princess in the White Stone Kingdom.

Princess Kaylee: Keeper of the book *Angels of the Ages*.

Other angels in the White Stone Kingdom: Eri the Watcher, Rehabiah , Rayuel, Mikneiah *(Mik nee yuh)*, Jathniel *(Jath nee el)*, Ismachiah *(Iz muh kigh uh)*.

OTHER ARMOR BEARERS

Dale Thomas: Armor Bearer of uncertain motivation.

Captain Adams: Armor Bearer of uncertain loyalties.

THE DARK KINGDOM WARRIORS
Soldiers are fallen angels.

Queen Jewel: Leader of the dark kingdom

Shemed/Ashbel: Evil leader of pain and deception, high ranking in Queen Jewel's kingdom.

Telmar/Acor: High ranking in the dark kingdom. Leader of sexual perversion, lust, all sinful use of sex.

Amash: Warrior in the dark kingdom.

Delilah: dark kingdom witch serving as leader for destroying families.

Prince David and Princess Caroline: Warriors from the White Stone Kingdom who became fallen angels.

Hannah: Fallen angel lured away by Acor but who repented and was forgiven by King Rayon.

Contents

Contents

Prologue

Stephen Daniel Harris thought nothing could be worse than losing his father five years earlier; however, the death of his mother had proven him wrong. After losing his mother and father and making the move from Todd's Creek, Virginia, to Calvins Point, Georgia, the realization of being alone for the first time in his life had kicked in. While sitting in the porch swing he had inherited from his father, Stephen looked around the old farm he had bought, and he had settled on a proper name for his farm: Eden's Gate. He missed his best friends in Todd's Creek. The Dawsons—Paul, Cordilia and their son Philip—had been a rock to him since his mother, Rachel, died. He missed Philip most of all. Rachel and Cordilia were pregnant at the same time with the boys. He and Philip were born eight minutes apart.

Rachel had told Stephen an angel named Eri had appeared to her and told her that God had heard her prayers and she would have a son. She told Stephen many times how special he was and the great part he would have in serving the Kingdom of Heaven. Stephen never felt special. Actually, just thinking about those words made him feel awkward. His mother told him about powerful angels, good and evil, who she, Cordilia and Paul had warred with. Rachel gave him their names and had written down the name of one evil demon that had sworn he would be back and kill her son. Stephen looked at the small piece of paper she had written the name on. He breathed the word, Shemed.

Stephen would for the first time encounter Shemed personally after the move. The stories his mother told him had paled in comparison to what he was now facing. His world as he knew it in Todd's Creek was now completely gone. If not for his memories and his friends the Dawsons, he would lose his mind.

A beautiful house guest, by the name of Victoria Stanton, would prove to be a challenge. He was desperate for money, so Victoria's Grandmother Brenda Stanton had offered Stephen $25,000 to allow Victoria to stay on the farm to write for her magazine a story about farm life in a small town in Calvins Point, Georgia. Needing the money, Stephen agreed, with the approval of his fiancée, Leann Conners.

Strange things began happening after his first day at Eden's Gate. His own private storm had opened many mysterious gates and doors he now encountered. He would learn of many Kingdoms, good and evil, along the way on the journey to find his destiny. How could he be gone days at a time and yet no one would know he was gone at all?

Life became a struggle for him. Arrested for a murder he didn't commit was just the latest challenge in his fight to find his place in the kingdom of the Most High God.

Through the garden gate.
Are riches yet unknown.
Through the garden gate
Is the pathway to the throne.

What treasures there await me?
What glory will I behold?
What mysteries there will unfold for me?
The half has not been told.

So I journey on, though most times,
Rough be the road;
The Spirit from the garden
Will not seem to let me go.

"Enter in, enter in,"
Are the words He spoke to me,
"And the glory of the throne room,
Your eyes will surely see."

Chapter One

The Storm

The swing screeched as Stephen slowly pushed back and forth, surveying the damage from the dreadful storm. Shingles were scattered around the yard. The mailbox had been blown down. The corn was lying flat in places but not touched in others.

The heavens had vacuumed away the gray clouds, and all that remained was a brilliant blue. The rain had ended, but the surplus was dripping from the roof, making long narrow puddles through Stephen's freshly planted flowers. The sun looked as if it were rising from the center of the earth, the terrain was so flat. As beams of light shot forth across the land, Stephen watched the moisture being drawn upward in clouds of fog.

Taking the final sip from his second cup of coffee, he walked to the edge of the porch, looked around, hoping to see Sally, his one and

1

only milk cow. Setting his coffee cup down on the banister, he walked toward the barn. The door was ajar, but he was sure he had closed it before retiring. Stopping at the door, Stephen saw the board he had secured the door with lying on the ground. He scratched his head, trying to figure out what had happened. There was no way the wind could have removed the board. He cautiously looked around the halfway opened door. "Hello! Is someone in here?"

Before entering his eyes darted toward the loft as he quickly seized a nearby hoe. Cautiously, Stephen stepped inside and called out, "Hello."

When no one replied, he took another step and froze when he saw the entrance on the other side of the building was open. His hands were feeling numb from gripping the hoe handle. It was obvious that neither the cow, nor his horse, Champion, were inside.

Moving carefully, he made his way to the other side of the dwelling. The dampness and the smell of hay were causing his allergies to act up. He wiggled his nose like a rabbit to ease the stinging sensation. Approaching Champion's stall, Stephen stopped and looked inside at the boards torn down. "Oh, my Lord! What happened in here?" he whispered.

Wanting to get out of there fast, he gradually moved backward toward the door. When something brushed against his leg, Stephen screamed and tried to run but tripped over the hoe he had hurled to the ground. His heart pounded so hard he could barely breathe. However, he wasn't the only one frightened. Ralph, his cat, ran halfway to the entrance and stopped with his back arched high. "Oh, Lord in heaven! Ralph, you scared me half to death." Stephen quickly secured the door and left the barn. He would check the dwelling again later, after he called Ian Jackson, one of the few people he had befriended since the move to Calvin's Point. First, he wanted to see if he could locate Sally and Champion.

Walking through the cornfield, he noticed the pattern that had been made where the corn was shredded and flattened. Squatting down to take a closer look, Stephen observed what appeared to be burnt strips, about two feet apart.

Feeling the hair on his arm rising, he walked hurriedly through the field, calling out to Sally and Champ. After a couple more steps, a smile spread across his face. "Come here, Champ." Grazing at the end of the cornfield, his horse raised his head and began making his way to Stephen. Thrilled, Stephen patted Champ's neck, grabbed his mane, mounted him and headed out to find Sally.

His anxiety calmed somewhat just by finding Champion and would be calmer still if he could find his cow. Jason and Jamie

Conners had given the cow to Stephen as a "farm-warming gift."

"Whoa, Champ," Stephen said as he pressed his legs against his ribs. Sitting erect, he squinted, trying to make out the dark mass near the fence line. A sober feeling shot through Stephen as he sensed an awareness that the next few minutes would reveal the horrible. "Surely that's not Sally," he uttered as he headed toward the fence. His worst fear was proven true. It was Sally. But what happened to her? Stunned, Stephen looked at her charred remains, forced to keep a distance due to the breath-taking stench that emanated from the area around her.

Not sure what to do, he rode back to the house and called Leann Conners, his closest neighbor and the girl he would marry in a couple of months.

"Leann! Did you get a lot of damage from the storm at your place?"

"Well!" Leann sighed. "Not even good morning or, 'How are you?'"

"I'm sorry. I . . . still feel a little shaken."

Leann could hear the distress in his voice, "What's the matter, Stephen? Are you all right?"

Stephen paused, and then replied, "Right now, I'm not sure."

Leann eagerly asked, "Are you sick or something? You don't sound like yourself."

"Sally's dead!"

"Dead? Stephen, why is she dead? What happened?"

There was no response.

"Stephen! Stephen! I'll be right over."

In silence, Stephen hung the telephone up. Dazed, he made his way to the front porch and sat in the swing waiting for Leann. As he waited, thoughts and feelings from the past encircled him. The swing had provided comfort through the years because it reminded him of his father. He missed his parents so much and the peaceful surroundings of his home in Todd's Creek, Virginia. Before moving to Calvin's Point, Georgia, Stephen had never really been on his own. So far, the experience was not favorable. At Todd's Creek, he at least had Cordilia, Paul and Philip who had been close friends with his family. He missed Philip most of all. Lately, thoughts of calling Philip were strong but shrugged off. Was it pride or the need to prove something to himself? His emotions were going wild, his insides were shaking, he wanted to cry, but the tears wouldn't come. Being alone in a huge empty house, he breathed silence in intense loneliness for his parents. Rachel and John appeared to know how to handle every situation. They always encouraged and prayed for him. At present, Stephen couldn't do either for himself.

The dreadful nightmare he had the night before infiltrated his mind. The green tint on everything and the nauseating taste in his mouth seemed so real. Was it real? Why would he awake and scream out the name his mother made him promise he would never forget, Shemed? Shemed was a powerful demon his parents had encountered many times. Now for the first time, Stephen sensed Shemed's evil presence. How could he possibly know it was Shemed's presence that awakened the unwanted feeling in the pit of his stomach? Why now? What did it mean? Names of the Gray Stone Kingdom rang loud in his ears. Shemed, Telmar, Delilah and Queen Jewel, the leader of the Gray Stone Kingdom. The threat Queen Jewel made to his mom rushed through his mind. She had vowed, "I may not have you, Rachel, but I'll be back for your son."

Rachel told Stephen how the dark kingdom sent its most powerful demons to stop the birth of this future mighty man of God that she called son. It embarrassed Stephen because he didn't feel special or mighty. He had no clue what the future held for him. Could it be the call to preach that changed the course of his life? Perhaps, he should forget preaching, but how could he? The call to the ministry burned like fire in his soul. He rubbed his face with both hands, groaned, and rolled his shoulders, hoping to clear his mind as he stretched his body.

***

Leann's car was a welcome sight. Stephen opened her car door, took her hand to help her out and embraced her so tightly it was uncomfortable.

"Stephen, stop!" Leann groaned as she tried to push back against the forcefulness. He only pulled her closer and kissed her passionately. With both hands, he held Leann's face, kissing her so hard Leann knew something was terribly wrong. This wasn't like Stephen at all!

Stunned, she again pushed away. Stephen immediately tried to pull her back to him. "Stop it, Stephen! What's wrong with you?"

"There's nothing wrong," Stephen snapped. "Can't I kiss you if I want to without something being wrong?"

Leann frowned. "That wasn't wanting to kiss me. You were hurting me."

Stephen's jaw tightened, and with a tone Leann had never heard before, erupted, "It wouldn't hurt you to show a little more fire toward me. We're going to be married in a couple of months. I hope this isn't a preview of what's to come."

Furious, Leann shouted, "Fire? Where did that come from?" In total shock, she stared at the man she loved.

Stephen turned his back to her and faced the cornfield.

She was speechless. *How can I respond? Stephen is acting like a wild man, not the sweet-mannered man I fell in love with.* She tried to put her hand on his shoulder.

He swiftly pulled away.

Leann exploded, "Stephen Daniel Harris! I don't deserve this kind of treatment. What's your problem? Please don't tell me these actions are all over a cow, or is it because I didn't let you manhandle me?"

Without turning around, Stephen groaned in a low tone, "Go home, Leann."

Devastated, she began to cry. "Fine! I'll go home. I wish I hadn't come to start with. I came because you sounded so upset. I was worried and wanted to help you. If your actions are a result of being upset or hurt, just say so. Don't take your feelings out on me. When you're ready to talk . . ." Leann paused, and looked at Stephen, who still had his back to her. She got in her car and called out. "When you're ready to talk, call me."

Stephen stared out across the field and listened as Leann drove away. When he knew she was out of sight, he fell to his knees and moaned in pain. Trembling in his anguish, his groans flowed upward to God. Then his groans turned into a yell, "Why, God! Why?"

Stephen stayed on his knees until he released the tears that were dammed up. He needed to call Leann but couldn't. No words could possibly explain his behavior. *Will she even listen if I could perhaps come up with an explanation? I have no idea why I behaved in such a manner. I will deal with it when I get my thoughts straight. Right now, I have to do something with my cow, but what?*

Chapter Two

Sheriff Bolton Investigates

Stephen drove into town to see Sheriff Ronnie Bolton. Sheriff Bolton was sitting on the porch in a straight-back chair. He was 45, tall, medium-built, with full eyebrows. His thinning brown hair was cut in the most profound flattop Stephen had ever seen. Ronnie had been the sheriff in Calvin's Point for three years. Before that, he served four years in Vietnam. He could tell the most horrendous stories. You couldn't be around him long before, one way or another, he would bring up the many causalities he saw with his own eyes in Vietnam. From time to time, he would enjoy a chew of fine-cured tobacco. This was one of those days.

As Stephen was getting out of his car, he saw Sheriff Bolton spit. The sheriff asked, "What brings you to town this great morning, Mr. Harris?"

"Hi, Sheriff. I wondered if you heard any damage reports after that storm, we had last night? I'm curious if there had been any damage reports on property or livestock due to the storm."

Sheriff Bolton scratched his head. "No. Should I have?"

Stephen shook his head. "I understand your puzzled look. As I drove into town, I didn't see any damage at all."

The Sheriff stood and spit in a bottle he was holding. "Did you have damage or something?"

"Yes! Quite a bit."

"Really? You mentioned livestock."

"Yes. I had only one cow. She was killed last night."

"Killed? How?"

Stephen shrugged his shoulders. "I don't know. She looks like she was burned."

"Burned?" Sheriff Bolton walked to the edge of the porch. "Maybe we better take a look and see what we got."

Stephen was thrilled at the sheriff's suggestion, which meant he would be checking the barn as well.

***

Sheriff Bolton looked at the corn. "Hey, Stephen, what in the world made these burnt looking strips in the corn and shredded the stalks like that?"

"It's a mystery to me, sheriff. I've never seen anything like it. Have you?"

The sheriff spit and replied. "Yeah. I've seen something like it, in Vietnam. Where's your cow?"

Stephen took him to the fence line. As Sheriff Bolton neared the remains, he took his handkerchief from his back pocket, held it over his mouth and moaned, "My goodness! This smells like a death camp. Did lightning strike her?"

Stephen moved back. "I don't know," he said.

"I don't know either, but I can tell you, it wouldn't be too healthy to breathe much of this foul air." Stepping away from the remains, Ronnie looked at Stephen and uttered, "It looks like you had your own private storm last night. There was a sprinkle of rain and a little wind in town, but nothing like this. Maybe the Big Man upstairs wants to get your attention."

The sheriff horse-laughed, but Stephen could only muster up a smile. Maybe there was some truth in what he said. After all, his was the only place in town with damage.

Back at the house, Ronnie said he would get a backhoe out to dig a hole and bury the cow. He helped Stephen check the barn but saw nothing that could explain the ruins.

Sheriff Bolton removed his hat and said, "My gosh! What happened to this stall?"

Stephen sighed. "I don't know."

Looking around, the sheriff said, "I'll file a report. From the looks of this stall . . . let me put it this way, the wind last night didn't do this!"

"Do you think somebody did this to my farm . . . to my cow?"

The sheriff stared into Stephen's eyes and said, "Well, it certainly wasn't a storm. If you really want to know my thoughts, I'll tell you."

"Please do, because, right now, I don't know what to think."

"Lightning didn't strike your cow, and the wind didn't blow your barn doors open. Not from the size of the boards they were secured with. As for the stall, no way did wind do this. I'll get somebody out here to check for fingerprints. Who knows what we'll find?"

Stunned, Stephen said, "I don't understand. I know very few people here in Calvin's Point—none of whom would do this. Sheriff, a human being couldn't do this."

"As a rule, I would agree with you." Sheriff Bolton put his arm around Stephen's shoulder as they walked back to the house. "However, let me tell you something about people. When I was in Nam, the commander sent my battalion into a small village called Yinpeg. We were to secure the village and check for mines. The people in the village were so good to us. We ate with them, drank with them and even slept with the women. Children 9 and 10 years old would pull their dresses above their waist and say 'I sleep with you for candy bar.' Some of the men slept with them and did everything imaginable to those little kids."

The sheriff lowered his head and continued, "What a disgrace! I'm sorry. The point I'm trying to make is we were there so long we became comfortable. Therefore, the enemy, which was the villagers, was able to blow two thirds of our men up. Their hate for us was so great, they killed half of the people in the village to kill us. We played right into their hands and let our defenses down. By doing so, we opened the gate wide, and they entered without notice— although we were trained to be alert and never nap while on watch. Just be careful, Stephen. Sometimes, we don't know people as well as we think we do. If you have an enemy, whether from Calvin's Point or elsewhere, they may sneak right up on you if you don't keep watch. Well, I guess I've taken enough of your time. I'll send a man out to check for prints, and to take care of your cow."

Sheriff Bolton shook Stephen's hand. "I'll be in touch. If you need me, you know where I am."

"Thanks, sheriff," Stephen said, and went inside. Sheriff Bolton's story was sobering. It reminded him of his mom. She too used stories to make a point. Stephen quickly picked the phone up and dialed Philip's number but hung up on the first ring. "No! I am not going to call Philip the first time something comes up. However, I need to call Leann!"

Stephen couldn't make that call either. The time just wasn't right.

Chapter Three

So Upset

*J*ason and Jamie were worried about their only daughter. Leann hadn't eaten and would start crying at nothing.

Jamie was looking to the top of the stairs at Leann's door, which had been locked all morning. Jason was watching the news when suddenly, rapid tapping on the shoulder prompted him to turn. Jamie, "Why are you tapping my shoulder?"

Jamie tilted her head and growled, "Just come into the kitchen a minute."

Jason took a deep breath. "Can it wait until the news goes off?"

Jamie marched over, turned the television off and stated, "No, it can't wait! Now come on."

Like a commanding officer, Jamie went stomping to the kitchen. Jason pulled his glasses off, rubbed his eyes and whispered, "Lord, help me." He then asked, "What is so important that it couldn't wait until after the

16

news?" he asked as he walked reluctantly to the kitchen.

Outraged that he would even have to ask, Jamie put her hands on her hips and snapped, "How dare you act as though our baby isn't locked in her room and won't come out. We need to get to the bottom of this."

"To the bottom of what? She told us yesterday that she had a fight with Stephen."

"Yes! But about what?" Jamie protested. "Stephen is the nicest boy I ever met. You know, if he can get my approval, he has to be extraordinary, so what could have happened?"

Irritated, Jason said, "Stephen is not a little boy, and Leann is not a little girl. They're grown-ups, so let them work out whatever it is by themselves."

Jamie stomped her foot and scolded, "Jason Conners, you make me so mad I could scream."

Jason frowned. "Why do I make you mad because I said let them work out their own problems? It's their problems, not ours."

Through clinched teeth, Jamie muttered, "Exactly! And we haven't bothered to find out what the problem is so we can help."

"If you are so bent on nosing into their business, then you march on up there and find out. I'm not going to. If she wants our help, she knows she can always come to us. But she hasn't come, so give her some space, why don't you?"

"I can't believe you don't care about our daughter."

Jason turned and headed toward the living room. "I'm going to watch what's left of the morning news."

Jamie stomped her foot again. "That's it. Walk away like you always do. You leave everything for me to handle alone."

Jason froze, turned and walked back toward Jamie. With tight lips, he growled, "If you stomp your foot one more time . . . do you realize the grace God has to give me to keep from forgetting you're a woman? I would never let a man get away with stomping his foot at me." Getting eye to eye with her, Jason said sternly, "I said I'm going to give her some space and that's what I mean. Now, I'm going to watch the news. If you would like to join me, you're welcome; otherwise, leave me alone until my program goes off. Do I make myself clear, dear?"

In disgust, Jamie snorted, "Well! I've never."

Before Jason could respond, Leann interrupted, "What in the world is going on down here? Are two fighting?"

Jamie was quick to say, "See, Jason! Leann asked if we're fighting, so what's the big deal about us asking her?"

Jason threw both hands in the air. "I give up!" He looked at Leann and said, "Your mother wants to know the details of your fight with Stephen. I, on the other hand, think we need to give you enough space to decide if you want to share the details or not."

Jamie took Leann's hands and explained, "Honey, you know I don't mean to pry, but when I know you're hurting, I want to fix it. I can't stand to think you're in pain, whatever the reason."

Aggravated, Jason said, "It's the stomping of the foot, Jamie, and the demands you make that drives me up a wall."

Before Jamie could respond, Leann said, "Mom, Dad, what is wrong with you two? You're worried about Stephen and me having a fight and look at you. I only told you we had a fight because there was no way I could hide the fact that something was wrong. I've prayed and asked God to show me or at least give me understanding of what Stephen is going through. We had some words, but nothing we can't work out. Now, I think you two need to pray and work your feelings out. I'm fine, and when I get back, I want to see your smiling faces."

Jamie timidly asked, "Where are you going?"

Leann took her keys from the rack. "I'm going to talk to Stephen. I should have gone last night. I love Stephen, and if I'm going to be his wife, I need to stand by him and help him work through whatever his problem is. I'll be back later."

Jason and Jamie watched Leann drive away. At first it was a standoff to see who would speak first, then Jason smiled, hugged Jamie and said, "She's right! The news wasn't worth all this fuss. I'm sorry, honey."

"No, no. I am the one who should apologize. I tend to be overbearing and I know that." Jamie began to cry. "I just can't stand to think that something's wrong with Leann. That's all!"

"Here, here," Jason said, as he took his handkerchief and wiped her tears. As Jason and Jamie held each other, they took Leann's advice and prayed.

Chapter Four

Trying to Explain

Stephen was sitting in the porch swing when Leann pulled up. Still feeling numb from the past twenty-four hours, he didn't move when he saw her. She walked slowly to the swing, smiled and said, "Do you mind if I join you?"

Stephen managed a grin. "Please do."

"I've heard a lot about this swing. Does it work as good as you say?"

That was all it took for Stephen to break. He gently stroked her cheek. His inner pain, evidenced in his facial expression, was plain for Leann to see.

"I wanted to call but didn't know what to say after my awful behavior. Leann, can you ever forgive me?"

"I already have," she whispered.

They embraced. After the tears dried, Stephen put his arm around Leann, and they watched as the sun began to set.

"The land is so flat here," Stephen said softly.

Leann stared at Stephen. "I have forgiven you, but I need to know what's bothering you."

Stephen walked to the edge of the porch and looked toward heaven. "I don't know exactly what it is. If I did, it would be easy just to tell you and get it over with. But I don't know for sure."

Leann joined Stephen. "I don't know either, but you were not yourself."

Stephen told her about the destruction to the barn, the burnt strips in the corn, and how the cow looked when he found her. He also shared what Sheriff Bolton had said.

"Baloney, Stephen! I see all the symptoms of something much deeper. I want us to be able to share, not only the good but the difficult as well. That's a big part of marriage to confide in and help each other overcome any obstacle. I prayed for you last night and today. Stephen, with God and our love for each other, nothing can keep us down or apart, but we must be able to talk."

Stephen looked at Leann and stroked her long auburn hair. "I don't know if you're ready for the things I have to tell. It's not your ordinary story."

"I'm listening."

Stephen patted the swing. "You may need to be sitting for this."

Leann joined him. "So, tell me, Stephen."

"My mother saw an ancient book at a weird old woman's house. Her name was Effie Brown. Mother said, 'The name Shemed was all through the book.' I've been hearing that name ringing through my mind for over a month now."

"Who is this Shemed?"

"Leann." Stephen paused. "There are good angels and bad angels. This Shemed is one of the worst." Stephen went on and on about good and bad angels and Jacob's ladder.

Finally, Leann could take it no longer. She pressed her fingertips to her temples. "I want to say two things. First, you're rambling. Second, why are you getting louder and louder? Since you first started talking about the angels, your voice has elevated to quite a high pitch. Why?"

Stephen shouted, "Because this is burning in my soul. I feel like I could explode."

Irritated, Leann stood. "This has nothing to do with us. I asked what was bothering you not about angels and Jacob's ladder. Are you trying to get off the subject to keep from telling me what's really wrong?"

Frustrated, Stephen shouted, "I knew you weren't ready for what's really bothering me, Leann."

"I want to be! I just don't understand."

23

Stephen put his arms around Leann. "I know. I've heard it all my life, and I still don't understand it all. I'll be merciful and share a little at a time, but enough for tonight. Okay?"

"Absolutely!" Leann sighed.

Chapter Five

Confused

*D*ark clouds scudded across the full moon that had slowly made its way to the middle of the sky. When Leann pulled away, Stephen lingered outside, taking in God's awesome creation clouds and all. Standing in the night, Stephen, with his mind racing, desperately tried to figure out what was going on with his undisciplined emotions. Thrilled that he and Leann had made-up, Stephen felt that a great deal of his anxiety had calmed. However, he needed to know more. Stephen prayed and asked God to give him understanding and direction. "God, I feel as though my insides are being pulled apart. What's happening to me? Why did I scream out the name Shemed? I've heard about him my whole life. Now I can sense something right in front of me and not be sure what it is. God, help me."

Stephen had drawn understanding from his parents about Shemed. After his parents' deaths, he still had Philip, Cordilia and Paul, but now so far away from Todd's Creek, he felt the void. It would take time for Leann to understand about Shemed.

Feeling desperate, Stephen put both hands on his head and wept loudly. "Help me, Father! Please help me! Give me your wisdom."

After a time, Stephen started to go inside, but froze when he heard what he thought was a cow mooing. He turned and looked toward the cornfield. Again, he heard the strange sound and the rustling of corn stalks as something moved through the rows. Stephen called out, "Sally!"

Listening intently, he began to step backward toward the porch without taking his eyes from the field. The rustling of the stalks grew louder. He grew short of breath and was beginning to feel faint. A blazing inferno parted the stalks and came into the edge of the yard. It was his cow, Sally! "Oh God! Oh God!" Stephen gasped as he managed to pull his feet backward toward the door.

"Stephen!" A voice called out. It sounded as though someone was trying to call out from under water. The gurgling sound echoed as again it called out, "Stephen!"

He wanted to move, but his body was frozen. Everything was so dark. As his knees buckled, he caught one last glimpse of the cow coming toward him. Suddenly, evil laughter echoed across the field.

When Stephen opened his eyes, he saw the large family portrait that hung on the wall directly across from the foot of the bed. He quickly sat up. His eyes wildly scanned the room. Looking down, Stephen touched the buttons on his pajama top. Pushing the covers down he put his feet on the floor continuing to survey the room as he gradually moved to the window that overlooked the countryside. Trembling, he pulled the curtain back but saw nothing. After raising the window, he looked around the yard, seeing nothing but a beautiful sunny morning. The only voice he heard was that of two robins that were building a nest in the huge magnolia tree right outside the bedroom window. Stephen sat on the side of his bed. "How did I get into my pajamas? Better yet, how did I get into the house, up the stairs and into bed?"

He looked at the telephone on the nightstand, raised his hand, rubbed his fingers together and then picked the phone up. "I've got to call Philip," he muttered.

Cordilia and Paul Dawson had bought the Harris home place from Stephen after his mother Rachel had died. Philip was living in the house now. The phone rang and rang, but no answer. "Come on, Philip," Stephen mumbled to no avail. He hung up and eagerly dialed Cordilia.

The Dawsons had been his mom and dad's best friends. Rachel and Cordilia were, as Stephen's mom put it, kindred spirits. They were prayer partners, Sunday school teachers, choir-singing, devil-fighting buddies. So different, yet their goal was the same—to war against Satan, set the captives free and bring them to the Kingdom of God. They had been pregnant together. Stephen and Philip were born only eight minutes apart. Angels, both good and bad, had visited Rachel and Cordilia on more than one occasion. The name of one of the bad angels had been invading Stephen's head. SHEMED!

Chapter Six

Leann's Explanation

*J*amie and Jason Conners heard Leann come in from Stephen's the night before but purposely tried to give her the space she needed. At breakfast, Jason looked across the table and smiled at Jamie. Curious, Jamie asked, "Why are you smiling? Do I have something in my teeth?" Jamie asked as she wiped the corners of her mouth.

"No, dear! I was just thinking how very proud I am of you. I know it's not easy for you not to ask Leann what happened between her and Stephen."

Jamie smiled. "Thank you, Jason, for noticing." Jamie was going to refill her coffee, but Jason insisted on getting it for her. "My goodness," she grunted, "had I known I would get this kind of attention, my words would have lessened a long time ago."

Jason raised his brows and patted her hand. "Let's not get carried away, dear."

Jamie was going to respond, but Leann entered the dining room.

Leann tried not to laugh as she sat down at the table. It was obvious her parents were trying not to say anything to her about Stephen. After making small talk, Leann decided to bring it up before her mom exploded. Jamie was in the middle of a question, so Leann waited.

"What time do you go into work today, Leann?"

Leann shook her head. "Mom, let's drop the charade. If you want, you can ask me about last night."

Jamie exhaled. "I thought you would never say those words."

"Leann," Jason interrupted, "I'm not sure you should give your mom that much leeway. I get her to shut up, and you give the green light."

Jason stood and kissed Jamie on the top of her head. "Honey, it was worth it to know you could hold out that long."

"Well, I'm not doing it anymore, so be quiet and let me get some details."

Anticipating, Jamie insisted, "So! What happened?"

"He's just going through a hard time right now. Recently losing his mom, moving to a new place, all new people."

"No, no, no!" Jamie said, slowly shaking her head. "Stephen has been here long enough to plant an acre of corn and watch it come up. Those things may be some of it, but there is something deeper that underlies it all."

"Actually, Mom, I think you're right. His thoughts seemed scattered. I asked him to share with me what was bothering him, and he started talking about Jacob's ladder, demons and angels. He was talking about them in a strange way. It's hard to explain. I didn't understand any of it."

Jamie propped her elbow on the table and stared straight ahead. After a moment, she tapped her lips. "I'm going to have to think about this. Stephen seems like a godly young man, so I'm sure he's not into witchcraft or demonic activity."

"Mother!"

Jamie frowned. "I'm just thinking out loud," she said.

Leann took a sip of orange juice and continued, "I guess I should tell you, as Paul Harvey would say, 'the rest of the story.' Remember the other night when we had that rain shower?"

Jason, who was standing at the sink, was quick to respond, "Yes, I remember. I was praying we would get a good downpour for the crops. We need it desperately."

31

Leann took her glass, put it in the sink and began running dishwater.

"Leann!" Jamie said, "leave the dishes, and come tell us why you asked about the rain."

Leann leaned against the sink. "Stephen got more than a downpour at his farm. The corn looked like the wind had taken vengeance on it."

"He only lives about a half mile away. How did he get a downpour and not us?"

Leann crossed her arms and replied, "That's not the half of it. There were burnt strips all through the field. In some places, the stalks looked like they had been shredded."

That perked Jason's attention, "What do you mean 'burnt strips'?"

"You know, like skid marks from tires. But wait, there's more. Sally, the cow you gave him, was struck by lightning or something. Stephen said she looked charred. And the barn doors were opened and Champion's stall was demolished. Sheriff Bolton said he'd have someone come out, bury the cow and check around for fingerprints."

Jason frowned and said, "Why would the sheriff do that? I mean if the damage was from the storm. Of course, what storm are they talking about? We surely didn't have one."

Leann looked at her watch. "I've got to be going." She got her purse, kissed her parents and headed for the door.

Jamie called out, "Leann!"

"Yes!"

"Ask Stephen if he would like to drive up to Garrison and have some fresh seafood. Our treat, of course."

"Mom, that's a wonderful idea. Don't you think, Daddy?"

"I do. We'll visit the Grand Surf. It's on the ocean, and their food is fabulous."

Leann thanked them for caring so much.

Jason added, "While we're at it, I'll take him another cow over and see if I can do anything to help."

"I love you so much," Leann said, "and thank you both!"

Tears welled in Jamie's eyes. "Now you go on before I start crying. You know when I cry, I get a headache. You be careful."

Jason picked one of his best milk cows to take to Stephen. He and Jamie had a three-hundred-acre peanut farm, and employed fifty workers on a seasonal basis, most of whom came from Clarksville, a suburb outside Augusta. He paid his workers well, so they didn't mind the drive. The appropriate name for his farm was Graceland. People thought it was because Jason and Jamie were fans of Elvis Presley. "Not so!" Jason said, "It's because of the enormous grace God gave me to run this beautiful place."

Jason was 50 years old. He worked hard all his life and vowed he would until the day he died. He was a medium-sized man with chestnut hair that was graying, hazel eyes and a dark tan, due to the amount of time he spent outside. Calluses, as hard as rocks, lined his palms. He would laugh, and say God gave him Jamie to mature his patience, but now he wished God would do a re-check and see that he had already matured several years back.

Jamie was an attractive 49-year-old woman, about thirty pounds overweight. She stood five foot nine and was as strong as an ox. The sun had highlighted her shoulder-length, light brown hair. She too was a worker. From driving the tractor to cleaning the barn, she could do it all. She was honored to serve God as president of the Women for Christ fundraising at Calvin's Point Baptist Church. She and Jason not only made money, they had set up a fund at the bank to help people in town who fell on hard times. Only two people at the bank knew Jason and Jamie were the sole contributors to the fund. The couple lived comfortably, but half of what they made each year went into this fund. They had been married thirty years. Leann was an only child, but she wasn't spoiled. She too worked on the farm, as well as part time for Ginger Banks, the only attorney in the town.

Ginger liked the small-town life, so she made her office in the downstairs of her home. She also had an office outside Augusta, where she acted as public defender, but brought most of her work home. Leann kept Ginger organized, reminding her constantly of what to do next, helping search for papers and typing closing arguments. Ginger loved the help.

Leann was a beautiful woman. She had long naturally curly auburn hair, fair skin and emerald green eyes. Stephen thought she had the most perfect lips and body in the world. A recent graduate of the University of Georgia, she had all the charm of a true Southern belle. She was very independent and felt a woman should never be totally dependent on any man. Her top priority, single or married, was serving God. She loved Stephen and knew God had brought her soulmate from Todd's Creek, Virginia.

Ginger Banks was a 38-year-old divorcée. Her ex-husband not only loved her, but every other woman who would give him the time of day. She was a giving woman, but not giving enough to share her husband. Ginger was of medium height and a little overweight, but only in her hips. She was the only red-haired person in Calvin's Point. She didn't attend church, although most other people in Calvin's Point did. Leann had asked Ginger to go, but she always had a firm answer. "No!"

As Public Defender, her caseload increased so much it seemed like all she did was work and sleep. She didn't mind the long hours—work helped keep her mind off her ex-husband.

Chapter Seven

Renovation

Stephen tried to numb his emotions, particularly his fear about work. He made up his mind to hire workers and develop the farm. The new cow was a treasured gift. He didn't understand his fascination with animals and farming, unlike his dad and grandfather before him who loved trains. Their goals had been to become engineers and both succeeded. Stephen, on the other hand, knew his call was to preach, although no doors had opened in over a year. At times he felt he might have been wrong about his calling. However, the burning desire in his soul was more intense than ever.

He looked at his two-story Victorian house. The gable roof and colossal wrap-around porch gave it a style all its own. The seven slender, sculptured pillars glistened a brilliant white. Matching pickets outlined the porch. The landscaping was perfect. Stephen planted many flowers, a trait he picked up from his mother, Rachel. She filled the yard at Todd's Creek with an array of flowers. She told Stephen, "Flowers are like people—all original, all beautiful and all necessary to fulfill the plan of creation."

One of the largest magnolia trees Stephen had ever seen cast a shadow over his bedroom window. He often opened the window, allowing the aroma to fill the room.

The spacious yard was bordered with a white, crafted picket fence. At certain points in the fence, there were seven rounded raised posts' gates. At the entrance of the yard was an elaborately designed gate. When Stephen purchased the farm, the gates, like the house, desperately needed renovation. Therefore, he hired Ian Jackson, the handy man in town, to come and help repair the effects of years of neglect. After many hours of hard work, the house and the gates were restored to their original condition.

The barn that was in plain view of the house was painted and restored. The terrain was very flat; Stephen's was the only house in Calvin's Point that sat on a rolling hill allowing him to see the entire town. The main attraction from the porch was Calvin's Point Baptist Church. The steeple towered into the sky. The bells of the church rang twice a day—at noon and sundown.

Stephen really wanted Cordilia, Paul and Philip to come for a visit since the work on the house was completed. Their last visit was before the renovations. He knew Cordilia would be thrilled with what he had done with the house.

Cordilia loved Emily and Jerry Jackson's huge Victorian house that adjoined Stephen's home place in Todd's Creek. The Jacksons' son, Chris, and his wife Paula Miller now lived in the house. Chris shared stories about his life with Stephen. One story in particular bothered Stephen. Chris's parents dedicated him to what they called the dark kingdom when he was born. Chris spoke of Shemed many times, calling him the demon of pain and death.

Chapter Eight
Jamie's Talk with Stephen

The trip to Garrison with Leann and her parents was filled with lots of laughs, a peaceful reminder of Todd's Creek.

The Grand Surf restaurant was situated on the fifteenth floor of a round conglomeration incased in glass.

Jason needed to make a phone call while Leann went to the bathroom. Jamie was hoping for a moment alone with Stephen. She watched as Stephen absorbed the view.

Clearing her throat, she said, "Stephen!"

He quickly responded, "I'm sorry, Jamie. I don't mean to be rude. The view is just . . . breathtaking."

"I know. Anyway, you're not being rude. But I did want to talk to you for a moment before Jason and Leann return."

"Of course, what is it?"

Jamie sat up straight. "You know me well enough to know I speak my mind."

Stephen grinned and replied, "Yes, I know."

"Then you know not to be shocked by anything I say."

"Absolutely!"

Jamie leaned toward Stephen and whispered, "You're not into something we should know about are you, son?" Before Stephen could answer or even understand the question, Jamie continued, "Because if you are, now is the time to say so. I won't tell Leann or Jason anything you say to me is in confidence."

Caught completely off guard, Stephen asked, "What do you mean?"

"Leann was very upset when she came home, the other day."

Wondering what Jamie was getting at, Stephen said, "Did Leann tell you how devastating the storm was at my place?"

Suddenly on the defensive, Jamie quickly responded, "Yes, she did! However, it wasn't gossip. Leann doesn't gossip. She told me only because I asked."

Stephen licked his lips to keep from smiling. "Jamie, I know Leann doesn't gossip. Now, let's get to the point before they get back."

Sternly, Jamie said, "My point is, are you into some kind of demonic activity?"

Stunned by the question, Stephen shook his head. "Did Leann tell you about the discussion we had about angels and demons?"

Jamie raised her brows, lifted her chin and said, "Well . . . yes, she did."

Stephen chuckled. "So, that's what this is about? Jamie, the Holy Spirit dwells inside you; surely you would know if I were into anything demonic. Would you not?"

A quick nod of her head and a deep breath, Jamie straightened her posture. "I knew you weren't!"

"Here comes Leann." Stephen squeezed Jamie's hand. "We will talk again later."

Quickly Jamie said, "Let's keep this between us, okay?"

"Of course!"

Stephen talked with Jason about hiring workers and developing his farm. He had raised a small field of corn, but he wanted to build the farm—a farm he could make a handsome living from. He knew he needed help to do that. After buying his place, the money from his inheritance was almost gone, so he had to do something. Since he now owned a farm, it only made sense that he would work it and have an income.

Stephen had hired six men to help in the fields. One of those men was Ian Jackson. He originally met Ian in church just after moving to Calvin's Point. They hit it off, and Ian had been a great help in renovating his house. As it turned out, Ian was great on a farm too. Stephen made him supervisor over the other workers. Stephen's only experience with farming was planting a half-acre of corn, that didn't do that good alone, so he had decided to raise corn and cattle. When Jason offered to help Stephen by sending some of his workers to prepare the fields for planting, Stephen gladly accepted.

Chapter Nine

A Call Home

One murky summer's day, Stephen was sitting on his front porch swing, looking out over the land and thanking God for His many blessings. He felt if he was going to have a functioning farm, he needed to give his farm a proper name. He looked around the yard hoping to get an idea. Gazing toward the sky, he asked, "Father, what should I name this land you have blessed me with?" Without hesitation, he said with confidence, *"EDEN's GATE!"*

He had barely spoken those words when he saw Pastor Don Reynolds coming up the driveway. Pastor Reynolds was a fiery preacher who had been at the church for fifteen years. Over the past year, Stephen had grown devotedly attached to him. He shared many spiritual and personal things with the pastor. He was a 48-year-old man, married, with four children. At six feet tall, he weighed two hundred pounds with graying thinned hair and a heavy salt and pepper mustache. His medium complexion carried a few acne scars. He drove a pristine 1957 yellow Ford Fairlane.

Stephen stood to greet him. After hello, a handshake and a glass of iced tea, Stephen and Pastor Reynolds took seats on the porch.

Stephen squinted and said, "You know you're always welcome, and you don't need a reason to stop by, but there is a reason for your visit today, right?"

Pastor Reynolds sat his glass down, looked straight ahead for a moment, took a deep breath and said, "Stephen, my spirit has recognized something very special about you."

Stephen pointed to himself. "Something special about me?"

"Yes!"

Curiosity piqued, Stephen asked, "What's special?"

"I'm not sure how to put it in words, but from the first day we met, the Holy Spirit told me you were a chosen vessel God has sent here for a very distinct purpose."

Stephen set his glass down. "Pastor Reynolds, we're all here on distinct missions. You, for instance."

Appearing apprehensive, Pastor Reynolds leaned toward Stephen and whispered, "Stephen! Listen to me. You are a chosen vessel! Of course, we're all here on distinct missions, but yours is on an immense scale. There's nothing ordinary about it."

Not understanding, Stephen questioned, "Why are you whispering? There's no one here but you and me."

Pastor Reynolds began to break out in a sweat. Aware something was extremely wrong, Stephen took hold of his arm and asked, "Are you all right?"

Pastor Reynolds took a handkerchief from his pocket and wiped his forehead. "I don't have much time, so listen carefully. The Holy Spirit has been revealing some very powerful things to me. I want you to study about the Garden of Eden."

Slightly shaking his head, Stephen asked, "Why?"

"You told me about your mother's theory of Jacob's Ladder, that angels that descend to the earth temporarily become human. That prompted me to search it out for myself. Stephen, she was right. As I was searching to disprove that theory, I saw more. I have such a strange feeling in my spirit." Pastor Reynolds, walked to the edge of the porch, took hold of the column and leaned against it.

Stephen quickly went to see if he was okay. "Should I call Dr. Taylor for you?"

Pastor Reynolds instantly calmed down. With a look of despondency, he said, "I'm going out of town this week, and I would like for you to fill in for me on Sunday."

Caught totally off guard, Stephen asked, "Do you mean that?"

"Yes, I do."

"I'm thrilled you would ask me, but will it be okay with the deacons?"

"Yes! I've already cleared it with them."

Stephen sternly asked, "What's wrong with you? It doesn't take a rocket scientist to see you're acting this way out of fear. Tell me what it is; maybe I can help."

Looking hopeless, Pastor Reynolds lowered his head. "I don't think I'll be coming back."

Confused by his statement, Stephen asked, "What . . . what do you mean?"

The pastor fixed his sober eyes on Stephen and took him by his shoulders. "If I don't come back, promise me you'll study the Garden of Eden. Promise me!"

"I promise! What do you feel is going to happen that you won't be back?"

"I don't know, but I *do* know . . . if that makes any sense."

Stephen paused. "It's strange you should be talking about the Garden of Eden. I've just named my farm, 'Eden's Gate.'"

Pastor Reynolds closed his eyes and said, "Thank you, Father! Stephen, you are the one. Go through 'Eden's Gate.' I've got to go. I'll pray for you, my brother. Know this, Stephen! You will speak, teach and preach about the Garden of Eden."

Pastor Reynolds hugged Stephen tightly. "Go through the Garden Gate! The Most High will show you the way."

As the pastor slowly walked away, Stephen was too stunned to even call out to him. He watched until he drove out of sight. What could have possibly had Pastor Reynolds in such a frame of mind? Being asked to preach was tremendous, but the demeanor of his friend had thoroughly dampened the invitation. After praying for him, Stephen called Leann. Before turning in that night, he made another call.

Stephen dialed the number and patiently waited for someone to answer. "Hello!" a voice said on the other end.

Stephen was so excited. With sheer exhilaration, he shouted, "Cordilia!"

"Stephen, is that you?"

"Yes, Yes, Yes."

Cordelia was elated. "Why haven't you called, dropped a letter in the mail, sent a pigeon or something? I've called several times, but didn't get an answer, even late at night. Where have you been spending your time?"

Stephen laughed. "I've been spreading myself around. Quite a bit of my time is with Leann and remodeling my house. How is Paul?"

"He is standing here with his head pressed against mine wanting to hear every word."

"Hi, Stephen!" Paul called out.

"Paul! It's so good to hear your voice. Cordilia, Paul, I have something exciting to tell you."

"You didn't elope, did you?" Cordilia shouted.

"Heaven's no! I would never do that to you. Pastor Reynolds asked me to fill in for him this Sunday."

"Stephen, that's wonderful."

"I would love for you to be here if possible."

"You know we'll be there." Paul said.

"I can't wait to see you," Stephen said. "I miss you so much."

"We love you and miss you terribly too," the couple responded in unison.

"How's Philip?" Stephen asked. "He's doing great. Working in Benson and taking a couple of classes. He'll be so sorry he missed your call. How about we come down Friday, so we can spend some time with you."

"I can't wait! I love you two so much."

Chapter Ten

A Talk with Sandra Reynolds

Stephen was ecstatic the Dawsons were coming to visit. He called Leann to share his good news. She insisted on helping Stephen make sure his house was spotless. He was so excited that night he could hardly go to sleep. Amid all the excitement, Stephen couldn't keep Pastor Reynolds off his mind. He kept seeing his face and hearing the fear in his voice.

The next morning Stephen called to make sure Pastor Reynolds was okay. His wife, Sandra said, "He left early for a retreat in Atlanta, but he will be back on Monday."

Sandra Mae Warren was born in Lawrence, Kansas. She was 46 and very thin. Her family moved to Atlanta, Georgia, twenty years earlier. She and Don Reynolds met at camp meeting, fell in love and were married one year later. They had four children—Maria, 14;

Tyler, 16; Scott, 19; and Karen, 21. Scott and Karen attended the University of Kansas.

Sandra worked part time at Andy's market to help with extra income. The church wasn't very big, and neither was the pay. She was the pianist and the secretary, and she filled almost any other job that needed to be done in the church. She and Don worked hard to get the church up to 70 faithful attendees. It was nothing like the church in Todd's Creek, with 260 members. Calvin's Point Church looked like a Norman Rockwell painting. It gleamed a brilliant white with a spectacular steeple. The church would hold 200 people. The Reynolds' desire was to see it filled for the kingdom of God.

Sandra was curious why Stephen called so early. Probing, she asked, "Is there something I can help you with, Stephen?"

"No . . . well, maybe you can. When Pastor came to visit yesterday, he appeared very anxious. I wondered if you noticed it or if it was just me?"

Breathing a sigh of relief, Sandra said, "I am so thankful you asked. Don didn't act like himself at all yesterday. He had been studying something in Genesis. He really hasn't acted right since he began the study. I've been concerned, but he's said repeatedly, 'There's nothing to worry about.' The other night, he acted very bizarre and was saying the strangest things. He said . . . he said, 'I entered the garden.' I've no idea what he meant by that since we don't have a garden. Last night, we were lying in bed, and he asked me, 'Do you think about dying?' My response was, 'Everyone does.' He hardly slept at all but fought with his pillow all night. He tossed and turned like a wild man. I finally went to the sofa so I could get some sleep. Did he say anything to you, Stephen, about what was bothering him?"

Stephen didn't want to worry Sandra with the statement Pastor Reynolds made about not coming back, so he replied, "He did say something about the Garden of Eden. I think the Holy Spirit has opened several avenues for him there. Well . . . I better get off and get to work."

"Thank you for calling, Stephen! Don has a deep regard for you as his brother in Christ. If you need anything before Sunday, just let me know."

"Thank you! That goes for me as well."

Stephen hung up the phone, and wondered what Don could have seen in his study about Eden that would cause his peculiar behavior."

Chapter Eleven

Ian Jackson

A knock at the door interrupted Stephen's reflection. Ian Jackson arrived for work early. He had the appearance of a real cowboy. His attire was straight from a John Wayne movie—a tall, medium-build man with a long, brown ponytail and his hair cut short around his face. A few of the church folk frowned at that, but he felt it was none of their business. The reverend had no problem with it. Ian felt the heart of a person was what counted. He was a single man of 43 years old, with a mustache that was a little long around the corners of his mouth, dark skin, and a smooth complexion. In addition, he wore a gold ring that read, "AOTA."

Ian was born in Houston, Texas. Why he moved to Calvin's Point was a mystery. He chose not to discuss his past. When people did ask, he would change the subject by saying, "The past is in the past and that's where it stays."

"Good morning, Ian! You're just in time to have a cup of coffee."

In his unique country drawl, Ian was quick to respond, "That sure sounds like a winner to me."

They took their coffee to the porch. Stephen sat in the swing and began slowly pushing back and forth.

Looking around, Ian said, "You sure have brought this place back to life, Stephen."

Beaming with pride, Stephen agreed. "With your help. When I heard the price of this place, I couldn't believe it. I was convinced it had to be a dump. When we came down to look at it, I felt God had shined a light and verbally declared, 'This is the place, Stephen.'"

"God chose well on your behalf. Stephen, have you thought any more about the storm that came through a few months ago?"

Stephen slowly shook his head, lifted his shoulders and replied, "Have I? Almost all the time. The sheriff didn't find anything, and for some reason, I'm not surprised. But there is one thing he said I can't get out of my mind."

Ian faced Stephen and asked, "What's that?"

"He said, I might find out who has something personal against me. An enemy that has crept in unnoticed."

"That's the way the enemy likes to come in. Unnoticed." Ian stood. "I better get to work; the men will be waiting. Thanks for the coffee."

Hastily, Stephen called out, "Pastor Reynolds asked me to fill in for him Sunday."

Ian smiled, "I think he made a good choice. I know God will give you bread for the people. See you later."

Stephen didn't have a clue what he would speak about Sunday. As he looked out the window, the words that Pastor Reynolds spoke to him raced through his mind. "Go through the garden gate!" *What did he mean by that?* Stephen wondered.

Stephen opened his Bible to Genesis and then quickly turned to Romans. He studied for a couple of hours and felt sure he had found the right topic for his message.

Chapter Twelve
The Visit

Leann and Stephen had the house immac-ulate. The refrigerator was stocked, and all the photo albums were nearby. Stephen could hardly wait for his family to arrive. It was late, Leann had gone home and Stephen was preparing for bed when he heard an unexpected knock on the living room door. He looked out the window, saw a car, but couldn't make out who it was. He put his robe on as he hurried down the stairs, turned the porch light on and asked, "Who is it?"

"The Queen of England!"

Stephen's mouth dropped open as he promptly opened the door. There in front of him was the most welcome sight ever. Overjoyed, Stephen jumped up and down like a little kid at the sight of his three friends. There were hugs, kisses and a few tears on Cordilia's part. The first ten minutes, everyone was so excited they couldn't even carry on a conversation.

Cordilia surveyed the house and uttered, "Is this the same house we helped you move into? This looks like a man-of-abundance estate."

Stephen put his arm around Cordilia. "After the renovation, the abundance is almost depleted. So, I'm praying God will fatten the cows and increase the corn."

Cordilia lowered her head and began to cry. "Stephen, I've missed you! You look so much like your mom, and I will never cease to miss her. I was thinking about what she said to me the day she died. She told me I was jealous because she would be climbing Jacob's ladder first."

Paul took Cordilia by the arm. "Honey, it's been a long day; you and I need some sleep. We'll leave the rest of the night to the youths."

Cordilia grinned and kidded, "You know, I think you're right. Stephen, do you have the feather bed fluffed?"

Stephen picked up a suitcase and said, "Your feather bed is fluffed and waiting. May I show you to your room?"

"Oh, my word. This boy will want a tip. Paul, make sure you have a quarter."

Cordilia, Paul and Philip settled into their rooms. But Philip wasn't going to let the night pass without some time with Stephen to recount the events of the past few months. The front door was open, but the screen was closed. He slowly walked toward the door and opened it. "I knew I would find you out here."

Stephen patted the swing. "Why don't you join me?"

Philip sat and the two began to push the swing back and forth. "How have you been, Stephen?"

Stephen blew his breath out and said, "Very busy. I wish you lived closer, Philip. How is the home place?"

"Just like you left it." Philip paused and asked, "Have you been studying for Sunday?"

Stephen raised his brows, "What do you think?"

"What are you going to speak on?"

Stephen smiled and replied promptly, "The Garden of Eden."

"What revelation are you going to bring us about Eden?"

Surprised, Stephen said, "Eden? I'm not speaking about the Garden of Eden. I'm speaking on Romans 8:28, 'All things work together for the good.' Why did you say that about the Garden?"

Stunned, Philip replied, "Only because you just told me you were going to speak about the Garden of Eden."

"I said that?"

"You did."

Lowering his head, Stephen asked, "Why would I say that?"

Jesting, Philip answered, "You tell me. Okay, let's get right to it. What's going on? And, don't try to patronize me. You know I can see right through you, so be straight with me."

Stephen stood, walked to the edge of the porch and braced his hand against the column. "There have been a couple of things taking place since I last talked to you in depth." Stephen, feeling perplexed, continued, "I felt Shemed's presence one night."

Philip quickly stood and asked, "When was this?"

"I had only been here a little while, and I think I had a dream, but I'm not sure. There was a storm . . . let me correct myself. *I* had a storm."

"What do you mean?"

Stephen faced Philip and continued, "I am the only person in town with any damage. My cow was charred. She looked as though she had been roasted. The corn was a mess! Half flattened with burned strips about two feet apart throughout most of the field. It wasn't just flattened, it was shredded. My barn was a mess, yet no one else had anything but a sprinkle of rain. That night, I felt as though someone was in my room. I could have sworn I saw a green tint on everything, yet there wasn't. My head hurt so bad, and the taste in my mouth was nauseating. I can't mentally conceive what actually took place, but I know something did."

Concerned, Philip put his hand on Stephen's shoulder. "I can't tell you everything, but you had better prepare yourself for battle with prayer and fasting. Not all these misfortunes are accidental. Shemed must be here! Which means, God is moving on your behalf. There is something God wants to reveal to you about the Garden of Eden."

Stephen asked, "But what . . . what could it be?"

"That's something you'll have to find out. Be careful, Stephen, not paranoid, but cautious." Trying to lighten the moment, Philip then asked, "Are you and Leann going to do any carving on the swing like the generations before you?"

Stephen smiled. "She is wonderful, Philip. I love her so much. She's everything a man could dream of having for a wife. She is—"

Philip interrupted, "You sound like a man who wants to say, 'I love her, but . . .!'"

"Philip, I do love her very much, but you're right. I can hardly talk about the wedding. Leann has said a million things about flowers, dresses and so on. But I can't tell you anything she's said. I want to marry her and have children with her. Sometimes I don't want to kiss her, because I want her so badly. Even so, I want to postpone the wedding for a little while. But how do I tell her that?"

"Tell her any way you choose, but you better do that and very soon. Listen, Stephen, where God is going to take you it may be best not to have a wife until you arrive at your destiny. Pray about it! We'll talk more tomorrow." Philip and Stephen hugged goodnight and settled in for some much-needed rest.

Chapter Thirteen

A New Voice

The aroma of freshly brewed coffee, mingled with the luscious smell of bacon, awakened Stephen from his peaceful sleep. He put his arms under his head and remembered the scrumptious aroma of his mom's cooking. Stephen dressed and hurried down stairs to see what Cordilia was making for breakfast. He stopped at the kitchen door and laughed. Paul was taking homemade biscuits out of the oven. "Uncle Paul, I should have known it was you driving me from the comfort of my bed with that heavenly scent."

Paul closed the oven door. "I thought I would give you a treat this morning."

"Hum, I thought sure it was Cordilia."

"Now, Stephen, I said I wanted to give you a treat. Cordilia would have given you a stomachache. She never did conquer the kitchen. Hollywood, she would have taken by storm, but not cooking. Between you and me, she has only two dishes she makes that are even pretty good. You know the saying 'the way to a man's heart is through his stomach.' That has nothing to do with Cordilia."

From the porch came a resounding, "Paul Dawson, I heard that. You know, I may be getting old, but Hollywood would take me in a minute. So, watch what you say."

Paul picked up a biscuit, handed it to Stephen, and said, "This reminds me of the morning you and Philip were born. Cordilia and Rachel were up most of the night with aching backs and swollen ankles. John and I were making breakfast, and just as I was taking the biscuits out of the oven, Rachel made the announcement, 'I have to go to the hospital.'" Paul laughed. "That didn't stop your dad and me from eating though. We wrapped the bacon and egg biscuits, poured a thermos of coffee and ate on the way."

"That sounds like you and dad. Where is Philip?" Stephen asked.

Cordilia called out, "Stephen!"

Stephen went out to see what she wanted. Cordilia was in the porch swing. Stephen gave her a kiss on the forehead. "Did you sleep well?"

"Like a rock! You asked about Philip. He's at the barn with Champion."

"I'll go tell him breakfast is ready. I'll be back in a minute."

Stephen jogged out to the barn, opened the door and watched a moment as Philip was brushing Champion's mane. "He's a beauty, don't you think?" Stephen asked.

Philip seemed not to hear Stephen. Stephen walked over and stood behind Philip. Putting his hand on his shoulder, he asked again, "He's a beauty, don't you think?"

Philip stopped brushing and answered without looking around. "Oh, yes, he's breathtaking."

Upon hearing the voice, Stephen stepped backward. The body was Philip's, but the voice was the sound of someone speaking into an empty barrel. Stephen was too scared to call out for help.

The creature who was possessing Philip's body turned and looked at Stephen as he continued to move backward. The being looked like Philip yet was repulsive. He grinned, and said, "Are you afraid, Stephen? You look like you did when you saw your beloved Sally burnt to a crisp."

In only a whisper, Stephen asked, "Who are you, and what are you doing here?"

The creature walked toward Stephen, who was now backed against a stall. In a voice that raised the hair on Stephen's neck, he said, "My name is Despair, and I'm here for you. You can't escape me!" He laughed so loudly that Stephen's ears were ringing.

Closing his eyes, Stephen was sure he was going to die, but instead he heard someone calling his name. "Stephen! Stephen!" When he felt someone grab hold of his arm, Stephen swung his fists wildly.

"Stephen, stop it! Stop it, Stephen!"

Recognizing the voice as Philip's, Stephen opened his eyes. "Philip! Is that really you?" Stephen was trembling uncontrollably.

Philip took hold of his shoulders and shouted, "What is wrong with you, Stephen? It's me, Philip."

Distraught, Stephen touched Philip's face and whispered, "Is . . . that really you, Philip?"

In unbelief of what he was seeing, Philip answered, "Yes! It's me, Stephen."

Stephen began to weep loudly. He leaned his head forward, placing it on Philip's chest. Philip reassured him that he was safe. When Stephen finally calmed down, he and Philip sat on a bale of hay while Stephen tried to tell what he had seen.

"Philip, this is like something you see in a horror movie. Not in real life."

Before Philip could respond, Cordilia called out, "Is everything okay out there?"

Philip quickly responded, "Yeah, Mom. Everything's fine."

"You better come to breakfast before it gets cold."

"We'll be right there," Philip replied.

Philip hugged Stephen. "Are you okay to go in now, buddy?"

"I think so. I feel much better. Philip, I don't want to say anything about this to your mom and dad okay?"

Philip nodded and agreed not to say anything. "Now, let's go eat before Dad has a fit."

At breakfast, Cordilia sensed something was wrong. She wasn't the kind of person who would let that feeling pass without asking questions. "Have you been taking care of yourself, Stephen?"

"Yes. I've been very busy, but now hopefully things will slow down, and I can get some rest."

Cordilia, Paul and Philip were all looking at Stephen as he rambled on. Aware of this, Stephen put his fork down and asked, "What's going on here? I feel like I'm under a microscope."

Cordilia took the napkin from her lap, placed it on the table, stood and continued to look at Stephen.

"Aunt Cordilia! What is it? I recognize that look, so just ask whatever you want."

Cordilia lowered her head, tightened her lips and stared into Stephen's eyes. "You've encountered Shemed, haven't you?"

Stephen looked at his plate without answering.

Cordilia insisted, "Tell me, Stephen, when this took place?"

Stephen stood, walked to the sink and looked out the window. "I'm not sure." He told them what had taken place, including the event in the barn earlier.

Cordilia joined Stephen at the sink. With deep concern, she pledged, "Shemed will not have you Stephen. Your mother and I fought Gray Stone Kingdom and Queen Jewel herself for you and Philip. By the grace of God and the power of the mighty Holy Spirit, you will dominate every situation that has been created to destroy you."

Paul inserted, "Cordilia's right, Stephen, but don't try to keep this to yourself. You can always call us. There is power in unity. The Bible says, 'Where two or three are gathered in My Name . . .'"

Philip only listened. Cordilia looked at Stephen, then Philip, and asked, "Philip, what are your thoughts? We need your input."

Philip looked at his mother and firmly stated, "This is something Stephen must do alone. Of course, we'll pray with him and for him, but the journey before him is his alone to take. I love him like a brother, but even *I* can do nothing."

Disturbed, Stephen began to massage his temples. "All this is so absurd! I don't know what to think. At times I feel like I've gone mad. The voices, the dreams, the cow, that-that thing I saw in the barn an hour ago. Pastor Reynolds telling me to go through the garden gate. What garden gate? Cordilia . . . Paul . . . Philip, I don't know what to do."

They listened as Stephen released the anxiety that was build up inside. When he finished speaking, he fell to his knees on the kitchen floor. Cordilia, Paul and Philip got on their knees around him and prayed until Stephen felt the overload of stress subside.

Chapter Fourteen

The Gifts

Sunday morning arrived. Stephen had studied and prayed. He felt ready to bring the Word to the people of Calvin's Point Church. He wanted to make a good impression, so he chose his navy blue suit, light blue shirt and navy and red-striped tie. His freshly polished wing tip shoes capped off his attire. After putting his Bible under his arm, he asked, "How do I look?"

Tears welled in Cordilia's eyes. "I've always thought you looked just like Rachel, but not today. You look so like your father. John would have been so proud of you. Especially knowing you have his extraordinarily good looks."

Stephen was 25 years old, six feet tall, well built, with ebony black hair like his mother, Rachel. His tanned complexion accented his perfect white teeth. Stephen had the palest, blue eyes that were a carbon copy of his dad's. Cordilia beamed with pride as she stared at

Stephen. Holding her stare, she asked, "What do you think, Paul?"

Paul nodded. "Exceptional is the word that comes to mind."

Stephen looked at Philip, did a profile pose, lifted his chin high and asked, "What do you think, my brother?"

Philip fluttered his lashes, tilted his head and, in a feminine voice, responded, "You look so pretty. You take my breath away."

Stephen punched his shoulder and shouted, "Shut up!" At those words, Stephen and Philip began to scuffle around. Cordilia interrupted, "Boys! We don't have time to play."

Stephen punched Philip's arm one last time and straightened his jacket.

"Hey, you two! Knock it off! Stephen, come here please." Cordilia straightened his tie and took a small box from her pocket. She opened it and said, "This tie pin belonged to your dad. I brought it for this special occasion." From the box, Cordilia took the gold pin in the shape of an engineer hat and put it on Stephen's tie. "Your dad gave it to Paul, but he wants you to have it."

Tears welled in Paul's eyes.

"It's from your dad and me. Whenever you wear it, I want you to think of us both."

Stephen hugged Paul and thanked him.

Cordilia said, "There is one more thing we want you to have. She took a box from a leather bag sitting beside the sofa. Stephen opened the box to reveal his mom's Bible. Surprised, Stephen looked at Cordilia. "Mom gave this to *you*."

Cordilia nodded. "True. However, the time has come to give it to the rightful owner. I wanted you to carry it today."

Overwhelmed, Stephen embraced Cordilia. "Aunt Cordilia, you have no idea what this means to me. Thank you so much."

"I might add, the margins of this Bible are filled with notes Rachel made as she studied. Now, we'd better get going. The preacher can't be late."

Chapter Fifteen

Humiliation

$\mathcal{E}$ighty people attended the morning worship service. Stephen had butterflies in his stomach but was ready to proclaim the Word of God. Inside the sanctuary, the sunlight glistened through the stained glass windows, causing a smoky effect toward the front of the church. The oak floors, darkened with age, glowed from the polyurethane that had been applied. The oak pews matched the floors perfectly. A table sat on the floor below the stage, which was bordered by a curved altar. On each side sat a gold offering plate filled with tithe envelopes. Directly above the table on the stage stood the oak pulpit. Between the table and the pulpit sat a brightly colored arrangement of fresh cut flowers. The A-frame ceiling supported a stained-glassed chandelier, which had been given in the memory of Jay Stanton III, by his wife, Brenda. Her father built the church in

1898. At 98 years old, with an extraordinary mind, Brenda was the oldest person in Calvin's Point. She also managed to get around quite well. She graced the second pew on the right side of the church every Sunday morning. She was a very wealthy woman whose father and grandfather made their money from growing rice in Charleston, South Carolina. After Jay died, Brenda sold the land in Charleston and settled in their home at Calvin's Point. Jay built the home in Calvin's Point as a vacation retreat, a place they could go to escape the world. Mrs. Stanton had a staff of four to help keep the house in operation.

She was a tall, slender woman with white hair that was finger waved around her face, and pulled into a bun in the back, the bun capped with a gold-lace-designed cover. Almost all her clothing had a high choker neckline on which she wore a pendant in the center. She loved Pastor Reynolds and his wife, Sandra. This Sunday she had come to check out Stephen Daniel and see if he even came close to the fiery pastor she loved to hear.

Brenda Stanton had also provided the church with a baby grand piano.

Tommy Sawyer, the music director, loved the old hymns. If the truth were known, Brenda Stanton had quite a bit to do with that as well.

Tommy led the choir in a couple of hymns, and one congregational song before turning the service over to Stephen. Stephen stepped up to the pulpit, laid his Bible down, and greeted the people. He introduced the Dawsons to the congregation. With a smile, he asked everyone to stand for the reading of God's Word. Feeling very confident, Stephen began, "I want us to turn to Genesis chapter three and start reading at verse one."

Philip quickly looked at Stephen, realizing he was saying the wrong text. Cordilia noticed Philip's uneasy stare. She nudged Philip and whispered, "What's wrong?"

Perplexed, Philip replied, "That's not his text."

"Are you sure?" Cordilia asked.

"Yes, Mom! I'm sure."

With zeal, Stephen said, "If everyone has it, say, Amen."

In unison, the congregation responded, "Amen."

"Now the serpent was more subtle than any beast of the field . . ." Stephen instantly broke out in a sweat. He was so embarrassed he would have loved to crawl into a hole and never come out. His mouth was as dry as cotton. He rubbed his chin and explained, "I am just a little nervous, so please bear with me. Would you please turn to Roman's 8:28. 'And we know that all things work together for the good of them that love God, to them who are called according to His purpose.'"

Stephen calmed down after the reading and went into his message. He was doing exceptionally well until he gave the altar call. Again, he went completely off the subject. "If there is one here today who doesn't know the way, you need to stand now and go through the garden gate. Only there will you find the answers to the mysteries that have been hidden from the foundation of the world. Come through the garden gate. Come just as you are."

Confused, the congregation glanced at each other. Stephen continued as if he was unaware of what he was saying. Cordilia looked at Paul in despair, "Oh, Lord . . . Paul, what can we do?"

Paul slowly replied, "There's nothing we can do."

Leann, who was sitting with her mom and dad, was hurting so deeply for Stephen, who again realized what he had done. He asked one of the deacons to close with prayer, and he went out the back door, too humiliated to face anyone. Leann rushed out to catch him. He was getting into his car when she finally caught up with him.

"Stephen!"

Without looking at her, he demanded, "Leann, please. I am not in any kind of mood to see or talk to anyone. Now please let me go before the people are dismissed."

Leann took hold of his arm and asked, "Why won't you let me get close to you? I love you! I know you're embarrassed, but you can't run from the people. You see most of them every day."

Desperate to get away, Stephen took hold of Leann's hand and pulled it from his arm. He frowned and sternly said, "I said, I want to go! Now excuse me."

Stephen got into the car and hastily drove away. Philip came out in time to see Stephen's behavior. Seeing that Leann was crushed, Philip put his hand on her shoulder and tried to comfort her.

Fighting back the tears, Leann said, "If this kind of behavior doesn't stop, there won't be a wedding."

Philip tried to take up for Stephen, but Leann wouldn't hear of it. Frustrated, she looked at Philip and confessed, "Stephen hasn't been the same since the storm. I don't know what to do. He won't let me help him."

Philip said, "I don't think you, me or anyone can help him right now."

Annoyed, Leann said, "I could help him if he would only allow me to. I could."

She turned and walked away. Cordilia and Paul joined Philip. "My heart breaks for him," Cordilia said.

Jamie and Jason asked Philip where Stephen had gone. "We're very concerned for him. We love him like he was our own son," Jamie said.

Jason spoke up. "Jamie and I were going to ask all of you out to dinner, but due to the recent circumstances we'll just ask you three to join us."

Philip looked at his parents. "You two go on. I need some time alone with Stephen."

Chapter Sixteen

Advice from Philip

The first place Philip went was back to Stephen's house. He looked everywhere, but no Stephen. Philip decided to check in the barn. Perhaps Stephen would be with Champion. He opened the barn door and called out, "Stephen! Stephen! Are you in here?" Philip knew he had to be around somewhere. His car was in the driveway. He left the barn and loudly called out, "Stephen! Where are you? I know you're around here somewhere." There was no answer. Philip began to walk through the cornfield, calling Stephen's name. After a short walk through the corn, he saw Stephen sitting in the middle of the field, with his arms wrapped around his knees. He stopped and looked at Stephen.

"You know, Stephen, it's okay to sit in the field, but it would have been nice if you would have answered me." Stephen still didn't acknowledge that Philip was there. Philip cleared a place and sat down beside him. Stephen lowered his head and rested it on his knees but still said nothing.

Philip looked straight ahead. "Do you remember when we were young boys, how we would go to the barn and play? We rarely played ordinary games. You would preach and I would be a prophet and tell our pretend congregation all the events that would befall each one of them. We didn't have a congregation, at least for a while. Then the angels appeared one day while you were preaching. It scared you so bad you almost wet your pants. One of them told us they came to observe the future. After that, they came all the time. There was one angel there named Haleb. Your mom encountered Haleb many times. Did you ever tell her that we met Haleb long before she did?"

There was silence for a moment before Stephen finally spoke, "No! I didn't. I don't know why. I just didn't. I never told her about the angels at all, until after Dad died. She wanted me to go back to Duke University and learn all a prominent school could offer. I told her I felt the call to be a minister of the Gospel. She questioned me, and I told her about the angels that came to the barn and how I was always afraid and you never were. I never did understand why you weren't afraid when I was so scared. You would go up and talk to them like they were your friends."

Stephen slowly turned, looked at his friend, and asked, "Tell me, Philip, why was it you were never afraid?"

Philip took a deep breath. "Some people are afraid of heights. Some people aren't and challenge the high places. You were afraid of the angels. I wasn't."

Looking ahead, Stephen asked, "Why did I say that about the garden gate? Why? I hadn't studied anything about the garden. I made a complete fool of myself. I can't believe for an altar call I was telling them to go through the garden gate." Stephen laughed. "Do you believe that? Come just as you are . . . through the garden gate." Shaking his head, Stephen whispered, "Lord, help me!"

By now, Philip was laughing with Stephen. When the laughter died down, Philip asked, "Why don't you go through the garden gate, Stephen? God is obviously calling you to go. Obedience is everything."

Stephen stared into Philip's eyes and confessed, "I don't have one clue how to go through the garden gate. It's easy to say 'go through,' but where is the gate? I don't know which way to turn."

Soberly, Philip said, "The garden is Eden. The gate is the entrance to Eden. The Bible holds the key to the gate. Go to the Word, and you'll find your way."

Philip and Stephen were walking back to the house when Philip said, "You hurt Leann. You know that don't you?"

Stephen stopped, lowered his head and confessed, "I can't go through with the marriage right now. There is so much spinning around in my head, Philip. I just pray she will understand and that . . . that she will wait for me. I do love her very much."

"I'll pray for the both of you. We'll be going home soon, but I'll be here with you in spirit."

Stephen took a deep breath. "I dread talking to Leann, and I sure pray Pastor Reynolds will be home tomorrow. It will be a load off me just to know he's okay."

The night was spent with reminiscing about days gone by in Todd's Creek. Too swiftly the night was consumed and the time for good-byes had arrived. Hugs, kisses and reassurance were given. The next morning, Cordilia, Paul and Philip were on their way back to Todd's Creek.

Chapter Seventeen

Postponing the Wedding

The first thing on the day's agenda for Stephen was to talk to Leann. He couldn't put if off any longer. It wasn't fair or honest to Leann, her not knowing his feeling about postponing the wedding. He called, but she had left for work. Stephen cut a red rose from his flower garden and headed for Ginger Banks' home. He knocked; Leann opened the door. She was as radiant as the sunshine after a stormy night. Her eyes connected with Stephen's, and she felt a burning heat well up inside her. Her passion was demanding Stephen to take her in his arms and make passionate love to her. Yet something within said that wouldn't be for a while.

She grinned and asked Stephen to come inside. Ginger had left for Augusta and would not be back until late evening. Stephen had one hand behind him as he entered the house.

Leann closed the door and leaned against it. Stephen brought the rose from behind his back, handed it to her and then told her how sorry he was for his behavior. As their eyes met, Stephen leaned forward and kissed Leann on the cheek. The exotic aroma of her perfume sent a tingle through Stephen's body, and he quickly kissed her lips. They stared into each other's eyes and a fiery passion shot through them both. Stephen gently took her face into his hands and pressed his lips against hers. The passion was so hot it burned from head to toe. Leann moved her fingers to unbutton Stephen's shirt and pulled it from his jeans, opened it and pulled him tightly to her. "I want you so desperately. Stephen." She whispered.

He kissed her again and again. Instantly, Stephen froze.

"Stephen! Don't stop." Leann groaned.

Stephen fought desperately not to become one with Leann. She stared into his eyes. "Leann, this is so wrong. I can't."

Leann straightened her blouse and in a low whisper agreed, "You're right, Stephen."

"I want you so much, but I can't sin against God." Stephen said with tears in his eyes.

"I know. I'm so sorry," Leann said as she and Stephen sat up on the sofa.

Stephen lowered his head and then faced Leann. Before he could say anything, Leann sadly said, "There's not going to be a wedding for a while, is there?"

Stephen felt relieved that Leann knew. Yet, he ached inside, knowing that she was hurting. Stephen held her hands and kissed them. "Will you wait for me, Leann?"

Without hesitation, Leann said, "You know I'll wait for you. The Holy Spirit told me this would happen. I didn't want it to. I thought I could hold you by giving my body to you. I not only ask you to forgive me, but above all, I ask God to forgive me. I'll be here anytime for you, Stephen. All you have to do is call."

"I love you, Leann! I pray the time will be short and God will bring us together as man and wife. Please pray for me."

"I will pray for you every day, Stephen."

Stephen embraced her and kissed her forehead. "I'll call you later."

Leann watched as Stephen drove away. Although her heart was breaking, she realized Stephen had to be obedient to what God was calling him to do. By doing so, he would come back to her even more blessed.

Chapter Eighteen

Good to Be Home

Stephen was relieved when Pastor Reynolds answered the phone. Ecstatic, Stephen said, "You have no idea how thankful I am to hear your voice."

"Thank you, Stephen. It's good to hear your voice. I want to thank you for filling in for me Sunday."

"Hum. I was so embarrassed. I slipped out the back door while Deacon Payne closed with prayer."

"Sandra told me you were saying something about the garden gate."

"Pastor . . ."

Before Stephen finished his statement, Pastor Reynolds interrupted, "Stephen, please call me Don. That is my name! Pastor is only a title."

"Sure, uh, Don. After what you told me last Wednesday about going through the garden gate, it bore on my mind so strong, it was all I could think about."

Pausing, Don asked, "What exactly did I say to leave such an impression?"

Surprised, Stephen responded, "You don't remember what you said about the Garden of Eden?"

"Of course, I remember, but was there one particular thing that burned in your mind?"

"There was more than one thing. The main thing being, you said you didn't think you would be coming back home. When you broke out in a sweat, I believed you. About the garden, you said God was revealing many things to you, and if you didn't come back, to promise you I would go through the gate into the Garden of Eden. So, what made you think you weren't coming back?"

"I was just under so much stress. I was dead tired; therefore, my emotions were a wreck. I apologize, Stephen. The retreat worked a miracle on my being. I feel like a new man."

Delighted, Stephen said, "Thank God for a retreat. Maybe that's what I need. Things have been crazy of late, but I know God will help me through it."

"How's Leann?" Don asked.

"I hope she's okay. I think she is. We . . . we postponed the wedding for a while. I need to get my direction straight before I try to take on a family."

"If that's what you feel, then that's what you need to do. Leann's a strong woman, I'm sure she'll be fine."

"Pastor . . . I mean, Don, I better go. Ian Jackson is coming through the gate. I am so pleased you're home."

"I'll come over soon, and we'll talk more, if you'd like," Don said.

"I would like that very much," Stephen said. "I want to hear what the Lord revealed to you about the Garden."

About the time Ian Jackson was going to knock at the door, Stephen opened it. Startled, Ian jerked his hand back, "Man, you gave me a bit of a scare."

Stephen laughed, "I'm sorry, Ian. I saw you coming."

Ian frowned. "Where did you get off to so fast after church yesterday?"

Stephen looked toward heaven. "Oh, Lord, how long will it take to live this down?"

Ian laughed. "I'd say 'awhile.'" After a hefty laugh, Ian said, "I hired a couple of extra men for harvesting the corn and getting the cows ready for market."

With a quick nod of the head, Stephen agreed the extra help was necessary. "Jason wanted us to combine with his workers and help with his crops, and he, in turn, will help us. I thought helping him out would give the workers a little overtime. God knows some of the workers need it. I thought if the cattle and corn bring a good price, I would give a little extra on their checks."

Ian took his hat off and wiped his forehead. "I know the men would be so thankful for that generous act of kindness. You're a good man, Stephen Harris." Ian put his hat on and headed toward his truck. About halfway, he turned and asked, "Are you coming out in the fields today?"

Stephen put his hands on his hips. "I may be out in a little while. I have to go to the market and by Jason Conner's first."

Chapter Nineteen

Ready for Work

*I*an threw his hand up, got in his truck and drove away. Stephen hurried to Andy's Market. He dreaded going but knew he would have to face the townspeople, sooner or later. Sooner was probably the better choice. He parked his dad's black 1937 Ford pickup, took a deep breath, straightened his shirt and went inside.

Upon entering the market, Andy Taylor, the owner called out, "Why, Mr. Harris, how are you doing?"

"Doing fine, Andy, and you?"

"Great! That was quite a message yesterday."

Humiliated, Stephen confessed, "Andy, you don't have to try and make me feel good. I messed up . . . and big time."

A voice from behind acknowledged, "Come on, Stephen, it wasn't that bad. You sounded like a man with a mission."

Stephen quickly turned to see who else was present to hear his blunder. "Sheriff Bolton!" Stephen said, as he extended his hand for a handshake. "How are you doing?"

Sheriff Bolton smiled. "Finer than a frog hair on an over-weight frog."

Stephen looked at Andy, "My, my."

"Have you had any more trouble out at your farm?" Sheriff Bolton asked.

With a sigh of relief, Stephen said, "No. Thank, God!"

"Tell me something, Stephen. In your opinion, do you think there is a chance your 'mission' you revealed yesterday has anything to do with what took place out at your farm?"

Stephen scratched his head and admitted, "I am beginning to think so. I just don't know what yet."

Sheriff Bolton got close to Stephen, gazed into his eyes and suggested, "You better watch your back, son. There is something evil breeding out there. In Vietnam, you could smell the evil. The stench was everywhere. You can't forget it. I recognized that same odor at your place the other day." The sheriff patted Stephen's shoulder and added, "If you need me, call."

"I will, and thanks for the concern."

Sheriff Bolton turned and threw his hand up. "See you, Andy!"

Chapter Twenty

Andy's Market

Stephen got the items he needed, put a paper bag in each arm and left the store. Looking down, he didn't notice the white stretch limousine parked on the passenger side of his truck. He put the bags in the truck bed and opened the door. Before he could get inside, he heard someone call his name. "Mr. Harris!" Stephen looked up and saw the limousine. Immediately, he knew it was Brenda Stanton. She was the only person in Calvin's Point that owned such an extravagant car. She even had a chauffeur to go with it. She had the window rolled down halfway and was calling him from inside the car.

"Stephen!"

Reluctantly, Stephen closed the truck door and walked over to her car.

With both hands, she held the top of the window. Facing him, her eyes were squinted to keep the sun's bright glare from blinding her view.

Stephen's mind was racing. Every step of the way, he wondered why she would be calling out to him. Suddenly dread griped his mind knowing she surely was going to say something about the service.

Stephen smiled. "Mrs. Stanton! What brings a lovely lady like you out this morning?"

Sternly, Mrs. Stanton said, "For heaven sakes, Stephen. I'm not out fishing for compliments. I happen to know I'm wrinkled and look somewhat like a prune, but I would like to talk to you for a moment. Would you join me in the car?"

Mystified, Stephen whispered, "Of course."

Charles Wilson, her chauffeur, had been with Brenda for twenty-five years—a large black man with salt and pepper hair that curled tightly to his head and who endured more than most people would. He boasted the pay was substantial; therefore, he could put up with whatever came his way.

Liz, Charles' wife, was a housekeeper for Mrs. Stanton. She and Charles had quarters in the main house. Liz was a fiery, five foot-two, light-skinned woman. She sang old spirituals all the time. Mrs. Stanton's only request was for her to please refrain from singing when she had guests. When alone, Mrs. Stanton joined Liz in the beloved spirituals. Brenda was paying the tuition for their only son, Grant, to attend the University of Georgia. Grant grew up in the Stanton house, and Brenda loved him as her own. He was a handsome young man. His skin color was brown. He had black curly hair, stood six feet three inches tall and weighed two hundred fifty pounds. He had played basketball from the time he was old enough to walk. He now played for the University of Georgia Bulldogs.

Charles quickly got out of the car and opened the door for Stephen. Inside, Stephen was looking from left to right, admiring the car. Impressed, Stephen expressed, "Wow! This is some car! I have never been in a limousine like this. I rode in one when my dad died, but it wasn't like this."

Brenda raised her chin, tilted her head slightly and confessed, "I bought this for status only. Knowing the money I have, people would make fun of me if I had Charles drive me around in something like your pickup."

Stephen shook his head and grinned. "You're absolutely right. You don't belong in my pickup."

Brenda furrowed her brows. "That was your father's truck, wasn't it?"

"Yes, it was."

Mrs. Stanton took a deep breath. "Stephen, I know you have to be curious as to why I asked you to join me in my car."

"Without a doubt," Stephen confessed.

"I have been doing some checking up on you and your finances."

Dumbfounded at the statement, Stephen asked, "Why would you do that? Pardon my frankness, but that's really none of your business."

Mrs. Stanton chuckled. "That is the kind of answer I expected and the kind I wanted, for what I have in mind."

Baffled, Stephen demanded, "Just what do you have in mind that would lead you to check my finances?"

Brenda sternly answered, "I want to offer you a business proposition. It's strictly business. So, please hear me out before you decide to call Sheriff Bolton, will you?"

Not sure how to feel or what to think, Stephen responded, "What kind of business proposition do you have in mind?"

"I have a granddaughter who lives in New York City. Her name is Victoria Lee Stanton. She is 43 years old, and she happens to be the only heir to the Stanton money. She is spoiled beyond means and works for *My Magazine* as a reporter. It cost me dearly to land that job for her—a well-educated person but not easy to get along with . . . period. She doesn't go to church, and she acts as though she is a purebred heathen at times. It's not that she wasn't taught about God; her father was a godly man. I miss him terribly. A child should never die before his parents." Brenda was fighting back tears but managed to contain herself. "Oh, well! As I was saying . . . twice a year she comes to visit. I'm sure she loves me, in her own way, but I am no fool. It's not her love for me that drives her to visit. It's her love for money."

Stephen interrupted, "I don't mean to be rude, but what does any of this have to do with me or my business?"

Brenda lifted her eyebrows. "Please, bear with me awhile longer, and you will see." She pointed to the limo bar and asked, "Would you like a cold drink? I have almost anything stocked."

"If you have a Pepsi, that would be nice."

Mrs. Stanton put ice in a wineglass, filled it with Pepsi and handed it to Stephen. She leaned back in the seat. "Let me get right to the point, Stephen. I asked the president of *My Magazine* to give my granddaughter a special assignment. I requested that she be assigned to a story about life on a farm. I not only want her to write about it, I want her to experience it. Right here in Calvin's Point. She will be expected to go out with the workers early in the morning. She will take hundreds of photos, and at night, she will write, study the photos and will do whatever else necessary to prepare the story. I want her to see firsthand that the money she is inheriting came from

95

hard work. Her deadline is set for two months from now."

Confused, Stephen said, "I don't understand. What does all this have to do with me?"

"I want to rent a room from you for the duration of Victoria's stay."

Abruptly, Stephen stated, "No! I don't rent rooms, especially to women. Leann would have a fit."

"Leann is not so insecure that a 43-year-old woman would bother her, is she? Victoria is almost twenty years older than you. Besides, that is a big house, and she needs to stay at the farm she writes about. She would never get up in time if she stayed with me, and I don't want to be too harsh. God knows she needs it, but nevertheless.

She will clean her own room and help with preparing dinner. That aside, I will give you twenty thousand dollars for the two months stay. Before you give me your answer, I know your money is almost depleted from buying the cattle and getting your first crops started. The twenty thousand could tide you over in case something unforeseen should arise."

Stephen thought a moment and then asked, "Is this going to be okay with your granddaughter?"

"Whatever I say, she will do. Yes, it will be fine with her. I also want you to witness to her about her soul. See, this could be fertile ground in which to plant a seed and watch good grow from all the mess she carries inside." Mrs. Stanton straightened her posture and declared, "All right. I'll give you twenty-five thousand, and that's it. Take it or leave it."

Stephen frowned and scratched his head. After thinking, he said, "That is a lot of money . . . but, I need to ask Leann before I decide."

Brenda picked the telephone up and handed it to Stephen. "Go ahead and call."

Stephen called and explained everything to Leann. Brenda also spoke to Leann about her granddaughter. Leann didn't hesitate with her answer. "Stephen, that's up to you. Not me. I don't think any 43-year-old woman will be a threat, if you love me. If anything, at her age, she should be more of a mother figure than anyone to be jealous over."

Stephen couldn't believe Leann's attitude. He thought he heard her snicker when she was hanging up the phone. Stephen placed the phone on the hook and said, "Okay. I'll do it." When will she be coming?"

"Charles is going to pick her up in Atlanta at 6:00 p.m."

Shocked, Stephen asked, "Today?"

"Yes . . . today!"

"That's pretty short notice, but I guess I can get everything ready."

Brenda took a check from her purse and handed it to Stephen. "Here is fifteen thousand. I will give you the rest when this is over." Mrs. Stanton specified the items Victoria would demand.

Stephen agreed, took the check and shook Mrs. Stanton's hand.

Charles opened the door. As Stephen stepped out of the car, he whispered, "Good luck!"

Mrs. Stanton asked, "What was that you said, Charles?"

Charles smiled at Stephen, and replied, "I was just wishing Mr. Harris a good day."

Snappy, Brenda made known her thoughts, "I don't think that was what I heard. I may not hear as well as I used to, but I'm not deaf yet. Now! Let's go."

Chapter Twenty-One
Brenda Stanton

All the way to Jason Conner's, Stephen tried to figure out what he had just agreed to. He also hated to discuss the news with Leann's parents about the wedding being postponed.

Leann called her mom and dad before Stephen arrived. They were disappointed, but wanted God's will for Stephen and Leann.

Stephen shared with Jason and Jamie the agreement he had just made with Mrs. Stanton. Jason was quick to say, "Lord help you, Stephen. If you needed money, you should have come to Jamie and me. I've met Victoria twice, and she is . . ." Jason paused, exhaled, shook his head and confessed, "I don't know the proper words to express my feelings about her."

Jamie was quick to speak up. "I know the words Jason is too embarrassed to say. She is a woman straight from hell."

Astonished at his wife, Jason said, "Honey! That's pretty harsh."

Tightening her lips and widening her eyes, Jamie was unrelenting in her statement. "I didn't intend for it to be nice. She's not nice. Leann has met her. Stephen, that's the reason Leann doesn't mind her renting a room from you. She knows she will be nothing but torment."

Wearied, Jason put his hand on the back of his neck and began to massage his tight muscles. "Jamie! Enough said, okay."

A quick nod, and Jamie agreed. "You're right, dear. Actions will speak louder than words." She hugged Stephen and assured him, "I will pray for you, because you will need it. And, if Jason takes up for her one more time, he will be renting a room from you as well. He evidently needs his memory refreshed. As far as you and Leann, in God's time, you two will be married. Now, I have some chores to do, so I'll talk to you later."

Stephen and Jason watched as Jamie walked toward the house. Jason lifted his hands, and said, "Lord, while you are giving Stephen grace, please add to mine."

Stephen laughed. "Is Victoria Stanton really that bad?"

Jason put his arm around Stephen's shoulder as they walked toward the truck. "Son, she's that bad and worse. I just can't give Jamie that

kind of leeway, or she would go on and on."
Jason clicked his tongue. "Sometimes, Jamie
is almost that bad." He slapped his hands
together and laughed. "But I'm scared to death
to tell her, so I just let her talk. However, there
is some good news, Stephen. Leann takes after
her dad."

After a short visit, Stephen hurried home
to prepare for the guest he wasn't sure he
wanted. But, hopefully two months would go
fast, and twenty-five thousand dollars was a
lot of money.

Chapter Twenty-Two

Visitor Arrives

The summer sun beat down and the humidity was dreadful. Stephen had set the air conditioning on sixty-five to make sure the house was cool. He had fluffed the down feather bed and put the one-thousand-thread-count sheets on his guest bed. As specified, he purchased a new down comforter and fresh cut flowers for the table that sat in front of the large bay window. For the finishing touch, he put a box of chocolates and a basket of fresh fruit on the desk she would be using to work on her article. He observed the oversized room decorated with yellow and the royal blue floral drapes with white sheer liners. A royal blue wing chair sat beside the table at the bay window. The thick, expensive towels were in the guest bathroom, and the room was dust free. Stephen felt touches of his mother, Rachel, popped out at the seams as he cleaned and decorated the bedroom and bath. His mom was a perfectionist when it came to those kinds of things. One last look, and Stephen closed the door. He felt confident there would be nothing left for criticism.

Stephen was sitting on the porch swing when he saw the limousine turn off the main road into his driveway. Feeling a little apprehensive, Stephen stood and waited to view this woman whom everyone thought to be appalling.

Charles got out of the car and called out, "Good evening, Mr. Harris."

Stephen smiled and walked toward the car to greet his guest. When Charles opened the door, a long slender leg was the first thing Stephen saw. Charles took the woman's hand and helped her from the car. A large brimmed hat prevented Stephen from viewing her face, but the rest of her was exquisite. As she slowly raised her head, Stephen's eyes widened to capacity. She was gorgeous. The most beautiful woman Stephen had ever seen. Victoria was five feet ten inches tall, and her figure was one every woman in America would desire to have. She looked as though she had stepped out of a fashion show, wearing a black velvet wide-brimmed hat with the front of the rim turned down toward her face. A narrow band around the hat was red silk, graced with a large red rose. The calf-length red dress, fit like a tight glove. A slit went up the right side of the dress, stopping half way up her thigh. A wide, black belt hugged her tiny waist. The dress was sleeveless, and the low V-neck revealed the top of her voluptuous breasts. Black high heels accented her sexy, long legs. A narrow strap fit across her toes and a buckle fastened around her small ankles. Her face looked like an angel with red full lips, white porcelain skin, rosy cheeks, large green eyes and high arched eyebrows. Platinum blond hair rested on her squared shoulders, revealing large red, hoop earrings.

The new houseguest who stood before him left Stephen overwhelmed. She was nothing like he had imagined. Charles could see Stephen was stunned, so he said, "Mr. Harris, this is Victoria Stanton. Victoria, meet Stephen Harris."

"Hi . . . hello," Stephen managed to get out.

Victoria gazed at Stephen and abruptly asked, "What's the matter with you, cat got your tongue? Or can you not possibly take your eyes off my breasts long enough to get your words together?"

Embarrassed, Stephen looked aside and apologized. "I'm sorry if I stared. I was expecting someone quite different."

Victoria tilted her head and confessed, "So was I." She grinned as she walked by Stephen to the porch. Stephen took a deep breath in to smell the captivating perfume that trailed behind her. He turned and watched her walk to the steps, moving her rounded hips from side to side. Charles again saw Stephen was staring. He nudged him and whispered, "Go on, before she calls you."

Stephen held his arm out and with pride announced, "Welcome to Eden's Gate, Victoria. It's good to have you."

Victoria sneered her nose; put one hand against her chest leaned her head forward, and ridiculed, "Have me? It's good to, 'Have me?' You may want me, which is obvious from the drool hanging from your lips, but you don't *have* me. But, if you're a good boy, you may have me before I leave. If you take a long bath."

Stephen was flabbergasted! He looked at Charles, then at Victoria. Words fled his being. He was beginning to understand what everyone had warned him about, but no one mentioned her beauty. All they had talked about was her disposition. He prayed it wouldn't be any worse than he had already encountered.

Rudely, Victoria snapped, "Charles, would you please get my bags from the car. Grandmother doesn't pay you the kind of money she does for you to stand around and do nothing. I need to get inside before I die from heat stroke. I think this place is hell itself."

Stephen turned to help Charles get a bag, but Charles stopped him, by whispering, "I'll get the bags. You take care of the wind bag."

Feeling uneasy, Stephen put the bag down, hurried to open the door for Victoria and welcomed her inside. Charles followed behind with her bags. She had a total of ten suitcases and a large make-up case.

Victoria was turning her head left to right checking the house.

"Would you like something cold to drink?" Stephen asked, not sure what to expect for an answer.

She faced Stephen and walked close enough to him that he could feel her breath on his face as she spoke. "What do you have to offer? Iced tea?" she snarled.

Stephen could take no more. Money or not, he wasn't going to listen to another sarcastic remark. "Listen here, Victoria! I don't care if you are old enough to be my mother; I want this rudeness stopped. You're in my home, and I am not going to hear this kind of outburst for two months. Now, I'll show you to your room."

Victoria raised one brow and said, "A good thing for you that I am too tired to respond to your outburst right now."

Stephen picked up a couple of suitcases, as did Charles. Stephen paused and looked at

Victoria, but said nothing. She frowned and snapped, "Well, what are you waiting for?"

Calmly, Stephen replied, "I'm waiting for you to get your make-up case."

Shocked at the response, Victoria frowned. "Me?"

"That's right. Your dainty little hands aren't broken, are they?"

Victoria jerked the case up and shouted, "Just show me to my room."

Chapter Twenty-Three

A Visit from Brenda Stanton

After Victoria was settled in her room, Charles went to pick up Brenda Stanton so she could see Victoria in her new surroundings.

Brenda came inside and immediately asked, "Well, Stephen, what do you think of my granddaughter?"

"Mrs. Stanton, I have no words to describe what I think."

Brenda grinned. "Just watch the display when she comes downstairs. It always amuses me."

A voice called from the top of the stairs, "Grandmother!"

Stephen didn't recognize the voice. This voice was sweet as honey, not the she-devil voice he heard earlier. Victoria embraced Mrs. Stanton and went on about how good it was to see her.

"How do you like this beautiful farm of Stephen's?" Mrs. Stanton asked.

"It's picture-perfect, Grandmother, and my room is wonderful. Stephen, I want to thank you for the candy and fruit." She hugged Mrs. Stanton, smiled and said, "I know my grandmother told you all the things I love, because my room is filled with them. Thank you again, Stephen. That was so thoughtful."

Stephen could have dropped over from watching the Oscar-winning performance. This was not the woman he met earlier.

The door opened. Liz and Charles brought in covered dishes. "Stephen, I had Liz prepare you and Victoria supper."

"Thank you, Grandmother, and you too, Liz. I can hardly wait to indulge myself. How about you, Stephen, are you hungry?"

Stunned, Stephen replied, "Yes, I am."

"Will you join us, Grandmother? Liz, you and Charles join us as well."

Mrs. Stanton replied, "Maybe another time. Charles better get Liz and me home. It's past our bedtime. Right, Liz?"

"Yes. It most certainly is. Goodnight, Mr. Harris," Liz said as she walked toward the door. Mrs. Stanton gave Victoria a hug. "You better get some sleep, dear. Seven o'clock comes early."

Puzzled by her grandmother's statement, Victoria asked, "Seven o'clock? Really? Why so early?"

"The men have to do the brunt of the work before the sun gets too hot," Stephen said with some satisfaction.

After everyone left, Stephen asked Victoria to come eat. She walked to the table and sat down, but said nothing.

"This meal is delicious," Stephen said.

Victoria didn't respond. She finished her meal, wiped her mouth and put the napkin on the table.

"Are you going to bed now?" Stephen asked.

Victoria leaned her body over the table toward Stephen and seductively asked, "What's it to you? Do you want to join me or something?"

Stephen looked her in the eye and said, "I set your alarm clock for six a.m."

After Victoria went to bed, Stephen called Leann to make sure she was all right. It was late, but Stephen knew how upset she had been that morning. She was in bed, but eagerly took the call.

"I'm sorry to call so late, Leann. Victoria Stanton went to bed only five minutes ago."

"So, how is it going with your guest?"

"You seem to take some delight in the matter. Is this true?" Stephen asked.

Leann laughed, "I must confess. I've met Victoria a few times. She's horrible! I don't think Satan himself could put up with her."

"So . . . that's why you didn't mind her long visit. Are we talking payback?"

"Stephen, I love and trust you. I'm sure you noticed Victoria is a knock out."

Stephen chuckled. "I saw her beauty only for a moment. After that, all I could see was her hateful, detestable, disgusting ways. I wanted to punch her."

"Honey, it's only for two months. You can make it. With twenty-five-thousand dollars at stake, you can tolerate quite a bit."

"I miss you, Leann."

"I miss you too, babe. I pray God will give you the direction you need very soon."

Chapter Twenty-Four

The Look

Stephen went to bed and intended to pray while lying there, but the next thing he knew the alarm clock was going off. Barely able to move, he dragged himself out of bed and took a cool shower to help get fully awake. He dressed and went to knock on Victoria's door to make sure she was awake. He was surprised her door was wide open. He thought, *She must have been up during the night, because the door was closed when I went to bed.*

Stephen called out, "Victoria! It's time to get up. Are you awake?"

She didn't answer.

Stephen reluctantly glanced into the room. Looking through to the bed, Stephen froze. He should have called out to her, but did not. Her beauty was enchanting. For a moment, Stephen had to fight the erotic emotions that were stirring in every ounce of his being. She was lying on her side, with no cover. The white, satin, short nighty was around her waist, exposing her white satin bikini panties. Stephen could feel his heart beating so hard he felt his chest moving.

"Oh, God, help me!" he whispered as he turned and went down the stairs.

As he put on the coffee, he fought the lustful fire that was burning inside. Stephen had never experienced this kind of raw emotion before. Not even with Leann. He fought the urge to go back to Victoria's room and take her by force, if necessary. Knowing that he needed help, he went to the sofa, made it an altar and asked God to cover his mind that could see only Victoria's alluring body as she lay sleeping.

Stephen had felt the same forceful urges with Leann the morning after the storm. His mouth had the same nauseating taste it had that morning. As Stephen prayed, Victoria walked into the living room. "Are you praying for me, Stephen?" she teased.

Startled, Stephen quickly turned and looked at Victoria.

"I'm sorry. Did I scare you? You didn't think I was the boogie man, did you?"

"You did startle me, but only because I'm just not used to anyone being in the house." Stephen stood and looked at Victoria standing there in her gown. "You ought to get dressed; the men will be here soon."

She smiled, put her hand on her hip and said, "You like what you see, don't you? Have you never viewed a mature woman before? I know you liked what you saw when you stared at me lying in bed."

Stephen trembled, unable to find words to answer her. "The-the coffee's ready," he stammered.

As he walked by her, she seized his arm. "You're a handsome young man, Stephen. I'll let you in on a secret. I wish you would have come to me satisfied your passion when you were staring at me." She softly whispered, "I burn inside just thinking about your lips touching me." Victoria leaned her head toward Stephen's, brushed her silky blonde hair across his face. The fragrance of her hair was exhilarating. She put her lips against his ear, still holding his arm. Stephen tingled as her warm breath gently blew against his skin. In a low tone she moaned, "I can make you feel like you have never dreamed possible."

Stephen couldn't move. He wanted to, but at that moment his sexual desire was greater than he could restrain. When he felt her tongue stroke against his ear, he could take no more. Like a wild animal, Stephen grabbed her shoulders and kissed her. They melted like hot wax from a burning candle onto the floor. Stephen slowly pulled the strap from her shoulder as he passionately kissed her neck, when the doorbell rang, Stephen froze as though he had been shot. He looked at Victoria in anguish, closed his eyes and groaned, "Oh, God. What am I doing?" The sound of the doorbell ringing sent an explosion of pain through Stephen's head. He raised his body from Victoria, sat in the floor, put both hands over his face and wept loudly. "God, please forgive me! What's wrong with me? Why am I acting like this?"

The doorbell stopped ringing. Victoria sat on the floor beside Stephen and watched as he cried out to God for forgiveness. She lightly put her hand on his shoulder. "Stephen, are you okay?"

Taking his hands from his face, Stephen wiped the tears from his chin, then whispered without looking at her, "I want you out of here. Today."

Stunned, Victoria slapped Stephen on the back and shouted, "Who do you think you are, telling me to get out?" She stood, put her hands on her hips and stormed, "I am not going anywhere."

Angered, Stephen stood, and through gritted teeth demanded, "I want you out of my house by noon. Do I make myself clear, Miss Stanton?" Stephen turned to leave the room.

Victoria was furious. "You're such a hypocrite!" she yelled.

Stephen stopped, turned and asked, "Just what do you mean by that?"

Victoria walked toward Stephen with her lips and eyebrows drawn tight. Stopping in front of him, she bluntly replied, "You want to throw me out because you can't control your lust."

Stephen protested, "My lust! What do you think you were doing?" Pointing to her gown, Stephen lashed out, "Why don't you get some clothes on?"

"You're trying to blame me for your actions," Victoria declared firmly.

Stephen shouted, "How is a man supposed to respond when he sees a beautiful woman before him with practically nothing on?"

Calming her tone, Victoria replied, "If you don't want to get turned on, don't look. When you were standing, staring into my bedroom, you knew if you were being aroused or not. You were aroused, and yet you continued to look. Tell me, Stephen, as a so-called 'Christian,' shouldn't you have walked away if you really didn't want what you saw?"

Stephen lowered his head. "You're right. I should have walked away, but you shouldn't have lain there knowing I was watching you."

Victoria shook her head in disgust. "How old are you, Stephen?"

Puzzled at the question, Stephen said, "Twenty-five."

Looking into his eyes, Victoria said, "Twenty-five is a grown man, not a two-year-old child. When you are 2, you can blame someone else for your actions. Not when you're 25. You know, Stephen, you sound just like Adam in the Garden of Eden." Victoria tilted her head and urged, "Correct me if I am wrong. Did Adam not whine to God that Eve was the reason he sinned? Did he not say, 'God, this woman you gave to me! She gave me the fruit and I did eat'? Tell me, Stephen, was the choice not Adam's to take of the fruit or not?"

Stephen was shocked at the response she gave. Repeatedly, as she talked, Stephen heard the words, "Go through the Garden Gate!" Curious, Stephen asked, "Why did you say that?"

Victoria replied sharply, "Because it was the truth!"

"But why Adam and Eve?"

Victoria threw her hands up. "Who else should I use? Is that not where it all began? With the flesh and blood man?"

Stephen paused. "Victoria, I want to apologize for my actions. You are right. I'm responsible for me. Not you or anyone else."

Arrogance leaped from Victoria. "That's what I have been saying for fifteen minutes! Look,

Stephen, I can't help the fact you've never encountered a fantasy like me before, but I want you to understand something. I'm used to men wanting my body. I am what you would call a yes-woman." Victoria put her index finger under Stephen's chin. "Maybe you are a yes-man, and you just don't know it."

Stephen buttoned his shirt and tucked it into his pants. "Again, you're right, Victoria. I didn't know that kind of behavior was in me. At least not until a while back, but that was with the girl I love, not someone I just met."

With a lift of a brow, Victoria said, "Since I am not leaving today, I am going to take a cold shower. Then I'll be down for toast and coffee. I'll take my coffee black, thank you."

Chapter Twenty-Five
Ian Meets Victoria

*V*ictoria went up the stairs, and Stephen went to the kitchen. The doorbell rang again. Stephen hurried to answer the door, thinking it would be Ian. When he opened the door, Ian was standing there with a smile on his face. "Well, good morning, Stephen!"

A little embarrassed, Stephen invited Ian in for a cup of coffee. Ian sat at the table; Stephen got the coffee and joined him.

"I came by earlier, but there was no answer. Did you sleep in or something?"

"I'm humiliated to confess the 'or something' fits my situation."

"Well, you just piqued my curiosity." Ian said. "It wouldn't have anything to do with Victoria Stanton, would it?"

Before Stephen could answer, Victoria entered the kitchen. "I'll respond to that, if I may." Victoria sat beside Ian and asked,

"Stephen, did you not pour my coffee, and where is my toast? I did tell you I only eat light toast, didn't I?"

Stephen smiled, as he put the bread in the toaster, "Forgive me. I'll try to be more prompt next time."

Ian chuckled, trying not to laugh aloud. Victoria was sizing up Ian when she noticed the tattoo on his fingers. Abruptly, she asked, "Were you in the Navy or some other branch of the military? Before you answer that . . ." Victoria looked at Stephen, "Were you not going to introduce me to this cowboy?"

Stephen looked at Ian and smiled. "I'm sorry! This is my supervisor, Ian Jackson. Ian, Victoria Stanton."

Ian extended his hand to Victoria, but to no avail.

She haughtily grinned. "What a joy! You may answer my question now."

Ian frowned. "What question was that?"

"You're a supervisor and don't pay any more attention than that? I asked if you were in the Armed Forces."

Ian frowned. "No, why?"

"The initials on your stunning gold ring, AOTA. Is that your sweetheart's initials or your mother's?"

"What difference does that make to you, Miss Stanton?" Ian asked.

Stephen jumped in before Victoria could answer. "Victoria will be going out with you today. I told Ian you were going to do a story about the farm. I have to go into town. Then I'll join you."

Ian stood. "Really? In that case are you ready, Miss Stanton?"

"How rude! You can see I haven't finished my coffee!"

"Then bring it with you. In the mornings, I'll pick you up at seven o'clock sharp. If you're going to wear make-up, you'll probably need to get up at five."

"I most certainly will not get up at five. Do I make myself clear?" Victoria said. "Now, if you will follow me, I'll show you where my supplies are for you to carry." Victoria raised her head and left the kitchen.

Ian looked at Stephen. "What was that?"

Stephen laughed, "I think God has sent some kind of trial for me, Ian."

Chapter Twenty-Six

Destiny is Back

When Ian and Victoria left for the fields, Stephen felt as though his heart was filled with anguish. He went to his place of solace, the porch swing. Remembering his father, John, he gently rubbed his fingers across the carved places in the back of the swing. One time his dad was going to pull one of his baby teeth that hung by a thread. Stephen was scared. Knowing this, his dad explained that under the baby tooth, there was a permanent tooth that would stay his whole life, if he took care of it. He then showed Stephen the letter "V" carved in the back of the swing. Stephen's grandfather had carved the "V" for victory after pulling one of John's baby teeth. John told Stephen they would pray and ask God to let it come out so fast it wouldn't have time to hurt. Stephen grinned, recollecting what happened. He ran his fingers over the "V" his dad had helped him carve. The words John said to him that day, as they carved the "V," burned in Stephen's mind forever. "This 'V' stands for victory over fear, victory for the things we have to do. Even though at times, they may be painful."

Pain from the morning was exactly what Stephen was feeling. He had never felt such passion and excitement over sin. Victoria aroused feelings and lust inside him that he would have sworn wasn't there. This confused him even more. In his mind, he questioned, "God, I don't want to hurt you. Search my heart. Clothe me with your holiness." Stephen looked toward heaven and confessed, "Father! I am afraid of the path you're calling me to go down. Why am I afraid? I've always been obedient to your call, so why is this different? Whatever you want me to do, I will do."

Stephen paused as the Holy Spirit burned inside his soul. No longer did Stephen wonder where the path he must travel would be. He closed his eyes and pledged, "Father! Show me the way to Eden's Gate. Open my eyes that I may see your truth. Let your wisdom guide my steps and your light brighten the hidden way."

Stephen decided to go to the Word of God and allow the Holy Spirit to direct his path.

***

That night, while Stephen was preparing the payroll, Ian brought back Victoria to the house. Stephen watched her as she got out of Ian's truck. He didn't see that spire-straight posture he had seen the day before. Stephen couldn't help but laugh, but only before she came in the house. When the door opened, he quickly looked down and began to write. Victoria said nothing as she walked through the kitchen.

"Victoria!" Stephen called out.

She stopped but didn't face him right away.

"How was your day?" Stephen asked.

With that question, Victoria slowly turned and stared at Stephen with no expression. She raised one eyebrow and muttered, "How was my day? How was my day?" She sluggishly walked toward Stephen and complained. "My day was straight from hell! I have sweated until I think I am dehydrated. My sinuses are filled with dust; therefore, my head is pounding. I was stared at by a group of men who had the smell of a pasture filled with cows on a steaming hot day. The water tastes terrible, and your supervisor is the most uncaring person I've ever met. He's a dog who needs obedience training. I'm hungry. I asked your supervisor for half of his sandwich, and he flatly refused. Some of the other men offered, but he told them no, they would need their strength. Then, he embarrassed me in front of those sweaty creatures by saying, 'She will learn to bring her own lunch. She should have known there was no restaurant in the middle of a cornfield.' I am so sore! That truck had no shocks at all."

Stephen managed to restrain the laughter that was struggling to be released. He watched and listened as Victoria continued her rant. Finally, she stopped. Her chin was quivering, and the look of bewilderment controlled her countenance. Tears welled up in her eyes. She put her hands to her head, and in a cry of anguish, wailed, "Just look at my hair! There's probably not a descent hairdresser in this grand city of Dog Patch."

At this point, Ian entered the house and came into the kitchen.

Pointing to Ian, she demanded of Stephen, "Well, are you going to say something to this animal who shouldn't be allowed loose in society, or not?"

Stephen answered, "Of course." He stood, faced Ian and tightened his lips trying not to burst into laughter. "Ian, are these accusations true?"

Ian twisted one side of his mustache and made a funny sound with his mouth. "They are."

Stephen nodded his head. "Okay."

Shocked, Victoria shouted, "Is that your discipline? He should be fired!"

Stephen raised his brows. "That's it!"

By this time, Victoria was sobbing and threatening to go to her Grandmother Stanton's estate. Stephen, trying to be sympathetic, put his hand on her shoulder and told her to take a bath. He said he would make supper.

Victoria stomped out of the room and up the stairs. With the slamming of the door, Stephen and Ian knew they were safe to release the laughter they could hold no longer.

Stephen squinted. "Were you really that bad?"

Ian nodded. "I guess I was. I asked the men to help me out a little. I want her broke in fast. I can't stand two months of whining."

Ian left, and Stephen prepared supper. He lit a candle, and placed it on the table. He heard Victoria coming and poured her ice water. Upon entering the room, she saw the candle and smiled. Stephen pointed the way to the table, pulled her chair out and went into the kitchen. He brought the plate, napkin and drink, and placed them in front of Victoria. Her smile soon turned to a frown. "Are you making fun of me?"

Stephen was seated. "No, I am not. Why do you ask?"

"What is this?" she growled.

"It's called a grilled cheese sandwich and potato chips. Have you never had grilled cheese sandwich?"

Victoria demanded, "I want something else and now."

Firmly, Stephen replied, "This is it. The kitchen is closed. You can eat this or cook what you want."

Enraged, Victoria stood, leaned over the table and stated, "Let me make one thing clear, I am here because I have to do whatever my grandmother says to inherit her estate. You're being paid an enormous amount of money for two months' rent. Did grandmother want you to try and run me off so she would have a reason to give it all to Charles and Liz?"

Stephen shouted, "You're a 43-year-old spoiled brat! Your grandmother loves you, and all you can think of is her money. If you were my granddaughter, I would leave you nothing. I feel sorry for you, Victoria. You have no regard for anyone but yourself. You haven't had a kind word for anyone since you've been here. That performance you put on for your grandmother was pitiful. Do you think you fooled her for one moment? She knows all you want is her money. All she wants is you . . . and your love. Not because she has money, but because she has a tender heart where you're concerned. She speaks of your father often, and his love for God. She can't understand how you can push aside everything you have been taught and act like a heretic."

Victoria protested, "I am not a heretic! I may not believe like you . . . or grandmother . . . but heretic is a bit strong."

Stephen braced his hands on the side of the table and leaned toward Victoria. "Did your father teach you about Adam and Eve? If you were not taught, you would not have known the details as you stated them this morning."

A somber look disclosed the fact that Stephen had touched a tender place in Victoria's rough exterior. She sat down, lowered her head, bit her lower lip, and confessed, "Yes. My father saw that I was taught 'the Word' as he called it. I don't really know when things got so messed up. My father left me an inheritance of money and knowledge. After his sudden death, I started drinking and partying. I tried drugs."

"Really?" Stephen asked.

"The combination of substances weakened my defenses to everything. I was so angry with God for taking my mother and my father away from me. I asked, 'God if you're in control of life and death, as I have been taught all my life, explain to me why you took them both.' I prayed, went to church and took classes at seminary. I thought I was really pleasing God. I was a fool to think that. He pulled my whole life out from under me. I got myself off the booze, drugs and some of the men."

"Some of the men?" Stephen was incredulous.

"I hardened myself. I couldn't take any more pain. I thought God's love was true love. When I found out differently, I went from man to man thinking sex was love. I needed to feel the warmth of someone's touch. I became one with so many men, I was spread all over New York City. I wasn't whole, but torn apart. The rude awakening came when I realized that too was a lie."

Stephen could not believe the woman that sat before him was the same Victoria Stanton who arrived the day before. He watched as she played with her sandwich, not lifting her head in arrogance, shouting or demanding anything. She looked like a little child who needed to be able to believe in something real again. Stephen put his hand on top of hers. She quickly pulled it away and straightened her posture. Stephen sympathetically implored Victoria not to give up on God.

"God is real, Victoria! He cares about you. I believe God has sent you here to Eden's Gate. Nothing is by chance. My destiny and yours are in His hands. Right now, for some reason, God is compelling me to go through the gate into the Garden of Eden. Why don't you go with me? Maybe God sent you here to bring back life to the uncultivated places in your heart. The seed has been sown, but it needs to be cultivated. You've allowed the circumstances of life to harden your heart. Seeds can't grow through that stubborn, unyielding exterior. Tonight, I can see a breakthrough. I've seen a small part of the real you. Let me help you, Victoria. Just give me a chance. We'll study the Garden of Eden together. As God reveals to us, He'll heal your heart. Will you help me?"

Trembling, Victoria stared into Stephen's eyes. "I am so afraid to believe again."

Stephen quickly responded, "I am afraid sometimes too, but faith overcomes fear. Can I pray with you?"

Apprehensive, Victoria confessed with tears, "I haven't prayed in so long, Stephen. I don't know if I remember what to say, and even if I did, I don't know if God will ever forgive me."

Stephen gently took Victoria by her shoulders and assured her, "The words don't matter to our Heavenly Father. He just wants us to come with our hearts open to Him."

"Stephen, I want you to sit down. I'll let you pray, but I want to share something with you before you do."

Stephen sat and waited anxiously to hear what she had to say.

Victoria wiped her nose, and after pausing for wahile, said, "When I was a little girl, I didn't play a lot of normal games like other kids. I had a very special doll my father brought me from England. Her name was Victoria, the same as mine. Therefore, I had to give her another name when we played because there couldn't be two Victorias. One day we had a tea party. I put her at the table, poured her tea, and said, 'What can your new name be?' I thought for a moment. Your new name will be Destiny. I don't know why or where the name came from. It just came out of my mouth. For almost a year, I played with her. She was my favorite toy, and I had many toys. I was in my room one day. It was in the spring of the year. I remember because the dogwood trees were in bloom. Destiny and I were sitting in the large bay window overlooking the garden. As I talked to her, I asked what she wanted to be when she grew up. A voice from behind me softly said, 'A prophetess.' I turned, and behind me stood a man in white."

Stephen stared without moving.

"I remember thinking he looked like a flashlight shining in a dark room because he was so bright," Victoria continued. I wasn't afraid of him, though. I asked who he was, and he said, 'My name is Destiny.' Now that scared me! He then told me that truly I was a prophetess of God and had great favor with God and I would see many mysteries unfold. This was my destiny preordained by God.

"I never told anyone about that. I was afraid they would think I was pretending or that I was crazy. I was sure they wouldn't believe me at all.

I saw many things when my father and I studied at church and seminary. The thing that confused me was that what I saw and what other people saw were different. It scared me. When I tried to explain what I was seeing, I was looked at as if I was a heretic or they ignored me all together. I really don't think my father, our pastor, or my teachers thought I saw anything mainly because of my age. All these things started when I was 7. By the time I was in seminary, I said very little about spirit things. I think I was waiting for the teachers to bring it up in some of the topics, but when they did, it was contrary to what I understood. It was probably best the topics didn't come up often. I would more than likely have been thrown out of school."

Stephen was in awe of what he was hearing. "Victoria, you saw an angel?"

Puzzled that Stephen was so excited, she answered, "Yes. I saw Destiny many times. The last time I saw him was after my father died. I was drinking a glass of red wine and satisfying an oversexed, married man. At first, I thought it was an illusion. Why would an angel appear to me in a hotel room, especially while I was making out with a married man? I closed my eyes, but each time I opened them, Destiny was standing right in front of me. I pushed the man halfway across the room. I knew I had to get out of there. He repeatedly asked, 'What's wrong with you?' Of course, he didn't see the angel standing at the foot of the bed. I grabbed my purse and headed for the door. When I took hold of the doorknob, Destiny put his hand on top of mine. His hand went through my hand and held the doorknob. His piercing eyes stared into mine, and he spoke these words, 'You can run from me, but you'll not get away from me.' When he said that, he vanished, and I have not seen him since." Victoria took a deep breath. "Does this sound like a fairy tale to you, Stephen? Am I crazy?"

Quickly Stephen answered, "No! It makes perfect sense. I've seen angels since I was a little boy. My best friend, Philip Dawson, and I saw them when we played in the barn. I was a preacher, and he was a prophet. The angels appeared one day while I was preaching. They would cheer on occasion, and other times they would say, 'The Most High be praised.'

"Philip talked to the angels. I was always too afraid. One angel there was named Haleb. My mom, Rachel, met Haleb many times. After I grew up, I stopped seeing the angels, but the burning in my soul to preach the gospel has never stopped. Speaking of Destiny, preaching the Word of God is my destiny. I just don't have all the missing pieces yet."

Victoria said, "Stephen, we need to pray now."

Stephen smiled and agreed. They joined hands, and Stephen began the prayer by thanking God for bringing Victoria to Eden's Gate. After the prayer, Victoria picked up the cold, grilled cheese sandwich and ate it as though she was starved.

The time had swiftly passed. Stephen took a bite of his sandwich, and the phone rang. He inhaled and moaned, "Oh, no!"

Concerned, Victoria asked, "What is it?"

Pushing his chair back, Stephen whispered, "I forgot to call Leann."

Leann was uneasy that Stephen hadn't called. "I wanted to make sure everything was all right. It's eleven thirty."

Immediately, Stephen responded, "Honey, I am so sorry. I got busy, and the time slipped away from me."

Curious Leann inquired, "What are you doing at eleven thirty at night, if you're not talking to me?"

Excited Stephen explained, "I am preparing to do a study on the Garden of Eden. That is definitely where God is directing me to go."

"I'm so glad, honey. I have been praying that God will hurry and bring you back to me."

Speaking softly, so Victoria wouldn't hear, Stephen uttered, "I love you and want to hold you so much. It won't be long, Leann. I feel that in my spirit."

Chapter Twenty-Seven

Victoria's First Full Day at Work

Stephen went to sleep as soon as his head hit the pillow. He was sleeping soundly when he heard someone whispering his name. He halfway opened his eyes to see a figure towering over him. Stephen hastened to sit up in the bed, scared half to death.

He sat up so quickly Victoria screamed.

In panic, Stephen shouted, "What are you doing beside my bed, Victoria? You scared the life out of me."

"You scared me too!"

Stephen ran his fingers through his hair and again asked, "What are you doing on my bed?"

Victoria spoke so low Stephen couldn't make out what she had said. "I can't hear you. What did you say?"

Trembling, Victoria said, "I saw Destiny in my room."

"Tonight?"

Victoria nodded yes.

"Did he say anything to you?"

Swallowing hard, Victoria replied, "Yes! He said he had come for me. Then he was gone. What do you think he meant by, 'I am coming for you'?"

"I . . . don't know. Maybe it has something to do with us praying and asking God to renew you tonight. After all, he said his name was Destiny." Stephen paused, lowered his head and looked at Victoria. "Victoria, the Garden of Eden may have something to do with *your* destiny."

Confused, Victoria asked, "What could your study have to do with me?"

"I don't know! However, I do know Ian will be here to pick you up early, so we need to get some sleep."

Victoria stood, went to the door, paused and said, "Stephen, I feel a little uneasy about sleeping in my room. May I sleep in here?"

Stephen had already laid down; nevertheless, at her words he raised his head and said, "You'll be fine in your room. I'll be right here if you need me. Now, try to get some sleep."

Stephen felt as though only minutes had passed when the alarm went off. He had to make himself get up and get dressed. As he was exiting his room, he called out to Victoria, and then he caught a glimpse of something from the corner of his eye. In unbelief, Stephen saw Victoria lying on the floor beside his bed, wrapped in a blanket. She looked like a child who had a nightmare and wanted to be close to someone. He squatted beside her and called her name. "Victoria! Victoria!"

She groaned and pulled the blanket over her head.

Stephen pulled the blanket away from her face. "Come on, sunshine, it's time to get up."

Victoria snapped, "Would you please let me sleep? I have had a horrible night and you know it."

Stephen shouted, "No! And don't start your hateful routine with me again. Get up or I will pour cold water on your head and see if that will wake you. I'll have the coffee ready in five minutes. Don't forget, you need to pack your lunch."

Stephen was pouring a cup of coffee when he heard footsteps coming down the stairs.

Victoria came bouncing into the kitchen.

Shocked, he whispered, "It can't be!" She was not the woman Stephen saw the day before, but a woman dressed in tight-fitting jeans and a white cotton sleeveless blouse with the tail tied in a knot around her waist. She wore white tennis shoes and turned-down white socks. On her white cap, the letter "S" was embroidered on the section above the bill. Her long blond hair was in a ponytail, pulled through the opening on the back of the cap. She looked gorgeous with no makeup. Stephen was amazed! All he could do was stare at this transformed creature who was now pouring coffee for herself.

"Good morning, Stephen! Did you sleep well?"

Stephen shook his head. "Ian is not going to believe this. Just look at you. You poured your own coffee, smiled and said good morning. I don't know what to say."

Victoria chuckled. "Ian will not see this side of me, nor anyone else for that matter. I'm going to be my sweet lovable self only when it is you and me. Not even Grandmother Stanton will get a peek, so please don't tell for the time being."

Stephen agreed, but didn't understand. When Ian arrived, Victoria was ready with lunch in hand. Ian had expected a long wait but found her ready and waiting on him. "Well, Miss Stanton! I must confess I am surprised to see you looking so fine, yet ready to go."

Victoria cautioned, "Don't mess with me today. You leave me alone, and I will most definitely elude you as much as possible. I do work for a living, and I am good at my job. I wish I could say the same for you, Mr. Jackson. However, you need to improve your performance from yesterday or else I will recommend Stephen have your severance pay waiting at the end of the day. Therefore, I suggest we get to work before the sun beats down on the workers and the perspiration smell nauseates me." She raised her chin and proceeded to go outside.

In disgust, Ian said, "I have never hit a woman before. As a matter of fact, I've never been tempted to hit a woman, until now." Shaking his head, Ian tightened his lips and said, "You better pray for me, Stephen, because as of right now, I would like to bend that woman over my knee and give her a good spanking."

Stephen slapped Ian on his shoulder and laughed. "It will be only seven weeks and three days and she'll be on her way back to New York."

Chapter Twenty-Seven
Coffee at Martha's

Stephen quickly locked the house and headed for town to see Leann. He missed her terribly but knew postponing the wedding was the right thing to do. When he stopped at Mitchell's service station to fill up with gas, he saw Pastor Reynolds. Eager to speak to him, Stephen called out, "Pastor Reynolds! How you doing?"

The pastor smiled and walked toward Stephen. Shaking his hand, Pastor Reynolds asked, "How are you doing, my brother? It feels as though I haven't seen you in weeks."

"I know," Stephen agreed.

"Martha Mitchell has some fresh coffee. Would you like to go inside and have a cup?"

"I was on my way to see Leann, but maybe one cup won't take too long."

They went inside and set at the counter. Martha had added to the station a small

dining room, complete with a soda fountain
and bar stools. Martha poured the coffee
and commented on the message Stephen
preached when Pastor Reynolds was out of
town. Martha was heavy set and faithfully
wore her dyed black hair in a French twist.
She was known for her long, dangling
earrings, heavy makeup and a wonderful
sense of humor, which she was about to use
on Stephen.

"Hey, Stephen, have you persuaded anyone
to come through the garden gate yet?"

Embarrassed, Stephen replied, "Not yet,
Martha, but when I do I'll be sure and let
you know."

She leaned on the counter and asked, "Would
you two handsome men like a fresh doughnut
with your coffee?"

Pastor Reynolds patted his tummy. "I don't
need the extra pounds. I think Sandra would
like for me to lose about ten pounds."

Martha put her hands on her hips and shook
her head. "Now, Pastor, I don't see any place
you need to lose anything; it all looks pretty
fine to me. Just ten more pounds to love."

Pastor Reynolds smiled. "Thank you, Martha.
I'm not detecting a sermon in your flattering
comment, am I?"

Martha winked at him. "Use me any way you
like, honey."

Stephen motioned for Martha to come close to him. "Martha, you shouldn't leave yourself wide open like that. Satan loves those little foxes. The Word says, 'It's the little foxes that spoil the vine.'"

Martha put her hands in the air. "Okay, boys, I get the message. I'll try to contain myself."

Pastor Reynolds laughed aloud. "Martha, you are a mess . . . but a good mess."

As Martha walked away, Stephen asked, "Have you studied any more in Genesis since you came home from the retreat?"

Excited about the question, Pastor Reynolds said, "I have been studying not only in Genesis, but I am going to start a Wednesday night study on the first four chapters next week. I will announce it Sunday morning. I don't want you to miss one session. I think you'll benefit greatly from it, Stephen."

Stephen and Pastor Reynolds finished their coffee and got up to leave, when the pastor paused and asked, "Is it true Victoria Stanton will be staying at your place for a few weeks?"

"Hum! So, you've heard?"

"Yes, Sandra said something about it. I'd like you to invite her to come to the worship service Sunday."

"I'll extend the invitation but can't promise anything."

Chapter Twenty-Nine
Ginger Banks

Stephen hurried to get to Ginger Banks' house to see Leann. When he arrived, Ginger answered the door. Surprised and a bit embarrassed, Stephen said, "Ginger, what a surprise."

"Stephen! It is my house you know . . . but it is a surprise to see you as well. Come in."

It was obvious to Ginger that Stephen was nervous. Repeatedly, he was tossing the coins in his pants pocket. Ginger called Leann, then took hold of Stephen's arm and demanded. "Stop playing with your change. You know in a court of law, that would be a dead giveaway you were guilty of something. You're not on trial here, so calm down. I don't mind you stopping by to visit Leann if her work is completed at day's end. I'm sure I don't have to worry about that."

Stammering, Stephen replied, "I . . . just wasn't expecting anyone to be here."

Ginger smiled. "Well, as a rule, I would have been out of here an hour ago. However, I don't have to be in court until noon, so I took advantage of the extra time and slept in. Stephen, do I make you nervous?"

Before he could answer, Leann entered the room. "Hi, Stephen!" Leann gave him a hug. "What brings you here this morning?"

Ginger laughed. "If this were a courtroom and Stephen said he was just passing by, the court would charge him with perjury. So, before I find him guilty, I am out of here."

Ginger got her briefcase and looked at Stephen. "If you ever need a good lawyer, Stephen, give me a call."

"God forbid," he said, "but if I do, you'll definitely be the one I call."

When Ginger closed the door, Stephen took a deep breath and blew it out, "Oh, my! I feel like a kid who has been caught with his hand in the cookie jar."

Leann spoke up. "Ginger's not like that at all. If she minded you coming by, she would let you know."

"I just didn't expect her to answer the door. It caught me off guard."

With a shy grin, Leann asked, "So, what *does* bring you here this morning?"

Stephen put his arms around Leann's waist and pulled her to him. "I miss you so much! I wanted to start the day with the smell of your perfume, the sight of your dazzling smile and the taste of your sweet lips."

Leann gently stroked his cheek and said, "You know, I can accommodate all three of your requests."

"It won't be long, Leann, until we can be together, I'm sure. I love you!"

"I love you too, Stephen, but now it's time for me to get to work."

"You're right! I told Ian I'd come out in the fields today."

Leann began to giggle. "How is it going with Queen Victoria?"

Stephen shook his head. "I can't believe the girl I love would laugh about my strange situation."

Leann straightened Stephen's shirt collar. "She'll only make you love me more. I like that thought."

Stephen gave Leann a quick goodbye kiss. "Oh, you think so, do you? Actually, Leann, she is very nice . . . sometimes."

"Yeah, of course she is."

Stephen grunted, "Hum!"

Chapter Thirty

Tempers Flare

Stephen joined the men and Victoria in the field. One of the funniest sights Stephen had ever seen was standing on the back of the pickup truck. Victoria had a white handkerchief tied like a mask around her nose and mouth. She was clicking pictures left and right. Ian was standing on the back of the truck beside her. Some of the workers were seated in the back of the truck and some were standing. The truck stopped, the workers unloaded and they went to work. Ian got out of the truck, frowned at Stephen and pointed at Victoria. "Is there not another way she can write her story other than coming out in the fields with us?"

Stephen was fighting the overpowering urge to laugh aloud at Ian. "What seems to be the problem?"

Stunned that Stephen even had to ask, Ian again pointed at Victoria and shouted, "It's this queen bee from the pit that you've sent out to kill everyone, me included."

Stephen looked at Victoria, and asked, "What have you done this time, Victoria?"

She walked to the tailgate of the truck and held out her hand for Stephen to help her down. She stood in front of Ian, pushed her handkerchief higher on her nose and scoffed, "Where did you find these so-called workers? All they have managed to do this morning is ride around in the truck burning your gasoline. The way I see it, they have cost you money. They haven't earned anything."

Ian looked at Stephen, furrowed his brows and shouted, "See what I mean?"

Puzzled, Stephen asked, "Victoria, why do you have the handkerchief over your mouth?"

Victoria stomped over to Stephen and stopped in front of him. "I have been forced to wear it due to the non-use of deodorant by this pack of so-called men."

Ian took a deep breath, gritted his teeth and headed toward Victoria. "That does it! I'm going to give you the spanking you have needed so desperately for some time."

Victoria boldly tightened her lips and balled up her fist. Stephen stepped in between them and said, "You two cut this out. Victoria! You can't go around telling people they stink. I may not be here next time to stop the brawl. You two are acting like brother and sister. I want you both to try to get along. Surely you can manage that. It'll only be for a few weeks." Stephen put his hand up and said, "Okay, Ian, I can tell you need a break. I'll take Victoria in for the rest of the day."

"You're right. I need a break. I have never witnessed a more disgusting female in my life. I'm having to repent because of her."

Victoria leaned forward and sarcastically asked, "Is it your lust for me that drives you to repentance? Cowboy!"

Ian put both hands up and roared, "That's what I mean." He squinted at Victoria and bellowed, "You arrogant witch!"

Irritated, Stephen stormed, "Victoria, get in the truck now! Ian, take a break and calm down. I'll see you later."

Shaking his head, Ian muttered, "I can't believe I called anybody a witch."

Stephen slapped him on his shoulder. "I think God will quickly forgive you for that justified outburst."

On the way back to the house, Stephen warned Victoria, "This has got to stop. Ian is a valuable worker. He knows his job, and I need him. So, please stop it and take the handkerchief off your mouth. You're both acting like children." Stephen glanced at Victoria. "Why are you smiling?"

"I love when Ian gets so riled the blood vessels in his temple almost burst."

Stephen said, "How can you say that? Life in the fields is hard enough with this heat. So please leave your torment out of the picture."

Victoria turned the rearview mirror, checked her hair and said, "It won't kill him. He's tough."

Chapter Thirty-One
So Many Questions

That night at supper, Brenda was visiting Stephen, and Victoria was as sweet as honey. Liz made Victoria's favorite foods and brought with her a big surprise. Grant—Charles and Liz's son—was home for a visit. He too came for supper. After eating, everyone retired to the living room except Grant, who went to the barn to see Champion. Victoria got her camera and insisted on going to take some pictures of Grant with Champion for the magazine. Forty-five minutes passed. Grant and Victoria still had not returned from the barn. Brenda Stanton asked Stephen to go tell Grant his mama was ready to go home.

The barn door was ajar. Stephen heard groaning and moaning as he slowly entered the barn door. There he saw Victoria and Grant all over each other. Victoria's back was against the wall, her eyes closed as Grant kissed her neck and shoulders. Instead of saying anything, Stephen watched the steaming passion between the two. Victoria opened her eyes and casually looked at Stephen, reached out to him and sensually begged, "Come join us, Stephen. I can see in your eyes you want to. Join us and I will fulfill your wildest desire."

Stephen slowly moved toward them. Drawn by the power of a seduction he had never experienced. He broke out in a cold sweat as his lips touched Victoria's. Instantly, Grant disappeared. Stephen covered Victoria's voluptuous body with his. He was groaning passionately when abruptly he heard someone shout, "Stephen! Stephen!"

Like a wild man, Stephen sat up in bed. Victoria watched as his eyes shifted around the room. "Where am I?" he gasped.

Stunned by his response, Victoria replied, "You're in your bedroom."

Stephen stood pacing back and forth. He stopped, looked at Victoria, took her by her arm, and demanded, "How did I get here?" Before she could respond, Stephen bluntly yelled, "How could you?"

Victoria didn't know what to say as Stephen trembled and wiped the sweat from his face. He grabbed her shoulders, shook her and demanded, "Answer me!"

Victoria slapped Stephen's face. "Stephen Daniel Harris, you better wake up or I am going to deck you. Get your hands off me."

Stephen felt numb. Slowly his trembling hand touched Victoria's cheek. He looked down and whispered, "I'm . . . I'm so sorry, Victoria."

Stephen felt as though he was moving in slow motion as he sat on the side of the bed. He put his elbows on his knees and rested his head in his hands. Repeatedly, Stephen groaned, "Oh, God!" His mouth tasted so bad he felt nauseated. He cautiously raised his head and whispered, "Shemed!"

He looked at his hands and arms that were covered with a green tint. In haste, he went to the bathroom and turned the hot water on. He braced himself by holding the sides of the sink as he moved his face close to the mirror and saw a green tint even on his tongue. Baffled, Victoria watched as Stephen rubbed a bar of soap up and down his arms, in his hands and then on his face. He grabbed his toothbrush and paste, and then intensely brushed his teeth and rinsed with mouthwash. Exhausted, he rubbed his hands across his hair, stopped at the crown of his head and firmly pressed down trying to stop the pounding in his head. Attentively, Stephen stared into the mirror and said in despair, "He's here!"

"Who's here, Stephen?"

Stephen faced Victoria. "Shemed."

Victoria shouted, "Who in the world is this Shemed? Who is he?"

"He's . . . he's a general in Queen Jewel's army. Jewel has sent him for me."

Stephen sat on the side of the bed. Victoria gently stroked his hair and asked, "Stephen, are you okay? Can I get you something to drink?"

Ignoring her question, Stephen asked, "When did your grandmother leave?"

"Right after you came to the barn and told Grant, Liz was ready to go home."

Stephen closed his eyes. "I don't remember leaving the barn. I remembered hearing groans and moans. I wasn't sure what it was until I went inside." Stephen raised his head and looked at Victoria. "Grant and you were getting . . . intimate. You asked me to join you, and I did. Grant vanished when I kissed you. You wanted me to kiss you and I did. I don't believe it. I don't remember anything else until you woke me a few minutes ago." Stephen took Victoria's hand and pleaded, "Please tell me what happened."

"Stephen, I didn't kiss or touch Grant in any way. You came in the barn and said, Liz was ready to go home. I snapped a picture of you, Grant and Champion, and we came inside. They left, you went to bed, and I took a shower. You woke me with all the groaning you were doing. That's it! Listen, Stephen, I'll be back in just a minute."

Victoria left the room, came back with a glass of warm milk and handed it to Stephen. "Drink this."

Victoria was relieved Stephen was calming down. "You scared me. I expect me to act like that but not you." Victoria smiled. "Did you enjoy kissing me?"

Stephen cut his eyes to Victoria, and, with tears in his eyes, said, "That's not funny."

Victoria quickly stated, "I'm only trying to help. I know this isn't funny. I just didn't know what to say to make you feel better. If you're okay, I'm going to bed. Ian will be here for the witch from the pit very early." Victoria stroked Stephen's hair one last time. "It's okay, Stephen. God is in control. Goodnight."

"Goodnight, Victoria, and thanks for everything."

Victoria grinned, nodded and started to leave the room. She stopped and asked, "Who areQueen Jewel and Shemed?"

"I . . . I don't feel like explaining right now. My head is pounding."

Victoria nodded. "You will tell me later, right?"

"Yeah, later. Goodnight."

Stephen didn't know what to think, do or how to pray, other than "God help me." He so wanted to call Philip, but not at 3:00 a.m. He turned the light out, climbed into bed and asked the question, *How and when did I get to bed from the barn?* He wasn't sure how to fight what he could feel, but not see. He tried to pray but drifted off to sleep.

Chapter Thirty-Two
Sheriff Bolton Visits Ginger

The next morning, Victoria promised to behave, keep the handkerchief off her face and try not to argue with Ian. When alone, Stephen spent time in prayer before going to work. He needed answers only God could give him. After work, he made up his mind that he was finally going to study about the Garden of Eden.

Ginger Banks was preparing to leave for Augusta as Leann arrived for work. Ginger was hurriedly putting papers into her briefcase when Sheriff Bolton knocked on the door. Leann opened the door and asked the sheriff to come inside. He looked at Ginger and said, "You're just the person I need to see, Miss Banks."

Ginger closed her briefcase. "Why could that be, Sheriff?"

"Your neighbor, Larry Weeks, is missing. His wife, Alma, called the station and said he went to the store but didn't come back. I found his car out next to the covered bridge on Clayton Road. I had Alex Mitchell pull the car in and check it. He said the radiator hose had busted. There were footprints leading away from the car. The prints ended with tire tracks beside them. Therefore, it looks like someone picked him up. The questions are, 'Who?' and 'Where did they take him?' I said all that to ask, 'Have you seen him?'"

Ginger shook her head. "No, I haven't. I use that road almost every day going to work. It's a dirt road, but it cuts at least ten miles off my daily trip to Augusta. When I was coming home last night, I saw only one vehicle and that was Stephen's old black truck." Ginger raised her brows and said, "There is no mistaking that truck."

Leann spoke up. "Stephen takes a couple of the workers home. He always uses that road."

"I guess I'll drive out and see if Stephen's home," Sheriff Bolton said.

"I don't think he is right now," Leann said. "He went out with the workers today. He should be in by 2:00 or 3:00."

Sheriff Bolton squinted and looked around the room. "I guess I'd better be going. Thanks. I'll drive out and talk to Stephen later. You ladies have a good day."

Leann looked at Ginger. "What do you think about that?"

Ginger frowned. "I have a strange feeling about this. One of those feelings you can't quite put your finger on, but you know it's not good. Well, I've got to get out of here or I'll be late."

Ginger hurried out the door. Leann wondered what Ginger was really thinking. The blank stare in her eyes clearly revealed she thought more than she shared.

Chapter Thirty-Three

A Late Evening Guest

*L*ater that night, Victoria and Stephen had a quick supper. Stephen cleared the table and prepared to study.

"I feel a little uncomfortable, Stephen."

Stephen put his pen down and looked at Victoria. "Why would you feel uncomfortable?"

Squirming, Victoria said, "I haven't studied the Bible in so long. Just looking at it sends a chill down my spine. I loved the Word so much. I just saw things differently. I don't understand how two people can read the same thing and not come close to the same meaning."

Stephen put his hand on Victoria's. "You can definitely share with me. One thing my mom taught me was to keep an open mind. Know where you stand, but also listen because God's Word is a proceeding Word: God changes not, but His Word can change for our life. Take Abraham for instance. God told him to sacrifice Isaac, but then told him not to. What if Abraham had closed his mind and only heard God say 'Sacrifice Isaac'? He would have killed his son. Killing Isaac wasn't God's desire. He was only testing Abraham's faith."

Stephen realized he was going on and on. "I'm sorry, I seemed to have kicked into preaching mode."

Victoria agreed. "You did, but I needed to hear it. So, thank you."

Stephen gave his Bible to Victoria, and he got his mom's Bible. As he opened the cover, he looked around the room. "The angels are standing all around the room, Victoria."

***

Stephen had begun to read only the first verse, when someone knocked on the door. Victoria quickly got up and said, "Don't say that we're studying. I am not ready to let anyone know yet. Please, Stephen, I'll go to my room, okay?"

Stephen nodded. "Okay, but hurry."

Stephen waited until Victoria got to the top of the stairs to open the door. "Sheriff Bolton! What a surprise! Come in."

Stepping inside the kitchen, Sheriff Bolton apologized for coming by so late.

Stephen asked, "Is something wrong, Sheriff?"

The sheriff put his thumbs inside his belt loops and said, "Leann told me you take a couple of your workers home sometimes and you travel Clayton Road when you do. Is that right?"

Curious, Stephen replied, "Yes, I do. Why do you ask?"

"Larry Weeks appears to be missing. Do you know him?"

"Yes, I gave him a ride yesterday. His radiator hose busted, he was walking down Clayton Road, and I gave him a lift."

"Where did you drop him off?"

"He asked me to drop him off at Neil Franklin's. It was kind of strange though. He wanted me to drop him off at the end of Neil's driveway. I told him I would take him to the house, but he insisted on getting out at the foot of the drive. So, I let him out. Sheriff, you said he appears to be missing. What's going on?"

Before he could answer, Victoria entered the kitchen. Sheriff Bolton nodded, "Good evening, Miss."

Victoria strutted around Sheriff Bolton, stopped in front of him, tilted her head and said, "Stephen, you failed to tell me Barney Fife was coming to visit."

Sheriff Bolton shifted his stern eyes to Stephen and frowned. "What?"

Shaking his head, Stephen said, "Don't mind her, or else you may want to arrest her. Let me introduce you to Victoria Stanton, Brenda Stanton's granddaughter."

The sheriff rubbed his lips and with a halfway grin. "Oh, yes! I've heard about you."

Flirting, Victoria ran her fingers up and down his badge and asked, "Are you married, Sheriff?"

Sheriff Bolton replied, "No, Miss Stanton, I'm not."

Victoria stroked his cheek. "Maybe you and I can get together, and I do mean real soon. The only lawman I have ever been out with was a hateful, New York City police detective. I think a Southern gentleman like you would be worth investigating."

Sheriff Bolton's face turned a bright shade of pink. Astounded, he came back with the only thing that came to mind, "Well, my goodness."

Stephen took Victoria's arm, pulled her aside and asked, "Don't you have some work to do on the story for the magazine?"

Not taking her eyes off Sheriff Bolton, she winked at him and said, "If I don't hear from you by noon Saturday, I'll call *you*." She brushed against him as she walked by. She growled and whispered, "At times, I love . . . to be the aggressor."

Stephen grinned as he watched Sheriff Bolton run his fingers through his thinning hair. He was stunned at this magnificent lioness and the mating growl she had sent his way. Stephen spoke up, since the sheriff was speechless.

"She's something, isn't she?"

In disbelief, Sheriff Bolton asked, "My Lord in heaven! She's staying here with you?"

Stephen lightly slapped the sheriff's shoulder. "Sheriff, you're the first one she has been civilized to. I think she likes you."

Sheriff Bolton put his hat on. "Me, really?"

Stephen smiled. "Honest. Now, what were you saying about Larry Weeks?"

Totally blank, Sheriff Bolton asked, "What did you say?"

Stephen laughed aloud. "Sheriff, have you been beamed up to the space ship?"

Sheriff Bolton rubbed his forehead and replied, "For a minute, I think I entered the heavenly realm. I don't think I have ever been at such a loss for words. I've been in many places, but I have never seen a woman more beautiful. I have to confess, when she growled at me, I almost hyperventilated."

Stephen shook his head. "She knew exactly how you would feel."

"Enough of that." Returning to the reason for the visit, Sheriff Bolton asked, "Stephen, do you remember Larry acting in an unusual way? Did he mention anything that would make you think he wasn't planning to go back home?"

Stephen thought a moment. "Nothing. It was just casual talk. When he got out, he thanked me for the ride, and that was it."

Sheriff Bolton walked toward the door, turned, and said, "If you think of anything that might be of help, give me a call." The sheriff gave a shy grin. "And, take care of your guest for me."

Chapter Thirty-Four

Acor

Stephen walked out to the porch with the sheriff. After he left, Stephen took a moment to sit and enjoy the clear summer night. Slowly he pushed the porch swing back and forth. He missed Leann, Cordilia and Paul. But above all, he missed Philip. He watched the fireflies that looked like a neon sign flashing in the darkness. The night sounds were so relaxing.

The door opened and Victoria asked, "Has the lawman gone?"

"Yes, he just left. I think you made quite an impression on him."

Smugly, Victoria agreed, "Of course I did! How could I not? There's something very special about that man."

"What would that be, Victoria?"

"He . . . is a very spiritual man. My gift, when I exercise it correctly, is to see a person as he truly is." Victoria sat on the swing beside Stephen and sternly said, "There's something not right about your Pastor Reynolds."

"What? Our Pastor Reynolds?"

"I know you're very fond of him and so is Grandmother Stanton, but the other night, when he was here, I saw a darkness about him. It wasn't good, Stephen. Grandmother would die if she heard me say that."

Stephen frowned. "What do you mean you saw a darkness?"

Victoria stood and looked Stephen in the eye. "It's not something you would see from the outside. It's on the inside. Now, let's talk for a while."

"Sure. What do you want to talk about?"

"About a place I . . . . I heard about a long time ago."

Curious, Stephen asked, "What place is that?"

Victoria took a deep breath. "It's called the White Stone Kingdom."

Stephen paused and then said, "My parents told me about the White Stone Kingdom. Who told you about that place?"

"I studied about White Stone when I was in college."

Stephen slowly shook his head. "That can't be," he said. "White Stone is in the third heaven. Very few know about it. Are you telling me you're one of the few?"

Victoria stood and crossed her arms. "I found out about White Stone when my professor had the senior class do a study on the Garden of Eden. I saw many revelations that others didn't see." Victoria fixed her eyes on Stephen and held the stare.

"What is it?" He asked.

"Will you listen to what I have to say without insisting I'm wrong?"

Stephen furrowed his brows and assured her he would listen. This pleased Victoria, because no one had really listened to her when it came to spiritual things.

"When I was very young, I saw things that sometimes scared me. When studying about Eden, I saw many things. I'll share them if you promise to keep an open mind. Will you do that, Stephen?"

Stephen said, "I already told you I would keep an open mind, so share!"

A quick nod and Victoria began by asking the question, "Do you believe in magic, Stephen?"

"Yes, I believe in magic, witchcraft and all that goes with it. Why?"

"Because if you don't believe in magic, then you won't believe what I'm about to tell you."

Stephen responded, "I believe and have an open mind, so please share."

Victoria nodded and began, "There's a place where the Most High dwells called The Crystal

Kingdom. It's over Wisdom's Mountain just past the field where a very special tree grows. It's called the Ancient Tree. This domain is beyond the White Stone Kingdom. Acor, was a great high priest who lived in the Crystal Kingdom. The Most High withheld nothing from him, including knowledge of the deep magic. He was given authority to visit all three heavens, The White Stone Kingdom, Emerald Shore Kingdom and the Highland Kingdom. It was in the Highland Kingdom that Acor fell from his position. The Highlanders were a unique people. They tended the many gardens God planted for them. The queen of the Highland people was a beautiful woman named Hannah. Acor saw her many times in the orchard.

"When the planets aligned, Acor was sent from the Crystal Kingdom by the Most High to ask the kings and queens from the three heavens to attend a special meeting in the White Stone Kingdom. Though Acor had visited the tree garden many times before, this visit was different. Instead of approaching Queen Hannah right away, he lingered at the giant willow tree and fixed his eyes on what he thought was the most extraordinary sight he had ever seen. As he held his stare, an emotion he had never felt before was birthed. His sentiments started spiraling out of control like a whirlwind. With all his wisdom screaming for him to move away from the garden, he did not. It wasn't until Hannah called his name that he remembered why he was there. Hannah respected Acor's position as high priest but could sense something was different this visit. His dark eyes were piercing, and his countenance sent a chill through her. Acor should have gone immediately and asked the Most High for strength to overcome this sudden passion for Hannah. Because he did not, the 'deep magic' took control—."

Stephen interrupted, "Tell me, what does being attracted to Hannah have to do with the deep magic?"

"As time passed Acor's passion became an obsession. Hannah's not returning the passion would drive Acor to use the deep magic to seduce her."

"How?"

"The kings and queens of the three heavens went on special feast days to the Garden of Fire to be rejuvenated in the fire of the Most High—"

Stephen interrupted, "Mom told me about the Garden of Fire and a high priest named Tashmere who looked after the two trees in the Garden. She explained the two trees burned but were never consumed. One tree blazed with the holy fire of the Most High. The other blazed with the flames of forbidden knowledge."

Victoria asked, "Did she tell you Queen Jewel used the deep magic to seduce Tashmere into the forbidden fire?"

"Yes."

Victoria rubbed the back of her neck and moaned, "I'm really tired."

Stephen frowned. "Come on, Victoria! It's not that late. What was Acor's plan?"

Victoria sighed and continued, "Acor became possessed with thoughts of having Hannah one way or another. He wanted her to have his child, so he did the unpardonable. Instead of going to the Most High, he went to the dark kingdom and sought counsel from none other than Queen Jewel. Jewel had set up her own domain. Using the deep magic, she gathered her own army to war against the Most High. She was ecstatic to see Acor enter her throne room. The thought of gaining yet another high priest from the Most High's altar was euphoric. Trembling, Acor stood before her and bowed his head as though she were God. She commanded him to look into her eyes. When he did, she began to sway and hum a song that left Acor spellbound. As Jewel slowly moved her feet and twirled, the hum grew louder. The enchantment of her moves left Acor spellbound. After a long while, Jewel suddenly stopped and fell to the floor. When she stood and removed the veil from her face, it wasn't Jewel Acor saw, but Hannah. Speechless, Acor shivered as Jewel neared him and ran her long fingers down his chest and whispered, 'If it's Hannah you want, you must serve me. Show your allegiance; drop to your knees.'

"Acor gradually bent his knees and lowered his head before her. Jewel stroked his shining hair. 'You must lure Hannah to the forbidden tree and take her into the flames, and there she will yield to your every need. In the mist of the flame, plant your seed, and she will bare you a son.'

"When Acor raised his head, it was Jewel he saw. She reminded him that he couldn't go back to the Crystal Kingdom or he would die suddenly. Knowing this to be true, Acor stayed with Jewel in the dark kingdom."

"What about the Most High?" Stephen asked.

"When the Most High felt the pain from Acor's sin, a cry was heard throughout all the kingdoms. God wailing over the loss of one of His sons shook the elements." Victoria's countenance saddened. She muttered, "I hear that cry often."

Stephen asked, "How did you see this from studying the Garden of Eden? I've studied the Garden many times and never saw it. Yet you and my mother saw things that I've only been told about."

Victoria grinned. "That, Stephen, is about to change for you very soon."

"How can you be so sure? I'm not sure of anything. Where did you learn all of this? It's not in the Bible."

Victoria raised her high arched brow. "Oh, it's there, Stephen. Believe me, I not only studied it, I lived it."

She stood and pushed her chair under the table. "We have to get some sleep. Ian will be here before the rooster crows, and I'm exhausted."

She patted the top of his head as she walked by. "Good night, Stephen."

Stephen ran his fingers through his hair. "Good night, Victoria. Sleep well."

He watched Victoria as she left the room. She sounded so like his mom talking about Queen Jewel and the White Stone Kingdom. He wondered aloud, "God, why is she really here?"

Chapter Thirty-Five

Stranger at the Gate

Stephen secured the house for the night and went to his bedroom. When he opened the door, the heat almost overpowered him.

"What's going on in here?" he groaned.

He went to the large bay window that faced the main gate and opened the four windows that encircled it, allowing the cool night air inside.

The area light just outside the gate cast forth an exceptional golden glow. Stephen pulled the curtain to one side as he opened the window. The air conditioning was set on 65 degrees and the rest of the house was cool. He sat down on the window seat and fixed his eyes on the largest full moon he had ever seen. It appeared to fill half the sky. Golden rays cast light over Calvin Point, turning it a shadowy blue appearance to the freshly painted white church he attended.

As Stephen sat fanning himself with a magazine and absorbing the beauty, something caught his attention from the corner of his eye. Squinting, he leaned toward the window, trying to discern what he was seeing. It looked like a man staggering up the drive. Stephen stood and watched as the man stopped at the gate. He was dressed in dark clothing and walked with his head and shoulders slumped over. He stopped, took hold of the gate, slowly raised his head and looked toward the window where Stephen was standing. Stephen pulled back. A fear gripped Stephen's heart as he felt an evil force from the approaching man.

He called out to waken Victoria, then immediately dialed Sheriff Bolton, and breathlessly told him about the man standing at the gate. The Sheriff assured Stephen he would be right over. Stephen called Victoria, but there was no response. He rushed to her room. The door was open, but Victoria wasn't in the bed. He shouted her name again, without reply.

He ran back to the window to see if the man was still at the gate. He wasn't there. Fear shot through Stephen's soul when he heard pounding at the front door. Still worried about Victoria, Stephen ran into her bedroom, bathroom and guest bedroom and screamed, "Victoria!"

The knocking stopped. Stephen seized the handrail and slowly descended the stairs. Suddenly, he heard pounding at the door again. It sounded like someone beating the inside of a large empty barrel with a sledgehammer. The sound was getting louder and louder. The house began to vibrate, and the chandelier in the formal dining room sounded as though someone had a stick knocking icicles onto a tin roof. Horror gripped Stephen as he ran back up the stairs.

"Where is Victoria? God help me!" he groaned.

Sensing the presence of someone behind him, Stephen cautiously turned. Standing there was the same repulsive being he had seen in the barn when Philip, Cordilia and Paul had come to visit. Without speaking or taking his eyes off the being, Stephen slowly moved backward toward the door. The man followed him.

"Who are you? How did you get in here?"

The being laughed aloud, snorted and snarled, "You will never get away from me. You're mine."

Stephen backed out the door and ran down the stairs, only to find the uninvited guest waiting there. Trembling, Stephen demanded, "Where is Victoria?"

He growled, "You'd better worry about yourself, Stephen."

At those words, Stephen lunged at the man, went through him and fell to the floor. He laughed at Stephen. "You will never get away from me," the being roared as he moved sluggishly toward Stephen who was scooting backward toward the main door. He managed to stand

and run for the door, praying Sheriff Bolton would be on the other side when he opened it. His hand almost stuck to the freezing door handle. He flung it open and ran outside. The door slammed shut behind him. Stephen shook his head and grabbed his chest. This was not his front yard, but a vast circle with two men standing in front of him, both dressed in white suits . . . unlike the other being he had just encountered. In haste, Stephen turned to see if the other man was behind him. As if reading his mind, one of the men in front of him said, "Don't worry, Stephen, he's gone. He did what he was sent to do, and that was to get you to this place."

Chapter Thirty-Six

Keeper of the Gates

Stephen wondered, *Where could Sheriff Bolton be?*

The other man answered his thought, "Sheriff Bolton can't help you here, Stephen."

Confused, Stephen asked, "Where am I?"

One of the men laughed aloud. "Well, you're definitely not in Kansas, Dorothy."

Numbed by what had taken place, Stephen solemnly asked, "Who are you?"

"We are the keepers of the gates."

Stephen looked from left to right. There were so many gates of all different shapes and sizes. Baffled, Stephen asked, "What . . . what are these gates?"

One of the men answered, "Each gate represents a choice. It's all about choice, you know. Behind each gate, you will find a different horizon to every possible avenue in life. You must choose carefully, Stephen.

I understand, and Fini agrees with me, that you are looking for a specific gate."

Stephen frowned, "Yes. I am, but I am not sure . . ."

One man stepped toward Stephen. "Is Wisdom with you, Stephen?"

Stephen nodded, "I've sought God for wisdom. I trust He has heard my prayers."

The other man stepped forward and said, "My name is Fini. I am a solider in the army of the living God. Behind each gate, there are countless numbers in the demonic army. The dark kingdom has them at every entrance. Their weapons are not swords and guns, but pride, jealousy, bitterness, lust and hate. The list goes on and on. The primary strategy of this army is to cause division on every level. Churches are coming against each other. Congregations are coming against their pastors. Husbands and wives are warring against each other, as well as children against their parents. Spies from the dark kingdom have been sent to find any opening they can exploit and make larger. The sad thing is, Stephen, they have found ways to go through every gate. Most of them are well-dressed, respectable and educated; there are representatives from every lifestyle. The power of this demonic army is rooted in deception—the very tool used in the Garden of Eden."

Stephen was attentive to all Fini was saying, but when he mentioned the Garden of Eden, he sternly interrupted. "That's the gate I need to find—*Eden's Gate*. Can you help me?"

The other man stepped forward. "My name is Kaman. I too am a warrior in the White Stone Kingdom. Fini and I can only alert you to what you will find in the assemblage. Look behind you, Stephen. God will never send you through any gate, except He sends his angels with you."

Stephen turned. Standing behind him was a host of ordinary looking people. Stephen immediately looked at Kaman and questioned, "Are *they* angels?"

Kaman nodded. "Yes," he confirmed. "They are all here to war on your behalf."

Stephen lowered his head.

Fini reprimanded him. "Hold your head up, soldier. Never look down! You must keep your head upward. You're entering the frontlines of the battle. A mistake like that could cause you to be mortally wounded. Your help comes from above, not from below."

Concerned, Stephen asked, "Can you tell me where Victoria is? I couldn't find her in the house."

Kaman put his hand on Stephen's shoulder. "Victoria arrived before you. She has already gone through a gate."

Stunned, Stephen asked, "She went through a gate?"

Fini smiled. "Destiny came for her immediately after she retired for the night." Fini pointed toward the gates. "It's time for you to choose, Stephen."

Chapter Thirty-Seven

Choice

Unsure, Stephen walked toward the gates. He walked around and stopped in front of many of them. His heart felt a pull from the first gate he saw. Was that the one to choose? His mind wasn't sure, but his heart said yes. He walked back to the first gate and stopped. He stared at the gate, gently ran his fingertips down the front of it and whispered, "My God, if this is the gate, show me."

He felt confident this was *Eden's Gate*. He looked back at Kaman and Fini, gave them a tight-lipped grin and took hold of the handle. After a deep breath, he slowly opened the gate. Apprehensive, yet determined, Stephen stepped inside, and the gate slammed shut. His jaw dropped as he beheld devastation, unlike anything he had ever seen. The land was filled with craters, most of the trees looked stripped. The sky was pregnant with brown clouds.

Stephen had seen black rain clouds before, but never anything like this. Most of the grass had the same brown appearance as the clouds. The surrounding mountains were either smoking or on fire. He heard many voices, but saw no one. Unexpectedly, the sound of women wailing pierced Stephen's ears. The sound was so close, he felt he could reach out and touch them, but where were they? What had taken place here?

"This is not Eden. Where am I?" Stephen whispered. "I have to choose another gate. This is definitely not the right one."

He turned to open the gate, when someone grabbed his arm and shouted, "It's about time you got here!" The man frowned, shook Stephen's arm and in bitter animosity asked, "Did you not bring the supplies we asked for? Well, speak up."

Bewildered at the fiendish stares and shouts of the gigantic man who was gripping his arm so tightly that it was growing numb from the pain, Stephen answered, "I don't know what you are talking about."

Another agonizing squeeze of his arm, and the man shoved him backward, releasing his grip. With a look of despondency, he lowered his head. "The troops aren't coming, are they?"

Stephen didn't know how to respond. How could he? Not knowing where he was, who the stranger was or what he was talking about.

The man was a towering six feet five inches tall, above average weight, with brown curly hair, green eyes, and a fair complexion. His hands were filthy. On his middle finger was a gold ring with the initial "A" stamped in the center. A large scar rested just under his right cheekbone, descended his neck and stopped at his collarbone. His clothes were dirty and he was in serious need of a bath. He stared hopelessly at the ground, biting his lower lip. His shoulders were slumped in despair. Stephen wanted to say something, to console the bold man who now appeared hopeless.

"What is your name?" he asked.

The man cut his eyes toward Stephen, and with a blank expression asked, "What difference does a name make here? If a person's integrity has been stripped away, what is a name?"

Stunned at the response, Stephen stammered, "I-I just wanted to know."

"What would *your* name be?"

Stephen put his hand out, offering a handshake, "I am Stephen Daniel Harris."

The man took hold of Stephen's hand and squeezed. "I'm Jim Lee." Jim managed a grin. "It sounds Chinese don't you think? Nevertheless, trust me, it's not. Who's ever seen a Chinaman who is six feet five inches tall?" Immediately, Jim looked back toward the burning mountains.

Still trying to figure out where he was, Stephen questioned, "Can you tell me where *Eden's Gate* would be? I came to a place where there were so many gates, I had to choose one, and this is definitely not *Eden's Gate.*"

Jim shook his head, and in disgust said, "My God in heaven! You sound as though you are the only one looking for *Eden's Gate*. We *all* are looking for *Eden's Gate*. Who doesn't want to be in a place of peace and plenty?"

Stephen took a deep breath and blew it out. "Can you please tell me where I am!"

Shocked at Stephen's response, Jim asked, "Where did you come from and what are you doing here?"

Stephen started to stand but Jim grabbed his arm and demanded, "Stay down! You'll get us both killed."

Stephen pulled his arm away. "What are you talking about? Killed by who?"

Harshly, Jim answered, "That's just it. We can never tell who the enemy is. They all look the same. That's why there is so much devastation. If we could determine who the enemy is, then we would have a chance to kill it. But when everyone looks the same, it's hopeless."

Confused, Stephen asked, "Why do you stay here? Why not go back to where you came from?"

Tears filled Jim's eyes as he explained, "I came from the Eden."

Surprised, Stephen asked, "You've been to the Garden of Eden?"

"Yes! I was there most of my life, even though I feel I've been *here* a lifetime."

"I don't understand, Jim. Why did you leave Eden and why not go back?"

Before Jim could answer, arrows sailed passed their heads. Jim pushed Stephen down and demanded, "Go toward the tree line, Stephen. They must have spotted us."

Stephen crawled as fast as he could toward the tree line, with Jim following close behind. In this area, there were still green trees and lots of underbrush. Out of breath, Stephen and Jim leaned against a tree trunk before they moved on. Stephen leaned his head back and closed his eyes. Jim was quick to remind him not leave his eyes closed too long. In a whisper, Stephen groaned, "God, what is going on? I want to go home."

Jim surveyed the area, stood and started to walk away.

Stephen called out, "Jim, where are you going? Don't leave me!"

Jim faced Stephen with his lips tight and his knuckles white from squeezing his fists together. Furious, he knelt down, grabbed Stephen by the collar of his shirt and growled,

"You make me sick! You barely come through the gate and have the audacity to cry like a baby wanting to go home. If you feel that way after a few minutes, how do you think others feel who have been here too many seasons to count? How about the ones who were born here? It's people like you wanting to live in the comfort of a home, closing their eyes to the truth, that keep people in this desolate wilderness. If you cared, you would want to help these people find *Eden's Gate*, that they too may leave this hell."

Releasing Stephen's shirt, Jim started to run away. Stephen grabbed hold of his leg and begged, "Don't leave me here, please. I don't mean to appear uncaring. I *do* care. I'm scared. I don't have a clue as to where I am or what I'm doing here. You talk about people, but I see only you. I hear crying, but I see no one to comfort. Please, be patient with me."

The frown on Jim's face loosened. He nodded and commanded, "Come on, soldier, we need to get to the cave before dark." Jim extended his hand to Stephen and pulled him to his feet.

Stephen had to run to keep up with Jim. The darkness was swallowing up what was left of daylight. As they neared the foot of a mountain, Stephen again heard wailing, moaning and cries of agony. The desolate land had signs of once being a utopia. He saw overrun flower gardens and broken fountains. Stephen wondered what had happened in this place.

Jim stopped so fast Stephen almost ran over him.

Jim knelt down and parted the grass. He was jubilant. "Look, Stephen," Jim whispered, "Praise be to God! Praise be to God!" At first, he was digging with his fingers, then grabbed a stick and dug with it. Suddenly, Jim threw the stick down, held up something that appeared to be a root and looked at Stephen. "Look what I've found."

Curious, Stephen asked, "A root? I thought you were digging for gold."

"Strange you would say gold. That is exactly what we call it. Gold root. I haven't seen any for a month now. We can make tea and medicine out of this root. God has blessed us today. My wife will be ecstatic."

Surprised, Stephen asked, "Did you say wife?"

"Yes, and two children. My son, Tim, is 5, and my daughter, Mary, is 10. Now, let's go and I'll introduce you.

Chapter Thirty-Eight

Jim Lee

As they approached the area, Jim called out as he neared his home.

Everything appeared to be more at ease. Jim was no longer bent over running but walking upright. Stephen saw a little boy come to the opening of a cave. A smile spread across the child's face as he came running with open arms. "Daddy, Daddy!" he cried.

Overjoyed, Jim picked up his son and swung him around. "How is daddy's little man?" Jim hugged and kissed his son. By then, a beautiful blue-eyed, blond-haired girl was making her way to hug her daddy.

While watching, Stephen remembered the countless times he ran to greet his dad with hugs and kisses—the difference being, he wasn't living in a cave, in an impoverished terrain. Stephen held back tears when he saw Jim's wife. Through his spirit, Stephen saw a black cloud hovering over her. The cloud moved slowly down and disappeared into her body. Stunned, Stephen lowered his eyes, trying not to hold his stare.

Jim's wife was pale and very thin. Stephen could tell by her appearance she was once a very attractive woman. Her shoulder-length brown hair was pushed behind her ears. She had big brown eyes, sunken cheekbones and protruding collarbones. Her dress was a dirty green. One of her shoes was tied on with strings. She, too, smiled and embraced Jim, but her eyes were empty.

Excited, Jim said, "Close your eyes. I have a surprise for you." They all three closed their eyes and reached their hands forward. Jim playfully said, "No peeking."

His little boy said, "I'm peeking, Daddy."

Jim tickled his tummy. "I said no peeking." Jim took the root from his pocket, held it in front of him and shouted, "Surprise!"

You would have thought it was Christmas the way they acted over a piece of root. Jim turned and apologized for his manners, "Honey, kids, this is Stephen Daniel Harris. Stephen, this is my family. My wife, Ellen; my son, Tim; and my daughter, Mary."

Ellen shyly nodded her head and ran her fingers across her hair. "It's good to meet you, Stephen. I must look a mess." Ellen widened her eyes and eagerly questioned, "Are you one of the reinforcement soldiers?"

Before Stephen could answer, Jim responded, "No, honey, he just came through the gate."

A look of total hopelessness swept across Ellen's face. Lowering her head, she began to cry, "No one is coming to help, are they?" She looked at Stephen. Her eyes pierced his soul. Again, she asked, "Is help coming?" She pushed her long slender fingers to her head and groaned. Before Stephen could respond, she hysterically screamed, "Does no one hear our cries for help on the other side of the gate? How many more will die before we are delivered from this waste?" A woman who frequently prayed, sometimes she felt too helpless to pray.

Stephen felt sick to his stomach, not knowing what she was talking about or how to answer her urgent question.

Ellen put her thin hand on Stephen's chest and pleaded, "Can you tell us the news from the other side of the gate. Are the plans for rescue in progress?"

In an attempt to encourage her, Stephen assured her, "Yes, plans are in progress. The Most High won't leave you in this place, I promise."

Ellen hit Stephen's chest and shouted, "I want to know about man's plan, not God's."

Jim took hold of Ellen's arm and tried to comfort her. "Ellen, please! God will send help. In time, He will."

Ellen pulled her arm from Jim and bluntly replied, "If God was going to do anything, He would've done it by now. I don't want to hear another word about a God who allows children to starve to death or die from thirst and keep their mother alive to see it."

Tim fixed his sad eyes on his mother. "Mommy, are we going to die?"

Ellen snapped, "More than likely!"

Just as fast, Ellen grabbed Tim, hugged him and said, "No, no, no, we are not going to die. Mommy's just not feeling too good." Ellen managed a smile and again hugged Tim and Mary. She dried her face with the sleeve of her dress and said, "Come on, I'll fix you two some tea."

Ellen took the children's hands and made her way further into the cave.

That night Ellen laid down on the ground with only her arm for a pillow, curled in a fetal position. After a short time, she began to weep.

Suddenly, a boundless mass of weeping echoed through the valley and pierced Stephen's soul. He felt so helpless. That night

Stephen's eyes wouldn't close. He questioned silently, *Why was I thrust into something I don't understand? Lord, I thought this was the right gate.* He watched Jim as he held Tim in one arm and Mary in the other. His heart broke, knowing all the children had for supper was warm tea and half a potato.

Stephen couldn't breathe. He had to get outside. Quietly he stood and looked at a family that would die soon if help didn't arrive. His insides wrenched with pain. He rushed outside to find a place where he could cry out to the Most High.

Once outside, Stephen moved cautiously. All around, the mountains were still burning and smoking. The air was contaminated with an unusual stench. He staggered around in the night for what seemed an eternity, then fell to his knees. After bowing his head, he remembered Fini's rebuke, "Never look down soldier, your help comes from above, not from below." Wanting to start his prayer with worship as usual failed. The oppression and death of this place had overwhelmed him. Where would praise come from? A joyful heart, a full stomach, a warm bath and bed—the dream of such simple things were not to be found in the cave where Jim and his family lived.

Stephen muttered, "How do you praise God for contaminated water, air and starvation?"

The words Tim had asked his mother burned like fire in Stephen's soul. "Are we going to die, Mommy?" Stephen repeatedly whispered Ellen's words to himself, "Does anyone hear our cries? How many will have to die before we are delivered from this waste?" Stephen looked toward heaven and asked God the same question. He could not look up, but lay with his face to the ground and lamented for the people stuck in this hell. As Stephen petitioned God for deliverance on behalf of the people, his body and soul began to rise. With his hands lifted, he worshipped the Most High in the mist of ruin.

Chapter Thirty-Nine

Discouraged

awn was breaking. Without realizing it, Stephen had prayed all night. He slowly opened his eyes, hoping he would be back home at Eden's Gate, but it was not to be today. Sluggishly, he raised himself up from the ground. His knees were stiff. His stomach growled from hunger, and his throat felt parched from thirst. A strange feeling swept over him as he licked his lips, trying to wet them. Instantly, he recognized the terrible taste in his mouth—the same taste he had encountered the night of the storm when his cow was charred. Discerning this, Stephen scanned the area and uttered, "Shemed!"

Stephen tried to find his way back to the cave but wasn't sure if he was going in the right direction. As he came off one trail and onto another, he wondered if he had gone that far out before.

He had taken only a few more steps when he came into a clearing. For the first time since he had been in this place, Stephen saw people other than Jim's family. Startled, Stephen stopped. Like lightning, the group of people turned to look at Stephen.

Immediately, one of the men stepped forward and shouted, "Who are you?"

Before Stephen could answer, two men came from the side and seized him. The man demanded again, "Who are you?"

Stephen struggled to loosen the firm hold the two men had on his arms, but could not. The hard-looking stranger standing before him grabbed his face with one hand and commanded, "For the last time, who are you?"

Stephen, now angrier than scared, replied, "I am Stephen Daniel Harris. Who are you?"

The man's eyes widened as he quickly loosened his grip from Stephen's face, stepped back, saluted and apologized.

Adding to Stephen's confusion, the two men who had seized his arms loosened him and joined the man in a salute to Stephen. About thirty more men in the group lined up with the three, stood at attention and saluted Stephen. The stranger who had held his face stepped forward. "Sir! We are the Seventh Armored Division! We war under the banner of the Crystal Kingdom."

195

Amazed, Stephen asked, "What is this? Why are you saluting me?"

At once the soldier replied, "It is only proper to give respect to a commanding officer of the Eagle Forces."

Shaking his head, Stephen said, "I don't know who you think I am, but I am not an officer of any kind. Why would you say or even think that?"

The soldier boldly replied, "Twenty-six years ago, a message was brought to us from the Most High. It said the Most High had commissioned two top-ranking angels to descend Jacob's Ladder and to be born of woman. One would be Eri, a top warring angel under King Rayon's command, and the other would be a 'top general from the White Stone Kingdom.' His name is Rakar. General Rakar's boldness still shakes Queen Jewel and the dark kingdom's emps. He stood with the Most High at the great rebellion. The message also told us the child's flesh name would be, Stephen Daniel Harris."

Puzzled, Stephen muttered, "I am Stephen Daniel Harris, but I'm surely not the one you are looking for."

The man lowered his head. "I did hope you would be Rakar, for all our sakes."

Feeling bewildered, Stephen said, "Help me understand something. If you are the Armor Bearers of King Rayon's army, why do you look for this Rakar? Why not call on the Most High, Himself?"

The soldier frowned. "Sir, even the Most High has leaders. He works through those leaders to give direction to His people. We know our calling is to war, but we need a leader to know where to confront the battle. Most people here claim to march under the Most High's Banner, but they're not free. The enemy keeps them underfoot. There're only a few who truly march under that banner."

Looking around, Stephen asked, "Where are all these people you speak of? I've seen only one family other than you since I came through the gate."

The man turned and pointed toward a mountain. "Come and I'll show you."

Stephen hesitated, thinking of Jim and his family. "I want to see the other people, but there is a family that is in desperate need of assistance. I fear if the mother doesn't get help soon, she will die."

The man soberly replied, "You've been touched by one family; we have been touched by millions. Nevertheless, where is the family and I will send as much help as possible?"

Stephen eagerly said, "The father's name is Jim Lee. He is very tall . . ."

Before Stephen could finish his description, the man interrupted, "I know Jim, his family

and the cave where they live. I haven't seen
him in a couple of days, but I'll send a man to
make sure all is well with them."

He motioned to a man standing nearby and
commanded, "Go, take a cup of water and some
hot bread to the cave."

Upon hearing that, Stephen asked, "You have
drinkable water and hot bread?"

"Yes, Sir! Would you like some?"

Stephen patted his stomach. "I feel sick, I'm
so hungry."

Stephen followed the soldier into a cave,
sat down and eagerly enjoyed the fresh bread
and water. "Umm, umm. This is wonderful."
Stephen paused and asked, "By the way, what
is your name?"

The soldier grinned and nodded. "Sir,
I'm Dale Thomas." He was about six feet tall
with long, sandy hair and hazel eyes. His dark
complexion was rough—a strongly built man.
Stephen finished his meal, such as it was.
"This is a miracle straight from God." he said.
"I've never really been hungry before. I could
hardly stand to watch Jim and his family,
knowing the small amount of food they've
had for days."

Dale stood and looked out the cave opening.

Stephen's attention turned to the gold
ring on Dale's middle finger, with the initial
"A" stamped in the center. "Your ring, does

it have significance? I noticed Jim has one almost like yours."

Dale picked up a sword that was propped against a rock, walked forward and said, "We'll talk as we walk. We must keep moving. I want you to view the deep valley."

Chapter Forty

The Ring

They left the cave and started down a dusty trail. Moving swiftly, Dale answered Stephen's question about the ring. "All Armor Bearers' leaders wear one. It serves as a signet showing we were hand-picked for our post."

Stephen paused when he thought of the ring Ian Jackson wore. "Dale, have you ever seen a ring like yours that has more than the letter 'A' on it?"

"Yes. There is another ring with more letters on it. Have you seen one?"

Dale was walking so fast Stephen could hardly keep up. He took hold of Dale's arm and said, "Dale, please slow down. I am out of breath."

Stephen put his hands on his hips, took a deep breath and responded to Dale's previous question, "Ian Jackson, my foreman, has a gold ring with the letters 'AOTA' stamped on it."

Dale turned and looked into Stephen's eyes. "You've seen that ring?"

"Yes, Ian has one."

Dale's countenance completely changed as he put his hand over his mouth. He whispered, "They're finally here."

"Who's here?" Stephen asked.

"A member of the elite. They alone wear that ring."

Again, they began to move forward. Stephen asked, "Do you know what the letters on the ring mean?"

Dale abruptly stopped and frowned at Stephen. "You don't know what the initials stand for?"

Stephen shook his head. "No, I don't have a clue."

Disappointment was evident by the look on Dale's face. With a broken voice, he said, "Then maybe you are not the one I thought you were sure to be."

Totally confused, Stephen asked, "Wait a minute. Why would not knowing what initials on the ring stand for change your mind about who you thought I was?"

Dale snapped, "A true leader of the people would know what the letters mean."

"Well, since I don't know, will you please tell me?"

Dale tightened his brows. "*Angels of the Ages*. Only the ancient ones who have warred from *the beginning* for the Most High were given that ring. If you've seen the ring, you are special indeed."

"Are you saying, Ian Jackson is one of the ancients you spoke of?"

Dale turned and began moving forward. "We need to be moving. We'll talk about it later.

The farther they went, the darker the sky grew, until the sky was so dark they could hardly see, but it was only noon. Stephen asked, "Dale, why is it so dark? Is it from all the smoke or what?"

Dale sighed. "Stephen! The dark kingdom has conquered this territory."

Stephen and Dale had crawled for about a half-mile when Dale abruptly stopped. He put his hand back toward Stephen and whispered, "Shhh! It's essential you stay low." Dale looked from left to right, turned, looked at Stephen and quietly demanded, "Control your breathing, breathe lightly. We have come into the vicinity of the Deep Valley. I can't stress the urgency of being alert to everything around you, including the grass."

Dismayed, Stephen said, "The grass? There's hardly any grass here."

Looking straight ahead, Dale said, "The grass here is covered with poison gases. The only way to detect the poison is through the Holy Spirit."

Dale faced Stephen. "Not everyone will see the Dark Valley. Man's natural eye will never view it. This war is spiritual. If you see the valley, you'll know the Most High has brought you here to see it. If not, I'll take you back to the gate immediately, or you too will be taken prisoner. Are you ready to see, Stephen?"

Stephen nodded. "I'm ready!"

Dale tightened his jaw. "Good."

Stephen and Dale crawled for a short way farther. The sounds of bombs, missiles, arrows and swords were piercing their ears. Stephen wondered, *If the war is only spiritual, why the deafening sounds of the war weapons?*

Unexpectedly, Dale stopped.

Stephen could see nothing, but felt only Dale's hand pressed against his shoulder. Apprehensive, Stephen asked softly, "What is it?"

Dale quietly replied, "We've reached our destination. Are you ready to see, Stephen?"

"Yes! Show me."

Holding Stephen's arm, Dale guided him to the crest of the Deep Valley. At first, it was so dark Stephen couldn't tell if his eyes were open or closed. He began to pray softly, "Father! Open my eyes to see what you want me to see."

In a twinkling, a miraculous light illuminated a boundless valley. Overwhelmed, Stephen felt uncertain. What could this signify? He looked toward Dale. He, too, was now clearly visible. Dale's eyes were fixed on him. "You are the leader sent from God, Stephen."

Stephen knew immediately that Dale was right. Still, he asked, "How do you know that?"

"God made the valley clear to you. Many have seen in part; but, Stephen, God has fully opened your eyes to see."

Stephen was fast to add, "I see clearly, but I am not sure what I am seeing. God will have to reveal that as well."

Dale looked toward the valley. "Tell me, Stephen, what do you see?"

Stephen stared into the valley and said, "I see why it is called the 'Deep' Valley. This valley is an abyss of deception."

Stephen put his hand over his mouth and a cry of anguish came from his soul. "Father, help me understand what I am seeing!"

Instantaneously, Stephen and Dale were in a dense population of the Deep Valley. Wailing, groans and expressions of sorrow in every possible form echoed through the valley.

Dale explained, "When one tries to stand, the demon of hopelessness puts his foot on the struggler's mind and shouts, 'No hope!' When one tries to reach up, the demon of rejection and low self-esteem kicks him down and dictates how sinful and worthless he is. All have been wounded and are in desperate need of healing." Dale looked toward Stephen with a broken heart and said, "They have suffered in this vast darkness so long, they have come to think pain and suffering is all there is to life. No one here has seen the light of our Lord in so long. Too many feel the veil has been stitched tightly together and God no longer hears their prayers. Jewel has spread a smoke screen of deception so thick that most have come to believe the light will never shine again. The majority are too weak to fight any longer. The bombs, missiles, swords and arrows you hear are only a deception. Queen Jewel wants them to think they are outnumbered to such a degree they won't even try to fight. They're afraid of being hit by something that seems to be real, even though it's not."

The cries for help pierced Stephen's soul. In heaviness of heart, Stephen walked through the valley viewing what appeared to be the primary sin. The dark kingdom had infiltrated the Word of God with a great degree of cunning deception. The lies had gone totally unnoticed. The shepherds of the sheep had accepted the deceit. Stephen took his eyes from the hurting people and began to make eye contact with their false shepherds, who kept them in oppression. So many had set themselves up as gods instead of their protectors and leaders. In arrogance, they themselves slaughtered the ones they were to protect. The pastors were so blind with arrogance they thought they were truly doing the work of God's kingdom.

Stephen saw many chained together, struggling to be freed. The ground rumbled from the force of the struggle.

Many were grabbing Stephen and Dale as they made their way through their midst. One man grabbed hold of Stephen and pleaded, "I did everything the church told me to do, and still I can't get free. Please, help me!"

Chapter Forty-One

Death of a Friend

Stephen and Dale walked for what seemed like hours. Up ahead, Stephen saw the most awesome sight he had ever seen—a gigantic gate made of solid gold adorned with every kind of precious stone. The entrance was immense. However, blocking the opening there was boiling, black smoke.

Stephen frowned. "Dale! What is this gate?"

Before Dale could answer, they were instantly back at the cave where the Armor Bearers were camped. Stephen turned in a circle, viewing his surroundings. He sighed deeply. Every muscle in his body tensed and ached. He released a long, wailing cry. He felt his heart and soul being transformed, as he stood, unable to make words, he was able only to groan in his spirit.

The Armor Bearers knelt in a circle around Stephen and cried out to the Lord God

Almighty to empower them and their leader, General Rakar.

After a time of worship and prayer, Stephen wanted to go to Jim Lee's cave and check on them. Dale led the way. Before they arrived at the entrance, Dale and Stephen heard Jim crying and knew something must be tragically wrong. They ran as fast as possible only to find Jim, Mary and Tim holding Ellen's lifeless body.

Frantic, Stephen knelt down and took Ellen's face in his hands. Excruciating pain gripped his heart as he looked at the frail malnourished body of a wife and mother, and a woman who had lost hope. Stephen and Dale embraced Jim and the children. The Armor Bearers came and helped bury Ellen and took Jim and the kids back to their camp.

The scene at the camp was very subdued. Stephen felt numb. He stood and started to walk away from the camp. Dale called out, "Stephen, do you need some company?"

Stephen shook his head No.

"If you do, please let me know. We're here to serve you."

Stephen gradually walked away from the light of the campfire. He couldn't walk far. He felt an intense heaviness. He sat down and looked toward the Deep Valley. The images of each face he had seen were flashing before his eyes. The words Ellen had spoken the day before added to his pain. Stephen raised his head and pleaded with God, "Father, I need to understand. Why did she have to die? You could have spared her, Father! She said, 'I don't want to hear about a God who allows children to starve to death and keeps the mother alive to watch.'"

Stephen was trembling as anger began to take custody of his heart. Through gritted teeth, he shouted, "I don't understand it either! Do something! Father, help Jim and his children. Release the people in the valley. If I am this, Rakar, help me make a difference. If not, take me home."

Dale spoke up, "I couldn't help but overhear your prayer. I want to agree with you on that request. Do you mind if I sit with you a moment?"

Without expression, Stephen said, "Please do, Dale."

Dale sat down, pushed his knees to his chest and embraced them with his arms. "You've had quite a lot thrust upon you since you came through the gate, but it's all a part of God's plan for your destiny, Stephen. You may not fully understand it all now, but you will soon."

Looking straight ahead, Stephen asked, "Will you tell me about the gate in the valley?"

That question caused a glimmer of excitement to cover Dale's face. "Of course, I will. The gate in the valley is the same as the gate spoken of in the testament writing. Two disciples were going to the temple to worship. In order to do so, they had to go through the gate called 'Beautiful.' A man lying there had never walked. He had people bring him and lay him at the gate every day. Not only him, but many others who were also sick and afflicted were laid there daily. They begged for alms or anything to help support themselves."

"The man that couldn't walk. What was his name?" Stephen asked.

"No one knows," Dale said. "His name was never mentioned."

Stephen lowered his head. "So, with no name, he could be anyone, including, me or you. The man knew about the gate and the temple inside of the gate. However, people passed him every day as they went through the gate into the temple to worship. Some people may have dropped a coin in his cup, but no one gave him what he needed, which was to be healed so that he too could stand and enter the gate and temple to worship for himself. He physically couldn't walk because of his circumstances. He needed truth in order to maintain hope and keep his spirit healed."

"Absolutely!" Dale said. "The entrance to the temple was blocked to those wounded or maimed who could not walk in on their own. So close to the gate, yet so far. Though the gate was called 'Beautiful,' it wasn't beautiful to the people who lay there daily and could only watch as others went through. They could only hope to go through. But, hope was diminished. How would it feel to lie and watch pious priests and lay persons alike walk by you as if you were not there? This is what happened. He begged for help. After a while, people didn't see the man as a man, but as a cripple. It's funny how easily that takes place. If a man is black, all we tend to see is his color. If a man is white, we see the same. If a person is rich, or a beggar as the lame man, it's all the same. We see the exterior and title it. He's rich. He's poor. He's black or white. We've lost sight of the person."

Stephen ran his fingers through his hair. "We can see the circumstance and feel bad about it, but if we're not moved with compassion to alleviate the condition, then we've done nothing except have a bit of outward emotion. Our God was moved with compassion. He felt the deep, inward pain, where a person lives. The kind we're feeling as I speak. The inward affliction moves a person to act, or to change a situation. You must see more than a person's condition; you must feel the person's need, or you'll never set them free."

Stephen shook his head. "This was no ordinary lame man. I know this story. This certain man had an anger that came from the intense anguish deep in his soul. He had grown furious with the ones who professed to know God, yet looked at him and his condition as though he deserved it. They dared to question, 'Why is he this way? Because of his mother's or father's sin or his own?' When he saw the Lord's servants, Peter and John, he fastened his eyes on them in anticipation that he would receive something. Maybe there had been a time he had hoped someone would come by and pray for his healing and it would happen, but now all hope for that was gone. Now he settled for alms and had pushed healing and hope to the back of his mind. He had accepted his condition as a way of life. When he was laid at the gate that morning, I feel sure he thought this would be like any other day. He would lie at the gate called Beautiful and beg for alms. If it was a good day, he just might take in a few coins. At first, the people had given coins to assist, but that too had dwindled. When he fastened his eyes on Peter and John, he was pleading from the depth of his heart through his eyes. He could see. He just couldn't walk."

Dale interrupted, "Peter and John were moved with that compassion we were talking about."

Stephen continued, "Remember in the *Book of Acts*, Chapter 3, when thousands had just been added to the church. The disciples were filled with the Holy Spirit. They were full of God's power. The amazing thing was that God had not lost sight of the man at the gate. He loved him and wanted him healed, so the man could make his own way through the Beautiful gate and not be dependent on other men."

"Stephen, true leaders will clear the smoke screen from the entrance of the Beautiful gate. The Most High has sent you and the men at the camp to war on behalf of the people in the valley." Dale stood erect. "Stephen! Not only the few you saw at the camp." Dale pulled his sword, pointed it behind Stephen and boldly stated, "Look behind you, sir!"

Stephen turned to behold a multitude standing behind him. Stunned, he asked, "All these are here to follow me?"

Dale frowned and rebuked him. "No, sir! None of us are here to follow you. We follow the mantel you wear."

Stephen looked at his clothing, then at the host of Armor Bearers. He shook his head and rejected the claim that his mantel was preferred over anyone else's.

Dale swiftly said, "Sir! It is imperative that you know your rank and who you are in the Most High's army. Until you do, you're not ready to fulfill your command."

"Then tell me who I am!" Stephen ordered.

Dale looked down then back at Stephen. "Our Lord wore the same mantel when He too walked among men of flesh. The mantel is called humility. Maybe it's not time for you to see the mantel that each one of us sees clearly. All of heaven and hell recognize the mantel. If you wear it, no power in hell can stand against you. Hell will come against you but will not prevail. The mantel is not given to produce pride, but to serve the Kingdom of God."

Stephen was beginning to feel the effects of the mantel; however, he did not see it as others did. As Stephen and Dale walked through the ranks of the Armor Bearers, each one lifted their swords and cheered. Stephen found himself having to fight pride. He had to remember this was not about him being something, but about the Most High being everything.

Chapter Forty-Two
Beautiful Gate

Stephen noticed that some of the Armor Bearer's rings had two letters, and some had three. He asked, "Dale, I noticed the different rings on the Armor Bearers. We talked about the 'A' on your ring and the 'AOTA' on Ian Jackson's, but what is the significance of two and three initials?"

Dale responded, "The more letters on the ring, the higher the rank and the closer to the throne position. The higher the rank, the clearer you see things. For instance, you clearly saw the Deep Valley today and God allowed you to see the gate. Very few see the gate, even if they see the valley.

Stephen thought a moment and then asked, "If that's true, where is my ring?"

Dale smiled. "When you see the ring on your finger, you will know you're ready to step into your swordsman position."

Stephen stopped and looked Dale in the eye. "Swordsman position? What do you mean by that?"

Dale shook his head. "It means the Word of God will be the sword you fight your battles with. Trust me, Stephen, your sword will cut every way you turn it. The truth will set people free, because it will cut the fetters, unlock the chains and open the 'GATE' to the Kingdom of God."

Chapter Forty-Three

A Surprise Visit

Stephen and Dale entered the camp with the assembly of Armor Bearers. The first person Stephen looked for was Jim Lee. He went into the command cave. There, he found Jim lying on a blanket holding Tim in one arm and Mary in the other. Stephen walked over and sat down beside the blanket. He gently stroked Mary's long blond hair. Concerned, he asked, "How are you doing, Jim?"

Pain filled Jim's face as he whispered, "Right now I feel numb. Ellen always feared she would live to see the children die. She couldn't stand the thought of that. God was merciful. I only wish she could have seen the mantel you wear."

Confused, Stephen asked, "Are you saying you saw the mantel?"

Jim's sober eyes looked at Stephen. "The minute you came through the gate. I am thankful God has sent you, General Rakar. Now, in a short time, with you leading the way, we will secure the valley and take back what the dark kingdom has stolen."

Stephen patted Jim's arm. "I feel sure it will be sooner than you think, Jim."

Jim slowly closed his eyes and moaned. "Praise God!"

Dale was standing outside the cave waiting for Stephen. "Sir!"

"Please, call me Stephen."

Dale nodded. "Stephen, you better try and get some rest. Tomorrow, I'll take you to the mountain, and you will experience the battle first hand."

"Thank you, Dale. You get some rest also."

Dale looked around the area. "Not tonight. I am on watch duty until 3:00 a.m. After that I'm sure I'll sleep like a baby. Come and I'll show you where to sleep."

Dale led Stephen to a knoll overlooking the camp. That night, instead of silence filling the camp as before, the Armor Bearers danced, clapped their hands, shook tambourines and sang a song unto the Most High. They rejoiced and shouted in unison "GLORY to the ANCIENT of DAYS!"

Before long, Stephen was on his feet, clapping his hands, dancing and singing praise with the Armor Bearers. He was so caught up in praise he didn't notice the Armor Bearers had fixed their eyes on their leader. He danced and praised God with all his might before the soldiers of the White Stone Kingdom who would liberate the incomprehensible number in the Deep Valley. The praise went on most of the night. When Stephen stopped dancing, he opened his eyes and saw the Armor Bearers on their knees, with their hands lifted toward heaven. The sound of worship was like the hum of a giant swarm of bees.

Stephen too knelt and worshipped. As he worshipped, he felt compelled to open his eyes. When he did, he was overwhelmed at what he saw. Radiant beams of light infiltrated the camp. An illustrious light from the Crystal Kingdom covered each soldier.

A voice coming from behind said, "It's an awesome sight, don't you think, sir?"

Stephen turned to see Dale looking over the camp.

He took a deep breath and said, "It's the most inconceivable thing I have ever experienced. The Most High has blessed us with His presence tonight."

Dale smiled. "The dark kingdom is surely trembling. Queen Jewel's army knows the Armor Bearers have been empowered. They also know General Rakar is in the camp."

Chapter Forty-Four

Night Watch

Stephen was awakened by someone shaking his shoulder and whispering, "Stephen, Stephen, wake up!"

Sluggishly, he opened his eyes. Jim was leaning over him. Propping himself up, Stephen asked, "Jim, is something wrong?"

Still whispering, Jim replied, "The enemy has attacked the foot of the mountain and taken many prisoners. The Armor Bearers are on their way to the mountain as we speak."

Stephen rubbed his eyes. "Why didn't someone wake me?"

Jim tensed his brows. "Wake you? You should have awakened the men and gone before them. That's what a leader does."

Stephen hurriedly stood and straightened his clothing. "Can you take me to where they are now?"

Jim nodded. "That's why I'm here, sir."

Jim started forward. Stephen took hold of his arm, "How are the children?"

"They're doing okay."

"Jim, did you get any rest?"

Jim sadly said, "Not much! A big part of me is gone. Nevertheless, I'll be fine. Rest will come again someday, but for now we'd better be going."

The peaceful surroundings soon dissipated as arrows sailed past Jim and Stephen Daniel's head. Continuously, the number of arrows increased as they neared the foot of the mountain. Stephen noticed something strange taking place as he paused and stared at the mountain. What he thought had been fire burning on the mountain was not fire at all but the shining armor of the Armor Bearers. As Stephen surveyed all areas of the peaks, little by little the light grew dimmer.

Puzzled, Stephen asked, "Jim, what's happening to the light?"

Jim's put his hand on his hip as he looked to the mountain. "When a light grows dimmer, it means the darkness is overshadowing a soldier, which means that soldier is no longer standing. He's been shot down. This makes it harder for the others to see the path. Our focus at this point is to free the believers in the valley. In order to do this, we must keep the fire burning brightly on the mountain. The fire will also encourage those who are not a part of either army to come forward. There have been so many 'angels of light' sent by the dark kingdom to deceive the powerless and uneducated. Their main goal is to generate pride and self-righteousness in the Armor Bearers—thus, causing their armor to shine so brightly but only in their own eyes. They lose sight of the real light. Little by little they begin to operate out of darkness and become soldiers for the enemy without even knowing it. In turn, they shoot their arrows into their own White Stone Army, wounding and killing many."

Stephen felt devastated as he watched the light on the mountain continuously grow dimmer. Frantic, Stephen asked, "I know you said pride and self-righteousness were weapons used on the Armor Bearers, but help me to understand. If those emotions were in their hearts, how did they rise to the level of Armor Bearers?"

Before Jim could reply, he pushed Stephen to the ground. Several extremely loud shots exploded over their heads. Jim yelled, "Keep down and follow me!"

They crawled on their bellies for what seemed forever. Men were being wounded and falling all around them. The bombs were unbearably loud. After crawling onto a ledge and resting his back against some rocks, Stephen realized he and Jim had traveled about halfway up the mountain.

Jim took hold of Stephen's arm and whispered, "Stay here! I'll be back in a few minutes."

Stephen leaned forward. "Where are you going, Jim?"

"I'm going to check on casualties. Please stay down until I get back."

Chapter Forty-Five

The Fight

$\mathcal{D}$ucking out of the way of arrows, Jim started around the mountain. Stephen watched until he was out of sight. He put his hands over his ears to soften the aching in his inner ears. Tears filled his eyes as he cried out seeking help for the soldiers. "God, let your light shine on the mountain so those in darkness can find their way to you."

Stephen was shaking uncontrollably. Until that moment, he had no idea his motivation had been driven as much by fear and hate for the enemy as it had been for furtherance of God's kingdom. Stephen lowered his head and wept bitterly. With a broken heart, he prayed, "Father! How could I have been so blind to what was in my own heart? Please forgive me. I thought I knew my motivations and myself. It appears, I know very little. Thank you for revealing this to me and opening my heart to know that what I do must be motivated by my love and faith in you. Not fear, hatred or disgust. Change my heart, Father. Mold it to be like your heart. Fill me . . . with You."

Dale, already on the mountain, watched without interrupting.

Stephen raised his head and wiped his eyes.

Dale continued to stare at Stephen, astounded at what he was beholding. Stephen's mantel illuminated so brightly that the dark clouds were retreating. For the first time in many days, a glimmer of blue sky shone, intermittently fragmenting the darkness. True worship had weakened the enemy's defense and driven them from the mountain, if only to provide momentary relief. In silence, the two warriors worshipped their King as they camped for the night.

Stephen smiled and confessed, "I didn't realize the sin hidden in my heart. I never want anything to take His place in my heart."

Dale agreed. "You should see your mantel, Stephen. It glows as the noonday sun in the darkness."

Tears again filled Stephen's eyes. "There is only one light. I've held so much pain inside since my mother died. For some reason, I felt if I released the pain, I would also release her from my heart. Tonight, God has rejuvenated my soul."

Stephen closed his eyes and absorbed the presence of the Lord. After what seemed like hours, he sensed a presence close behind him. He stood and held his breath as he extended his hand to touch the person standing before him. "Mama!" Stephen whispered.

With open arms, Rachel greeted her son. Stephen held her tight and begged, "Please don't tell me this isn't real. Please!"

Rachel smiled. "It's very real, honey. God saw me beaming with pride as I watched your mantle light up as you worshipped. He nodded and told me to come to you."

"I miss you so much, Mom."

"I don't want you to miss me that much. I'm with you all the time, Stephen, in spirit. I am among a great cloud of witnesses that observe the battlefield you're standing in now."

Rachel took Stephen's hands. "Listen, Stephen, I have only a few minutes here, then I must go back. God is revealing many things to you, and more will come. I want to remind you, 'Don't forget the things I told you about Shemed and all the others who tried to prevent your birth. Don't forget."

With those words, Rachel slowly vanished. In anguish, Stephen called out, "Mom, Mom! Don't go yet." Stephen slumped down and leaned his head back against the rocks.

"Stephen, are you okay?" Dale asked, as he came running.

Stephen nodded his head. "Yeah," he said.

Stephen said nothing about Rachel, but did ask about Jim. "Dale, do you know where Jim is? He said he would be back in a few minutes. It's been at least three hours."

Dale replied, "He went back to the camp to be with his children."

Stephen nodded. "Good, he should be with them. They've just lost their mother, so they need their father with them as much as possible. Dale, have you noticed how quiet it is tonight? It's as though a silence has fallen over heaven and earth."

"Yes sir, and it is a great feeling. I have watch duty, so I had better get to my post. Good night, sir."

Dale turned to walk away, when Stephen called out, "Dale! You had watch duty last night. Let me take your watch tonight."

Surprised, Dale said, "That would be highly irregular, sir."

Stephen patted Dale's shoulder. "Get some sleep, soldier. Tonight, the watch is mine. Just show me where to watch."

Dale saluted Stephen. "Thank you, sir! Right here is a perfect place to watch. You can see every angle of the mountain, and we have a bit of moonlight to help for the first time in months. If you need me, just call. I'll be inside the first cave over there."

Chapter Forty-Six
Victoria's Imposter

Stephen looked across the terrain, which was quite beautiful as the yellowish glow of moonlight glistened along the mountainside. He desperately wanted to reach out and touch his mother again. He thought also of Philip, Cordilia and Paul. He wished they were sitting there with him on the night watch. He thought also of Eden's Gate. He had lost track of how many days he had been away. A week, two weeks, he didn't know. He did know it seemed like an eternity since he had taken a hot bath. He smiled as he remembered Victoria on the back of the truck with a handkerchief tied around her nose and mouth, declaring every worker needed a hot bath and deodorant. He chuckled, thinking she would surely grab a bath towel and cover her whole head if she was with him now.

As he looked at the almost full moon, he thought of Leann. He closed his eyes and could smell her enchanting perfume. He could taste her sweet lips and feel the warmth of her body.

He thought also of Victoria and the raw sexual desire that aroused him the day he stared at her, as she lay in her bed. He could see her long, sexy legs, tiny waist and all-but-bare, voluptuous breasts. He could feel the excitement he felt that morning as she brushed her long, blond, perfumed hair across his face. He felt her warm breath on top of his ear. The erotic passion Stephen was feeling scared him. Why was he feeling this excitement, when moments earlier all he felt was the spirit of God? Was God revealing something else that was perhaps still in his heart? Until the night of the storm, he had never known that kind of uncontrolled lustful feelings. As he had watched Victoria lying in her bed, why did he not just walk away? He should have thought, *Wow*, and dismissed it from his mind. When he did walk away, he wanted to go back. As Stephen thought about Victoria, a green mist began to form in the sky and fall toward the ground in the shape of a spiral funnel. It was creeping its way toward Stephen. He stood and watched as it came down in front of him. A hypnotic state suddenly controlled him, leaving him unable to call out. It stopped in front of him and a figure began to form. As it materialized fully, Victoria stood before him. She swayed and stroked her hair and neck. Stephen couldn't move. He could only whisper her name. She looked like a goddess. She slightly lowered her head and moved toward him. He slowly stood up with his back against the rocks and his arms down to his sides, enjoying the smell of her intoxicating perfume. Everything was moving in slow motion, even her words. Victoria sensually breathed Stephen's name and urged him to come into her arms. Stephen wanted her so desperately.

Victoria groaned his name. Stephen trembled as she touched her fingertips to his lips. Trying to move his arms, he found he could not. His breathing was so shallow he felt dizzy.

Victoria gently kissed his lips, snuggled her cheek against his and whispered in his ear, "Come with me to the fire, and I will open your senses to a whole new world. There are no words to describe the pleasure it will bring you." Victoria passionately kissed Stephen. This time, Stephen kissed back. The lustful feeling had seized Stephen's body. Suddenly, he moved freely.

They fell to the ground, when Dale came running around the corner screaming, "Stephen! Stephen!"

Terrified, Stephen looked up at Dale and then back at Victoria, who was no longer there. Stephen heard laughter and the smell of sulfur was breathtaking.

Dale stopped abruptly, looking at Stephen sitting on the ground. "Sir, what are you doing?"

Stephen hurriedly stood and adjusted his clothing. Embarrassed, instead of answering the question, he asked, "What is it, Dale?"

Confused by Stephen's behavior, Dale sternly asked, "Did you not see the enemy advancing on the north side of the mountain?"

Stephen eyes widened, as panic overtook his countenance. Out of breath, Stephen said, "No . . . no I didn't."

Dale shouted, "Why? Tell me why. The north side is in full view. There is no reason you shouldn't have sounded the alarm to warn the camp below."

Stammering, Stephen asked, "What . . . happened?"

Dale was furious. "Did you not hear the bombs and the cries of our soldiers?"

Stephen swallowed hard. "No, I didn't hear anything."

Dale looked away and quickly back at Stephen and shouted, "What! Were you in a trance or something? When you're on watch that is all you do—watch. Not sleep, daydream or fantasize. You watch. You watch because soldier's lives are in your hands. Some of those lives were lost tonight because you were not watching. Their blood is on your hands, Stephen. Obviously, you're not ready to wear the mantel of your office. What happened to the light that shone so brightly from your mantel just a few hours ago? Now, there is no light at all."

Stephen shook his head, tears filled his eyes, and his chin began to quiver as he tried to answer. "I . . . I don't know."

Dale stood firm and rebuked Stephen, "That is a lie! You do know. You know what took place on your watch. You asked Jim earlier how a person could reach this level of the mountain and still be wounded. Well, you tell me, Stephen. Was it pride, arrogance or were you seduced with an illusion of some sort? Whatever your answer, I want you to know, Jim was wounded and may not make it. Because you were not at your watch-post, lives were lost. You are supposed to be the 'Watchman.'"

Dale turned and walked a few steps. Without turning around, he shouted, "WATCHMAN! WHAT OF THE NIGHT?" He then walked away.

Chapter Forty-Seven

Explaining

The moonlight had faded as darkness once again surrounded the mountain.

Breathless, Stephen tried to call out to God, but he could find no words. He fell to his knees, put both hands over his face, wept aloud and finally cried out, "Father, what have I done?"

Stephen felt so dizzy, he couldn't open his eyes for a moment.

"Father!" he pleaded, "Let Jim live. Take me if someone must die, but not Jim. You know he has two small children, and they have just lost their mother. Father, I beg you, let Jim live."

Stephen's head was spinning out of control as he lost consciousness.

"Stephen! Stephen! Wake up, Stephen!"

Victoria called as she shook his shoulder. Stephen was lying on his stomach, groaning, crying and repeatedly asking God to let Jim live. Victoria continued to shake Stephen, trying to wake him. Unsuccessful, she had to do something to get him out of the dream he was in. Using both hands, she took hold of Stephen's arm and turned him onto his back. When she did, Stephen jumped out of the bed like a wild man. He grabbed Victoria and threw her against the wall. Groaning in pain, she watched Stephen act as though he had been using hallucinogenic drugs. Stephen went to the window and frantically tried to open the blinds. Victoria could not imagine what Stephen's horrendous nightmare could possibly be about. It was so bad she couldn't wake him up.

Stephen stood and looked at Victoria in disgust. He moved gradually toward her with his fists clinched. Glancing from left to right, Victoria searched for something to use in her defense if necessary. As Stephen drew closer, she again made another attempt to rouse him.

"Stephen Daniel Harris! You had better wake up, or I will personally knock you into next week. WAKE UP!"

Stephen's eyes were glazed, and his teeth were tight together. In rage, he came toward Victoria and growled, "You whore. When I am through with you, you will wish you had never seen me or any man."

Victoria tried to run, but Stephen grabbed her around her waist and dragged her toward the bed. Victoria was slapping, kicking and scratching all the way. Stephen pushed her down onto the bed. She tried to roll off, but couldn't. He slapped Victoria's face, leaving an outline of his hand on her cheek. She was struggling to push Stephen off. He ripped her gown down the front and continued to mutter something about someone named Jim.

Stephen took a piece of her gown and tied it around one of her wrists. Victoria managed to use her other hand to grab the phone from the nightstand and hit Stephen with it in the side of his head and again on his chest. He fell over. Finally, Victoria was able to push him off. She stood, shaken by what had happened, never expecting this type of behavior from Stephen. She quickly tied Stephen's hands and feet to keep it from happening again. She thought about calling Sheriff Bolton, but didn't. After securing Stephen, she grabbed her robe, put it on and then checked Stephen's temple, which was bleeding. As she cleaned the blood off, she nervously rambled, "I'm sorry I had to hit you so hard. What in the world came over you, Stephen? If I have a bruise on my face, I will kill you. I just might anyway, if you don't have an excellent excuse for all this craziness. And look what you did to my negligee. You will pay for it."

Victoria checked Stephen's chest, which was now visibly bruised. She got cotton balls and peroxide to doctor the cuts and scratches she had inflicted.

Stephen groaned and slowly turned his head to the side.

Victoria continued to put the peroxide on the wounds. "Be still, Stephen!" she shouted.

He opened his eyes, frantically looked from left to right and breathlessly asked, "Where am I?"

Victoria frowned. "Oh! So that's what you have to say for yourself, 'Where am I?' Please, Stephen, you can do better than that."

Worried about Jim, Stephen pleaded, "Victoria! Untie me. I have to get back to the battle."

"Uh! Get back to the battle! The battle has been right here in your bedroom. So, you were dreaming of battle? That's why you hit me? That's a sorry reason."

Stephen shouted, "Untie me! I need to find out about Jim and . . . and . . ." Stephen soberly looked around the room. Confused, he asked, "Victoria, how long have I been here?"

Aggravated, Victoria growled, "Is this some kind of crazy game you're playing, Stephen? If it is, I don't like it."

Stephen took a deep breath and said, "I hit you? You said I hit you?"

Victoria was furious. "Yes! Look at my face. It isn't bruised yet, but if it does, God have mercy on you, Stephen Daniel Harris."

Stephen closed his eyes. "I have never hit a girl in my life."

Victoria furrowed her brows. "I figured you were having a nightmare, in shock or something. To be honest, you acted like someone who was on hard drugs."

"I'm so sorry I hit you. I wanted to hit you when you first arrived here, but that feeling passed. Please untie me. I won't hit you again, I promise."

Victoria frowned and bit her lower lip. "Do you promise, and I mean promise?"

"I promise."

"Okay, but if you start anything, I am going to take you out. Have you got that?"

"Yes, my head is pounding."

Victoria untied him. "What kind of dream were you having?"

"Let's get some coffee first and then we will talk about it."

Chapter Forty-Eight
The Argument

Stephen made coffee and asked Victoria to join him on the porch swing. He said nothing, just glided back and forth, sipping his coffee. Victoria was getting inpatient, . She stared at Stephen, who was looking straight ahead.

"I'm waiting for details. What caused your vigorous advances?"

Staring toward the barn, Stephen said, "I wish I could say it was only vigorous advances."

Surprised at his response, Victoria said, "You mean it wasn't?"

"No, Victoria, it wasn't."

"Then, I demand to know what possessed you to hit me."

Stephen walked to the edge of the steps, seized the column and groaned, "I wanted to kill you, Victoria."

Victoria's eyes widened as she shouted, "You what?"

Stephen slowly lowered his head. "I wanted to kill you."

"But . . . why? Kill is a bit much, don't you think, Stephen?"

"Because of what happened at the battle!"

Victoria shouted, "Well tell me what happened at the battle, Stephen."

Stephen turned and faced Victoria. "You won't believe me. I don't even believe it. How can you?"

With her hands on her hips, she said, "At this point, after what you have put me through, I want to hear every word. Better yet, I *need* to hear it. So, you better start talking."

Stephen tried to take hold of Victoria's hand, but she jerked it away.

"Victoria, at least sit with me, and I'll try to explain."

Stephen told her what happened before blacking out.

Victoria pressed her fingertips to her temples. "Let me get this straight. You're saying, there was a green mist that turned into me?"

"Yes. I can't believe what I did on my watch. I hated you so bad for distracting me. I wanted to kill you."

"Stephen Daniel Harris! You are such a whiny baby.

"A baby! How do you figure?"

Victoria shook her head in disgust. "You're so self-righteous! Is it so shocking to you that perhaps *you* have these emotions and desires? And, no one else is to blame? You're not exempt from demented behavior, you know. What are you thinking, you're privileged or something? Do you want to know what I think, Stephen?"

"I am assuming you are going to tell me whether I want to know or not."

Victoria frowned. "My, my, you're getting to be a regular genius; or else, you would not have been able to make that accurate prediction. Now, listen up! I think, for the first time in your life, God has let the hedge of protection down that has guarded you. He's letting you get a taste of the real Stephen. That doesn't mean you are not a good person, or in your case, a chosen vessel. It means, you need to experience life to save life. It's obvious you haven't experienced anything. Your whole life has consisted of a *Leave it to Beaver* mentality. That's not where the real world lives, Stephen. There's another thing I want to point out. You tend to believe I am spoiled without ever considering how spoiled *you* are. Sometimes God allows us to see all the hidden junk that is planted deep inside our hearts. He is what we would call the 'great exposer.' If He doesn't reveal the sin inside our hearts, how would we know that there is anything for us to deal with? We never know how we will respond to something, unless we experience it. Look at it like this, Stephen. God is putting you through boot camp. It's not pleasant while you're in training, but the lessons are essential. Even leaders like you have to be trained."

Stephen sat down, propped his elbow on the armrest of the swing and massaged his pounding forehead.

Victoria sympathized with Stephen's anguish. She, too, had been in that place. She patted Stephen's shoulder. "I'll get you some aspirin for your headache."

Without looking up, Stephen said, "Thank you. I'm sure that will help."

Chapter Forty-Nine

Facing the People

Stephen could hear the phone ringing but made no move to answer it, so Victoria did. She came to the door and said, "Stephen, it's Leann."

Frantic, Stephen shook his head, No. He said, "Tell her I'll call her back."

Victoria lifted the receiver and said, "Yes, Leann, he's sitting right here." She handed him the phone.

He breathed in disgust and took the telephone. "Hi, honey! How are you?"

"I'm fine. I just called to remind you about our appointment to have our first portrait together taken together at 11:00 this morning."

Stephen put his hand over the receiver. "Oh, man, I forgot about the pictures."

"Leann could you please reschedule? There's no way I can make it this morning. Besides we haven't got a new date for the wedding yet."

Aggravated, Leann snapped, "Stephen! This isn't for the wedding. It's our first portrait since we started going together. You've known about this appointment for three months.

"Honey, I know and I want the photos as much as you. I just can't go this morning. Call and reschedule, please. I love you so much, but I don't feel well and have so many things to do. Please try and understand."

Leann paused, then reluctantly agreed. Stephen was so relieved. Right now, he had no idea how to explain to Leann the cuts, bruises and scratches.

Just as Stephen was saying goodbye to Leann, Ian Jackson drove up.

Victoria turned to go into the house. "I better go get my things. You know how impatient Ian gets."

Stephen hurriedly stood and asked Victoria to tell Ian he would join them later.

"Hum," Victoria said, "you never cease to amaze me. You tell Ian what you like. I am not telling him anything. Now, if you will excuse me, I have to go get my camera."

Stephen was so embarrassed. He didn't know how to explain his wounds to Ian.

Feeling helpless, Stephen sat back down on the swing. Ian came onto the porch and whistled. "What happened to you? You look like you were in a fight and got the bad end."

At that moment, Victoria came out of the screen door to the porch. She pointed toward Stephen's injuries and said, "I promise you, Ian, if you don't get me back home before the employees work up a sweat and start smelling, this is only a drop in the bucket compared to what I will do to you. Now! Let's get going. Time is wasting."

Victoria started toward the truck with a strut that beat anything Ian had ever seen. "Stephen, surely she didn't do this to you, did she?"

Stephen avoided the question. "I know what the letters on your ring stand for."

Suddenly solemn, Ian said, "Is that right?"

Stephen stood and looked into Ian's eyes. "Yes."

"There are only two ways you could possibly know what the letters stand for. Either God revealed it to you, or you have been through a gate. Which is it?"

Stephen was going to answer, but Victoria was repeatedly blowing the horn.

"I had better go now, or Victoria may leave without me. We'll talk later."

Stephen nodded and Ian left to join Victoria in the truck.

Chapter Fifty

Bible Study

Wednesday evening, Pastor Reynolds was going to start a Bible study on the Garden of Eden. Stephen didn't want to miss a session. He wanted all the information he could possibly get on the Garden, but how could he explain the cuts and bruises on his face? He started to back out and not go, but Victoria insisted he would be fine. She ranted about needing some time alone. She got her makeup and tried to cover the scratch on his cheek and the cut on his temple as much as possible.

He stopped halfway up the church steps, took a deep breath, and entered the church. It was as bad as he thought it would be. Everyone commented about the condition of his face. He did his best trying to pass it off as an accident. Stephen felt pretty good and thought sure everyone had bought his story until Brenda

Stanton grinned and asked, "Does Victoria look as bad as you, Stephen?"

Trying to appear as though he didn't know what she was talking about, Stephen replied with, "What?"

"Don't try to fool me, Stephen. I happen to be her grandmother and know what she can do. Those are her marks, not marks from an accident. If I were you, I don't think I would try to persuade anyone else with that story."

Stephen was going to say something but stopped when Brenda put her finger to Stephen's lips and said, "Shhh! Save your explanations. I know what happened. It was Victoria. Please don't bother trying to convince me it was anything else. I'm no fool." Brenda took Stephen's arm. "Would you please take me to my seat, Stephen?"

After helping Brenda to her seat, Stephen saw Pastor Reynolds approach to shake his hand. "Good . . . my goodness, Stephen. What in the world happened to your face?"

Stephen started to say it was an accident, but saw Brenda looking at him and said, "I really don't want to talk about it now."

Pastor Reynolds smiled, raised his brows and whispered, "I'll come over and we'll discuss it later."

Stephen felt miserable. He really dreaded seeing Leann and her parents. Would they, like

Brenda Stanton, be convinced it was a catfight with Victoria? His main concern was Leann. As he was going to his seat, Leann came through the door. Stephen hurried to sit down before she got to him. Pastor Reynolds was opening the service as Leann sat down by Stephen. She put her Bible down, squeezed his hand and looked at him. Her smile abruptly diminished. In shock, her jaw dropped open, and she took a deep breath. Still holding her breath, she asked, "Stephen, what happened? Were you in a wreck or something?"

Before Stephen could answer, Leann, having seen the scratches on Stephen's cheek, looked forward and said nothing. Stephen took hold of Leann's hand.

"Honey, let me explain."

Leann continued to look forward and said, "We will talk after church. Now is not the time."

In more ways than one, Stephen found himself in a mess. He wanted to get up and run out of the church. On the other hand, church was the very place he needed to be.

Chapter Fifty-One

No Revelation

astor Reynolds read from Genesis chapter three. Stephen was expecting something astounding, considering the way he had talked before he went to the retreat in Atlanta. The pastor went through the first six verses . . . and nothing. Stephen continued to think things would surely pick up, but they didn't. The same thing that had been traditionally taught for years was being taught tonight. Stephen was disappointed and confused. Where was all the revelation Pastor Reynolds had spoken of while sitting on his front porch? In his heart, Stephen knew there was more to the Garden of Eden than Satan telling a lie and Adam and Eve eating fruit from a tree.

After service, Leann told Stephen she would meet him outside. Everyone was shaking Pastor Reynolds' hand, while saying how much they enjoyed the lecture. Stephen was in line to shake his hand as well, but he couldn't say he enjoyed anything.

Pastor Reynolds shook Stephen's hand and asked, "Well, Stephen, did you learn something from the lesson tonight?"

With a blank expression, Stephen said, "No, I didn't. I thought you were going to share what had been revealed to you before your trip to Atlanta."

Surprised, Pastor Reynolds said, "I did, Stephen."

Stephen shook his head. "That was what the Holy Spirit revealed to you? Adam and Eve eating an apple."

As if rebuked, Pastor Reynolds asked, "Just what do you think took place in the Garden of Eden?"

"I don't know for sure, but I know I'm going to keep seeking until I find out."

Sandra Reynolds heard Stephen's conversation with her husband. When Stephen came outside, Sandra called out to him, "Stephen!"

Stephen turned to see who was calling him. "Hello, Sandra. How are you?"

With heartfelt emotion, Sandra asked Stephen if she could talk with him for a moment . . . in private. Walking out to the parking lot, Sandra looked at Stephen. "I know I probably shouldn't say anything, but I have noticed a drastic change in Don since he came back from Atlanta. He would be furious if he knew I was saying anything, so please keep this between us."

Puzzled, Stephen said, "I can't imagine him being upset over you being concerned."

Sandra looked down and said, "As a rule, you would be right, but not lately. Even with the children, he's not acting the same. And, when he . . . when we are intimate, something's not right. I am very embarrassed to mention our private life, but I don't know what to do. Have you noticed anything different about him?"

Before Stephen could answer, Pastor Reynolds called out to Sandra, "We had better be going, dear. I'll be over soon, Stephen, and we will have that talk."

Sandra looked at Stephen and whispered, "Let me know if you think of anything, Stephen."

Stephen nodded okay and Sandra joined Pastor Reynolds at the top of the stairs.

Just then, Leann came out of the church and soberly stared at Stephen as she made her way to him. Stephen thought aloud, "Oh, Lord, how am I going to explain the scratches. I might as well prepare myself. She will never believe the truth."

As she approached Stephen, he held his hand out to take hers. Leann took his hand but immediately inquired about the scratches. Stephen hesitated, not knowing what to say.

She gently touched his face. "Those scratches were made by Victoria, weren't they?"

Looking down, Stephen said, "Yes, they were."

"An explanation would be great right about now. You know how the enemy can mess with your mind when you wonder about things too long. We surely don't want that happening to me, do we?"

"Leann, am I detecting a bit of sarcasm in your voice?"

Leann tilted her head. "What do you think this looks like to me? You're staying in the same house with one of the most beautiful, yet despicable, women I've ever met. I would like to know what's going on at Eden's Gate."

Distraught at Leann's behavior, Stephen firmly replied, "Look at me, Leann. Does this look as though Victoria and I have been romantically involved? I don't think so. If this is what happens when you make love, I want no part of it. You're the one that said, 'Yes, let her stay.' You do remember that I asked you before I agreed to this. You insisted, 'She's almost old enough to be your mother.' You agreed she could stay because you knew she would make my life a living hell. Isn't that right?"

Mellowing, Leann said, "You're right, Stephen."

Leann took Stephen's hands. "I'm sorry. I was just a little jealous. I love you and miss you terribly. Will you forgive me?"

A sigh of relief swept over Stephen. "You know I will."

Leann hugged Stephen just a little too tightly. He groaned, putting his hand on his chest.

"Stephen! What's wrong with your chest?" Leann unbuttoned the top button on his shirt to see a large bruise close to Stephen's collarbone. "Did Victoria do that to you too?"

Stephen pulled his shirt together. "Yes! But I don't want to talk about it now. Okay?"

Furious, Leann, through gritted teeth said, "I want to know why she would do this to you."

Reluctantly, Stephen said, "I had a terrible nightmare. She heard me groaning and calling out. She came to wake me up. Evidently, I wasn't fully awake. I hit her only in self-defense, and she knocked me out."

Speechless, Leann squinted her eyes and tried to respond. It took her several attempts before she could speak.

Finally, she, giggled and said, "My goodness, she is quite the fighter, isn't she?"

Chapter Fifty-Two

Wisdom from Charles

When Stephen arrived home, Brenda Stanton's limousine was sitting in front of his house. Charles was sitting on the porch, in the swing.

"Hi, Charles," Stephen said as he wiped the sweat from his forehead.

Charles nodded and tipped his cap. "Mr. Harris! How are you this hot, hell day?"

Surprised at the greeting, Stephen replied, "Hell day? Don't you know every day is given from God, even if it's steaming hot like today?"

Charles chuckled. "Yes sir, I know that for sure. I don't think my mama knew it though. She used to say any day that would reach the one-hundred-degree mark was a hell day. Mama and Daddy worked on the Miller plantation outside Atlanta. Mama said there was one day when Daddy was working in the field, and she was doing the wash . . . she did all the workers' wash on a washboard. Her knuckles were bleeding and sweat was pouring off her body. Had she gone by her feelings, she said she would have sat down and cried. But, not with people watching every move she made. She said, 'That day's temperature hit 120 degrees.' She also said, 'Anything that hot must be hell breathing on you.' It reminded me a bit of Victoria when she arrived at Eden's Gate."

Stephen sat in the rocker beside the swing. "That's definitely one way to look at it."

Stephen looked toward the door. "I suppose Mrs. Stanton is inside."

"You suppose right. I heard Miss Victoria telling how she had to knock you out. She said something about a nightmare. Is that true, Stephen?"

Feeling exhausted, Stephen reluctantly answered, "Yes, Victoria beat my head half off." Stephen, pointing to his face, turned toward Charles. "Look at the damage."

"My, my," Charles moaned. "I want her on my side, if I ever get into a fight."

"That's for sure. Charles, have you ever been so tired mentally, physically and spiritually you don't know what to do?"

"A countless number of times."

Charles leaned toward Stephen. "When I get that tired, I ask for a day off, and I go to bed. When you're worn out, you don't think straight.

Soon, you start making all kinds of mistakes. My advice to you is to take a day off and sleep. If you can't sleep all day, at least lie still and get some rest."

Brenda and Victoria came out to the porch. Holding her head high, Mrs. Stanton said, "Charles, we need to get home. Liz will be furious if dinner gets too cold. Stephen, would you and Victoria like to join us?"

Stephen stood and thanked Mrs. Stanton but declined. "I think I'm going to get some rest. Victoria, feel free to go if you like."

Victoria kissed her grandmother's cheek. "I think I'm going to have a peanut butter sandwich and work on my article for the magazine."

Mrs. Stanton stared at her granddaughter. "You're going to eat a peanut butter sandwich?"

Wide-eyed, Victoria hugged Charles and said, "I love peanut butter. Don't you, Charles?"

In unbelief, Charles replied, "It happens to be one of my favorites."

Victoria took Charles' arm and walked to the car with him.

Mrs. Stanton lifted her head and winked at Stephen. "Keep up the good work. I knew you could make a difference. That is, if it doesn't kill you first."

Chapter Fifty-Three

Sheriff Bolton's Visit

Victoria and Stephen went inside. Stephen put his hand on his chest and groaned. Victoria asked, "Do you think you may need to see a doctor, Stephen?"

Looking down, trying to check his bruise, Stephen muttered, "No. I'll be fine. I just need some rest."

Stephen was walking toward the stairs when Victoria called out, "Stephen!"

He looked around. "Yes?"

"May I talk to you, before you go to bed?"

Stephen walked toward her. "Sure. What is it?" he asked.

Victoria motioned toward the living room. "Is it okay if we sit in here?"

Puzzled, Stephen sat down on the sofa. "You're scaring me. What's up?"

Victoria's countenance revealed her seriousness. "Sheriff Bolton came by after you left for church. He said there was still no word from Larry Weeks."

"Really?"

"He also said 'a young woman named Linda Scott is missing.' Do you know her, Stephen?"

Stephen thought a moment. "No, I don't think so. I might know her if I saw her, but the name doesn't sound familiar."

Victoria snapped, "I hope you aren't lying to me, Stephen!"

Confused, Stephen asked, "Why would I lie about that?"

"I don't know! That's why I am asking you."

Stephen felt overwhelmed with everything that was going on. He shouted, "Victoria, I am tired and hurting! If you have something to say, please say it. Otherwise, I am going to get some sleep."

"If you go to Georgia State Prison, you'll get all the sleep you want."

Stephen stood, frowning. "What in the world are you talking about, Victoria? You went from asking if I know someone to having me in prison. What are you getting at?"

Distressed, Victoria stood, got in Stephen's face and shouted, "How can you forget a person that you gave a ride to yesterday?"

"Victoria, I wasn't even here yesterday!"

"Then tell me, Stephen, where were you?"

Shaking, Stephen yelled, "I was at the battle!"

"Boloney! You had supper with me, and then you went to bed. You appear to have been in a battle, but I made those battle scars you're wearing."

Stephen was furious. "I know where I was at. I know what I was doing, and I don't need you to tell me that I'm lying."

Stephen turned and headed toward the stairs.

Victoria shouted, "You may know where you were, Stephen, but someone else is saying you were at a totally different place. Your stories aren't even close."

Stephen turned and came back to where Victoria was standing. "Just what are you talking about?"

"When Sheriff Bolton came by just after you left for church, he said . . ."

Stephen frowned. "He said what?"

"He said that someone saw you with Linda Scott yesterday. That you were parked down by the covered bridge."

Stephen was furious and shouted. "I suppose I was making out with her, too."

With a blank expression, Victoria said, "Funny you would use those words. Those are the exact words that were told to Sheriff Bolton."

Troubled that someone would even *think* such a thing, Stephen said, "That is a lie! Who told the sheriff they saw me with this Linda Scott? Who and why?"

Victoria looked down and then raised her head. "Someone who is highly regarded in Calvin's Point. Someone the people would believe over you, especially with your story about going through a gate and being in a battle."

Stephen took Victoria by her shoulders, shook her, and demanded, "Who was it?"

Victoria abruptly pushed Stephen away from her. "Stephen Daniel Harris! Don't you ever grab me or use that tone with me again. Do I make myself clear? Now, let me answer your question. Pastor Don Reynolds told the sheriff he saw you with Linda Scott."

"What! Pastor Reynolds? I don't understand. Victoria, I'm sorry for grabbing you. My emotions are a wreck, and I haven't been myself for a few days now. There is a lot that I don't understand lately. I can't explain my irrational behavior, but I was certainly not with Linda Scott. I don't even know her. It hurts to think Pastor Reynolds would say such a thing."

Stephen picked up the phone and through his frustration said, "I'll call him right now and clear this up."

Stephen greeted Pastor Reynolds with a friendly hello and went straight to the point. "Pastor Reynolds, I need to ask you a question."

"Sure, Stephen, anything."

"Did . . . did you tell Sheriff Bolton you saw me with Linda Scott at the covered bridge and that we were being intimate?"

"Stephen, this is a little embarrassing, but yes I did. I didn't want to say anything, but he asked me, and I had to tell the truth."

No longer friendly, Stephen snapped, "That is *not* the truth! I don't even know Linda Scott. I don't understand how you could say such a thing. You may have seen someone, but it certainly was not me. Will you please call Sheriff Bolton and get this straightened out?"

"Stephen, calm down. I can't call Sheriff Bolton and tell him anything, except what I saw. There is only one 1937 black Ford pickup in Calvin's Point, and that's yours. I'm telling you, that's what I saw."

Stephen shouted, "Well, there must be another one. It was not my truck! I wasn't with this woman, nor was I at the bridge."

Surprised, Pastor Reynolds asked, "Are you asking me to lie, Stephen?"

"No! I'm asking you to rethink what you thought you saw. It wasn't me."

"To be honest, Stephen, I hoped it wasn't you. On the other hand, I know what I saw. I saw you and Linda Scott parked by the covered bridge, necking heavily. I am sorry, Stephen, but I can't change the truth. I am surprised that you would ask me to lie. No, let me rephrase that. I am *hurt* that you would ask a man of God to help cover up your lustful actions. I'll pray for you, Stephen, but I will not lie for you. If there isn't anything else, I need to go. Good-bye."

Pastor Reynolds hung up. Stephen stood in shock at what he had just heard.

Victoria watched Stephen as he held the phone down to his side and stared across the room. "Stephen, are you okay?"

Stephen looked at Victoria. "He's lying. How can he say those things? I don't understand."

Stephen thought a moment and looked at Victoria. "Sandra Reynolds said . . ."

Stephen remembered that Sandra had asked him to keep their conversation private, so he said no more.

"What is it, Stephen, what did she say?"

Stephen ignored her question. "By the help and grace of God, I am not going to let this get me down. Victoria, God has been pulling me for some time now to the Garden of Eden. I've let everything stand in my way and haven't been obedient. This too is another distraction. It's time I do what I feel compelled to do and that is, to find what God wants me to know about the garden. Let's you and I study about the Garden of Eden together, like we planned. It's time. Do you still feel the pull?"

Victoria nodded. "More than ever."

Chapter Fifty-Four

Victoria's Story

As Victoria and Stephen studied Rachel's Bible about the garden, Stephen began to read. "Genesis chapter three, verse one: 'Now the serpent was more subtle than any beast of the field which the Lord God had made.' Why do you think the writer starts with the word now?"

"You tell me why, Stephen."

Stephen rubbed his chin. "The word now in the Hebrew means, 'to beat regularly, to impel or agitate, to trouble, to stroke.'"

"Exactly," Victoria said. "It sounds as though the serpent was going to do whatever he had to do to get Eve's attention. Like little kids pulling at your shirt or pants leg to get you to look at them. They pull until you look and hear what they have to say." A somber look captured Victoria's countenance.

"What is it?" Stephen asked.

"This all reminds me of Acor," Victoria said. "Queen Jewel intended to gain Acor's attention, thus set her plan in motion to overcome him. She used her magic to disturb his mind. While telling you about Acor and Hannah the other night, I didn't tell the entire story. When the Most High sent Acor to invite the kings and queens to the Garden of Fire, Jewel knew the path Acor would use to get to the Highland Kingdom. She waited for him in the top of a giant willow tree that sat just before the entrance to the Highland Kingdom. As he neared the tree, Jewel blew an invisible dust into the air as Acor passed by. The dust was so powerful, Acor's mind went into a spin. His will and emotions were arrested by her power. The moment the dust touched him he was powerless. She began to stroke him endearingly. Endearingly means, With fondness or affection. With her sorcery, she breathed a demon into him that he would never shake."

"So, why aren't people taught about the witchcraft?" Stephen asked.

"Most people don't know about it. They can't teach something they don't know. You see Satan and Jewel are so alike. The Word tells us, 'The Old Serpent' cast his spell on Eve. The word, serpent in the Hebrew means, to hiss, whisper, a magic spell, incantation, or enchanter. He appeared to Eve in a cunning sense. That's why the Word says, Satan was more 'subtle' than any beast in the field. Subtle means naked, either partial or total. Naked means, 'not having the usual or natural covering.' Therefore, Satan, like Jewel, didn't use his natural covering to seduce his victims. Both appeared as illusions as anyone or anything they wanted to be. Anything it took to deceive. That's why we must be careful. Jewel and her leaders will always use something to disguise who they really are. What you sometimes see may be a total deception."

"Victoria! That's what happened at the mountain while I was on watch. The form that appeared before me was you, but not really you. It was an illusion, but it was so real."

Victoria took Stephen's hand. "Stephen, listen to me carefully. A lot of things are being exposed to you and fast. Be careful, Stephen. Guard your mind. Acor didn't guard his mind, or he never would have been swayed by the deep magic. To prove His children, God sometimes allows us to enter forbidden places. Maybe I can explain by using the word 'field.' After her fall, Jewel was forced to live in the field that was an open area beyond the garden gate. A fortified wall enclosed the garden and was guarded by elite angels and the Red Eagles Guards. No longer a part of the garden. Jewel could still come from the field into the garden, but only as God allowed."

"Like Satan?" Stephen said.

"Exactly. Remember Satan and Jewel have many different titles and forms, and they use the deep magic always.

Before Stephen could reply, someone knocked at the door.

Chapter Fifty-Five

Body in the Barn

Stephen answered the door to find Ian Jackson standing there looking exhausted. "Ian! What's wrong with you?"

"May I come in?"

"Yes . . . yes, I'm sorry. Of course, come in. What is it?"

Victoria came into the room. Sarcastically, she said, "Hi, Ian. You surely aren't working on Sunday. If you are, you can forget me. Did I state that clearly enough for you or do I need to be a bit louder?"

With a forceful voice, Ian shouted, "Shut up, Victoria! I have no time for your spoiled-brat attitude."

Victoria put both hands on her hips and shouted, "Just who do you think you are talking to? I am not one of the hired hands you can boss around."

Ian frowned at Victoria. "Shut up! I don't have time for this."

Stephen looked at Victoria. "Victoria, would you please give Ian a moment."

She looked at Ian and growled, "Only because you asked, Stephen." Victoria leaned forward, all but touching her nose to Ian's. "You're exhausting my last nerve."

Ian put his hand on Victoria's shoulder and pushed her aside. She in turn punched his shoulder. Ian jerked away and shouted, "Stephen, there's a dead woman in the barn!"

Stunned, Stephen and Victoria both looked at him. "What did you say?" Stephen asked.

"There's a dead woman in a cow stall."

Victoria grabbed Ian's arm, "You better not be playing around about something like that."

Ian pulled his arm away from her. "I think it's Linda Scott."

In shock, Stephen opened the door and raced toward the barn. Ian and Victoria followed behind. Running inside, Stephen looked in the first stall. His mouth opened and he inhaled deeply, holding his breath. Frozen in place, he stood looking at the partially clothed woman.

Victoria put her hands over her mouth and breathlessly whispered, "Oh, God, Stephen! Is that . . .?"

Stephen turned pasty white as he looked at Ian. "What is this? What's going on? How did she get here?"

Ian didn't answer the question but looked Stephen in the eyes and said, "Stephen, dimensions are colliding all around you. The time for turning back has passed."

Frantic, Stephen said, "I don't know what you're talking about."

"Stephen, you better get control of yourself. Shemed has entered Eden's Gate."

Stephen ran his fingers through his hair. "Victoria, call Sheriff Bolton."

"What do you want me to say?" she asked.

"Tell him Linda Scott has been found."

Ian put his hand on Stephen's shoulder. "Stephen, listen to me. Before Victoria calls the sheriff, you need to go through the gate you visited one more time."

Bewildered, Stephen rubbed his face with both hands. "I don't know where the gate is. I didn't know where it was the first time I went through it."

Victoria demanded, "Think, Stephen! Close your eyes and think."

Chapter Fifty-Six
Dumbfounded

Stephen slowly opened his eyes. Around him were tall marble columns, marble floors and ceilings that were at least forty feet tall. There were no windows or doors. Stephen felt faint. He didn't know where he was, how he got there or what he was doing there. Cautiously, he began to walk forward. His footsteps echoed through the great hall. Looking left to right, he prayed, "Father! What am I doing here? Please help me." Stephen paused, then added, "None the less, thy will be done."

Stephen walked around a corridor and entered an immense open area, embellished with half-human and half-animal sculptures. There was a smell so sweet that it was almost nauseating. Stephen continued to look for windows or a door of any kind. Entering another enormous room filled with highly polished black and white marble, he noted at the entrance, a gold carpet in the center of the room led to a solid gold throne, embellished with diamonds and emeralds. The walls of the great room were lined with gold cobras, standing twenty feet tall.

Stephen could hear running water, but didn't see any. Instantly, the gold rug became a running stream. The water was cold as ice. He gasped when freezing water soaked his shoes. Then, the water was gone as swiftly as it had appeared. Stephen was again standing on the gold rug, with dry shoes. He turned in a circle to see if someone was there.

The consuming sweet smell was unwavering. He put one hand on his stomach and lowered his head due to the sick feeling that was overtaking him. He coughed and groaned. His stomach began to cramp with intense pain. Stephen could go no farther and collapsed on the gold rug. He curled up in a fetal position, groaning in agony.

A voice thundered through the vast hall. Stephen felt a vibration as the deep voice asked, "Stephen, would you like for me to take care of your pain?"

Before Stephen could answer, the pain strengthened, gripping his stomach to such a degree he screamed in anguish. The voice again roared, "Stephen!"

At once, the pain ended. Stephen looked around to see where the voice was coming from. The first time he looked at the throne, he saw no one. When he turned back, he froze. Before him was the most radiant celestial being he had ever imagined. The being was gigantic in stature, with broad shoulders, long curly brown hair and eyes black as charcoal. His skin was pale and his lips were full. A long, royal blue robe fit loosely on his muscled body. His feet were covered with gold sandals. Sitting on the spectacular throne, propping his elbow, he lifted his pointer finger to his chin and stared at Stephen, who was still sitting on the gold rug.

"Who are you?" Stephen asked as he cautiously sat upon his knees.

The man stood, put his hands on his hips and said, "I like you on your knees, Stephen. I am the one to whom you should bow. I am the keeper of the gate."

Stephen's eyes darted around the area. "Keeper of the gate! What gate? There is no gate."

The man laughed loudly, waved his hand in a circle above his head and announced. "Behold the gates!"

In awe, Stephen gazed at the now seven magnificent gates that lined the hall. He rapidly fixed his eyes on the man in front of him. Baffled, he demanded, "Who are you?"

The man came down the seven steps that led to the throne and stopped in front of Stephen. "Calm down. With all the adrenaline that is racing through your body, you just might have a heart attack and die a young man. That would be a shame."

Stephen said nothing. He continued to stare at the man in front of him.

"Things haven't been going too well for you, have they?"

Stephen asked, "What do you mean?"

The man raised his brows and began to walk in a circle around Stephen. "Since you have moved to Calvin's Point, your cow met with hell itself and was burned to a crisp." The man frowned and continued, "Let's go back a little further. Let's go back to the night of the storm. Your bedroom window was slightly open. Tell me, what did you think about that awful green mist that touched everything in your room, including you?"

Shocked, Stephen demanded, "How do you know about that? Who are you?"

The man clicked his tongue several times. "I know everything. You can hide nothing from me. I also know poor Linda Scott is lying in your barn. She met with such a tragic end. Just tragic."

"How did she get in my barn?"

"Do you want to see what happened?"

The man raised the palm of his hand in front of Stephen's face and moved it in a circle. Stephen saw a truck that looked like his, pull alongside the covered bridge and park. He could tell two people were in the truck. The driver of the truck took the girl by the hair of her head and pushed it against the passenger window. The girl was fighting, but suddenly stopped. He could tell the driver was attacking her, but couldn't see who the driver was. The scene changed. He saw the man pulling the girl into the barn by the hair of her head.

Stephen watched in unbelief. He whispered, "Who's that man pulling Linda Scott's body into my barn? How did he get my truck?"

The man laughed. "Patience, Stephen. Watch and you will see."

Stephen watched as the man took his foot and pushed her into the stall, wiped his hands on his pants and laughed. Tenaciously, he watched to see who had committed this hideous crime. Bewildered, Stephen put his hand over his mouth and sighed in unbelief as he whispered, "NO! Not Pastor Reynolds."

"Yes, Stephen, Pastor Reynolds. Believe me, he enjoyed every minute of it. The sad thing is, you are about to be charged for that gruesome crime."

Stephen swallowed hard and demanded again, "Who are you?"

The being laughed and shouted, "I can be whoever you want me to be!"

Instantaneously, the man turned into Leann. She reached her hand out to Stephen and said, "I want you, Stephen. I love you."

Stephen slowly moved backward, as the man changed again. This time, it was Victoria. She was standing in front of him, wearing almost nothing, and passionately groaning trying to kiss him. He pulled away, only to see his dad coming toward him.

"Son, I miss you. I miss you."

The last one scared the life out of Stephen. He saw a man with a crown of thorns on his head. Blood was running down his face. He held his hands toward Stephen. There were nail prints in them and in his feet. There was also a wound in his side. "I am the Messiah. Worship me and me alone."

Stephen stood and boldly cried, "There is only one God! The Most High God alone is to be exalted." Stephen stood and fixed his eyes on the stranger and shouted, "Who is your God? How is it that you can conjure up such illusions?"

The man put forth his hand to touch Stephen's shoulder. Stephen quickly pulled away. Tilting his head, the man asked, "Are you afraid of my touch?"

"Afraid, no. Cautious, yes."

"You weren't cautious when you were the watchman. Many fell because you were doing everything but watching for the enemy. You volunteered to be the watchman. Your attention span was that of a small child."

Dumbfounded, Stephen asked, "How do you know about the mountain?"

"Stephen, Stephen. I was there. I was the one that seduced you. I'm sure I would have enjoyed your company, had Dale not interrupted. You were like a wild man. I like that."

Stephen felt sick, realizing how he had become prey to his own carnality. Something he hadn't been aware of before. He stared at the man, standing in front of him. Repeatedly, he asked himself, *Could this be Shemed?*

Stephen felt sure that it must be. Therefore, he decided to find out. Wanting to appear confident, Stephen shouted, "You may have fooled me on the mountain, but you're not fooling me again, Shemed."

In an outburst of laughter, the man tried to speak, but it took two attempts before he could. "You think I am Shemed? What a joke! Shemed would have never kissed you as I did. He's brutal."

Furious, Stephen yelled, "You tricked me! I would have never touched you, had I known you were a man."

"That's right, Stephen. I did trick you. However, you enjoyed your passion flaming inside you like an inferno. How can you be so easily tricked? A man who wants to blaze a trail preaching the so-called gospel."

Enraged, Stephen shouted, "You make me so sick!"

The man frowned and growled, "You want sick? I'll make you really sick."

The man raised his hand above his head and made a fist, and then, like throwing a baseball, he brought his arm down and opened his fist, extending it toward Stephen. Stephen fell to the floor in excruciating pain. His stomach felt as though it was being torn apart. Each time the man tightened his fist, the pain increased. He felt as though he was inside the man's fist and every bone in his body was being crushed.

Unexpectedly, a voice firmly called out, "Enough, Telmar! Don't overstep your limit."

Immediately, the pain was gone. Stephen lay looking at the man who had intervened on his behalf. He felt as if he knew this man; yet, he did not.

Telmar walked toward the man and shouted, "Haleb! You have no authority here. I was given permission to come through the gate."

Chapter Fifty-Seven
Stephen Meets Telmar

*I*n awe, Stephen remembered the names of both of the two men standing before him. He had met Haleb many times as a child. Haleb was a high-ranking angel of the White Stone Kingdom. He warred under King Rayon, ruler of the three heavens. Rachel, his mother, had spoken of Haleb many times. The day Rachel first met Haleb, he had shoved her from the path of a falling tree that had been cut and pushed in her direction. She had no way of knowing that Chris Jackson had purposely felled the tree in her direction, with the intent to kill her. Chris' parents, Emily and Jerry Jackson, were neighbors of John and Rachel, Stephen's parents. Chris was dedicated to Satan by his parents at birth. They had been placed in Todd's Creek to help take Rachel out before Stephen could be born . . . but, to no avail. Haleb was commissioned by King

Rayon to protect Rachel and her baby. There was something different about Haleb, different than Stephen had remembered. Stephen had not even recognized him until he heard his name called. However, it had been several years since he had seen him.

Stephen had not only been told about Haleb, but Telmar as well. Many times, Stephen's mom and dad had stressed the importance of remembering Telmar, the demon of lust and seduction. However, to see him and realize from experience his power of illusion was overwhelming.

Haleb looked Telmar in the eyes and declared, "The Lord rebukes you, Telmar. You are not to go beyond the bounds that have been allotted you. If you do, you will be sent to the pit."

Upon saying those words, Haleb disappeared.

Telmar fixed his eyes on Stephen, tightened his lips and growled, "I hate you, Haleb."

Stephen breathed a sigh of relief since Haleb reminded Telmar of his boundaries. Stephen shook his head. "So, you're Telmar? I've heard my mom speak of you often. However, she had nothing good to say."

Telmar leaned toward Stephen and through clinched teeth uttered in a voice of disgust, "Rachel! She vexed my being. I would have loved to seduce her, but she wouldn't give any leeway for it. She was quite a woman. I think she would be disgusted with you, Stephen. The way you fell for me on the mountain. She never would have been so untaught."

Stephen tightened his fist and roared, "You'd better shut up about my mother!"

Telmar cut his dark eyes at Stephen. "Is that some kind of threat? You have no power over me, Stephen."

"Did you tell my mother the same thing, Telmar? I know about Boone's Crossing and how she not only put you to shame, but Queen Jewel as well. You had no power over her, and you have no power over me."

Telmar slapped Stephen's face so hard it knocked him down. The evil being roared like a lion and commanded two of his guards to come forth. He pointed at Stephen and ordered, "Take him through the gate! Maybe a few more will be killed as he pretends to be the watchman."

The two soldiers grabbed Stephen's arms and pulled him toward one of the gates. Before they got to the gate, Telmar called out, "Wait! I've changed my mind. Let him choose his own gate."

Stephen looked at him. "You said you were the keeper of the gate, but you don't hold all the keys. I doubt you actually hold any of the keys."

Telmar lifted his shoulders and scoffed, "All these gates are open. I'm anxious to see how long you will last when you return to the front lines. I'll be waiting there for you."

The two guards shoved Stephen toward the gates. Stephen didn't have a clue which one to take. He breathed a prayer as he walked toward each gate. The second time around, he picked the gate he felt would be the one. He lifted the latch and slowly pushed the gate open. When he stepped through, the gate slammed shut behind him. Stephen turned to reopen the gate, but the gate was sealed and the handle was no longer there.

Chapter Fifty-Eight
The Poem

Stephen looked around the terrain, trying to get some concept of where he might be. Had he gone through the gate that would lead him back to Jim Lee, Dale and the Armor Bearers? He wasn't sure.

A white mist hid everything from view. Stephen began to tremble. "Father," he whispered. "What is this place? Why do I feel such hurt?"

Stephen began to weep uncontrollably. He dropped to his knees, put both hands over his face and wept loudly. The sound of his weeping echoed as though he was on the top of a very high mountain. The echo multiplied to the point that his sobs were deafening. Eventually, Stephen's sobs ended, but his pain continued. The mist was so thick he could feel the dampness against his skin. He closed his eyes, lifted his head toward heaven and asked, "Father! Why all the hurt, pain and sadness? Why?"

An unexpected voice startled Stephen. In haste, he turned to see who was speaking. Standing beside him was a tall, muscular soldier, arrayed in a white knee-length tunic. His chest was garnished with a gold breastplate, imprinted with the head of a lion wearing a crown. Underneath the lion were the initials, "AOTA." A gold helmet was grasped in one hand, and a distinctively marked gold sword was in the other. The blade of the sword was enormous. Deeply engraved on the blade was the word, "TRUTH."

The soldier, with eyes as blue as the sky on a clear day, looked at Stephen, "Jewel has entered the Garden Gate and Prince David and Princess Caroline have fallen."

Bewildered, Stephen asked, "Who are you?"

Sternly, the soldier answered, "Here, it is not who I am, but whom I serve that matters."

"Then tell me," Stephen said, "whom do you serve?"

The soldier stood at attention, placed the sword over his heart and declared, "I serve the Almighty. He alone is worthy of our allegiance. Declare to me, Stephen, who you have pledged *your* allegiance to."

Stephen made a fist with his right hand, put it over his heart and professed, "I too serve the True and Living God. The Most High whose throne is in the Crystal Kingdom."

Puzzled by what the soldier had said, Stephen asked, "May I ask something of you?"

The soldier looked at Stephen. "Because I see your mantel, you may ask anything you like."

Stephen questioned, "You said Queen Jewel had entered the garden gate and Prince David and Princess Caroline have fallen. Can you tell me who they are, and where I am?"

The soldier frowned. "You don't know where you are?"

Stephen shook his head. "No, I don't, but I would like to know."

Again, the soldier frowned. "How did you get here? To gain entrance, you must have been seeking this place. Did the Holy Spirit invite you?"

Stephen looked down, then quickly back at the soldier. "Not long ago, I entered a gate. Inside the gate, I saw a great mountain with different levels. Also, in that place, there was a deep valley filled with people. They were chained, lame and hopeless, yet their struggle to be free was tremendous. At the end of the valley was a gigantic, gold gate embellished with diamonds and emeralds. But the people trapped in the valley couldn't get through the gate. That night, after seeing the valley, I went back to camp. The Holy Spirit offered the invitation to the garden with these words:

Through the garden,
Are riches yet unknown.
Through the garden gate,
Is the pathway to the throne.
What treasures there await me?
What glory will I behold?
What mysteries there will unfold for me?
The half has not been told.
Therefore, I journey on, though most times,
Rough be the road;
The spirit from the garden
Will not seem to let me go.
Enter in, enter in,
Are the words he speaks to me,
And the glory of the throne room,
Your eyes will surely see.

Upon completion of Stephen's words, the soldier instantly dropped to one knee, lowered his head, and said, "Rakar! You have come."

Stephen touched the soldier's shoulder and insisted, "Please stand. That's not necessary for me."

The soldier looked at Stephen. "I bowed not to you. I bow only in respect of the mantel you wear. Seeing your mantel means the time has come."

Stephen looked sternly at the soldier. "What is your name?"

"My name is Machiah. Sir, tell me, when did you enter the gate?"

"Only a few minutes ago. Why do you call me sir?" Stephen asked.

The soldier raised his sword and said, "Tell me, Rakar, what is written on the blade of my sword?"

Stephen swallowed hard and said, "Truth."

"Exactly! The host of King Rayon's army has been waiting for the time when two profound things would take place in this age. One is for the garden gate to be opened. The other is for the mantel of Truth to cover the leaders of King Rayon's army. That would bring forth the end time. The army rejoices because now we see that time has come. You're not the only one to wear this mantel, but your rank as general puts you in front to lead the way of the other soldiers. Many will teach locally, but your mantel is global."

Stunned at the statement, Stephen asked, "What do you mean, global?"

Machiah looked deeply into Stephen's eyes. "You will preach the word of Truth to the common man and to kings of nations. That is why you have been summoned through *Eden's Gate*. Many mysteries will be unveiled to you. However, you must understand what took place in the Garden of Eden, before you can fully understand the rest of the Word."

Instantly, Machiah turned his back to Stephen. Stephen watched Machiah, trying to figure out what he was doing.

But, before he could ask, Machiah bowed his head, put his sword over his heart and said, "Yes, my King." He faced Stephen and said, "We've been summoned to the White Stone Kingdom's throne room. We must hurry."

Chapter Fifty-Nine

A Called Meeting

Machiah waved his hand in front of Stephen. Astonished, Stephen looked down at his clothes. No longer was he wearing jeans, a tee shirt and tennis shoes; but he was arrayed in the same uniform as Machiah.

Stephen took hold of Machiah's arm and asked, "What is this uniform? What do you mean we have been summoned to the throne room? Do you mean before King Rayon?"

"Exactly! You have so many questions, but time does not allow me to answer. We're called at different intervals to report to God."

"Report what?" Stephen asked.

"We report about our duty assignment. I report about warfare that is taking place on different fronts and subjects that have been placed under our watch. You, for instance. I was commissioned to be here and meet you today. Enough talk," Machiah said.

"Please, be patient with me," Stephen said. "What do I do before the Most High?"

Surprised, Machiah questioned, "What do you do now? You worship! Don't worry, Stephen, you don't have to be told what to do. When you enter His presence, you'll know what to do."

Stephen stopped and admitted, "I'm afraid."

Machiah put his hand on Stephen's shoulder and assured him, "It's only natural to feel apprehensive when you are being allowed to see tremendous truth. Now come."

Machiah took hold of the mist and pulled it back like a curtain. When he did, the sight was immeasurable. Stephen and Machiah entered an immense amphitheater. Angels; red, brown, and bald eagle guards; and a great number of witnesses were filing into the theater. They were seated according to rank. Many had the same breastplate as Machiah, with the lion wearing a gold crown and with the initials "AOTA" underneath the lion. Many wore gold rings with the same initials. Stephen also watched many enter the arena who wore a totally different shield, and others with no shield at all.

"Machiah, who are those that have no shield?"

"Some have not followed the Most High because of deception. God in His love and mercy has made a way to redeem them, but until such a time they are not allowed to wear the armor."

Stephen quickly interjected, "My mother told me about Queen Jewel and the many she drew with deception. I also know about Jacob's Ladder. Each angel would descend the ladder. At death, they would ascend the ladder back to God. She taught me that even King Rayon would descend and ascend that ladder."

Machiah grinned and said, "Opal is a true woman of God. In the flesh body and in the spirit body."

Surprised, Stephen asked, "You know my mom?"

"Yes, I do."

Puzzled, Stephen said, "You called her Opal."

Machiah nodded. "Yes. Opal is her eternal name. Rachel was only her flesh name. Flesh man is for a season. Spirit man will live forever."

"Do you know my dad?" Stephen asked.

Machiah smiled. "Oh, yes. I know Jathniel. He warred against Satan at the rebellion. He is a mighty warrior. So is his son."

"It's a little strange to hear them called by different names. All I've ever known is John and Rachel. While on the subject of names, Cordilia and Paul Dawson, Mom and Dad's best friends, do they also have angelic names. I wondered . . ."

Before Stephen could finish his statement, Machiah interrupted. "Cordilia's eternal name is Rehabiah and Paul's is Rayuel. They both are awesome in service and battle for the Crystal Kingdom."

"Michiah, who are Prince David and Princess Caroline?"

"David and Caroline are members of King Rayon's family. Jewel drew them to the Garden of Fire and into the strange flames that reveal the knowledge of evil."

Chapter Sixty

White Stallion

Suddenly, trumpet sounds erupted, causing the arena to vibrate. The angel's voices exploded in praise.

"Machiah, what is it?" Stephen asked.

With great enthusiasm, Machiah stood and said, "The White Stallion and Raptor are coming through the gate."

Stephen's gasped, and his eyes widened. "The White Stallion and Raptor?"

The White Stallion pranced down the center of the theater, his head held high and his long silky mane flowing. He was whiter than snow. Stephen slapped his hands together as the magnificent seven-foot-tall eagle walked with authority beside the stallion. His white head glistened. He spread his white tail feathers as he walked and unfurled his enormous dark brown wings to greet the guest.

Following behind the White Stallion and Raptor, was a beautiful, tall, blond-haired woman, carrying a large black book, with crimson letters on the cover.

"Who is she?" Stephen asked.

"Princess Kaylee."

Princess Kaylee was followed by beings taller than anyone Stephen had ever seen. The crowd again erupted in shouts and cheers. They all had long blond or black oiled hair that shimmered like diamonds. They wore long, flowing, red robes trimmed with gold piping and tassels. On their fingers wore a bold, gold ring with AOTA stamped in the center.

"Who are these?" Stephen asked.

"They are the Ancient Ones. They have been with the Most High since the beginning. They help guard the book that Princess Kaylee is carrying. The book title reads *Angels of the Ages*."

At the end of the arena in a semi-circle, twelve kings and queens who made up the high court were seated in twelve gold thrones.

Amid a gigantic blast of the trumpets and eruptions of praise, sheets of lightning, thunderclaps and massive smoke, Stephen felt the awesome presence nearing but saw only a vague image with his face shrouded with a white mist. He did see a billowing white cloud descending to the front of the arena. Bolts of lightning filled the cloud, giving the appearance

of a fireball landing. Thunderbolts shook everything as the cloud settled.

"Who is it, Michiah? I can't see his face."

"That's because you've not yet reached the
pinnacle of the mountain. Only then will you
see King Rayon clearly."

Although, Stephen couldn't see his face,
his heart connected with King Rayon at once.
A burning fire shot through his soul as he
felt Rayon's radiant light touch his being. The
praise of the angels was resounding. After a
long period of praise, silence fell. King Rayon
stood. His long, white hair was filled with gold
dust. He wore a large, crystal crown with three
perfect emeralds. His long, white robe glistened
with gold dust, and long, gold tassels rested on
his massive shoulders. His eyes sparkled like
the sun shining on clear blue water.

When King Rayon raised his golden scepter,
all beings, including Stephen, dropped to their
knees and lowered their heads. Rayon smiled,
opened his arms and shouted, "We offer praise
to the Most High God."

Again, all beings were on their feet, cheering.
Stephen too cheered with every bit of his
essence. After a while, Rayon brought the
scepter down, bringing the meeting to order.

Chapter Sixty-One

Shemed at the Meeting

The first angel to report came aggressively through the entrance. A gigantic being taking long strides was making his way to the throne. This one Stephen could see clearly. His tunic was black; his sandals, helmet and breastplate were black as well. Stephen felt nauseous when he saw his sword. The wrist of the sword had three stones. A ruby, a diamond and a huge emerald that rested between the two.

Stephen sighed when he recalled the sword his mother bought his dad for Christmas from an antique shop called "A Journey in Time" in Norfolk, Virginia. Delilah, the old woman who sold the sword to Rachel, was a witch for the dark kingdom. Telmar, the demon of seduction, would come forth from the emerald stone when the stone was touched or when he was summoned.

"Who is the bulky man with the sword?" Stephen asked.

"His name is Shemed. He's an evil force to be reckoned with."

Stephen stared in unbelief at the man he had heard about all his life. To finally see him was staggering. The blade of Shemed's sword was highly polished silver. Etched in the blade—with gigantic letters—was the word. DEATH.

Astounded, Stephen whispered, "Machiah, that's Shemed?"

Machiah soberly responded, "Yes, the archenemy of the Crystal Kingdom and tormentor of the souls of man."

Shemed approached the throne. Stephen so wished he could see Rayon's expression as Shemed approached. Machiah looked at Stephen and answered his thought.

"If you could see his face, you would see the pain of a king, who in the end will destroy his brother forever."

Surprised, Stephen asked, "You knew what I was thinking?"

Machiah nodded. "Yes, I know. I had the same thought when I was brought here the first time."

Machiah put his pointer finger to his lips and said, "Say no more, Stephen. Shemed is about to plead his case."

Total silence draped the arena. King Rayon leaned forward and asked, "Shemed! Where have you been?"

"I have been in the field. I have walked up and down in it. From the mountain to the sea, covering the area I have been assigned to."

"Why have you entered here today? Do you have something to report?" Rayon asked.

Shemed looked down, then faced Rayon. "I have a question?"

Rayon leaned back in His throne and asked, "Would that question have to do with Stephen Daniel Harris?"

Stephen's jaw dropped, and his breathing grew shallow when he heard his name. He took hold of Machiah's arm and whispered, "He said my . . . my name."

"Shhh. Listen, Stephen."

Shemed lifted his shoulder. "My position, as was given to me by You, has been hindered. How can I do my job if you shield your mighty men and women? Did I not prove that one third of your sons would not be faithful if they were tried? Have I not revealed to you what is in their souls?"

Rayon's eyes pierced Shemed as He answered, "Have you not revealed what is in your own soul? You are quick to accuse. Prince David and Princess Caroline were formed by the Most High's hand and were perfect, as you once were."

Shemed interrupted, "There, you said it. They were perfect, but no more. Even though you placed them in Eden and closed the gate. I proved they would yield to the dark kingdom's test. Therefore, I come once again to ask your permission to enter Eden's Gate to prove Stephen Daniel Harris. Or should I call him by his real name, General Rakar? I know you have put a hedge around him and prevented me, but now I ask your permission for entrance. Otherwise, as you know, I can't touch him."

Rayon sternly replied, "Why not say what you really mean? You came to challenge me for his soul."

Shemed laughed. "You know me so well. That is exactly why I came. He honored you once, but will he remain faithful or choose to follow me? I can be very persuasive. Ask anyone. You promoted me to the position of prosecutor—to uncover any weakness that may lurk in your sons and daughters. Rakar isn't exempt from being proven, is he? I mean everyone else has to be proved."

Shemed lifted his hand in the air, pointed toward the arena filled with God's children and declared, "Tell all these witnesses that you are no respecter of persons, yet you will not allow Rakar to be proven. Open the gate! But not only the gate, you must remove every protection. It is not enough to touch the outside, if you will not allow me to touch the inside as well. Do this, and I will reveal the darkness in his soul; I will go further and guarantee you that Queen Jewel will bear General Rakar's son. Open Eden's Gate and I will prove what I say to you."

King Rayon paused, then acknowledged, "I will grant your request. Before you go, I want to say, 'The Most High created you, the essence of beauty. He filled you with wisdom, and promoted you to your position because of your faithfulness. He made you and all of my children with choice that will not be controlled. You made the wrong choices. You've grieved the heart of the Most High and the White Stone Kingdom. You grieved my father's heart when you turned to the dark kingdom. His heart will be grieved again, when a fire from within you will consume you. You will be turned to ashes and it will be as though you had never been."

Shemed gritted his teeth. "Yes, but you gave me a set amount of time. Until the time has run out, I will continue doing the job assigned me. I will find every weakness in White Stone and use it to destroy every being and the Crystal Kingdom. I will not burn alone."

King Rayon frowned and demanded, "Depart from me!"

Shemed turned to leave, then stopped when Rayon called him. He turned and faced the king.

With the voice of authority, Rayon shouted, "Shemed! You better remember you're a man, and not God. You are a created being. You are not the Creator. Never forget that."

Shemed turned and went out from King Rayon's presence.

Chapter Sixty-Two
The Ancient Stump

*I*nstantly, Stephen and Machiah were back at the gate. Stephen put his hand on his chest and saw that he was back in his own clothing. Trembling, he fixed his eyes on Machiah. "My God! What did I just see?"

"I thought you wanted to know truth."

"I do! I do."

"It's time for you to leave this gate. When I wave my hand in front of you, you will be back at the barn with Ian and Victoria. Sheriff Bolton is on his way. You're about to face the truth of what you saw in the arena, when you're charged with murder."

"What?

"Keep the faith, General."

"Machiah, when I saw Raptor and the White Stallion in the arena, I remembered my mom told me about Raptor and the Stallion taking her to a place beyond Wisdom's Mountain.

She spoke about a crystal clear river that was filled with gold and every precious stone. She described to me the Ancient Tree with emerald leaves covered with diamond flakes. She said inside the tree was an ancient chest that held the hallowed book of souls. The White Stallion led her to what she called the Ancient Stump that holds the sweet nectar of the Most High. She was allowed to drink from the stump!"

As Stephen spoke, his legs grew weak, and he slowly knelt. "To see Shemed challenge King Rayon for my soul, I . . . I."

Machiah placed his hand on Stephen's arm. "It's time for you to go back."

Stephen gasped, "Will I . . .?

Machiah raised his hand and brought it down in front of Stephen. Instantly, Stephen was back at the barn with Victoria and Ian who watched as Stephen frantically looked around the barn.

Stephen fixed his eyes on Ian. "How long was I gone this time?"

"Long enough for Sheriff Bolton to be on his way here," Ian said.

Stephen took Victoria's hand. "I didn't ask you before, but now I need to know. Did you really go through a gate?"

Victoria hesitated, looked down and said, "Yes, I did. But I am not ready to share my experience."

Stephen was bewildered. He looked at Ian. "Ian, I finally saw Shemed. I heard Shemed challenged King Rayon for me."

"What kind of a challenge?"

"For my soul. He told King Rayon that he gave him the position of prosecutor, but he closed *Eden's Gate* and had not allowed him to enter."

"Think about what you're saying, Stephen. What did you name your farm?" Ian asked.

Stephen massaged the back of his neck and groaned. "*Eden's Gate.*"

Victoria rubbed her forearm. "Stephen! I'm getting cold chills. That's what we are studying about."

Stephen's mind was on overload, when he remembered Linda Scott. He put his hands on top of his head and cried, "Oh, God above, what am I going to do? Machiah said I would be charged with Linda Scott's murder."

Ian put his hand on Stephen's shoulder. "Stephen, where is your faith? Even jail bars can't stop the work of the kingdom. Sometimes the greatest revelations come when we are in the worst circumstances."

Victoria spoke up. "That's right, Stephen. Look at John on the Isle of Patmos. He received the book of Revelation while in prison. Even when Daniel was in the lions' den, the angel came and closed the mouths of the lions. That, my friend, is a great revelation. Just to know

God sees you where you are and will protect you accordingly. I can't imagine a big mouth lion breathing on me with drool oozing all over the place. Not to mention his breath that would be unbearable. Yuck!"

Victoria noticed Stephen and Ian both staring at her. She frowned and asked, "What are you two gazing at? You do know about those stories, right?"

Ian shook his head. "No lion in the world has a bigger mouth than you, my dear."

Victoria tightened her brows and pushed Ian's shoulder. "You are the most despicable person on God's green earth. You constantly look for any reason to make hateful remarks to me. That better stop or I will . . ."

Victoria paused and looked toward the window. "Stephen, Sheriff Bolton's coming."

Stephen looked at Ian and asked, "What? He's here now?"

Ian boldly asked, "Are you in God's hands or not?"

"Yes!"

"Do you trust him with your life?"

"Yes!"

"This is your proving time, Stephen. Without a doubt, Shemed has entered *Eden's Gate*."

Chapter Sixty-Three

A Warning

Sheriff Bolton parked the car and walked toward the barn. Victoria straightened her posture and said, "You know Stephen, Sheriff Bolton and I never did have that date."

Ian sighed. "How can you think about a date right now? I've never witnessed anyone like you in my life."

Victoria snapped, "Shut-up, Ian. I know what I'm doing!"

Sheriff Bolton smiled. "How are you doing, Stephen, Ian?"

He took his hat off, looked at Victoria, grinned and nodded. "Miss Stanton, it's good to see you again."

Victoria held her head high. She took her pointer finger and glided it across his badge. "I'm doing fine. Just to know you are the law in Calvin's Point brings a secure feeling to my heart."

Victoria took the sheriff's hand, put it to her chest and whispered, "Just feel how at ease my heart is with you here."

Sheriff Bolton swallowed hard, widened his eyes, and quickly glanced side to side. Ian and Stephen watched as Victoria went even further with her acting skills.

"I would like you to check my room sometime and give me some security tips. Before you do that, I need to tell you about a weird thing that happens when I lock the door. At times I can't get it to unlock."

Victoria straightened the sheriff's shirt collar. "Of course, you may not be able to get out for a few hours. Sometimes, you must let the lock rest before trying again, but I'm sure we could find something to do. Don't you think?"

Sheriff Bolton's face glowed a bright red. Stammering, he said, "Why, Miss Stanton. I-I-I had better get to the reason why I came out here. You have a charming way of making me forget."

Victoria ran her finger down his cheek. "I am sorry. If you and these two boys will excuse me, I've had an exhausting day."

She turned and walked toward the house. Ian shook his head. "I have never heard such a line in my life. That woman is full of it."

Sheriff Bolton faced Ian. "Did you say something?"

Stephen spoke up, "I guess you are here because of Linda Scott's body."

Shocked, Sheriff Bolton asked, "What did you say? Linda Scott?"

Stephen looked at Ian, then at the sheriff. "That's not why you're here?"

Confused, the sheriff said, "No! I just had you on my mind. I've been praying for you today. Things were quiet, so I thought I would drop by. I won't say that you were the only one I was thinking of, but enough of that. What about Linda Scott?"

"Her body is in the barn," Stephen said.

"Then, show me where she is."

Stephen led the way to the stall and stopped. Sheriff Bolton squatted beside the body. "My, my, what a waste of life. She was so young."

The sheriff stood, looked at Stephen and questioned, "How did her body get in your barn?"

Before Stephen could answer, Ian said, "I found her when I came into the barn."

"What can you tell me about this, Stephen?" the sheriff asked.

Stephen thought of what Telmar had shown him about the murder when they spoke inside the marble hall, but felt sure the sheriff wouldn't understand. Not sure how to respond, Stephen said, "I really can't tell you anything, except I came out to the barn with Ian, and she was lying here."

The sheriff asked, "Did you see or hear anything?"

"No, nothing."

"I better call and get the coroner out here. I'll need him to do an autopsy."

Sheriff Bolton walked outside and put his hands on his hips. "I remember something like this happening in Vietnam. An Army friend of mine was in camp one night. He couldn't sleep. He had been restless for three days. That night he went outside to smoke a cigarette. He stood there a few minutes, put his cigarette out and started back inside when he thought he heard a struggle and moans not far from the side of the tent.

"Then he did a foolish thing. He grabbed his bayonet and went to investigate without telling anyone. In the bushes, he found a young girl's body. She was bleeding profusely. Naturally, he bent down over the girl to see if she was still alive. He jumped almost out of his skin when a voice shouted, 'Private!' There was blood everywhere, including all over the private. Her jugular had been cut and blood was spouting. It was on him and his bayonet. He was arrested. At the trial, the circumstantial evidence was really against him. We were at war. One didn't go into the jungle and not tell someone. The enemy could be setting you up to kill you. The girl could have been strapped with explosives.

"My Army friend left the camp and safety for a jungle filled with reptiles. I saw some of the biggest snakes I've ever seen in my life there. But the point is, he was found guilty and then sentenced to death. Then a soldier came forward and said he saw a man come out of the bushes that night, but it wasn't the private. It was the commander the soldier identified. The commander had told the soldier he would immediately see that he would be sent back to the states with his family in exchange for his silence. When he was promised a secure place away from the war, the soldier accepted. He agreed and went home the next day. Of course, the commander was the one to find my friend standing over the girl and was, therefore, to be the star witness.

"Five years later, the day before my friend was to be put to death, the commander came forth and told the truth. After five years, he confessed because he said, 'The war in my mind was worse than the war in Nam.'"

Stephen stared out the barn door. "I understand war in the mind," he said.

"We all can, Stephen. After his release, the private saw the man who could have cleared him on the spot. Though he was wrongly accused, the private was so thankful that he came forward when he did. Before it was too late. The private learned never go into the night without being covered. The other soldier learned there is no peace in this world when you sell out and do what's wrong. He escaped the war in Nam, but the war zone moved to his mind. How could he have peace when he knew someone was sentenced to death for a crime he didn't commit?

"That soldier now preaches the gospel. In the mist of the turmoil that raged in his mind, God made his destiny clear to him. We never know where the next road will lead. Both these men were in prison. One, a literal prison, and the other, a spiritual prison. In the end, they were both set free and the real killer was put to death."

Sheriff Bolton looked at Stephen. "Draw from that what you will, my friend. I'd better get someone out here to pick up the body. Then, I'll need to inform Miss Scott's parents."

The sheriff turned to go to his car, stopped, looked at Stephen and said, "Pastor Reynolds said he saw you with Linda Scott down by the covered bridge, and you were very intimate. Is that right, Stephen?"

Furious, Stephen defended himself. "What's going on here, Sheriff? I don't even know Linda Scott! And why would you take his word over mine anyway? How do you know he's not the one who did this? He . . ."

Sheriff Bolton watched as Stephen put on a defense that would make Perry Mason look like an amateur. After a couple of minutes, he put his hand up to stop him. "Hold it, Stephen! I am going to ask you the same question that you asked me a couple of minutes ago. What's going on here? Why the long defense speech over a question about what Pastor Reynolds said he saw? All I wanted was a yes or no. I don't believe you had anything to do with this, but actions like these reek with guilt. Keep your head straight, Stephen. The truth will come out. Please try to remember you haven't been charged with anything . . . yet."

Sheriff Bolton started toward his car, stopped, turned back, and asked, "Stephen, if you didn't know Linda Scott, how did you know that was her body in your barn?"

Before Stephen could reply, the sheriff said, "We'll talk later. Why don't you and Ian go on to the house? I'll wait here for the coroner and check for any clues the killer may have left behind."

Chapter Sixty-Four

A Call to Friends

Entering the house, Stephen and Ian were greeted by Victoria, who had been watching and listening from the kitchen window. She was standing with one hand on her hip and her head slightly tilted. The men stopped in front of her. Before they could ask what she was doing, she shook her head. "Stephen Daniel Harris! What was that outburst? Don't you know the sheriff has been trained to observe the actions of possible suspects?"

Stephen said nothing. He walked by her to the telephone and began dialing a number.

"Stephen! We need to talk," Victoria snapped.

Concerned, Ian said, "Victoria, I know this will be an almost impossible request, but for once will you be quiet?"

Victoria shocked Ian by saying, "You're right."

Astonished, Ian whispered, "Really?"

She frowned at him. "Shhh!" she said.

Victoria felt sure Stephen was calling Leann. She was surprised when Stephen said, "Cordilia." Immediately, Stephen's eyes brightened and a smile appeared. After asking about Paul and Phillip, his smile diminished. His lively voice changed to somber. Cordilia must have been able to tell something was wrong. Stephen tried to assure her everything was fine, but she wouldn't buy that. Stephen broke down and told her everything. Cordilia assured him they would be on their way to Calvin's Point first thing in the morning.

Stephen looked at Ian and Victoria. With some excitement he said, "The Dawsons will be here by lunch tomorrow."

Victoria smiled. "I have wanted to meet this Cordilia ever since you first told me about her. Now my time has come."

Stephen pointed at Victoria. "Victoria, you had better be on your best behavior, and I mean it!"

Ian chuckled. Victoria squinted and faced Ian.

Stephen demanded, "Ian, please do not provoke her."

Sheriff Bolton knocked at the screen door. Ian opened the door, and the sheriff came inside but didn't speak for a moment.

"Sheriff Bolton, what are you doing here?" Stephen asked. "Is there something new with the case? Is everything all right?"

"Yeah. We got everything removed. I . . . I don't want you to leave town, Stephen, at least until the investigation is over."

Puzzled, Stephen asked, "Why?"

"The fact she was found in your barn is enough, but there is more."

"What?" Stephen asked.

"I'm not at liberty to say right now. However, as the sheriff and your friend, I will say you need to get yourself a good attorney."

Victoria spoke up. "Sheriff Bolton, as much as I am attracted to you, and I am, and as much as I respect your position as sheriff, and I do, I must say, Stephen has a right to know if he is being charged. If not, he also has the right to come and go as he pleases."

Sheriff Bolton removed his hat, twisted his mustache and responded. "Miss Stanton, as much as I am attracted to you, and I am. And as much as I would love to pick you up, take you up those stairs, close the door and pray it doesn't unlock for hours, I am still the law here and this is official business. By the way, beautiful lady, I am the aggressor in this field. Therefore, Stephen, if you would cooperate, I would appreciate it."

Sheriff Bolton then shocked everyone, especially Victoria, when he took her by the shoulders and pressed his lips hard against hers. He put his hat on, licked his lips and said as he went out the door, "Lady, your lips are as sweet as a honeycomb. I'll be in touch with you soon, Stephen."

Stephen, Ian and Victoria looked at each other in disbelief at the sheriff's actions.

Chapter Sixty-Five

Destiny Returns

Much to Stephen's surprise, Victoria assisted him in preparing the house for the Dawsons' visit.

Later that evening, Stephen went to the porch swing, wanting to revive some of the secure feelings he had known in Todd's Creek—those times when he and his dad would share everything together while sitting in the swing. Leann would be here soon, but Stephen knew he had to have this quiet time for himself.

His heart ached as he looked toward Calvin's Point. The church was in plain view and served as a reminder that Pastor Reynolds had either intentionally lied or made a horrible mistake about seeing him with Linda Scott.

Stephen knew his strength must come from God for the road ahead. He also breathed a prayer for Linda Scott's family. How devastated they must feel to lose their daughter under such horrendous circumstances!

He was excited, knowing he would see Cordilia and Paul, but was ecstatic about seeing Philip.

The sky was breathtaking. The gold, red and yellow gave the mountain the appearance of being blanketed with fall colors. Victoria had been at Eden's Gate a month already. Time was swiftly passing.

An unusually quiet Victoria joined Stephen on the porch swing.

"A penny for your thoughts," Stephen said, remembering his mom used that saying often with him and his dad.

Victoria stared into Stephen's eyes and asked, "How did you and Ian know the girl in the barn was Linda Scott. If you didn't know her, how could you possibly just assume it was she?"

Stephen shook his head. "Like everything else, I don't know why I assumed it was Linda Scott. I just don't know."

"The other thing on my mind is . . . you said you saw Shemed challenge King Rayon for your soul. Did you see anything else while you were away?"

"Like what" he asked.

"Did you see the Garden of Eden?"

"No. Why do you ask?"

"You asked me if I went through a gate."

"Yes, I did."

Victoria paused, and continued, "As I told you, I did go through a gate. I . . . I went through Eden's Gate."

Stephen's eyes widened. "Oh my heavens! You saw the Garden of Eden? Please tell me what you saw."

Victoria licked her dry lips and began, "That night after dinner, you had gone to bed. I went to bed too, but couldn't sleep. As I lay there, I realized someone was in the room with me. I looked up and Destiny was standing at the foot of my bed. He was only partially there, not totally. When I sat up, he fully appeared. He called my name and said, 'Victoria, you can no longer run from me. You are a chosen vessel. The Most High has brought you to Eden's Gate to revive your soul.' He held his hand out toward me and said, 'Come.' Instantly, I was in a battlefield. The smell of blood and death was everywhere. My heart was heavy, until someone spoke to me."

"Who was it?"

"He was a Watchman named, Eri. He told me a dear friend of mine had turned to the dark kingdom."

"Who was your friend?"

"His name was Lester. I . . . here comes Leann. I want to take a hot bath and have a glass of wine, and we will talk later."

Stephen stood. "I love Leann and want to visit with her, but her timing couldn't be worse."

Leann walked toward the porch with a puzzled look on her face. With a forced smile, she said hello and kissed Stephen.

Victoria smiled. "Well, how are you, Leann?" she asked.

"Fine, and you?"

"Good. I was just going to my room. Have a lovely visit."

Chapter Sixty-Six

Don't Leave Town

Leann stroked Stephen's forehead. "What is this about Linda Scott's body being found in your barn?"

Stephen took a deep breath and tried to explain all he knew to Leann.

Confused, Leann questioned, "Who and why would anyone try to frame you?"

"I can't say for sure," Stephen said.

"Does that statement mean you have a clue as to who would do this against you?"

"Yes, but, it's only a clue."

"Then, tell me. I'm sure you've told Victoria all about it."

"For heaven's sake, Leann. Don't start this jealous routine. I've been through quite an ordeal, and I don't have the energy to defend myself when it comes to Victoria. I think I'm going to be charged with murder, and I can't fight with you about Victoria right now."

Leann hugged Stephen and apologized. "I just want you to share everything with me. That's all. You think you're going to be charged with murder?"

"Yes."

Tears filled Leann's eyes as she asked, "Stephen, tell me, who would do this to you?"

"Okay, Leann, I'll tell you. Stephen paused and said, "Pastor Reynolds."

Leann frowned. "You have got to be kidding! Pastor Reynolds would never do that. Where did you get such a notion?"

Stephen sternly replied, "See! That's why I didn't want to tell you. I didn't think you would believe me. But it was he, Leann! He said he saw me in my truck, parked down by the covered bridge, making out with Linda Scott. Can you believe that? I don't believe it, because it isn't true."

"I don't understand. Pastor Reynolds is one of the most gentle men I have ever known."

"Really! I used to think that too. Well, there's more to this messy story," Stephen said.

"Then tell me, Stephen. I need to know."

"And what if you're not really ready to accept the truth?"

Leann stared ahead in silence.

"All right! I'll tell you the truth," Stephen said.

Stephen shared about the gate that led him to the marble hall, the statues and Telmar. He shared how Telmar waved his hand in front of his face, allowing him to see what happened to Linda Scott. How she was dragged by the hair of her head into his barn and pushed, with this man's foot, into the stall. "That person who did this horrendous act was Pastor Reynolds."

Leann thought a moment and slowly shook her head. "What's wrong with you, Stephen? You're insisting that you were beamed into a world of demons and angels alike. A move of the hand and you see into yet another dimension. I think you need a vacation."

Stephen erupted, "I knew you would respond exactly that way. I'm telling you the truth, whether you accept it or not."

Leann took hold of Stephen's arm and apologized. "I want to believe you. I just haven't been to the place you are now. So please try to be patient with me. If you say that's what happened, then I believe you."

Stephen softly held Leann's face and tenderly kissed her. "I love you, Leann. I don't understand all of this myself. I don't even understand half of it. However, I do know God is preparing me for my destiny, and right now, you're a part of that destiny. I wish we could run away and be married tonight. My flesh is screaming for that, but my spirit will not let me go. Not yet."

Leann stroked his cheek and assured him no matter what, God was in control. "I'll be here for you, and when this time has passed, we'll be together."

Quickly, Stephen smiled and changed the subject by telling Leann that Cordilia, Paul and Philip would be at Eden's Gate tomorrow morning. Leann watched and listened as Stephen acted like a little boy at Christmas time.

"Stephen! Why don't you take a week and visit Todd's Creek? I know the Dawsons are coming here tomorrow, but maybe later. I think that would be like a dose of medicine to your soul."

"You don't know how desperately I've wanted to do that very thing. Maybe you could come with me."

"No . . . no, I don't think so. Not the first time. The first trip you need for yourself."

"I think you're right, Leann. After this is over with Linda Scott, I'll definitely go."

Curious, Leann questioned, "Why after it's over? Why not go back with the Dawsons?"

"Sheriff Bolton asked me not to leave town until things were cleared up."

Shocked, Leann asked, "Things are that bad? You can't leave town?"

Stephen sighed. "Yes, the hard part is that I know I haven't done anything, but I was told I should find myself an attorney."

"Oh my, Stephen." Leann groaned. "Oh, I know what you can do! You can talk to Ginger

Banks. She'll be glad to help you. I'll go with you if you like."

Stephen said, "That sounds like a good idea. I'll call her tomorrow and set up an appointment."

Leann stood. "Speaking of tomorrow, I have to go to work early, so I better get home. You need to get some rest anyway." Leann tilted her head and then asked, "Is it strange to wake up with a woman in the house? Especially such a beautiful woman?"

"Victoria is beautiful, but she usually stays in her space, and I stay in mine. She has her own bath, so there's no problem there. It's not bad. Especially, when I love you so much."

Leann kidded, "Is she still the arrogant, spoiled brat people know and hate?"

Stephen chuckled. "I think you need to ask Ian Jackson about that."

Leann smiled. "I'll see you tomorrow. I'll tell Ginger you'll be calling her. If you need Mom and Daddy for any reason, please let them know. They love you too."

"I will."

Stephen watched Leann drive out of sight. He then walked slowly to the entrance that led into Eden's Gate. He placed his hand on the post that held the gate, then on the gate. Victoria watched from her bedroom window as Stephen held his head back and his arms out from his body and turned around and around in a circle. He stopped, lifted his hands toward heaven, fell to his knees and wept loudly as he called out to the Most High. Victoria inhaled and covered her mouth with her hand as she beheld a light descend from heaven in a funnel shape, encircling Stephen. She, too, was moved to worship.

Chapter Sixty-Seven

Stephen Needs an Attorney

Stephen was up early, anticipating the arrival of the Dawsons. He poured a second cup of coffee and made his way to the porch swing. It was only 6:30 a.m. and the sun was beginning to rise. The humidity was low and 70 degrees felt great. Stephen finished his coffee and was going to call Victoria before Ian arrived. To his surprise, he saw her jogging up the long drive that led to the gate. Her hair was pulled back in a ponytail and a white towel was around her neck. She had on a bright yellow tank top, white shorts, yellow socks and white tennis shoes. She saw Stephen standing on the porch and waved as she came through the open gate.

Stephen smiled and called out, "You'd better save some of your energy for the field."

Victoria stopped in front of the porch and began to march in place. "I have lots of energy. It wouldn't hurt you to get a little more exercise."

Victoria was doing stretches, when Stephen squinted and said, "Why in the world would Brenda Stanton be coming out here this early in the morning?"

Surprised, Victoria quickly turned around, "Grandmother?" she said as she wiped her face with the towel. Charles got out of the limousine and called out, "Good morning, Mr. Harris, Miss Stanton." He hurried around to open the door for Brenda Stanton.

Charles took hold of her hand, and she slowly got out of the car. Victoria ran out to greet her. "Grandmother Stanton! What brings you out this early in the morning?"

She gave Victoria a hug. "Does a grandmother have to have a reason to visit her granddaughter?"

"Yes! This early, there must be a reason. How are you, Charles?"

He smiled. "I am doing great, Miss Victoria. Mrs. Stanton woke me early this morning. Liz put the coffee on, we had a cup and waited until 6:30 to head out to Eden's Gate."

Stephen took Brenda's hand and helped her up the steps. She took a seat on the swing. Brenda looked like a portrait out of a 1910 magazine. Her hair was styled in a loose bun, with finger waves lying like rows from the crown of her head to her forehead. She was wearing a pale pink cotton blouse with puffy elbow-length sleeves that buttoned up the back. Four small lines of lace garnished the front of the blouse. The high collar rested underneath her chin. A bold, gold broach with a large pink stone surrounded with small, white pearls was secured in the center of the collar. Her long, black, ankle-length skirt served only to accent the size five, black pumps that closed on top of her feet with at least ten small buttons.

She patted the seat of the swing and said, "Stephen, come sit with me a moment, please. I would like to speak with you."

Stephen joined her. "What can I do for you?"

Brenda lifted her chin and said, "You can start by assuring me that you had nothing to do with Linda Scott's death."

Stephen put his hand on Brenda's and said, "That will be my pleasure. No! I had nothing to do with her death. I didn't even know her."

With a quick nod of her head, a tightlipped grin and a sigh of relief, Brenda said, "I knew you had nothing to do with all this. Tell me, Stephen, do you need an attorney?"

"Sheriff Bolton suggested I get one. I'm going to call Ginger Banks later this morning."

Brenda frowned. "Ginger Banks, hum. I have an attorney in Charleston who would be excellent. If you like, I'll call him. Don't worry about the money. He owes me dearly."

"I . . . I don't think that will be necessary. I'm sure Ginger Banks will be fine. I pray I don't need one. Nevertheless, the offer means a great deal." Stephen kissed Brenda's cheek. Thank you."

"Tell me, Stephen, has my granddaughter stressed your last nerve?"

Victoria hugged Brenda. "Now, Grandmother, you know I am just like you, as sweet as honey."

Brenda stood and pulled at her skirt. "I've found out what I need to know. Charles, we better get home before Liz goes back to bed and you have to do her chores."

Charles chuckled. "That sounds like a good idea."

He nodded at Stephen. "It's been a pleasure, Mr. Harris, Miss Victoria."

Mrs. Stanton took Stephen's arm and said, "Victoria, walk Charles to the car. Stephen and I will be right there."

Victoria took Charles' hand. "Come on, Charles. We can let grandmother talk about me to Stephen."

"Victoria is right," Brenda said. "I am going to talk about her. How is she doing?"

Stephen shook his head. "I've been shocked at the transformation that has taken place. Her wisdom on the Bible is astounding. I was expecting someone who knew nothing, and then to have someone who has so much knowledge. Wow!"

"I can tell by looking at her, Eden's Gate is exactly what she needed. Now, if you can get her to church, that may be worth a bonus to you. Do you need money? Don't be shy. I'm loaded, and everyone knows it, including you. So, speak up if you need anything."

"That's so sweet of you, but really, I'm fine. I'll let you know if matters change."

"Please do! I'll be calling daily to see how things are going."

Stephen and Victoria waved as Mrs. Stanton and Charles drove away.

Victoria went inside and poured herself a glass of orange juice. "Would you like a glass of juice, Stephen?"

Stephen walked to the table and said, "I want to know more about the Watcher and your friend Lester."

Victoria looked at her watch. "Ian will be here soon."

Stephen insisted, "Stay home today. Surely Ian won't mind."

Victoria sighed. "You have company coming."

"Share it with them too. They would love it. Please!"

"What about Ginger Banks? You need to go in to see her."

Stephen rubbed his eyes. "I don't think you have a clue how important this is to me. I need to hear every word."

Victoria grinned and finished her orange juice.

"What is that look on your face?" Stephen asked.

Victoria giggled.

"What is it?" Stephen insisted.

"I was thinking about Sheriff Bolton's kiss. Hum!"

"You like him, don't you?"

Victoria shrugged her shoulders. "A little. Now I am going to shower and then have some cereal. When I meet Cordilia, I want to look superb."

"You look beautiful," Stephen assured her.

Chapter Sixty-Eight

Dawsons Come for a Visit

Victoria stroked her hair and said, "I do look beautiful, I mean . . . I know I do." She put her hands on her waist. "How could this eighteen-inch waist not look fabulous?" She put her hands under her breasts, pushed them together. "I have incredible breasts." She took Stephen's hand, put it to her breast and said, "Just feel the firmness."

Before Stephen could pull his hand away, someone coughed. Stephen immediately pulled his hand out of Victoria's, thinking Ian had arrived early, but turned and saw Cordilia, Paul and Philip looking through the screen door. For a moment they all looked at each other; then Cordilia chuckled, "Stephen do you two need a minute or can we come in now?" Stephen's face was a bright shade of red. He put one hand over his face and muttered, "Oh, Lord! Please come in. I pictured myself running out to meet you with hugs and kisses, not this."

Cordilia hugged Stephen and whispered, "Rachel would have died if she had seen this, but I think it's hysterical. You should see the color of your face."

Paul followed suit. "Wow, Stephen, how are you doing?"

Stephen then looked at Philip, who was grinning shyly. Stephen lowered his head, and joined Philip who burst into laughter. That was all it took for everyone to join the laughter. Stephen confessed, "I have never been so embarrassed in my life!"

Cordilia inspected Victoria for a moment and said, "Well have mercy, you must be Victoria!"

Victoria pulled the ponytail holder from her hair, shook her hair and replied, "And you must be the renowned Cordilia Dawson."

"I'm sorry, forgive my manners," Stephen said. "I want you to meet Victoria Stanton, the houseguest I told you about. Victoria this is . . ."

Victoria stepped forward. "Don't tell me. Let me guess." She stood in front of Paul, held her hand out for him to kiss and said, "You must be Paul."

Paul took her hand and lightly kissed it. Victoria squeezed his forearm. "My goodness, you are a blessed woman, Cordilia."

She moved in front of Philip and stroked his cheek. "My, my, you are a beautiful young man, just like . . ." Victoria stared into Philip's eyes. A look of astonishment filled her countenance.

"What is it Victoria?" Stephen asked.

She immediately turned her head and changed the subject. "Cordilia! I've been looking forward to this day. Stephen has told me so much about you and Rachel. I feel I've known you for years."

Ian knocked at the door and called out, "Hello, everybody! It's good to see you nice people again. I just stopped by to pick Victoria up for work."

Stephen spoke up. "Victoria is taking the day off to visit with my family."

Ian looked upward, closed his eyes and said, "Thank you, God. You are so good to me."

Victoria growled, "Say what you will, Ian Jackson. I am smearing your name all through my article to let people have a real view of your hateful attitude. If that isn't enough, I'll see about getting your name smeared on a tombstone."

Stephen pulled Victoria away from Ian. "Victoria, I want this stopped. Ian, don't provoke her. My family's here, so please, for my sake, behave! Victoria, go take your shower and give me a few minutes alone with the Dawsons. I want to catch up on all the news from Todd's

Creek. Ian, you know what to do in the field, and I will talk to you later."

Ian went to work and Victoria went to take her shower. As soon as the rest were alone, a group hug was shared and they gathered around the table, enjoying a fresh brewed pot of coffee. Cordilia laughed and came straight to the point, "Why were your holding Victoria's breast?"

"I wasn't holding her breast. She grabbed my hand and put it there before I knew what was going on. She's really come a long way since she's has been here. She and Ian are worse than brother and sister, though. I have to correct them like children, or Victoria might tear into him, literally. God's working in her life, though. She has a vast amount of wisdom about the things of God. I asked her to share some of that wisdom with us today. But now I want to hear the news from home."

Paul asked, "Do you remember the hermit Cordilia and Rachel called Mr. Spook?"

"Yes! How could I forget him?"

"He passed away last week. After the battle at Boone's Crossing, he moved back to town. He joined Todd's Creek Church and became a Sunday school teacher. Most people didn't accept what he taught during the last few weeks of his life."

Cordilia interrupted, "I accepted it. He taught about a gate that he had gone through. He said the gate took him to a place much like the one you said you went to, Stephen. The one where you met Jim Lee."

Stephen sighed. "Cordilia, are you serious?"

"I'm as serious as a heart attack. He talked about the mountain and the valley filled with people as far as the eye could see."

Stephen asked, "How did the church people respond to that?"

"Some said he had 'gone off the deep end' and others said he needed to 'go back to the mountain to live.' He taught on Sunday morning, which was going to be his last Sunday because he had been asked to resign. He stood and looked across the people for at least two or three minutes before saying a word. Some were very restless at his stares. They knew he was looking through them. He opened the lesson by saying, 'Queen Jewel walked in the midst of the stones of fire on the mountain of God.' Someone called out, 'That's not the lesson topic. We have an outline. Didn't you study it?' To that Mr. Spook responded, 'It is essential that we reach the pinnacle of the mountain, and you will never reach it with an outline.' He died that night in his sleep."

Astounded, Stephen whispered, "He saw the mountain?"

Cordilia put her hand on Stephen's and said, "I want to know every detail about what has been happening in your life since we were last here. Have you encountered Shemed again?"

Stephen paused and said, "Yes, I finally saw Shemed in a setting I never would have imagined. I also came face to face with Telmar. And I talked with Haleb."

Surprised, Cordilia said, "You saw Haleb! I want details."

Stephen shared about Machiah taking him to the throne room; hearing Shemed challenging King Rayon for his soul; relating about Haleb, Telmar and the events of the last gate he had gone through.

Philip said nothing until Stephen finished. He then cleared his throat and uttered, "If Haleb has arrived on the scene, you can bet the battle is intensifying."

Stephen exhaled. "With the threat of being arrested for a murder I didn't commit, to me it's *beyond* intense."

Chapter Sixty-Nine

Garden of Fire

*A*fter a short time, Victoria joined them in the kitchen. Stephen asked her to share more about the Garden of Fire. Victoria took a deep breath and began.

"I want to start by saying what took place in the Garden of Fire is not taught by teachers or preachers. I've heard so much about you and would not even consider sharing what I know to be the truth, if Stephen had not assured me about your open minds."

Victoria told the events that took place with Acor, Hannah and Queen Jewel.

"Stephen asked the question," she continued, 'How did Acor would lure Hannah away from White Stone Kingdom and away from her faithfulness to the Most High God?' Jewel taught Acor about the deep magic. She took him to the Garden of Fire and into the flame of forbidden knowledge. He became a skilled

337

master of the magical powers. Acor knew if he were to gain Hannah's attention, he would have to start by asking her a question. He saw Hannah sitting in the meadow one day and made his move. He asked, 'Queen Hannah, is it really true what I've heard about the Most High not wanting His children to have every pleasure He has to offer?'

Cordilia spoke up. "So he was playing with her psychologically. By asking, is it really true, Acor is wanting to appear confused by what he's heard and wants to clear the confusion."

Victoria nodded. "Exactly. He wanted to arouse Hannah's curiosity about his confusion. Curiosity is a key word. It means 'an eager desire to learn, especially to learn what does not concern one.' Hannah's dormant desire for knowledge was awakened by the question. When he had her attention, Acor used his powerful sorcery to put Hannah into a hypnotic condition. He shredded her alertness, working her watchfulness into a tranquilized slumber. Acor blinded Hannah to his fallen state with sorcery. All she saw was the high priest Acor before he was deceived by Queen Jewel. He covered his true appearance with deception. Like false religion, deception takes on the covering of truth. Hannah knew truth, but so did Acor before he allowed the influence of the dark kingdom to distort the truth he knew.

"Hannah, now under his spell, asked, 'What pleasure has God kept from His children? He fulfills our every desire.'

"Acor quickly added, 'If He withheld nothing from His children, why are we to stay away from the tree in the Garden of Fire that holds the forbidden knowledge. Why is it forbidden?'

"Hannah thought a moment and said, 'I don't know why it's forbidden other than that God said it was strange fire and would hurt His children.'"

Cordilia said, "It sounds like Acor wanted to draw Hannah out of the boundaries God had set for her."

Paul added, "Away from the safety zone of truth into Queen Jewel's playing field."

Victoria continued, "Leaving Hannah unprotected, her holy covering was removed by her choice to allow Acor's words of deceit to penetrate her heart and give his evil entrance to her mind."

Stephen said, "Away from her proper place, which was in the Most High, she had no authority. Therefore, Acor could overpower her because outside of God, she was no match for the deep magic that Acor himself possessed."

"That's right, Stephen." Cordilia said, "It's the same for us all. Outside the Most High, we have no power, only chaos."

"So, what happened?" Philip asked.

"Acor assured Hannah that he knew many that had entered the forbidden flames and who had said there was a pleasure there that was indescribable. Hannah wanted to know what pleasure could be more than God had given them. Acor gave the invitation to join him and they would enter the flame together and find out what this forbidden mystery could possibly be. Hannah accepted and entered the forbidden flames that opened her eyes to a knowledge that was never intended for her."

"What was the knowledge Hannah gained?" Paul asked.

"Acor lured Hannah to the Garden of Fire, and they stood together before the forbidden flames. Acor exhibited himself before Hannah with all the seductive tenderness he could produce. By this time, Acor was moving erotically before Hannah, who was now very receptive to Acor's proposal."

Everyone was so caught up in what Victoria was saying, the ringing of the phone caused them all to jump. Stephen went to answer the phone in the kitchen.

"Good grief, that scared the life out of me," Cordilia said.

Paul put his hand on his chest, "I think my heart jumped a little also."

Victoria looked at Philip, expecting a similar response. Their eyes connected and for a moment, Victoria got chill bumps as she and Philip looked at each other. Cordilia and Paul noticed the baffled look on Victoria's face. Victoria turned her head and glanced at the floor.

Concerned by her pale appearance, Cordilia asked, "Victoria! Are you okay? You're as white as a sheet."

Victoria glanced at Philip and assured her, "Yes. I'm fine. I just need a drink of water."

Cordilia looked at Philip. "Do you two know each other?"

Victoria spoke up. "Not unless Philip has been to New York. I'm just very tired, that's all."

"I'm quite taken by your knowledge of the Garden of Fire," Philip said.

Victoria nervously whispered, "I wonder what's keeping Stephen?"

Chapter Seventy

Fall of a Warrior

Stephen entered the dining room. "That was Leann. She's bringing Ginger Banks over at lunch to talk about representing me. I just can't believe any of this big mess."

Cordilia embraced Stephen. "You don't worry about anything. God has His hand on your life, Stephen. He knows what's ahead of you and why."

Stephen hugged Cordilia tightly. "I am so glad you're here." He hugged Paul and said the same. He looked at Philip. They embraced and wept on each other's shoulder.

Victoria began to weep as well. Wiping her eyes, she whined, "Stop all this crying. I'm wearing waterproof mascara, but I am ruining my foundation."

Paul chuckled. "My word, Cordilia! She sounds exactly like you."

Victoria said, "I am certain you mean that in the highest regard, Mr. Dawson."

Paul looked at Stephen, shook his head and pointed toward Victoria. "I rest my case."

Stephen was eager to know what happened to Hannah before Leann and Ginger arrived.

Everyone agreed with Stephen.

Victoria, said yes and shocked them by saying, "I stood with Destiny and watched as this beautiful woman, formed in total perfection, followed Acor into the forbidden flames." Victoria raised her hands slowly and continued, "At one point when I first met Acor, I touched his chest and had never felt such pain, not even when my father died. The Garden of Fire was the most inconceivably, wonderful place I could have ever imagined. Unfortunately, Hannah lost sight of God and her surroundings. The forbidden became more desirable to her than God and the Highland Kingdom of which she was queen. She gave in to her selfish desires, not considering the cost."

Victoria shook her head. "Acor's plan was to draw Hannah—not because of love, but because of his desire for her to carry his seed."

Stephen furrowed his brows and asked, "Victoria, when you touched Acor's chest, you said you felt terrible pain, but the place you were in was so wonderful, how could that be?"

Victoria put one hand over her mouth and the other on her stomach as she fought back the tears. "Did I say that? What I meant to say was, the place was amazing but the pain of Acor's devastating choice to follow Jewel was heartbreaking."

There was silence. Everyone wondered what was wrong with Victoria. Cordilia broke the silence by asking, "Victoria, you are with friends now that you can trust. Please tell us why you are having to hold back tears?"

Victoria blew her nose and moaned, "I just got too involved when telling the story. I feel as though I'm there watching, with Destiny by my side. To realize the fall of one of the ancient ones is beyond overwhelming."

Hearing a car door close, Stephen turned and looked out the window. "It's Leann and Ginger Banks."

Cordilia took hold of Stephen's arm. "We'll go outside for a while and let you and Ginger talk."

Stephen nodded.

"Victoria," Cordilia said, "I would be honored if you would walk awhile with me."

Victoria said, "It would be a pleasure."

Philip, would you and Paul like to join us?" Cordilia asked.

"No. I think Philip and I will drive into town and have lunch. You two ladies can do all the talking you want without us along. What do you think of that, son?" Paul asked as he winked at Philip.

A smile from Philip and they were on their way.

Chapter Seventy-One
Ginger Stunned

Ginger and Leann sat at the table. Stephen poured the ladies ice tea and joined them. Ginger took a yellow legal pad and pen from her briefcase and placed the pad on the table. She looked at Stephen and held the pen firmly in her hand. After tapping the table a couple of times and writing something at the top of the blank page, she began her questioning. "Stephen, why don't you start by telling me what's been going on and why Linda Scott's body was found in your barn?"

Stephen took a deep breath. Leann put her hand on top of Stephen's and assured him everything was all right.

Stephen rubbed his forehead and fixed his eyes on Ginger. "I will tell you all I know. In my mind, it all started with the storm that appears to have ushered in all these crazy events." He proceeded to explain about the many characters he had met thus far, although he didn't fully understand their roles.

Ginger was quiet, listened to what Stephen had to say and occasionally took notes.

Leann noticed Ginger wasn't writing very much. "Ginger, aren't you going to write down more of the details? I mean you haven't written but two half sentences."

Ginger leaned back in her chair and laid her pen down. "I have tried hundreds of cases in my years as an attorney. I thought I had heard every kind of story imaginable. Some believable, some so far out no one could buy them. Then, just when you think you have heard it all and there would be no room for shock, I hear an intelligent young man shoot me a fairy tale that God Himself would laugh at." Irritated, Ginger stood, took hold of the edge of the table, leaned toward Stephen and demanded, "You tell me the truth or I'm out of here. I'm a busy woman. My caseload is enough for three people as we speak, but all that aside, I agreed to take your case because of Leann. You have ten seconds to start telling me the truth or I'm leaving."

Stephen stood and shouted! "Then go. All I have told you is the truth. Of course, I know it sounds like a fairy tale. It wasn't easy for me to tell you because I knew this would be your response. Every word I have told you is the truth. Now, you do what you have to do. I'll understand, but don't ask me to change my story to fit your mind set. I have told you the truth."

Leann put her hand on Stephen's arm and said, "Honey, some of this is pretty wild. It's not your ordinary story, you know that. I love you, but most of this makes no sense to me. I realize God deals with people in unconventional ways at times, but this goes way beyond unconventional."

Ginger sighed and tried to explain. "Okay, Stephen, let's say what you told me is true and I go to court and try to defend you on what you've told me thus far. The best case I could possibly make would be an insanity plea. That, my friend, would be a breeze."

Stephen looked Ginger in the eyes. "I don't want someone to defend me if they don't believe me. I am not insane! If you can't make my defense on the facts that I have given you, then I'll have to find another attorney."

Leann stood and said, "Stephen, try to understand where Ginger is coming from. She is not Cordilia or your mom. She hasn't been in the realm of the spirit world that you're talking about. Neither have I, Stephen, but I know you need help. I don't want you to go to jail for something you didn't do."

Ginger put both hands in the air. "Stephen, there is no way I can call this Haleb or Telmar for a witness. Do you get my meaning?"

Stephen nodded. "Yes, I do. I want to thank you for coming out and hearing what I had to say, whether you believe me or not."

Ginger put her note pad and pen in her briefcase. "I wish you well, Stephen."

Uneasy, Leann leaned toward Ginger. "Does this mean you're not going to help him?"

"I'm sorry, Leann." Ginger turned and walked toward the door.

Leann hugged Stephen. "Don't worry. I'll call Scott Ward. My dad knows him from Atlanta. I'm sure he will represent you."

"Leann, it's not enough to have someone represent you, if they don't believe you," Stephen said.

"I'll call him anyway, okay?"

Leann and Ginger were walking toward the car, when, suddenly, Ginger turned around and began walking back toward Stephen. "Okay Stephen, I will represent you. I can't believe Leann would even suggest calling Scott Ward. Besides, I love being stretched beyond my safety zone."

Leann hugged Ginger. "I knew you would!"

Stephen soberly asked, "Do you believe me, Ginger?"

Ginger took a deep breath and responded, "Do I understand what you told me? No! Do I believe you are telling the truth, as you know it? Yes! You're going to have to help me understand and see from your eyes what you're saying. Otherwise, we don't stand a chance. I can't believe that I'm doing this! I want you to come to my office first thing in the morning so we can fine tune this Oscar-winning story of yours."

Chapter Seventy-Two

Two Witnesses

Victoria and Cordilia rushed through the door. "Stephen!" Victoria gasped. "Sheriff Bolton is coming up the drive."

Before Stephen could say anything, Philip and Paul, who had just driven up, hurried inside the house.

Frantic, Leann said, "Why would Sheriff Bolton be coming back so soon?"

Ginger put her briefcase on the table. "I don't have a clue, but we will find out in a minute."

Sheriff Bolton came to the door and stopped when he saw everyone gathered in the kitchen. He jokingly asked, "Is it safe to come in or should I approach with great caution?"

Stephen pushed the screen door open for him. "I think we may be a bit apprehensive, but there's no harm in us. Please come in."

The sheriff nodded and removed his hat. He took a piece of paper from his pocket and handed it toward Stephen. Before Stephen could take the paper, Ginger stepped in front of Stephen and questioned, "Now, now, Sheriff, just what kind of paper are you giving my client?"

"Not one that I'm pleased to deliver. From that, you can gather it's not a party invitation. Just a few minutes ago, Judge Patton issued a warrant for Stephen's arrest."

Leann grabbed Ginger's arm and frantically pleaded, "Ginger! Do something."

Bewildered, Stephen softly asked, "How did it come to this? Sheriff, there's not been enough time to determine anything."

"It is highly unusual to issue a warrant before the ink dries on the report. District Attorney Buddy Crisp was hurriedly, and I mean hurriedly, assigned to the case. Judge Patton said there was more than enough evidence to issue a warrant, so he did."

Puzzled, Ginger asked, "Who wanted Buddy Crisp to try this case?"

Sheriff Bolton raised his brows. "I can't tell you that, but I can tell you I was told to serve the warrant on Stephen, citing the case as first degree murder."

Stephen started to speak, but Ginger held her hand up, stopping him. She took the warrant and read over it. Shocked, Ginger held the warrant up. "This warrant says they have two eye witnesses."

Stephen was furious. "What! How could there be witnesses? I didn't do it!"

"Don't panic, Stephen. I will petition Judge Patton to release you on your own recognizance. You have no priors, you're not a threat to anyone and you're not a flight risk."

Sheriff Bolton's expression was somber as he looked at Stephen. "Nevertheless, I still have to take Stephen in today."

Victoria stepped in front of Sheriff Bolton. "Sheriff, I will bring Stephen to the jail within the hour, if you will only allow him time to say goodbye to his family. Please, for me."

All eyes were on the sheriff. He tightened his lips, put his hat on and nodded. "Only because I know in my heart Stephen is innocent will I agree to that. I hold you and you alone responsible for him, Victoria."

Sheriff Bolton turned and walked to the door. Then he stopped, looked at Victoria and sternly said, "One hour. I can count on that, right?"

Victoria held her head high. "I am a woman of my word. I said I would bring him in within the hour and I will. I might add, I feel a bit crushed that it's because you feel Stephen is innocent that you would give him the hour with his family. I felt sure it would be because you trusted me to do as I said."

Sheriff Bolton lightly tapped Victoria's nose and with no expression, said, "Victoria, honey, I feel a bit crushed that you think I didn't consider your promise before I gave Stephen the hour. One hour."

He bowed his head and went out the door, leaving Victoria with a smile.

"Stephen," Ginger said, "I'll try to get in touch with Judge Patton and Buddy Crisp before the day is over and get you out of jail this afternoon. I'll come by the jail and let you know."

Feeling overwhelmed, Stephen shook her hand. "Thank you, Ginger."

Ginger picked up her briefcase. "Don't thank me yet, Stephen. You better keep that on reserve for now. I'll call you later. Leann, do you want a ride with me, or are you going to stay awhile?"

Leann hugged Stephen and said, "I'll go with you, Ginger, and give Stephen this time with his family. Stephen, I'll meet you at the jail in an hour."

Chapter Seventy-Three

Sandra Reynolds' Visit

When Ginger and Leann left, total silence filled the room. After a moment, Cordilia led the way to the living room.

When everyone was seated, Cordilia put her fingers to her temples and said, "Recalling the many obstacles that John, Rachel, Paul and I had to go through on the mountain sends chills down my spine. I can't stress enough that we had to go *through*, not *around*. Stephen, you know we're behind you all the way. We will go with you as much as God will allow. For now, we need to go home for a couple of days to get some things taken care of. You know we will be here with you every minute possible."

Victoria spoke up. "I'm rich and will share my wealth any way possible to help you, Stephen. I can also take off work as long as I like and help take care of the house."

Philip put his hand on Stephen's shoulder. "I'll be right here with you, Stephen, until this is over."

With tears of gratitude in his eyes, Stephen thanked everyone. He put his arms around Cordilia and Paul and insisted that they go home. "When the trial comes up, I want you here. Until then, I'll be fine. With Philip and Victoria both here, there's no doubt I'll be in good hands."

"Hum! Are you sure about that, Stephen?" Cordilia teased.

"I'm sure. I do expect you two to pray for me with every breath though."

Paul assured Stephen, "We pray for you whether you are in trouble or not."

Stephen hugged Paul. "I know you do, Paul. You're like a second father to me. I love you and Cordilia so much. Now, go home. We'll keep you posted on everything that goes on here."

Cordilia held Stephen's face in her hands. "I don't understand why, but the Holy Spirit is *also* telling us to go home. Therefore, Paul and I will leave right away."

Cordilia and Paul went to their room to get their things together.

Victoria called out as she headed up the stairs, "I need to call Grandmother Stanton. I'll be down shortly."

Stephen looked at Philip. "I think this would be a perfect time to visit the porch swing for a few minutes."

Philip put his arm around Stephen's shoulder and agreed. Stephen and Phillip sat and pushed the swing back and forth without speaking.

Stephen finally broke the silence, "Do you remember when we were 15? Mom and Cordilia took us to Norfolk for Christmas shopping. It was the coldest December on record. When I breathed in, the cold air hurt my lungs. Mom constantly told me to hold my scarf over my mouth, but of course, I didn't. I was too embarrassed. I didn't want to be a teenage wimp." Stephen stopped the swing and stared into Philip's eyes. "I feel that same cold feeling now that I felt that day—even though it's eighty degrees today." He leaned forward and propped his elbows on his knees and held his face in his hands. "I really miss Mom and Dad. Mom would know the exact words to say and exactly what to do. My dad was always a tower of strength, and so are you, Philip. I desperately need to draw from that strength right now."

Philip fixed his eyes toward Calvin's Point. "The judge is not going to release you, Stephen."

Surprised, Stephen faced Philip. "He's not?"

"No."

"But, why not?"

"Stephen, remember all the things we talked about with Victoria concerning the Garden of Eden?"

"Of course."

"God is going to show you so much more."

"In jail?" Stephen asked.

"That's all I can say for now."

"That's it? Stephen blew his breath out hard. "I'm sorry, Philip. I know if you could tell me more, you would. Listen, Philip, do you think you'll be okay here with Victoria? She can be offensive, unpleasant and disgusting when she wants to be."

Philip chuckled. "I promise I'll stay out of her way. Thanks for the warning."

In the distance, Stephen could see what appeared to be Pastor Reynolds' car coming toward Eden's Gate. Feeling disgust, Stephen muttered, "Oh, God, help me!"

Not sure what was wrong, Philip asked, "What is it?"

Stephen shook his head and moaned. "Surely, on top of everything else that's happened, Pastor Reynolds doesn't have the nerve to come here."

Stephen gripped the arm of the swing so hard his knuckles were white. He released his grip when he saw it was Sandra Reynolds.

"That's his wife isn't it?" Philip asked.

"Yes! Thank God for His mercy."

Chapter Seventy-Four

A Call from the Pastor

Stephen stood, curious to see what would bring Sandra to Eden's Gate. Timidly, Sandra got out of her car and walked to the porch.

Stephen put his hands in his jeans' pocket and greeted her. "Sandra Reynolds, what in the world brings you to Eden's Gate?"

Sandra gave a half-smile and looked around the yard. "I wonder if I might have a word with you, Stephen."

"Of course. Come have a seat on the porch with us."

As Sandra stepped onto the porch, Stephen asked, "Do you remember Philip Dawson?"

Sandra smiled and moved forward to shake Philip's hand. "Yes, I remember Mr. Dawson. How are you?"

"I'm fine, and you?"

"Good, thank you."

"Would you like something cold to drink?" Stephen asked.

"No . . . no, thank you. I can stay only a few minutes."

Stephen sat down on the swing beside Philip. "What is it you want to talk to me about?"

Sandra looked at Philip. "Would you mind if I speak to Stephen alone, please?"

Philip stood. "Of course I don't mind. I'll go check on Mom and Dad."

Sandra looked pale and kept wiping the corners of her mouth.

Stephen felt concerned for her. "What is it, Sandra? I can tell by the look on your face that something is wrong."

She leaned forward and softly asked, "Stephen, do you remember, after Don came back from Atlanta, I told you he wasn't himself?"

"Yes, I remember it very vividly."

Sandra placed her fingers on her forehead and closed her eyes for a moment. Stephen waited anxiously to hear what Sandra had to say but didn't want to pressure her. She exhaled and fixed her eyes on Stephen's.

"I don't have words to express how I feel inside. When you are married to a person as long as I have been married to Don, you know that person inside and out. You know what makes him tick. Since his return from Atlanta, Don has been like a total stranger. He vows that he doesn't like his favorite foods. The same dishes that I have fixed him for years. He spends no time with the children. He used to pray and study a lot. Now he never does. He hasn't picked up his Bible for weeks, yet he preaches and teaches like always."

Sandra paused, then continued, "When it comes to me, he is appalling. He doesn't like anything I do. At times he talks like a pagan. Most of the time, he is brutal when we make love. He has always been the most gentle man alive. Now suddenly, he treats me like trash. At times . . . well, enough said. I think I've made my point. I told him I couldn't take it any longer. He only laughed and forced me to do things that I won't even talk about."

Sandra stood and put her hand on Stephen's arm. "He would be furious if he knew I was here. If he knew what I just told you, I . . . I don't know what he would do. Please, Stephen, pray for me and my children, please."

Stephen nodded, assuring Sandra he would pray and say nothing about their conversation. "Trust me, Sandra. I can understand some of what you are talking about. I don't have a clue why he is telling lies on me either, but he is."

Victoria came to the door. "Excuse me for the interruption, Stephen, but you have a phone call."

"Who is it?"

"It's Pastor Reynolds."

Upon hearing it was Pastor Reynolds, Sandra began to tremble. Hysterically, she pleaded, "Please! Don't mention I am here, Stephen. Please."

Stephen assured Sandra that he would say nothing about her visit.

Sandra glanced at her watch and panicked. "Oh, God above! I've got to get home. Just whisper a prayer for me." Sandra took hold of Stephen's hand and managed a slight smile. "Thank you for listening, Stephen. I will pray for you as well."

Sandra released Stephen's hand and hurried toward her car.

Chapter Seventy-Five

Warrant Served

Stephen wasn't sure what to think as he watched Sandra swiftly pull away. Victoria stepped outside so Stephen could have privacy for his call. As he went inside, he could not imagine why Don Reynolds would be calling.

After picking up the phone, Stephen paused, closed his eyes, slowly raised the phone to his ear and said, "Hello."

"Stephen! This is Pastor Reynolds. I wanted to call and let you know if there is anything I can do for you, all you have to do is give me a call, and I'll be right there. Even though I must tell the truth about what I saw, I am still your pastor and friend."

Stephen was appalled. Just the sound of Don Reynolds' voice infuriated him. Without responding, Stephen hung up the phone. Victoria watched Stephen stare at the floor, saying nothing.

Victoria came inside and closed the door. "Stephen, we have only ten minutes before we head to town."

Stephen tightened his lips and nodded. "I know," he said softly.

Cordilia, Paul and Philip came into the room. Tears welled up in Stephen's eyes. They embraced and said a quick prayer. Afterward, Paul and Cordilia were on their way back to Todd's Creek.

Stephen left written instructions for Ian Jackson concerning the farm. He then turned to Philip. "Are you going to ride with us into town, Philip?"

Philip shook his head. "No. I'll wait here for Ian to come." Philip hugged Stephen and reminded him, "Don't forget the things I have told you. Go! Find your destiny, my brother."

"I hope I'll be back soon, Philip," Victoria said as she opened the screen door for Stephen.

Philip walked to the car with them. Before Stephen opened the car door, he paused and looked back at Eden's Gate. "I, too, will be back soon," Stephen said, trying to convince himself as he got into the car.

With a warm smile, Philip said, "I know you will, Stephen."

Chapter Seventy-Six
Stephen Goes to Jail

On the way into town, Stephen addressed Victoria. "I want you and Philip to get along. I know Philip and I know you. If there's going to be any trouble, it will come from you, Victoria."

Victoria glanced at Stephen and frowned. "Me! I think you, of all people, would have noticed that I am a changed woman. You've got some nerve to even suggest I would cause trouble, Stephen."

Stephen grinned. "You have changed, to some degree, since you came to Eden's Gate, but not that much. Please, behave until I can get out of jail. For heaven's sake! Jail! I can't even fathom me being in jail. My mom would have a fit."

Victoria parked the car in front of the jailhouse. Sheriff Bolton came out to meet them. "It's good to see you're a woman of your word, Miss Stanton."

Victoria stopped in front of him. "You, playing like Barney Fife, scare me. I said I would be here and I am. Try not to confuse me with the Daisy Mae of Dog Patch."

Stephen frowned. "Victoria! You just told me how much you have changed, and then you act like this."

"I am only calling it like I see it, Stephen."

Sheriff Bolton took his hat off and looked at Victoria. "I had thought of asking you out to dinner tonight, but I think I've just changed my mind."

Victoria snarled. "That's good. I don't want you cutting your wrist because of the rejection you would have gotten."

Stephen spoke up. "Victoria, go home . . . and don't bother Philip. Do you hear me?"

Victoria raised her head. "I'll check on you later, Stephen."

"Thank you, Victoria."

They watched as Victoria drove away.

"I declare, I have never seen a woman quite like her in my life," Sheriff Bolton said.

Stephen gave the sheriff a hardy "amen to that."

Sheriff Bolton took Stephen inside. "I'm sorry about having to do this, Stephen, but I have no choice."

"I know, and I appreciate you giving me the time to say goodbye to my family."

"My pleasure."

Sheriff Bolton asked Stephen to take every-thing out of his pockets, and then he put him in a cell.

"Stephen, I meant to tell you, Ginger Banks called. She said it will be tomorrow morning before she can see Judge Patton or Buddy Crisp, so you will have to make yourself comfortable for the night. I'll bring you some supper around 6:00. I need to go out for a while. Can I get you anything before I go?"

"No. It looks like the bathroom is right here beside my bed, and I don't care for anything to eat, so, I guess I'm fine."

"I'll be back shortly," Sheriff Bolton said as he opened the door. He looked toward the sky and clicked his tongue. "The way the clouds are moving in, we may get some rain tonight. By the way, I put some books on the table in case you would like to read. I included my Bible and a note pad."

"Thanks, Sheriff."

"Sure thing. I'll see you later."

Stephen's emotions were chaotic. He had never felt more alone or more afraid. He knew all the right spiritual things to do, such as falling on his knees and crying out to God, but he could do nothing. Not even a "God help me" would come out of his mouth. He tightly clutched the steel bars that restrained him. Feeling incapable of doing anything else, Stephen decided to lie down on the small, not so comfortable bed and closed his eyes. He knew if he could sleep, the hours would pass swiftly and the morning would bring Ginger Banks and release. However, he had not forgotten that Philip had said he would not be released. He hoped this would be the one time Philip would be wrong.

Chapter Seventy-Seven

The Lights Go Out

Stephen heard the stirring turbulence of thunder arousing friction in the heavens. The sound sent a cold chill through his body. Pictures of the storm that had swept through Eden's Gate, leaving a green tint on everything, flashed through his mind. Stephen sat up and frowned as the horrid taste engrossed his mouth once again, just as it did that morning.

Stephen groaned, "Lord! What is happening to me? My normal life has turned into a three-ring circus. I can't keep up with everything. My God, help me! I'm in trouble here. The kind that I have only heard about from my mom and dad. Hearing about is so different than what I feel right now. I don't feel brave. I feel scared to death! Here I am in the dark, sitting in a jail cell, charged with murder of a girl I didn't even know. Stephen lay back down on the small bed and closed his eyes. As he was drifting off to sleep, he whispered,

"Lord, please let me open my eyes and this all will be a bad dream."

Stephen abruptly opened his eyes as his bed began to vibrate. He sat up on the edge of the bed and put his hands over his ears to try and soften the deafening force of thunder. The air was so musty he could hardly catch his breath. Utter darkness occupied the jail as Stephen's eyes tried to survey the dark room, but he could see nothing. He held the bars to the cell as he called out to Sheriff Bolton. But, he really didn't expect an answer. The air conditioning wasn't working and the heat was suffocating. In the darkness, Stephen cautiously began to move toward the area where he thought he had seen a small window when he entered the cell. With his hands outstretched, he touched the wall and guided his way until a flash of lightning shone through the window only inches away. Gripping the bars of the window, Stephen squinted, trying to see anything. The downpour of huge raindrops battering the roof, sounded as though he was standing underneath a gigantic waterfall. Questions raced through his mind. *Where is Sheriff Bolton, and how long have I been asleep?*

Releasing the bars, Stephen leaned against the wall and took a deep breath, trying to dispel his overwhelming anxiety. The continuing thunderclaps had drastically shaken him.

His worry intensified as the building began to rumble. The rumble peaked with a clap of thunder that had the sound of a thousand wild horses running through an open field. His cell was illuminated from a sheet of lightning. Frantic, Stephen rushed to the front of the cell, grabbed the bars and cried out again for Sheriff Bolton.

Stephen's breath escaped him when he heard a loud deep voice shout out, "Sheriff Bolton is not here, Stephen. It is only you and me."

Numb from fear, Stephen cautiously turned to see who had spoken. Darkness prevented him from seeing anything at first. Then another flash of lightning exposed an unfamiliar man, who was standing in the corner with his arms folded. Stephen, moving only his eyes, glanced from side to side. "Who are you and how did you get into my cell?"

The man unfolded his arms and slowly walked toward Stephen. He scoffed at Stephen and adamantly said, "Iron bars cannot prevent me, Stephen. Surely, with all your wisdom, you should know better than that."

Stephen tilted his head, squinted his eye's and asked, "Are you Satan?"

A deafening laugh burst forth from the man. When he stopped laughing, he wiped his eyes. "It's evident that you think very highly of yourself to assume King Satan would give audience to you personally. Just who do you think you are, and what would give you that kind of status?"

Although his head was throbbing from fear, Stephen attempted to appear confident, "I am a son of the living God. Who is your father?"

"Stephen, Stephen. I've not come here to talk to you about the family tree, who is my father or who isn't. I have come because it would appear you have gotten yourself into an overwhelming predicament. I'm here to offer my assistance. I have inconceivable connections that are willing to relieve you of this duress. One word from me, and you could be back at Eden's Gate in thirty minutes or less."

"I don't want your help!" Stephen responded without hesitation.

The man shook his head. "I was hoping that would not be your answer. I didn't want to resort to a more drastic measure."

The man bit his lower lip and clicked his tongue. "I personally like you, Stephen. Therefore, I will give you one more chance to accept my assistance. Otherwise, you are going to see a whole different side of me."

The man put his face close to Stephen's. "Tell me, Stephen, would you like to get out of here? Before you answer, let me say this. It was tragic, what happen to Linda Scott. She was such a sweet, young girl. I would hate to hear that something like that had happened to Leann."

Stephen pushed the man's shoulders. "You better not touch Leann! Do you hear me?"

The man frowned and growled, "Does that mean your answer is 'yes' or 'no'? Remember, you can't protect anyone in this jail cell, now can you?"

Stephen shouted, "I want nothing to do with you. I rebuke you in Jesus' name. I call forth warring angels to surround Leann and her family. You have no authority over me or my family."

Stephen moved toward the man who was now backing up. Stephen put forth his hand to push the man. Upon his touch, a bolt of lightning rendered Stephen unconscious.

Chapter Seventy-Eight

You're Fired

When Victoria returned to Eden's Gate, Philip was sitting on the sofa in the living room, reading. As she entered the room, Philip closed the book. "How was Stephen when you left?" he asked.

Victoria shook her head. "Oh, he was trying to be like King Kong but was a nervous wreck. By the way, he won't be coming home tonight. I saw Sheriff Bolton at Andy's Market. He said Ginger wouldn't be able to talk to anyone until tomorrow."

Philip stood. "I know, and he won't be home tomorrow either."

Puzzled, Victoria said, "I'm not sure how I know, but I know he won't be home tomorrow or even the next day."

"You're right, Victoria, he won't."

As Philip walked by Victoria, she took hold of his arm. "I confess. I don't know how or why I know Stephen isn't coming home, but you seem to know both the how and the why. Would you mind telling me how that knowledge entered your handsome head?"

Philip looked down at the hand gripping his arm, then at Victoria. "Why are you squeezing my arm? If you would like to ask me something, you may do so without digging your fingers into my flesh."

Victoria snapped as she released her grip, "Pardon me! Do I need to call a doctor for you? Do you have a boo-boo?"

"No, I don't have a boo-boo and your sarcasm isn't warranted either. Now, to answer your question, I know because I know." Philip turned to walk away.

Victoria was furious at that answer. She rushed to catch up with him, grabbed his arm, turned him around and shouted, "That's it? You know because you know."

Calmly, Philip took Victoria's hand and pulled it loose from his arm. "That's it. Now, let me ask you a question. Why do you have such a build-up of anger to the point you feel you must grab someone as though you are challenging him to a fist fight every time you want to ask a question?"

Victoria put her nose to Philip's and screamed, "You pompous . . ."

Before she could finish, Philip put his finger to her lips and whispered, "Shhh!"

Victoria eyes connected with his. It was as if someone had shot her with a stun gun. She couldn't say or do anything. She stood numb, yet not understanding why. Every time she had looked into Philip's eyes it brought the same effect. She took a couple of steps backward and questioned softly, "Who are you?"

Philip grinned. "Why, Victoria, you know who I am . . . I'm Philip Dawson."

Victoria shook her head and adamantly argued, "No! No! I mean, who are you really? There is something about you. I can't put my finger on it right now, but I will."

"Without a doubt, you will. But, while I wait for your conclusion, I'll ask God to do something about your temper."

Ian Jackson called from the kitchen. "Hello, is anyone here?"

Victoria pushed by Philip and said, "Excuse me, I'll see what Ian wants."

Philip lifted his brows and grinned. "By all means, Miss Stanton."

Without saying hello, Victoria took a list from the table, handed it to Ian. "Here's a list of chores Stephen left for you and your band of merry men to do today. Now, why don't you get going and try to finish at least half of them?"

Ian laughed as he looked at the list. "I don't take my orders from you. Where is Stephen?"

"Stephen will be incarcerated for a few days. I'm in charge until he gets home. and you *will* take your orders from me. I wouldn't mind for my first official order to be sending you down the road without severance pay. Do I make myself clear?"

Ian didn't acknowledge Victoria's ranting. He looked past her to Philip. "Stephen has gone to jail already?"

Philip nodded. "Yes. You know what to do."

Victoria was furious that Ian paid no attention to her orders. "I am talking to you, not Philip," she snapped.

Ian took hold of her shoulders. "You have more mouth than any woman I have ever met. I want you to shut up."

He turned to walk out the door. Victoria screamed at the top of her voice, "You're fired!"

"You wish!" Ian said as he slammed shut the screen door.

Philip walked past Victoria. "I think I'm going for a long walk. I'll be back later."

"Philip, I'm going to call Grandmother Stanton and get her to have Charles bring dinner over later. I'll see that he brings enough for you."

Philip smiled. "Thank you, Victoria. I'm not sure when I'll be back, so please don't wait for me."

Puzzled, Victoria asked, "Where are you going that could possibly take that long? You don't know the area that well, do you?"

Philip didn't look back, but called out, "I'll see you later."

Victoria stomped her foot and sulked. "Why won't anybody listen to me? I'm going to take a hot bath and try to relieve some of this awful tension."

Chapter Seventy-Nine

Back to the Battle

Stephen turned his head to one side, trying to avoid the water dripping on his cheek. Feeling dazed, his body extremely sore, he attempted to raise his head, but to no avail. He tightly closed his eyes and rested his head on the damp ground for a moment. Again, Stephen attempted to sit up but could not. "Oh, God!" he groaned. "Where am I?"

He could hear what seemed to be a brook running nearby. He was immersed in a mass of damp leaves that were sticking to his clothing as though they had been glued on. He groaned as he tried to sit upright again without the support of his elbows. He was chilled from the dampness, and his ribs ached. Before he could move, Stephen felt a rumble underneath him and the deafening sound of horses' hooves pounding the ground. His heart raced. Not knowing where he was and positive he could not run, he quickly lay down, pulling the leaves over him. The horses stopped only a few feet from where he was lying. The breathless panting of the horses let Stephen know that they had been running hard, for a while. A voice filled with rage cried out, "He could not have gone far. He must be around here somewhere. Split up! Shemed wants Rakar by sundown. Blow the trumpet when you find him. Don't leave one stone unturned, or it will mean your head!"

The horses split and went in every direction. Fear gripped Stephen's mind. He knew he had to get out of this place. He pulled himself from the conglomerate of leaves while continuously asking God to help. He would have to help him. Otherwise, Stephen would be helpless. He had gone only a short distance when he heard someone coming. He tried to hide behind a large evergreen tree. His ribs hurt so badly he knew some of them must be broken. A wagon pulled up in front of the tree and stopped. An old, white-haired, black woman got down from the wagon and walked to where Stephen had squatted down to hide. Stephen's heart was pounding. The woman looked at Stephen and ordered, "Come quickly, the soldiers are right behind me."

She extended her hand to help him up. "Don't be afraid, Stephen. I have been sent to help you. Come, we must hurry."

Stephen groaned in pain as she pulled on his hand.

"When I get you to the safe place, someone will take a look at your ribs for you."

Stephen still had not spoken but listened intently to every word the woman had to say. The wagon was old, and Stephen could tell by looking that the horse looked as old as the woman. In the bed of the wagon was a wood cage filled with chickens and overlaid with mesh wire. A bale of hay sat underneath it. In the center of the wagon was a large, wood keg that had the staggering smell of whisky. In the distance, they could hear the sound of horses coming.

The woman shouted, "Quick, get under the wagon. Fast!"

Stephen dropped to the ground and pushed himself up under the wagon. "There's a door on the bottom of the keg. Get in and push your hands and feet firmly on the ends of the keg and I will close the door. I don't care how badly you hurt. Don't make a sound."

The intense pain brought tears to Stephen's eyes as he braced himself in the bottom of the keg.

"You can relax after I close the door."

Stephen moaned when she slammed shut the door and then relaxed his body to rest on it, but every muscle was rigid. He closed his eyes and held his breath when he heard the horses come to a halt at the foot of the wagon. Stephen recognized the rasping voice of the man who spoke as the same voice he had heard earlier while hiding in the leaves.

"What are you doing on this road, old woman? Did you not see the 'no trespassing' sign?" The man scoffed.

"I'm going into camp up ahead to deliver this keg of whisky."

"Deliver it to whom?"

"A sorcerer named Amash sent orders to get a keg of whisky to his camp before nightfall. Would you like to try a cup?"

"Who signed your papers to allow travel on this road? Amash, or not, you still have to have signed permission from the king, or someone in his office, to travel this road."

"Why sir, the king himself signed them."

"I want to see the papers now, and you better be telling the truth or I will skin you alive."

"Sir, I know better than to lie to you. Here are the papers. I'm sure you will find them in order."

The man looked over the papers, then quizzed, "Where do you live. I don't recall seeing you around here before?"

"I suppose I'm not one that stands out in a crowd, but I do recall seeing you many, many times."

"I did not ask if you had seen me before," he snapped. "I asked where do you live?"

"I'm sorry, I didn't mean not to acknowledge your question. I live over close to the foot of the mountain."

"We are searching for a man named Rakar. He's a general from the White Stone Kingdom. Have you heard of him or seen anyone in this section of the forest?"

"There was someone back toward the brook. A young man with black hair, but he surely did not look like a soldier. He looked like a bum to me. He was in desperate need of a bath."

"Be on your way, old woman, and tell Amash I'll be by for a drink of whisky after we catch Rakar."

"I'll be sure and tell him, sir," she said.

The soldier commanded the men to turn and go back to the brook. The old woman softly asked, "Stephen, are you all right in there?"

"Yes, I'll be okay."

"Let's get out of here and get you to the safe place. I'll try not to hit too many bumps."

Stephen thanked God for keeping him. He also remembered the soldier saying they were searching for Rakar. The same name that Dale Thomas, Jim Lee, the Armor Bearers and Machiah had called him. He felt sure he had entered the gate that would take him to the mountain again.

Chapter Eighty

Mylo Arrives

*I*n haste, the woman climbed aboard the wagon, took the reins, popped them and shouted out, "Come on, Lightning, let's get out of here!" The ride was close to unbearable for Stephen. He would have bounced all over the wagon, had he been able to move. It was a dirt road filled with craters. The ride took only ten minutes, but it seemed like a lifetime to him, as he groaned in agonizing pain. The wagon came to a sliding halt, forcing Stephen forward, hitting his head on the wooden keg and bringing him to a dazed state. He was so confused, he only remembered someone telling him they were going to open the door but to relax on a stretcher being placed underneath him. The next thing Stephen comprehended was hearing voices, one of which asked the old lady where he was found. Trying desperately to open his eyes, Stephen could barely make out the one who appeared to be the black woman who had rescued him. His ribs were sore, but the intense pain had ended. A man came close to the bed and put his hand on Stephen's shoulder, tapping lightly. "Stephen! Stephen, can you hear me?"

"Yes, I can hear you," Stephen replied softly. "Where am I?" Stephen tried to raise his head.

The man pushed lightly on Stephen's shoulder. "You're in a safe place. For now, we want you to stay in bed and get some rest."

Confused, Stephen questioned, "Where is this safe place?"

A woman stroked Stephen on his forehead. "Don't you worry about that. You will feel like a new man after you rest a while."

"Who are you?" Stephen asked.

She smiled and said, "My name is Mylo."

Stephen took hold of her hand and with deep emotion expressed, "Thank you for saving my life. I will always be indebted to you."

Mylo frowned. "Why would that be, Stephen? I did only as I was commanded. Therefore, any gratitude should be directed to our commander, the Most High. Now, go to sleep. When you awaken, there's someone very eager to see you."

Curious, Stephen asked, "Who is it?"

Mylo pulled the sheet over his arms and chuckled. "You're worse than a little kid."

Mylo bowed her head toward Stephen and whispered, "Sleep tight, Rakar."

Stephen yawned loudly, stretching his arms over his head. He quickly opened his eyes, realizing the pain in his ribs was completely gone. He sat up and looked around the room, that was not a room at all, but a large cave. He was lying on a red, wool blanket. His pillow was a folded, checked coat with a blue fleece lining.

Stephen stood and looked around the cave to see if anyone was there, but saw no one.

Dawn was breaking, allowing the mouth of the cave to be illuminated. Through rays of light, the fog gave a whitish glow. Stephen looked around the cave again and then back to the opening. Startled by someone standing amid the fog, Stephen gasped. The figure walked out of the smoky light to reveal Jim Lee's smiling face. He quickly made a fist, tapped his chest, lowered his head and with great exultation embraced Stephen. Stephen was thrilled to see his friend.

"Rakar! When I heard you were back, I could hardly wait for you to wake up. How are you, my brother?"

"I was in such pain, but now I'm fine. God is so good to us, Jim. How have you and your children been?"

"I have taken a couple of arrows, but I am fine now. The children are so excited that you are back."

"There have been so many things that have occurred since I last saw you. I don't know how or where to begin telling you."

Jim Lee put his hand on Stephen's shoulder. "I know all about the events that have taken place in your life. I'm just glad they led you back to the mountain."

Stephen soberly stared at Jim Lee but didn't bother to ask how he knew.

"We need to get out of this cave. The Armor Bearers are waiting to meet with you," Jim Lee said.

Stephen wiped his lips. "Is there a possibility of getting some food and water? My throat and lips feel as dry as the dessert sand."

"The Armor Bearers have some fresh bread in the camp. If we hurry, I'm sure you can eat your fill."

Stephen and Jim Lee exited the cave. Stephen was glancing around him, trying to find something familiar, but nothing was recognizable. "Jim, I don't recognize this place."

"Nor *will* you. We're in a different camp. We move all the time."

Again, Stephen looked around the location. "Jim! Where's the mountain?"

"You will face the mountain soon enough, but, for now, let's have some breakfast."

Chapter Eighty-One

At the Mountain

The Armor Bearers were exuberant. Great celebration was in the camp. Amid all the excitement, Stephen was searching for one he had not seen. "Jim, where's Dale Thomas?"

"He's on the mountain. I haven't seen him for two weeks. I'm beginning to worry. He always checks in, but not this time."

"Should we go look for him?" Stephen asked.

"There are many souls on the mountain. Each one is important. Each one will have to climb the mountain for himself. He's in God's hands, and I trust God to accomplish his perfect will in his life. As well as in everyone else's."

A cry came from the watch post, "A rider is coming."

The Armor Bearers dropped everything. In haste, they grabbed their swords. The rider stopped his horse in front of Stephen and Jim Lee. He tapped his chest with his fist and announced. "The enemy has sent ground troops to stop the people at the bottom level of the mountain. The enemy is marching under the banner of discouragement and oppression." He had barely finished speaking those words when he groaned and fell from his horse. Stephen rushed to see what had happened to the rider. In the back of his neck was a poison dart, shot from a close distance. Jim Lee took a trumpet and gave three distinct blasts. The Armor Bearers shouted and went in every direction. Jim Lee thrust a sword and a shield into Stephen's hands and ordered, "Come, Stephen. We must get to the foot of the mountain."

Shocked that Jim would leave one of the soldiers, Stephen shouted, "You can't just leave him here!"

Jim grabbed Stephen's arm and said, "He's dead, Stephen! Many more will die if we don't go and help defend the attack. Now come on! That's an order."

With one last look at the soldier, Stephen mounted a horse. He and Jim went in haste toward the mountain.

The noise was deafening as they made their way through a barrage of explosions and gunfire. Arrows were coming from every direction. Wounded soldiers lay all along the trail. Stephen called out, "Jim, what about these soldiers?"

"Someone will be back for them. We must get to the mountain."

Upon arrival, they dismounted and ran toward the attack. The enemy had inflicted devastating blows to the army of the Most High. Jim Lee rushed to the aid of a soldier who was surrounded by the enemy. Stephen watched in dismay as Jim Lee used the sword of TRUTH to annihilate the opposing force that attempted to bring down the warrior. Upon freeing the soldier, he and Jim Lee ran to aid another. As he watched, Stephen heard the whine of a torched arrow whistle by his head. It caused him to dodge right just as another whizzed by his left temple. The fiery sting brought the immediate realization of how closely an enflamed arrow had just missed hitting his head. Before Stephen could move, a bomb exploded in the area where Jim Lee was fighting, spraying everyone within fifty feet with shrapnel. Stephen was knocked to the ground by the blast. Recovering his senses, Stephen frantically looked for his sword. Blood from a gash on his forehead nearly blinded him. He was gripped with horror, seeing Jim Lee mortally wounded, lying only a few feet away. In his despair, Stephen screamed, "Jim! Jim!"

He had not even noticed the ugly wound in his own leg until he tried to rise. Unable to stand, he crawled to Jim's side calling on God, "Please, let Jim be alive." When he reached his friend, he saw no sign of life. Stephen wiped the blood from his face and managed to lift Jim's head, which was covered with small cuts. Stephen held Jim closely and wept aloud. "Father! Father! Why? Help me to understand why." The pain in Stephen's heart was worse than the wounds in his flesh.

Just then, an unearthly roaring noise, which grew increasingly, arrested Stephen's thoughts. He hopelessly stared toward the knoll. He knew another attack, like the one they had just suffered, would bring total defeat. He whispered, "Father, please help us. Please."

The Armor Bearers pushed forward, intent on breaking through the enemy's strongholds. Through the oppressive smell of sulfur and choking smoke, Stephen saw a ray of hope when a massive cavalry of white horses came over the knoll. He could hardly discern who the riders were until he saw the illuminated white flag carrying the crest of the Lion of the tribe of Judah. The reinforcements renewed the spirits of the Armor Bearers who were exhausted and in desperate need of rest. In only a few minutes, the aggressors had retreated. The air was deathly still, hanging like a thick blanket all about them. The horrid cries, moans and groans filled the vicinity around the foot of the mountain. Stephen sat dumfounded amid the devastation.

As far as his eyes could see, the Armor Bearers had come on the scene to assist and care for the wounded.

Stephen shouted, "I need help over here! My friend is mortally wounded."

Through the smoke, a white horse walked slowly in Stephen's direction. Blood was dripping into Stephen's eyes. He turned his head to the side, wiping blood onto his shoulder. The voice Stephen heard, as he wiped his eyes, caused him to sigh and quickly face the man standing before him. Through a cracked voice, Stephen responded, "Dale Thomas! I am so glad to see you. I fear Jim Lee is dead or dying."

Dale knelt and put his fingers on Jim Lee's neck. "He's not dead, Stephen. I feel a heartbeat."

"Thank you, God!" Stephen gasped.

Dale turned and told Mylo, "Bring a couple of people and get these men attended to."

Mylo rushed to Dale's side. She hesitated when she saw Stephen. "Rakar!" She ordered the men with her to take Jim Lee directly to the top level.

She knelt, took a cloth from the pouch on her belt and cleaned Stephen's face. "What in the world happened to you? It appears you have suffered some nasty wounds. Let me check your leg."

Stephen groaned when Mylo helped straighten his leg. "Hum, this is going to require some immediate care."

She reached into her pouch and pulled out a red stone. Red, glowing rays emanated from it. Astonishment gripped Stephen as Mylo slowly moved the stone over his wounds. She chanted, "Thank you, Jesus, for your blood that heals both body and soul."

A burning sensation shot through the wounds, causing Stephen to gasp. He felt faint as the skin miraculously knitted together and only a scar remained. Astounded, Stephen looked at Mylo, then Dale. Dale extended his hand to help him stand. Stephen put his hand on his head where the wound had been and then on his leg. He tried to speak, but there were no words to express the emotions that had welled up inside him.

Mylo patted Stephen's shoulder. "That's all right. You don't have to say anything. God knows your heart."

Dale embraced Stephen and reassured him Jim Lee would be okay.

"Enough of this! There are many warriors to treat. How about you two, giving us a helping hand."

Chapter Eighty-Two
Battle Rages

$\mathcal{E}$veryone worked late into the night. A watchman was posted around the wounded. Stephen and the Armor Bearers made camp close by in case the enemy would try another attack before morning. All the Armor Bearers gathered and recounted the events of the day. Their prayerful thanks for being alive came with sober remembrance of their fallen brothers. As they stood in silence, a message was delivered to Stephen. Jim Lee wanted to see him. Stephen looked at Dale, awaiting permission. Dale grinned and nodded. Stephen went in haste.

Upon entering the cave, Stephen was surprised to see Jim Lee sitting up, with his face basically free from the cuts he had received.

"Jim!" Stephen whispered in exhilaration.

Joining hands, they worshipped the Most High for His faithfulness in keeping and healing them. After a brief visit, Stephen said goodnight and

393

headed back to camp. He stood on the knoll looking toward the campfire, but his heart drew him to a high crest that gave a clear view of the mountain. Stephen gazed at the mountain illuminated by the shimmering glow of the perfectly rounded moon.

The high pitched whine of the wind sweeping through the enormous evergreens was the only sound Stephen could hear. No explosions, no horses' hooves pounding the earth and no fiery arrows to bring another warrior down. He gently touched the scar on his forehead. The reality of his brush with death was sobering. A greater reality was that many had died today. Stephen propped his elbows on his knees and lowered his head, groaning as his heart broke for the ones who had died fighting for the mountain before him. The memory of how helpless he felt in the battle left him gasping for breath.

The piercing cry of the wind had intensified even more. Dark clouds were beginning to gather and skirt about the bright radiance of the moon. As the shadows deepened, so did the jumbled mess of confusion that Stephen had been harboring the past few months.

Progressively, an unfamiliar feeling grew inside him. He became conscious of a figure watching him closely. Through narrow eyes he tried to make out who it was. Then, the dark shadow settled down beside him. Something deep was stirred within Stephen by this figure. Without thinking, Stephen asked the same question to the figure that stood by his side that Joshua had asked thousands of years before. "Are you for us or against us?"

Without hesitation the man replied, "I am for the Most High God and the White Stone Kingdom; therefore, I am with you."

Recognizing the voice, Stephen quickly turned to view Machiah. "It's so good to see you," Stephen whispered softly.

Machiah placed his hand on Stephen's arm and confirmed the feeling was mutual.

Stephen's smile faded fast. He stared at Machiah in stony silence.

Reading his thoughts, Machiah said, "Ask me the question that is burning in your soul, Stephen."

Unable to wrestle with his fears any longer, Stephen said, "Who are you really? Are you real or some dead spirit roaming around? Is all this a figment of my imagination? Have I lost my mind? Do I belong here looking at a mountain I don't understand at all, or do I belong at Eden's Gate? Not to mention being in some suffocating jail cell in Calvin's Point for a murder I know nothing about. One thing I do know for sure is I don't belong in a jail cell." Stephen threw up his hands in exasperation. "I need to know why so many died today and yet

I could live. I should have died from the loss of blood alone. Nevertheless, here I am with no sign of weakness, nor did the enormous gashes in my head and leg even require stitches. Am I of more worth then those who didn't make it? If Jim Lee and I could be healed, why weren't *all* the warriors healed?"

Stephen fought to regain control of the emotions in his voice and spoke his next words barely above a whisper. "If God is no respecter of persons, how can He allow this to happen to all the soldiers that are called by His name? How?"

Machiah took a deep breath. "Stephen, have you forgotten what you were allowed to see in the arena? You saw how Shemed challenged King Rayon for your soul. With that challenge, *Eden's Gate* was opened. From that day the battle began for you. The warriors that died today have finished their battles. They fought well and were given the honor of martyrdom. Therefore, a greater reward was bestowed upon them. To be martyred is the ultimate sacrifice for not only White Stone Kingdom, but for the Crystal Kingdom. They died that others may live as our King died that we may live. Stephen, there are times you cannot trust your own heart. You can be deceived by those emotions. Your feelings will pull you in a hundred different directions. Soon, so many voices will be telling you what to think and feel, you won't know which one to trust. When your feelings cease to exist and you need something strong, something that won't move out from underneath you, you must turn to your faith, not your feelings. To serve in this army, it is imperative that you have total faith in our commander King Rayon. To answer your questions, no, you have not lost your mind. You're exactly where you are supposed to be at this time."

Confused, Stephen asked, "Then tell me, what is the purpose of allowing me to be charged with Linda Scott's murder? I didn't do it!"

Machiah stood. "Let's go for a walk, Stephen."

Stephen hesitated, then stood. "Where are we going?" he asked, dusting off the seat of his pants.

"You will see. Come, walk with me."

Machiah swiftly walked into the forest laden with towering evergreens.

Stephen hastened to keep up. At times the pace was so rapid, Stephen had to run to keep sight of Machiah. Panting, Stephen shouted, "Machiah, slow down!"

Instantly, Machiah halted. Stephen leaned forward, placing his hands on his knees and gasped for air. Machiah walked slowly back to Stephen. Stephen looked up and asked, "What are you trying to do, kill me?"

Machiah sternly replied, "No, Stephen, but if you don't keep up, you will kill yourself."

Breathing easier, Stephen straightened his posture. "Just what do you mean by that?"

"I mean this is not a time to move like a snail. It's imperative that you move with the speed of light."

Angered, Stephen shouted, "I'm not a supernatural being! I'm flesh and blood. I can't appear and disappear with the fog, like you do."

"Did you not question me concerning the battle that took place at the foot of the mountain today?"

Puzzled, Stephen nodded. "Yes, I asked, but what has that got to do with you sprinting through a forest that is so dark, I have to guess where I'm putting my feet. Then you have the nerve to rebuke me because I can't keep up."

Machiah tightened his jaw as he looked into Stephen's eyes. "There's a final attack that is coming soon. The people at the base of the mountain will not be able to stand if they don't have leaders. They struggle repeatedly until hopelessness overtakes them. The greater battle is not physical, but mental. Queen Jewel will use her magic to destroy the mind, but Jewel is a liar! People can make it to the top of the mountain, but only if leaders make it to the top and return to show them the way. You saw only some of the battle today. It's obvious the attack is doomed before it ever begins. It should also be obvious by now that the mountain has never been, or never will be, an easy quest. Without competent leaders, the people will never stop the enemy. Thus, they will die at the foot of the mountain without ever knowing the glory of reaching the pinnacle. This is not a game, Stephen! You are a chosen vessel. You have no choices. Your destiny has been set. You need to allow your heart and soul to grasp that fact."

Overwhelmed, Stephen said, "My mom told me about the chosen vessels."

Machiah placed his hand on Stephen's shoulder. "I'm sure Rachel told you that she too was a chosen vessel. We need go now. There's a place we must visit before you return to the camp. Are you ready, Stephen?"

Stephen nodded. "Yes, I am ready."

Without looking back, Machiah asked, "Are you passionate about being ready?"

"Yes . . . yes, I am ready."

Looking forward, Machiah said, "Yes, you are ready, Stephen."

Chapter Eighty-Three
Summoned to Eden

The darkness had consumed the light of the moon, and dampness from the fog was growing. Stephen slowed from sprinting to a fast-paced walk. His lungs burned like fire from overexertion. Endeavoring to catch his breath was a challenge. He panicked when he realized Machiah was too far ahead for him to catch up. He wanted to sit down but couldn't see to do so. Stephen wiped the mounting fog from his face. Instantly, there was such an acute silence that Stephen swallowed so hard it hurt. Instantaneously, the blast of many trumpets sounded. At once, the earth shook from footsteps that hurried past him. The enormity of power that passed caused Stephen to bury his face in his hands.

In a voice of authority, Machiah said, "Come on, Stephen! We have been summoned to the garden."

Immediately, Stephen stood. "The garden?"

"Stephen, we don't have time for questions now. We must hurry." Machiah waved his hand in front of Stephen, and immediately their garments became white linen tunics, with wide gold belts. The trumpets continued to blast, and the earth shook as if a massive earthquake was consuming it. Stephen and Machiah moved with the force of the crowd. Stephen's energy was totally depleted from trying to keep up with Machiah. Out of breath and irritated, Stephen shouted, "Where are we going?"

Machiah stopped and shook his head. Without looking at Stephen. he said, "We have been summoned to Eden."

Stephen looked down and then up. "The Garden of Eden?"

Machiah took hold of his arm and pulled him. "Come on, Stephen. We can't be late."

They continued to race toward the garden. Suddenly, Stephen halted unexpectedly. He trembled like a frightened child. Instantly, the darkness gave way to light. Before him was an enormous, foreboding door over which was written: "Forum of Justice." Dread and uncertainty gripped Stephen as he looked at the door.

Machiah insisted that he hurry inside, but Stephen didn't want to enter the door.

"Machiah! What is wrong with me?" Stephen said. "I feel paralyzed."

401

"The fear you feel now is the result of great truth God is about to reveal to you. Now, open the door, Stephen, and go through."

Stephen nervously placed his hand over his mouth as he stared at the door. He swallowed so hard he gulped. As Stephen's trembling fingers touched the doorknob, a gale force wind thrust the door open from Stephen's hand.

Inside the great hall, the crowd was too numerous to count. The blasts of the trumpets ended and silence fell. After a moment, a single trumpet sounded long and hard. At once, the ground quaked and radiant beams of light illuminated the area. The sky was pulled back like a theater curtain, revealing unimaginable grandeur. Stephen shivered at the magnitude of what he saw. Dimensions shattered, revealing everything in the universe. He gasped when he saw the thrones with the Ancients seated upon them. Above them he observed the seven spirits of God, with their hands clasped together rotating in a circle. They stood with their backs facing the inner circle and their faces were set forward to constantly view everything in creation. Stephen witnessed the throne of the Most High God above the seven spirits. In a tight circle around the throne were the Ancient Ones standing at attention. Their musical composition consisted of few words. In unison they sang:

"HOLY, HOLY, HOLY IS THE
LORD GOD ALMIGHTY."

In a thunderous resound, everyone joined the Ancients in song. For a moment, the breath went out of Stephen's lungs, and he could only stare.

Over the throne was a massive rainbow with radiant colors filled the air. Behind the rainbow, underneath the throne of the Most High, a gentle radiance of emerald green gleamed forth, sending shafts of lights in dazzling beams across the floor. The Ancients' thrones sat on both sides of the hall that was centered in the midst of Eden. The seven spirits of the Most High moved to the center of the hall and rotated constantly . . . above everything. The throne of the Most High came to rest between, yet above the Ancients'. A shout of praise froze in Stephen's throat when the Most High stood. Intense silence filled the universe. The Most High's eyes of fire examined everything. Shattering the silence with a groaning cry that shook the world, the Most High wailed, "Acor! Acor! Where art thou?"

Stephen put his hands over his ears to ease the thunderous voice that felt as though it was puncturing his eardrums. For an instant, he remembered what Victoria told them about the throne and the Ancients in the garden. With that in mind, he observed everything in sight, including the gigantic beings that had filled the garden.

Chapter Eighty-Four

The Trial

Again, the Most High wailed "Acor!" Everyone stared as a man and woman slowly emerged from among the crowd and moved toward the center of the garden. Their heads were lowered and their chins were pressed against their chests. Their hands were clasped together over the fig leaves that covered their loins.

Breathlessly, Stephen whispered, "Is that . . .?"

"Yes, Stephen. That is Acor and Hannah."

Acor and Hannah went sluggishly toward the throne. God stood and roared, "Jewel! Jewel!"

From the midst of the beings, a clamor evolved. Stephen watched as a stunning woman arrayed in a black, flowing gown. A gold crown laced with rubies sat atop her raven black hair. In arrogance, she marched from amid the other beings and halted at the foot of the throne beside Acor and Hannah. God's heart was broken as He looked at His son and daughter whom He had carefully formed. God lovingly, yet firmly asked, "What jurisdiction did you come from, Acor? Why would you come from someone else's territory into mine? You are my son, Acor, so tell me, why you were in another's region? Tell me, Acor, why is your head lowered? Can you not look into the face of your Father?"

Acor raised his head and without looking at his Father's face, replied, "I heard your voice and I was afraid."

"Why would you be fearful of me, Acor?"

"I . . . I clearly heard the call for an assemblage. Your breathing was cool and filled with anger; therefore, I was afraid."

The Most High slowly shook His head. "What is the reason you would fear coming into my presence? I have always given you entrance, and you have never been afraid. So, why were you afraid this time?"

"My mantel had been torn; therefore, I had no covering. I was troubled to come before you naked, so I hid myself."

"Who told you that you were naked, and why is only one area of your body covered? With fig leaves? If you considered yourself to be naked, why did you not cover your whole body?

"I Am the Vine; you are the branches." What is the shoot you have inserted into the branch? Those leaves are not from *my* family tree. Have you severed yourself from me and stitched yourself to a family tree that is cursed? Have you entered the strange fire and allowed yourself to be engulfed with its doom?"

Acor pointed to Hannah. "Queen Hannah's beauty overpowered me. She stirred feelings inside me that I had never encountered."

God roared, "Don't you dare lie to me!"

Hannah lowered her head and tears filled her eyes. "Father, I take full blame for what happened. I should have never listened to Acor. I should have rebuked him and come to you. I entered the Garden of Fire and went with Acor into the flames, and now I carry his child. I'm so sorry that I've hurt you. Will you forgive me?"

God touched Hannah's shoulder and pro-claimed, "Queen Hannah, I do forgive you. Later you will reign with Me again. For now, you must face many hard times because of your choice to enter the forbidden flame."

God's anger blazed as He turned to Jewel. "Jewel, because you have used the deep magic to lure my children away from me, you will never again ascend to the grandeur of the position that you once held in my court. Your evil has leveled your position in my kingdom. Your devious ways have worn smooth the stones of your breastplate. I enlarged you in my kingdom, now I curse you and drive you from my kingdom, you daughter of perdition.

Your evil will devour you. I will bring you to ashes, and you will never be remembered."

Jewel smugly spoke, "I told you that if you would take the hedge down, they would crown me as their god, and I was right. A little temptation and your queen eagerly fell prey, and now she carries your fallen high priest's seed."

The Most High stood and shouted, "Enough!" He raised His right hand and proclaimed, "I call the Forum of Justice and the three heavens as witnesses this day for the judgment that I will declare against you, Jewel. There will be warfare, and you will not win!"

The Most High sadly faced Acor. "Acor, why did you not listen to me? And because you came before me with an unrepentant heart, you will never return to your place as high priest. You, like the leader you chose, will be consumed from within and it will be as though you never existed. Your name will be blotted out of the ancient book."

The Most High faced Jewel and ordered, "Depart from Me!"

Jewel jeered, "I will sit on your throne, and your people will worship me."

Jewel swiftly turned and disappeared into the field. God faced the Ancients and the seven spirits. Then, He faced Acor and Hannah. "The battle has truly begun. Go from me, and when the appointed time comes, I will call you back before my throne. Hannah, I want you to know that your son shall be among the great warriors for the White Stone Kingdom.

The Most High then faced the ones gathered in the great arena. "Today, the war to set the people in the dark valley free will be full blown. The red eagle guards and the brown eagle foot soldiers will be sent to the battle under the command of The Ancient Eagle warrior that has warred for the White Stone Kingdom since the Beginning, General Raptor.

After the Most High had spoken those words, line after line of red and brown eagles marched into the courtroom. Stephen gasped when again he saw the giant seven-foot eagle emerge, raise his massive wings and his white head and scream a scream that shook the heavens. In unison the eagles flapped their wings and disappeared from the theater. The Most High had only to think it . . . and King Rayon and Haleb were standing before him. Haleb bowed on his knees and lowered his head. King Rayon took the sword from his side and handed it to the Most High. The Most High touched the sword to Haleb's head and said, "Haleb, true and faithful one, go to the mountain and minister to and support the Amour Bearers."

"Yes, my God."

Through saddened eyes, the Most High looked at Acor and Hannah and ordered, "Depart from me."

The red eagle guard took Acor and Hannah by their arms and escorted them through the gate. One of the Ancient Ones closed the gate, and instantly the gate was ablaze with an unquenchable fire. They could not enter the gate again unless permission was given by the Most High.

The arena rumbled as the crowd of witnesses exploded with an ovation of praise.

The Most High raised his hand, and massive sheets of lightning and thunderclaps shook the universe. The severity of the light forced Stephen to bury his face in his hands. The wind force was as if a tornado was passing over him. When the rumbling ceased, the untamed wind turned viciously cold. Stephen cautiously removed his hands from his face. In a panic, he scanned the region. The force of the wind pounded sand against Stephen's skin. Rubbing his eyes, Stephen shouted, "Machiah! Where are you? Machiah!"

Chapter Eighty-Five
Finding His Way

Stephen couldn't tell where he was, but he knew he was no longer in the garden. He put his hand in front of his face to shield his eyes from the sand. In only a few moments, the sand diminished. As the cold wind went through his thin shirt, Stephen chilled. He rubbed his arms and gazed upward at the scudding clouds that were a deep shade of gray. Exhausted from following Machiah and from the freezing cold that started abruptly and from sheer exhilaration of spirit and soul, Stephen began to shiver uncontrollably. He thought of the indescribable scenes he had experienced in the Garden of Eden. Everything seemed unreal except the bitter cold that lashed against his skin. Stephen tried to move but was so cold every muscle in his body had tightened to the point he couldn't. Lowering his head, he whispered, "Father, help me." Immediately, the wind began to subside until there was total calm. Stephen could tell by the gigantic evergreens that he was back in the forest where he and Machiah began their walk. However, Machiah was not with him. Stephen's scream pierced the silence of the forest as he yelled, "Machiah! Where are you?"

It was almost dark, and Stephen knew he had to do something. At least the furious wind had ended and there was still enough light to try and find his way back to the entrance of the forest. He moved cautiously, yet swiftly, through the trees, calling for Machiah. He walked for what seemed like hours only to end up back where he had started. "My God above!" he cried. "I've been going in a circle."

The temperature had begun to drop even more as daylight had totally dimmed. In the dark, fatigued, hungry and freezing, Stephen knew he must find shelter. Squinting, Stephen looked around the area. He thought he saw something. As he slowly walked toward it, he recognized a welcomed embankment holding a good-sized rock cliff. Only the scanty rays, from the half-moon allowed Stephen enough light to determine when he was under the large rock. Before he sat down, he called out once again to Machiah, to no avail.

Stephen sat and scooted backward until his back rested against rugged rocks. He leaned his head against the rock formation and closed his eyes, reflecting on the awesome events that had been revealed to him from the garden. At once, he opened his eyes as his head nodded. Stephen didn't want to fall into a sound sleep in his unpleasant surroundings. Listening to the night sounds of the forest began to calm his anxiety.

"Oh, Father . . ." Stephen wanted to pray, but a prayer would not form as words escaped him. He bowed his head and wept aloud. After all the excitement of the spiritual events that had taken place earlier in the day, Stephen was suddenly overwhelmed with loneliness. He had never felt so alone. Why had Machiah left him alone in the dark in a strange place? Stephen was also having to fight his emotions that were telling him that maybe God had left him, too. How could it be: one minute he would shiver from the awesome presence of God, as he did in the garden. In the next breath, he would be sitting under a rock cliff in utter darkness. At this point, all Stephen wanted to do was go home. Dealing with Victoria when she first arrived at Eden's Gate was a piece of cake compared to being in a petrifying, dark domain.

Chapter Eighty-Six

Remember the Threat

Stephen had not intended to sleep, only to lay his head back and rest his eyes. However, he was startled out of a sound sleep, by twigs breaking. Stephen stood, praying it was Machiah. He walked forward and quietly called out, "Machiah, is that you?"

Stephen licked his lips and turned in a circle trying to see what had broken the twigs, but the darkness prevented that. He froze, when he heard a low growl. "Oh, God, help me!" he whispered in terror.

His blood chilled when he looked up to see two red eyes in front of him. In the background were many more red eyes. With agonizing care, Stephen stepped back slowly, wanting to turn and run through the rock cliff. Tentatively, he inched backward. With each step, the shadowy figures with blazing red eyes advanced clandestinely toward him.

Stephen's pulse raced when a glowing yellow and orange light surrounded the being in front of him. He was tall with bleached skin. His long, black hair was saturated with silver streaks. His eyes were red and his teeth were like that of a lion. His laughter echoed through the trees as he questioned, "What are you going to do, cut a path through solid rock, Stephen?"

His voice raised the hair on Stephen's neck. He recognized the voice as the same voice heard in the jail cell, but the appearance was shockingly different.

The being moved closer toward him. Stephen's back was against the rocks. He could go no further. The creature put his face close to Stephen's and stared directly into his eyes. The strange being's hands were that of a man, but the fingernails were like animal claws. He pressed his long finger against Stephen's cheek and chided, "It's not safe for a little boy like you to be in the forest alone on such a dark night."

With those chilling words, he pulled his claw down Stephen's cheek, cutting into the skin. Stephen groaned in pain and placed his hand on his face, which was now covered in blood. Panicked, he questioned, "Who are you and what do you want with me?"

The being smiled, showing his teeth, which resembled his claws. "That's the question I wanted you to ask. Of course, who I am is not important to you, but what I *want* is very important. I can still have you back at Eden's Gate in only a moment's notice or have you put in the electric chair for the death of Linda Scott. The choice is yours."

Stephen tightened his lips. "I told you before, I will not surrender to you or your offers."

The being motioned for a couple of men to come forth. Stephen trembled, knowing their intent was to hurt or maybe kill him. In his mind, he called on God to deliver him, whether in death or from his dilemma.

One of the men asked, "What should we do to him, Shemed?"

A sudden cold gripped Stephen's soul. So, this was the man, wearing another disguise, who his mother had warned him about. Stunned, Stephen whispered, "You're Shemed?"

Shemed scoffed, "Oh, Stephen knows who I am. I'm sure your wretched mother and Cordilia warned you about me. I think they would be disappointed in your stupidity. Where is all your help, Stephen? You're out here alone in the darkness. It would appear you have been forsaken."

Calmly, Stephen responded, "The Most High would never abandon me . . . the way you abandoned Him."

In a rage, Shemed yelled, "Silence! I am through playing. Need I remind you that Leann is all alone?"

Stephen fell silent as he remembered the threat Shemed made in the jail cell.

Shemed grinned. "It's good to see you remember."

"What do you want from me? You make threats, but you never make clear what it is you want."

Shemed raised his head and sighed. "Ah, I think I finally have your attention."

Shemed nodded for the two men to restrain Stephen. They grabbed him and pushed him against the rocks. Stephen groaned in pain and shouted, "What is it you want? Tell me!"

Shemed put his face close to Stephen's and growled, "I want you to kill Victoria."

"What?"

"You heard me. You kill her, or I will slowly kill Leann. It's that simple, Stephen."

Shocked by the request, Stephen sighed. "But . . . but why Victoria? What is she to you?"

Furious, Shemed turned away from Stephen and snapped, "I don't have to explain myself, or my reasons, to you. Your trial is scheduled in two weeks. I will see that you make bail. I will also see that you are cleared of all charges . . . if you cooperate. One week after the trial, which will be a short one, I want her dead!"

Shemed faced Stephen. "Are my terms clear to you?" he asked.

He grabbed Stephen's face in his hand and snarled, "You kill Victoria or I'll savagely kill Leann. As they say, 'The ball is in your court.'"

Trying to grasp what had been said to him, Stephen shook his head. "I can't kill Victoria!"

"Come on, Stephen. It's not that big of a deal." Shemed sighed, raised his brows and said, "Ah yes, I know what's wrong with you. You're worried about going to jail for Victoria's murder. Don't let that trouble you. Someone else will take the fall. I'll see to that. I'm good at that, you know. You can kill her fast or you can skin her alive, it makes no difference to me. Just do it!" Shemed turned to walk away, then turned back and in a low growl said, "If you tell anyone about our conversation, I will not only kill Leann, but will sever your head from your shoulders." With those chilling words, Shemed disappeared into the darkness.

The men who were holding Stephen pushed him away from the rocks. Quickly, several of them formed a circle around Stephen. They pushed him from one to another. Stephen fell to the ground. His hand seized a stick and he came up, swinging furiously and screaming at the top of his lungs. Without warning, Stephen felt an agonizing blow to his lower back that knocked him to his knees, then another blow to the back of his head. Stephen remembered hearing a blood-curdling howl nearby, which rumbled through the chilled darkness. Then another long wail sounded closer. Stephen couldn't move, and everything was blurry. At once a loud cry pierced the darkness, followed by a dreadful rumble of yells and metal clanging. Stephen's eyes closed, just as he felt someone lift him into their arms.

Eighty-Seven

Stephen Cried with Friends

$\mathcal{B}$efore Stephen could open his eyes, he smelled the rich aroma of freshly brewed coffee. He groaned from the pulsating pain that throbbed in the back of his head. Sluggishly, his eyes opened, but his focus was too obscured to determine the identity of the three figures looking down at him. A woman put her hand on his cheek and called his name. Stephen recognized the voice as that of Mylo.

She leaned close to Stephen. "How are you doing, my brother? We're going to have to stop meeting like this. Looks like you've taken a nasty blow to the back of your head. It must be pounding, and your face is also a mess."

Stephen could now hear, and his eyes were beginning to focus. He opened his mouth, but the words would not come forth. He felt relieved, sensing the fact that he was back in the camp with the Armor Bearers. He felt better still to recognize that the men standing with Mylo were Jim Lee and Dale Thomas. Dale and Jim Lee moved closer to Stephen and smiled. Stephen managed a slight grin, but only for a second. He tightened his lips and closed his eyes as his chin began to quiver. Taking short breaths, he groaned and the tears flowed freely. Jim Lee and Dale put their hand on Stephen's shoulder and cried with him and for him. Mylo prayed, wiped her eyes and said, "Ok, Stephen, it's time to make you feel better."

Mylo unzipped the pouch that hugged tightly around her waist and took a red stone from it. She had Stephen lie down and close his eyes. She closed her eyes and smiled as she moved the stone slowly over Stephen's head and all the way to his feet. His body burned like fire as she moved the stone over it. He could feel the pain diminish, but he continued lie as still as a dead man. Mylo put the stone back into her pouch and shouted, "Praise be to the Most High!" She took hold of Stephen's hand and raised him up. "Come on, Stephen. Let's get you a cup of coffee and something to eat."

Baffled, Stephen touched his cheek. "Come now, Stephen, you surely didn't think our king would leave your pretty face scared, did you?"

Stephen's countenance was seized with worry. Jim Lee put his arm around Stephen's shoulder.

"It's okay, Stephen, you're safe now. You went through some pretty hard things in the forest."

Confused, Stephen asked, "Who brought me here?"

Dale spoke up, "We'll discuss that, after you eat. Right now, you need nourishment."

Stephen exited the cave with Dale, Mylo and Jim Lee. When he emerged, he couldn't believe what he saw. There were Armor Bearers as far as his eyes could see. He looked at Dale, then back at the accumulation of warriors. Each one put his right fist over his heart and lowered his head. A thunderous shout exploded from the camp. Every voice, in unison, shouted, "Rakar! Rakar! Rakar!"

Stephen faced Dale. "What is this?"

"This is an army that has been waiting for their leader for a very long time."

Jim Lee brought a cup of coffee and a basket of hot bread. "Come, Stephen, let's eat together."

As the three men sat down to eat, Dale and Jim Lee noticed Stephen was unusually quiet, and his eyes were focused straight ahead.

"What has captured your thoughts to such a degree?" Dale asked.

Stephen sighed. "The simplicity of my life at Todd's Creek. I knew from day to day what was going to take place. Now, I don't know what's going to take place from second to second. God forbid that I try to plan a full day. My mother and Cordilia would thrive on this sort of thing, but I am not like them. On top of everything else, I've turned into a crybaby. I don't know if I am coming or going. I have been beat half to death. I have watched men and women die over a mountain I really know nothing about. And, if that's not enough . . ."

Stephen paused and lowered his head. Jim Lee assured Stephen that they understood how he felt, but he didn't understand how they could. Jim Lee explained, "We, too, had to come to the place that you are now, Stephen. It was just as confusing to us, but I clearly see that there is more bothering you than you are sharing at this time."

In disgust, Stephen questioned, "Where is Machiah? He abandoned me, leaving me prey to Shemed. I called and called, and he wouldn't even answer me."

Dale spoke up, "You're wrong about Machiah, Stephen. Machiah carried you to our camp."

Irritated, Stephen snapped, "Sure, after I'm beat half to death and threatened if I don't . . . All I know is, if you can't depend on someone in a time of trouble, what good is he? When things are going great, you don't need that person's help."

"What did Shemed threaten you with?" Jim Lee asked.

Stephen stood without answering and walked toward the cave. "I'm really very tired. I just want to rest for a while."

Dale and Jim Lee watched as Stephen disappeared into the cave.

Dale looked across the camp and whispered, "Jim, it's time for Stephen to take a short trip to Todd's Creek."

Jim smiled and agreed. Dale raised his hand toward the mouth of the cave and quickly pulled it down. "Enjoy the trip, Stephen." Dale said.

Eighty-Eight

Back Home

Stephen lay down and pulled the blanket tight around his neck. As soon as he closed his eyes, he could smell his mother's perfume. Faintly, he heard someone call out, "Stephen, you be home in one hour. No later." Stephen was afraid to open his eyes. He wasn't dreaming. He had closed his eyes-only seconds ago. Again, he heard a familiar voice. "Stephen, come sit with me in the porch swing."

At once, Stephen opened his eyes and breathed heavily. "Daddy . . . Daddy?"

He trembled when he saw he was lying in his mom and dad's dark cherry poster bed. He got up and moved to the antique cherry dresser. He glided his fingers across the edge of the dresser. Pulling the curtains back, he looked out over the lawn and the many flowers his mother had planted. As he opened the closet door, he saw his dad's favorite jacket. Taking it from the hanger, he held it tightly against his chest. He gently stroked his mom's favorite dress. In his mind, he could see her in this bright yellow dress with a wide black belt and elegant white lace collar. Stephen took the dress from the hanger and held it to his face. He could still smell the sweet fragrance of her perfume that lingered on the dress. He carried both the jacket and dress through the house, holding them tightly as a child might clutch a security blanket.

Stephen walked outside and went into the barn. Rays of sunlight came through the cracks in the loft. Startled by the voice of a child, Stephen turned and faced the platform his dad put together for him, as a stage when he was a young boy. In the corner, at the end of the stage, was a small worn-out table Rachel had given him and Philip to use. They would color, write or have lunch at that table. Stephen put the jacket and dress over his shoulder and moved the table to the center of the stage. He envisioned Phillip standing and prophesying to the imaginary congregation. Smiling, he took hold of the sides of the table and shouted out, "There's no one like the Most High God!" He remembered the countless times he would preach and Philip would give a hardy "Amen." Stephen remembered vividly his conversation with Rachel when he told her he had received the call to preach. Standing at the table, he had said the words aloud.

"Mom, even as a child, I would pretend to be a preacher. I dreamt of preaching. Being a minister is a part of my life that I could never get away from, nor did I want to. Many times Philip and I played in the barn, and we would see angels. One time, I heard them talking. It was as though they had gathered in the barn to hear me preach. Philip was never afraid of them. He boldly talked to them. I, on the other hand, ended up shaking in my shoes. I don't think Philip was afraid of anything."

Stephen gripped the sides of the table, leaned his head backward and rested it on his shoulders. He closed his eyes and absorbed the words he had just spoken. His soul tingled and the Holy Spirit renewed those words in his heart. He knelt and sought God for direction and strength, and thanked Him for allowing this special time of renewing. When Stephen opened his eyes, he was astounded. The barn was again filled with angels. He lost his breath, as he held tightly to the jacket and dress. A very distinct angel came out from the assemblage. Stephen stood unafraid and greeted him with a smile. "Haleb."

"It's good to see that you have refreshed your spirit with the words of your destiny. Stephen you can cherish your memories, but you can't live there. John's jacket and Rachel's dress are empty. The house is empty. Though filled with memories, they are only memories."

Haleb placed his hand on Stephen's shoulder and warned, "You have some serious battles ahead of you, but 'no weapon formed against you shall prosper.' Don't fear, Stephen, I'll be with you as well when you take the mountain. It's time for you to go back to Calvin's Point. God's speed, my brother."

Haleb and the other angels were gone. Stephen hugged and smelled the jacket and dress one last time. He carefully folded them, placed them on the table and walked away. After putting his hand on the door, he turned one last time to view the place he cherished. When he pushed the door open, a blinding light shone on him. Pausing a moment and holding his hand in front of his eyes, he let them adjust to the dimly lit room, only to reveal the small jail cell at Calvin's Point.

Stephen stretched out on the bunk and contemplated all that had taken place. In a short time, Sheriff Bolton entered the door with a covered plate and a glass jar filled with ice tea. Stephen stood and walked to the bars.

"Howdy, Stephen. I'm sure glad that storm passed. I would have been back sooner, but something came up that took longer than I thought it would."

Sheriff Bolton gave Stephen the plate and poured him a glass of tea. Stephen wondered how long he had been gone this time.

"Sheriff, what time is it?"

"It's six p.m. I'll hang the clock over where you can see it, if you like."

"Thanks, I would appreciate that." Stephen frowned and asked, "Sheriff?"

He looked at Stephen. "What's on your mind?" he asked.

Stephen stuttered, "I-I know this may sound crazy to you, but please bear with me."

Sheriff Bolton lifted his brows. "Well, you've got my attention."

"How . . . how long have I been in jail?"

Sheriff Bolton laughed. "It may seem like a life time, but it's been only six hours."

Eighty-Nine
Questions

Stephen slept like a baby through the night. He awoke when Sheriff Bolton called out his name.

"Stephen! Wake up. You've got company."

Stephen quickly stood and ran fingers through his disarrayed hair. The sleep had refreshed him. Sheriff Bolton opened the cell door for Stephen. He and Ginger Banks sat at a table.

Ginger again listened to Stephen's story. She exhaled and remarked, "I knew it! I had hoped you would come up with something different after a night's sleep. The trial is scheduled in two weeks, and I pray a lightning bolt, or something, will jolt your memory to anything a bit more believable."

Remembering, Shemed too had said the trial would be in two weeks. "Are you sure it's in two weeks?" Stephen asked.

"I'm afraid so. I told the judge it wasn't enough time, but he could have cared less."

"Ginger?"

"Yes."

"Where is Leann?"

"She'll be here as soon as I get through. And unless you want to change your story, I'm through."

"I've told you the truth. Why would I want to change it?"

Ginger put her papers into her briefcase and closed it. "Stephen, I am going to try and get you out of here this morning. However, I want to be up front with you. Judge Patton is not known for leniency, especially in murder cases. He's never allowed bail in a murder case. Nevertheless, I'll call right now and see what the good judge has to say. I'll be right back."

Ginger returned with a puzzled look.

"What is it?" Stephen asked.

"I've never known Judge Patton to let a person out on his own merit . . . under any circumstances. Something doesn't make sense. He didn't ask me anything. He just said to let you sign the papers, and you can go home."

Stephen was happy, yet uneasy recalling this was what Shemed said would happen.

Ginger gave Stephen a ride home and promised to tell Leann to come over. Victoria saw Ginger and Stephen pull through the gate. Surprised, she called out "Philip! Stephen's home."

Philip hurried to the door, looked at Victoria and questioned, "How could this be? The Holy Spirit said he wouldn't be home for several days."

"I know. I must have been wrong. How could that be that he is coming home so soon?"

"If you're wrong, so am I. Let's go find out what happened," Philip said.

Victoria and Philip hurried out to greet Stephen. They were excited, yet puzzled. After waving goodbye to Ginger, they hurried inside.

Victoria put her hands on her hips. "You certainly have a way of making a beautiful woman feel wanted, hurrying home like this. On the other hand, I might think you didn't trust me enough to run Eden's Gate for one day. Ian's heart will be broken. But, it's good to have you back. I'm sure I would have fired him by the end of the week."

Stephen grinned. "Victoria, I am so glad to be home. And, I can assure you, it's not because I thought for one moment that you were incapable of being a boss. I'm sure by now, Philip will agree with me. It's just good to be home."

"Stephen, what did Ginger have to say about your defense?" Philip asked.

"Only that she wishes I would change my story to something vaguely believable. Right now, I want to clear my head, take a hot shower and change my clothes."

Victoria rubbed his cheek. "Hum, if you need to borrow a razor, feel free to let me know. I wouldn't want you to chaff Leann's tender skin with that stubble."

"Thanks, Victoria, but I have my own razor. Why don't you two make some French toast and coffee. When I come down, I have something to tell you."

Victoria asked, "Do I look like a maid to you? I want to be the boss, not the cook."

Philip shook his head. "I'll make the French toast, and you can make the coffee."

"Uh! I will not make the coffee. That's so domestic. I am going to call Grandmother Stanton and let her know Stephen is home. You can make breakfast all by yourself."

"That's probably best, Victoria," Philip said.

"Stephen," Victoria said, "what do you want to share with us? Would it be the remarkable things Sheriff Bolton had to say about me, or does it have to do with the Garden of Eden?"

"To your first question, no! To the second part of your question, maybe." Stephen headed up the stairs.

Ninety

A Visit to Todd's Creek

Over breakfast, Stephen told almost everything that took place with Shemed, except the part about Shemed wanting him to kill Victoria. Victoria went to the door and gazed toward the church that had a golden glow from the morning sun. Stephen and Philip noticed she grew quiet when Stephen was talking about Shemed.

Philip smiled as he considered what Stephen had said about his visit to Todd's Creek. "You know, Stephen, I go to the barn often when I'm home. I'm glad you could go even if it was only for a short visit."

"Stephen," Victoria said without turning around, "you better pop a breath mint. Your honey is coming up the driveway."

Stephen joined Victoria at the door. She laughed and asked, "Have you ever made love to Leann?"

Shocked by the question, he replied, "Good Lord, Victoria! What kind of question is that?"

Philip laughed out loud.

"What's so funny, Philip?" Victoria asked. "I was only curious. She looks so dull. I just wonder if her looks are deceiving. Who knows, she could be a wild woman. On the other hand, I might need to teach her a few things and . . ."

"Victoria!" Stephen interrupted. "My love life is none of your business. No, we haven't made love, and she isn't dull at all. I don't want you to teach her anything. Behave yourself."

Stephen was surprised to see Jason and Jamie, Leann's mom and dad, with her. He hadn't seen or talked to them in a few days. He could only imagine what kind of questions Leann's mother would have for him.

Stephen smiled and hurried out to see Leann. A quick kiss, tight hug and a stroke of her shiny hair had to suffice until later. Jamie and Jason also gave Stephen a hug. Stephen then asked everybody to sit on the porch.

"Jamie, Jason, do you remember Philip Dawson and Victoria Stanton?" Stephen asked.

Jamie warmly smiled at Philip, then sternly stared at Victoria. "Yes, I remember them. So, tell me, Victoria, how does someone like you tolerate country life?"

Victoria smugly responded, "Someone like me? Just what do you mean by that?" Victoria was pulling and looking at her shirt. "Am I wearing a sign on my shirt that identifies me as, *someone like me*?"

Jamie raised her head. "I simply meant that New York City is quite different from Calvin's Point. My word, you're a bit testy, aren't you, Victoria?"

Victoria moved close to Jamie. "I am only testy when I detect sarcasm. And you, Jamie, are full of it."

Seeing the conversation needed to change and fast, Jason asked, "How is your grandmother, Victoria?"

Victoria shyly smiled, ran her finger down Jason's cheek and winked, "Good, very good."

Jamie snapped, "Well, I never! You keep your hands off my husband. I know all about your reputation."

Stephen stepped between Jamie and Victoria. "Victoria, don't you have something to do upstairs?"

"No, I don't!"

Stephen frowned. "Yes. I'm sure you do."

"Maybe you're right." Victoria smiled and fixed her eyes on Jason. "It was a pleasure to see you again, Jason."

She looked sternly at Jamie. "You too, Jamie."

After Victoria left the room, Jamie straightened her shirt and said, "I tell you, Stephen, that woman is bad news. I am a good judge of character and she has none. Put her hands on Jason like a prostitute. There, I said it. Has she ever made advances toward you, Stephen?"

Caught off guard by the question, Stephen replied, "Victoria is really not that bad. She puts on an act, but down deep that's all it is."

Embarrassed, Jason ordered, "Jamie, that's enough! This is a bunch of nonsense. We came to check on Stephen, not browbeat Victoria."

"Maybe I was a little out of hand. For that I ask your forgiveness, Stephen."

Stephen put his arm around Jamie's shoulder. "Consider it forgiven."

"I suppose what I am about to ask you, Stephen, will make me what people call a heavy, but I need to know."

"Jamie, feel free to ask whatever you like."

Jamie sat erect then and stared into Stephens eyes. "Stephen, you know that I am straightforward with you, and I always have been. Therefore, I'll ask you outright. Is there any truth to the many rumors floating around Calvin's Point, concerning you and Linda Scott?"

"No, Jamie. I don't know what you've heard, but there is no truth to it. I didn't even know Linda Scott."

Jamie tightened her lips and tilted her head. "I love you like a son, Stephen; however, Leann is our daughter and our only child. I don't want her hurt. I'm sure you understand that."

Irritated by the statement, Leann spoke up. "Mother, I am a grown woman, and while I appreciate your concern for me, I feel hurt that you would even say something like that to Stephen. Your good sense of character should have told you that. I thought you were coming to check on Stephen's well-being, not to interrogate him."

"Jamie, Leann's right. I think we better be going." Jason said.

Stephen hurriedly spoke up. "In Jamie's defense, let me say, I understand why she wants to know. If I had a daughter in Leann's position, I would probably ask the same questions."

Jamie hugged Stephen. "Stephen, you know I love you, and I'm thrilled about having you for a son-in-law one day, and I meant no harm."

About that time, Victoria came down the stairs. Jamie called out to her, "Victoria!"

"Yes, Jamie."

With tight lips Jamie said, "When I am wrong, I say I'm wrong. I feel I was a bit out of line with you; therefore, I ask your forgiveness."

Victoria smiled. "Ah, how sweet of you. Of course, I'll forgive you; but only if you will forgive me as well."

Victoria shocked everyone when she hugged Jamie. Jamie stiffened her body, held her arms tight to her side and had a look of horror on her face. Victoria then turned, hugged Jason and kissed him leaving bright red lips prints on his cheek. He held his breath and touched his cheek. Victoria chuckled. "Now that we're friends, let's do lunch soon."

Victoria turned and went outside. Jason and Jamie said nothing. Jamie took hold of Jason's arm and headed for the door.

"I'll get Stephen to bring me home later," Leann said.

"That's fine, honey," Jason said. Jamie continued to pull Jason toward the car.

As Leann watched as her parents go to the car, she shook her head. "Poor daddy, he'll hear about this up into the night. About how he didn't have to allow Victoria to kiss him."

Philip grabbed an apple and headed for the door. "I think I'll see what Victoria's motives were."

Stephen closed his eyes and put his arms around Leann. The thought of Shemed touching her made him furious. He knew this battle would be the worst of all. After a moment, Stephen asked Leann to sit with him in the porch swing. They talked for a while about the trial and the possibility of him going to jail. They reassured each other that God held all things in His hands. As they pushed the swing back and forth, Stephen recounted how his dad would say, "The best way to be in God's presence is to be outside. There you could soothe your soul, talk to God and breathe the fresh air."

Ninety-One

Philip's Question

$\mathcal{T}$hat night, when Stephen came back from taking Leann home, Philip was sitting on the porch swing. Stephen joined him. Philip fixed his eyes on Stephen.

Puzzled by the stare, Stephen asked, "Why the look?"

Philip tilted his head. "You tell me, Stephen, why the look."

Stephen swiftly responded, "I don't know, so tell me what's on your mind."

Philip nodded. "Okay. I want to know why you didn't tell all that happened between you and Shemed?"

Stephen walked to the edge of the porch. "What do you mean?"

Philip stood beside Stephen. "You can't fool me, Stephen. You never could and you never will. For you to withhold something means

Shemed threatened you, or someone close to you, someone very close, like Leann."

Stephen trembled as he faced Philip. "I can't tell anyone, including you, Philip."

Philip took Stephen by his shoulders. "You don't have to tell me anything. I know."

Desperate, Stephen replied, "You don't know everything! You might know some of it, but not all. There's no way."

Philip frowned. "Shemed wants something from you or he will hurt, no . . . *kill*, Leann."

Stephen lowered his head.

"What is it Shemed wants you to do? He wants you to kill, or he will kill Leann. Is that what he threatened you with?"

Stephen said nothing. Philip took Stephen's face in his hands, "Who is it he wants you to kill: me, mom, dad or someone else? Answer me, Stephen!" Philip demanded.

Stephen sluggishly muttered, "Victoria."

A voice came from the doorway, "What about me?" Victoria asked, as she came out to the porch. "You can't do without me for one minute? If I'm not with you, I am in your conversation. Should I be flattered?"

Stephen anxiously looked at Victoria and turned away. Victoria nudged Stephen's arm. "I feel being flattered is out the door. What's the matter, Stephen? You know, I apologized to Jamie and Jason."

"Victoria, I can't talk about it right now."

Victoria could tell Stephen wasn't going to face her; therefore, she stepped in front of him, "Are you saying something about me doesn't concern me? You know I won't settle for that."

"I can't talk about it now."

"So, Philip, you tell me?"

Philip assured Victoria when the time was right, she would be the first to know. For reasons unknown to both Stephen and Philip, Victoria accepted the answer.

Ninety-Two

The Gathering

The trial was only two days away. Ginger Banks was still bewildered that she accepted the case and still had no reasonable defense. She had thought of dropping the case or even faking an illness, so someone else would have to take it.

Cordilia and Paul were back at Eden's Gate to support Stephen through the trial. Victoria was busy checking her wardrobe, trying to decide which color schemes would go with the drab lighting in the courtroom.

Philip was staying extremely close Stephen. Stephen told Cordilia and Paul about what he saw inside Eden's Gate at White Stone Kingdom.

Cordilia said, "As Rachel would say, God has a natural order. Had Acor and Hannah been allowed to stay inside Eden, they would have died in their sins. It was God's mercy that drove them out. For that I am thankful. I hate Shemed, Jewel,

Telmar and all of Gray Stone. I look forward to the day Gray Stone crumbles."

Stephen grinned. "You know, Shemed mentioned you and mom by name."

Shocked, Cordilia replied, "Me? What did he say?"

"It wasn't in a good sense," Stephen said.

"Hum! Why am I not surprised?"

Stephen kissed Cordilia's cheek and hugged Paul goodnight. "I'll probably spend most of tomorrow with Ginger Banks. I know she will do her best to convince me to plead temporary insanity."

Cordilia asked Paul to give her a minute alone with Stephen. She took Stephen's hand and grinned. "I saw John's jacket and Rachel's dress on your pulpit in the barn. I knew you had been there and I rejoiced."

Cordilia squeezed Stephen's hand. "I love you, Stephen."

***

Stephen indeed spent most of the day with Ginger, but there were no changes. That night, Grandmother Stanton had a seafood feast prepared for everyone at Eden's Gate. Charles and Liz came early to prepare the table. The humidity was stifling. Stephen had the air conditioning on high to relieve the smoldering effect. Sheriff Bolton, Ian Jackson, Jason and

Jamie had been invited as well. When everyone was seated at the table, they joined hands and Stephen asked Cordilia to bless the food.

Stephen had warned Victoria to be on her best behavior. Victoria laughed when everyone was served. "Grandmother, I pray this is a celebration dinner. Not a last supper."

"Victoria, darling, you never cease to amaze me." Grandmother Stanton raised her glass, tapped the side of it carefully with her fork and announced, "I would like to propose a toast to my only grandchild and the heir to the Stanton fortune. To Victoria Stanton."

Everyone called out, "To Victoria." However, Jamie did not raise her glass as high as the others did.

Victoria stood and kissed her grandmother on her forehead. "What a surprise. To what do I owe this honor, Grandmother?"

Brenda Stanton chuckled and said with pride, "You're my granddaughter, aren't you?"

Victoria put her hands on her hips and raised her head. "Yes, Grandmother, I am your granddaughter. I'm beautiful, rich and a Stanton. Therefore, that should qualify me for a dozen toasts."

Cordilia's face was aglow. She squeezed Paul's hand and breathlessly said, "That is exactly what I would have said, Victoria. We are kindred spirits!"

Victoria raised her glass. "Let's lift our glasses and salute my first kindred spirit, Cordilia Dawson."

Everyone stood, raised his or her glass and called out, "To Cordilia!" Jamie spoke up in the middle of the toast. "I thought we were here to honor Stephen. Somehow, the table has turned, and we're toasting everyone but Stephen."

Victoria responded, "Everyone, I am so sorry for overlooking you, Stephen, but right now before we go any further, I would like to toast one of the most elegant women in Calvin's Point, Jamie Conners."

Jamie's face turned a bright shade of red as all raised their glasses and called out, "Jamie!"

Stephen knew he had better get away from the toasting before Jamie came up with one for Victoria. "I would like to thank all of you for being here tonight. Mrs. Stanton, Charles and Liz for this wonderful dinner, good friends, and family to share it with. Thank you, from the bottom of my heart, for everything."

Everyone was having a good time and peace prevailed. Brenda Stanton leaned forward and squinted her eyes when she noticed letters tattooed on Ian's hand. "Tell me, Ian, what do the letters AOTA on your fingers mean?"

Ian smiled and replied, "It's some letters from my early army days. All my battalion had the letters tattooed on their fingers."

Victoria, who was sitting beside Ian, said, "So, you were in the army. I thought it was a girlfriend's call letters. Take Sheriff Bolton, it's so obvious that he is a military man. By the way, I love men in uniforms." Victoria slipped her shoe off and ran her foot up Sheriff Bolton's pant leg.

Sheriff Bolton dropped his fork, took a deep breath, sat straight up and quickly looked around the table. All eyes were on him when Stephen asked, "Are you okay, Sheriff?"

Before he could answer, Victoria began to laugh uncontrollably. The sheriff wiped his forehead, which was beaded with sweat. Victoria laughed so hard she began to cough and had to leave the table. A chain reaction started as everyone was laughing aloud, yet no one was sure why. Sheriff Bolton regained the color in his face and laughed with them. He never did say what happened, but Stephen had a good idea. The laughter brought a welcome change that carried through the rest of the evening.

Ninety-Three

Stranger on the Porch

Everyone said a prayer together before saying goodnight. Stephen again thanked Brenda Stanton for the food. She, Charles and Liz were the first to leave. Ian Jackson followed. On his way out, Victoria smiled and said, "Now don't you be nervous on the stand when it's your turn to testify. Just be your sweet and charming self, and I'm sure they'll execute Stephen before Christmas."

Ian patted her cheek. "With any luck, they may find you guilty and fry you instead."

Victoria frowned and slapped Ian's hand. "Don't touch me! Get out of here, go home and get some beauty sleep; otherwise, you will scare Champion to death when you feed him in the morning."

Sheriff Bolton had said good night to everyone except Victoria. He stopped in front of her and looked down at his Stetson hat that he was holding in his hand. He shyly grinned and confessed, "You gave me a scare at the table tonight and quite a rush. My first response was to a thing that happened often in Nam. You could be sleeping or wide-awake and at times, a big rat would try to go up your pant leg. My second was personal, and I will keep to myself. Don't you worry about going to bed any time soon. You, unlike Ian, don't need any beauty sleep."

Victoria seductively whispered in his ear, "I think I need to be arrested."

Sheriff Bolton whispered back, "Victoria, darling, the jail is closed tonight. At this stage of the game, there is no time for anything but focus. Goodnight, sweet soldier."

Victoria watched Sheriff Bolton put his hat on and walk away. Cordilia, Paul, Philip and Victoria all retired for some much needed sleep.

Stephen was unable to sleep. He dressed and went to the porch swing. When he sat down, he shivered as he saw Shemed sitting in a rocking chair at the end of the deck. Stephen gripped the armrest on the swing. "What are you doing here?" he shouted.

Shemed stood and walked toward Stephen. "I've been enjoying the party. I knew you wouldn't be able to sleep with all the excitement; therefore, I came by to let you know your trial will be a short one."

Curious, Stephen questioned, "What do you mean by that?"

Shemed leaned toward Stephen's face. "I mean, the slob that actually killed poor Linda Scott has had a bout with his conscience and will be confessing to Sheriff Bolton first thing tomorrow morning."

Shemed walked to the edge of the porch and turned to face Stephen. "You see, Stephen, I am a man of my word. You have one week from tomorrow to keep your end of the bargain, or else you will have to find yourself a new girlfriend."

The door opened and Shemed vanished. Philip stepped outside. "Who were you talking to, Stephen?"

Stephen was breathing heavily and hesitated to reply.

"Was it Shemed?"

Stephen nodded yes. Philip sat down beside Stephen. "What did he say to you?"

"He said the trial would be short. That someone would confess to Sheriff Bolton tomorrow, and he wants Victoria dead in a week. You know the rest. I don't know what to do."

"You don't, but God does. He will guide you through this, Stephen. Don't worry. You won't have to do anything to Victoria." Philip stood and quickly opened the screen door

Victoria screamed and grabbed her chest.

"So, you were caught eavesdropping!" Philip said sternly.

Victoria stammered, "N-no, that's not true."

"Yes, it is true!" Philip boldly stated.

Victoria put her hands on her hips and ranted, "So what if it is true? You were talking about me again. I'll tell you what's true. You're making me paranoid, whispering behind my back. If you have something to say, say it to my face."

Stephen stood and tried to smooth things over by saying how sweet she was at dinner.

"That's a bunch of crap!" Victoria shouted. "Now, you tell me what you were talking about or I will knock you out!"

Stephen shouted, "NO!"

Before he could move, Victoria punched him in the nose. Blood gushed. Stephen pushed by her to go inside. He paused and shouted, "You're crazy!"

Victoria started to go after Stephen when Philip took hold of her arm. "You had better save your fighting for the battlefield, soldier."

Victoria stared into Philip's eyes. For a moment, she was unable to move. She breathlessly asked, "Who are you? You're not Philip Dawson. You may have that name, but you're not him. I know who you are, yet I don't. I can't explain it, but it will come to me."

"You better go to bed," Philip said. "Morning will be here soon."

Philip walked off the porch and down toward the barn. "Where are you going, Philip?" Victoria called out. Philip didn't answer but continued to walk away.

Victoria went inside feeling really bad about punching Stephen in the nose. She heard the water running in his bathroom. The door was ajar, so she slowly pushed it open. Stephen was propped against the sink with a washcloth held firmly against his nose. Victoria was playing with her necklace as she entered. "Stephen, are you okay? I didn't mean to hurt you. It was just a bad response, and I am so sorry."

Stephen had pulled his bloody shirt off and had on only his jeans. He took the cloth from his nose. Victoria quickly wet another one and held up the trashcan for him to drop the bloody one in. The flow of blood had all but stopped.

Victoria suggested, "Hold your head back and let me see how it looks."

Stephen leaned his head backward as Victoria took a closer look. "Does it hurt much?"

Stephen glared at her. "Victoria, don't you ever hit me again. Do I make myself clear?"

"You're right, Stephen. I was out of line. I won't do it again, I promise. Although, you're being a bit of a baby. Didn't you ever get into fights at school? Anyway, will you forgive me?"

"If you will get me something for my headache, I'll forgive you."

Victoria hurried to her bathroom to get some aspirin. Stephen was checking his nose for any possible broken bones when Victoria hurried back through the door. She froze when she entered. In the mirror, Stephen could see the expression on her face. "What is it?"

Startled, Victoria groaned, "My Lord, Stephen, what happed to your back?"

Stephen turned to look in the mirror. A black and blue mark covered the width of his back. Stephen knew Shemed's men had left the marks. His first thought was, *Why did the mark not go away when Mylo ran the red stone across my body?'*

Victoria whispered, "What happened to your back?"

Stephen quickly grabbed his robe and put it on. "It's nothing to worry about. It doesn't even hurt."

"Is this mark from the forest that you told Philip and I about? Remember, you said that some of Shemed's thugs were hitting you."

"Yes, it is, now you go to bed."

"I'm sorry, I hit you." Victoria gently hugged Stephen and said, "They will pay for this."

Ninety-Four

Freedom

The next morning at the courthouse, Ginger
Banks met Stephen in the corridor and
assured him she would do the best she could
to defend him. The courtroom was crammed
with the people from Calvin's Point. Stephen
sat beside Ginger. The bailiff entered through a
side door and called out, "All rise. Hear ye, hear
ye. Court is now in session. The Honorable Jack
Patton residing."

When everyone was seated, Judge Patton
picked up some papers, looked at them and
said, "Would the attorneys please approach
the bench?"

Ginger and the prosecutor both approached.
The Judge covered the microphone and said,
"Miss Banks, it would appear the person who
murdered Linda Scott has confessed and is in
the custody of Sheriff Bolton. I will announce
this, and your client will be released."

Ginger smiled from ear to ear and whispered, "Thank you, your honor."

Ginger sat down with a look of sheer delight on her face. She held Stephen's hand and said, "You're not going to believe this."

Before she could say anything else, Judge Patton announced, "In light of new evidence that has been placed before me, Stephen Daniel Harris, all charges against you have been dropped. A man has confessed to the murder of Linda Scott. He is now in the custody of Sheriff Ronnie Bolton; therefore, you're are free to go." The Judge pounded the gavel and shouted, "Court dismissed."

Everyone rushed to congratulate Stephen. Ginger Banks was so relieved. Just to know she didn't have to face the humiliation of presenting Stephen's defense brought a smile. Pastor Reynolds made his way toward Stephen. "Stephen, I want you to know how happy I am that I was wrong. Can you ever forgive me? I could have sworn the man I saw was you. He looked just like you."

Stephen was skeptical and showed little emotion toward Pastor Reynolds' apology.

Sheriff Bolton said, "On Pastor Reynolds behalf, I have to say the man who confessed looks like your brother, and get this, he has a black 1937 Ford pickup truck exactly like yours, Stephen."

Stunned, Stephen asked, "Who is he?"

Leann interrupted, "Honey, what difference does it make? You're free."

Outside, Brenda Stanton was talking of a celebration party. Stephen said he wanted to wait a few days and allow time for everything to settle down. Victoria was going by her grandmother's for a visit. Cordilia, Paul and Philip were going back to Eden's Gate. Stephen told Leann he would see her later in the day. He needed some time alone.

Stephen could not help himself. He had to go by the jail and see the person who looked so much like him. Sheriff Bolton was sitting on the plank porch of the jailhouse when Stephen arrived. He was leaning back in a straight back chair, holding a spit bottle, enjoying a chew. When Stephen got out of his car, Sheriff Bolton spit and said, "Mr. Harris, why am I not surprised to see you here?"

"Maybe because you know me too well. I had to see him for myself. Do you mind?"

Spitting again, Sheriff Bolton said, "I don't mind at all, come on in."

They entered the jail and Stephen was astonished when he saw the young man. "He looks almost like me."

The sheriff nodded. "That he does."

The young man stood, took hold of the bars and gazed at Stephen.

"Sheriff, do you mind if I talk with him?" Stephen asked.

"I don't mind a bit. I'll go pick up his lunch. I should be back in about ten minutes."

"Okay. I'll stay here until you get back." Stephen asked, "What's his name?"

The young man answered, "My name is Gene Price."

"I'll be back in a few minutes, Stephen." Sheriff Bolton said as he closed the door behind him.

Stephen brought a chair and set it in front of the cell. "Why don't you sit down, Gene."

Gene slowly sat on the edge of the bed and looked at Stephen. "You sure look a lot like me."

Stephen nodded. "I was thinking the same thing. Tell me, Gene, what brought you to Calvin's Point?"

"Actually, I was only passing through on my way to Charleston. I saw a young woman, who turned out to be Linda Scott, walking down by the covered bridge. I asked her if she wanted a ride. I've never asked anyone if they want a ride. Why I did, I don't know. It was like I was doing things, but it wasn't me doing them. When she got into the truck, I pulled off the road, and it was like something took over my body." Gene shook his head and began to cry. "The things that was done to that poor girl, I could have never done. I was biting her like a wild animal. I ravaged her. I remember at one point she clawed my arm. When I looked at my arm, it wasn't my arm at all. I don't know whose it was, but it wasn't mine. Does any of this make sense to you?"

"Yes, sadly enough it makes perfect sense. It wasn't you, it was Shemed."

"I don't know any Shemed, but I will tell you another strange thing. You and I look so much alike . . . but we are not the only ones."

Stephen stood, curious to hear what Gene had to say, "What do you mean we're not the only ones."

"The preacher the sheriff was talking to earlier looks exactly like a man they found outside Atlanta a few months ago. Someone sliced his throat. It made my skin crawl when I saw this preacher. They never did find out who the man was or where he was from."

"You said it was a few months ago when they found him?"

"Yes."

About that time, Sheriff Bolton came through the door with Gene's lunch. "I hope you like clam chowder and a grilled cheese sandwich. That seems to be what was on the menu today."

Stephen put the chair back beside the desk. "Gene, it's been more than interesting talking with you."

Sheriff Bolton slid the tray through the bars and told Stephen to wait, and he would walk out with him.

The weather had cooled overnight with just the hint of an early fall. The breeze whispered through the drying grass and leaves. Stephen stood on the porch, watching the leaves blow across the road. Sheriff Bolton patted Stephen's shoulder, "One time, in Yinpeg, some of my battalion was out on patrols. We knew to stay together and not lag behind. Suddenly, I found myself in a clearing. The terrain in the jungle is all the same. There's nothing distinct that you can look for to help guide you out of a situation, should it arise. The seasons there are not like they are here. So, to see colored leaves being spun around in a funnel was a strange sight. I watched the leaves until the wind stopped and they fell to the ground, which was when I realized I was alone. I should have had a compass, but I didn't. So, I wasn't sure which way to go. I looked around to get my bearings, but I was as lost as I could be. The sun had set and the thought of being lost in the jungle at night, alone was more than I could stand. When I heard someone call my name, I was ecstatic. I turned and walked toward the voice. I walked right into a trap. The enemy grabbed me. They blindfolded me, and tied me up. They surrounded me in a circle, shoving me from one to another, hitting me with their fists, sticks or whatever they happened to have. When I gained consciousness, I was back in my camp. My commander had made me the example. He allowed some of the people in the village to take me captive in order to teach a valuable lesson. When you're in a war, you can't allow anything to take your mind off your safety. I allowed leaves blowing in a circle to draw me to a clearing and hold me captive. Stephen, don't allow anything to get your focus off the battle. You know what you have to do, and soon you will do it. Don't be drawn from the path by dancing leaves or dancing women. You must have a plan in battle. If I can be of any help, let me know."

Ninety-Five

Time Alone

Stephen thanked Sheriff Bolton and headed for Eden's Gate. Stephen knew he had let many things cloud his vision. Sheriff Bolton was right. In order to defeat the enemy, he must have a battle plan. Stephen drove home but didn't go inside. He led Champion from the barn and rode east from Eden's Gate to the far end of his property. After getting off his horse, he sat on the grass and prayed for a while. He could feel the pull that would soon take him back to the mountain and the Armor Bearers. He was no longer satisfied to be on the sideline. The call to lead the warriors on the frontlines filled his spirit. To take that position, he had to mentally readjust his own protective shield. Now in the field, everything seemed so clear, but in the battle to take the mountain, everything had been cloudy.

He had been resting there for a long time when he heard horses coming through the field. Victoria and Philip had come looking for him. Victoria was fussing. "I thought you may have gone to Atlanta. Philip and I have ridden all over the country looking for you. I think my perfectly rounded bottom is bruised from pounding that saddle."

"I needed some time alone to thank God and to seek God," Stephen said.

"Before I forget," Philip said, "Mom wanted me to tell you that Daddy will have supper ready by the time we get back."

Victoria rubbed her bottom and grumbled, "Philip, I want to make one thing clear, I can't ride as fast going back as we did coming. I would like to enjoy supper without an upset stomach."

Philip laughed. "Stephen and I will try and accommodate your stomach and your bottom."

They mounted and headed back to the house. Stephen looked at Philip, smiled and shouted, "I'll race you."

Victoria was furious, but she managed to keep up.

They had barely put the horses in the barn when it began to rain. Paul had prepared spaghetti with Italian meatballs, tossed salad, garlic bread and his signature, German chocolate cake for dessert.

Cordilia was especially quiet during supper.

"Mom, I haven't seen you this quiet in a long time. Is something bothering you?" Philip asked.

Cordilia stood, walked to the sink and looked out the window.

"Honey, what is it?" Paul asked.

Cordilia slowly moved behind Stephen's chair. She massaged his shoulders and kissed the top of his head. "In my spirit, I see a mountain. Many are wounded and dying. They're calling for a leader to show them the way. Stephen, you will go to that mountain soon, and there your mantel will shine like the noonday sun. I am feeling the pull to that mountain myself." Cordilia smiled at Paul. "When John, Rachel, Paul and I went to Boone's Crossing, I was very pregnant with Philip, and Rachel was with you. My ankles were swollen, but we were ready for whatever was ahead."

Victoria said, "Stephen told me that you actually confronted Queen Jewel herself. Is that right?"

Cordilia smiled and nodded. "Yes, we did. Rachel came against her with boldness like I had never seen before. Every time Rachel would confront her with the Word of God, John, Paul and I would shout at the top of our voices, 'Glory to the Ancient of Days.' With every word, Jewel became fragmented, until finally, she vanished. That was when she said, and I quote, 'I may not have you, Rachel, but I will be back for your son.' Wow, what a day that was!"

"Cordilia, at that time, didn't Shemed use Dr. Fred Wells as his cover?" Stephen asked.

"Yes, he did, but we didn't know that until right before Boone's Crossing. We just thought he was a hateful man who loved to stir up trouble. He was the one who wanted to hang Mr. Spook. Matt Wilson, Sheriff Allen Butler's deputy, was killed at the Crossing. There had been reports of green lights hovering over the Crossing area.

Everyone knew the Crossing had been a vacant area, for who knows how long. Therefore, Sheriff Butler and Matt went to check it out. Sheriff Butler vowed that the trees moved like people and some of them even looked like people. Matt went crazy, shooting his pistol at random. According to Sheriff Butler, the trees killed Matt and would have killed him too, but Mr. Spook carried him out away from the trees. Jewel, Shemed, Telmar and Delilah had ruled over Todd's Creek for over one hundred years. I . . . I didn't mean to get so carried away. But, yes we did face Jewel and her trinity. The good news is the White Stone Kingdom prevailed."

Paul shook his head. "Sometimes it seems as though that never happened. Then again, it seems like it was only yesterday."

Victoria was thrilled. "It is so exciting to hear about the battle! I can see you and Paul at Boone's Crossing fighting like wildcats."

Without warning, the lights flickered, and the power went off. The glow from a candle lit the table, providing enough light for them to finish supper. Afterward, the intermittent flashes of lightning helped to light the kitchen long enough for Stephen to find his stockpile of candles. Victoria and Cordilia went upstairs to change into their pajamas. The thunder had the sound of cannon balls exploding. The wind was fierce. At one point, Stephen heard one of the rocking chairs scrape across the porch as the wind blew it into the yard.

"Man!" Stephen said, as he raced upstairs, remembering he had opened his bedroom window earlier to allow fresh air inside. After closing the window, he called into Victoria's room to check on her and Cordilia. "Victoria, Cordilia?" No one answered. He thought, *They must be in Cordilia's room.* Stephen would have proceeded down the hallway, but a flash of lightning reflected off something shiny lying on Victoria's bed. Stephen was distracted when the hot wax from the candle rolled onto his hand. The candle had burned out. Another flash of lightning froze Stephen. On her bed lay the most magnificent sword he had ever seen. The long gold blade had the word TRUTH engraved in the center of the blade. The handle was of purest gold with a glowing red stone in the middle. Stephen carefully moved his hand toward the sword. Victoria startled him by calling his name as she entered the room. "Stephen! We were looking for you."

He looked at Victoria. "Where did you get this sword?"

Puzzled by the question, Victoria jeered, "Did you get struck by lightning or something? What sword?"

The lights flickered and then shone brightly. "I'm sure glad the power is back on." Cordilia said from the hallway.

Stephen was stunned to see that there was no sword on Victoria's bed. Pointing to the bed, he shouted, "It was right here! I saw it. It had a gold blade with TRUTH etched in the center of the blade. The handle was gold with a glowing red stone in it."

Cordilia and Victoria stared at Stephen, seeing that there was no sword on the bed. "Why don't we go down stairs and clear the table before the power goes off again." Cordilia said.

Feeling weary, Stephen agreed.

Ninety-Six

Victoria Missing

After they cleared the table, the power went off again. The storm was dreadful. The thunderclaps and flashes of lightning seemed endless. The rain beat against the roof, mixed with hail the size of a penny. Everyone was in bed except Stephen and Victoria. They were going up the stairs when the living room door burst open. Startled, Victoria and Stephen hurried back down the steps to secure it. Stephen had to use the full weight of his body before the door would budge. Wiping the rain from his face, he looked at Victoria and frowned. "How did that door get unlocked? I locked it when Philip and I came in from putting the rocking chair back on the porch. I know I did."

Victoria shrugged her shoulders. "I have no idea how the door came open. I also have no idea how the rain and wind are so hypnotic.

My bed is calling my name to hurry upstairs and snuggle under my covers. Goodnight, Sweet Stephen."

Victoria began to stir and moan as she lay in bed. Trying to open her eyes, she saw a man's face close to hers. She tried to scream, but the man put his hand over her mouth. Victoria's blood chilled when she saw the enormous blade of his knife, which was now pressed against her throat.

Through horrid breath and clinched teeth, the man growled, "You scream and I'll slit your throat."

A low sinister chuckle caused Victoria to shiver. She knew she had to do something to break free. The man pushed his face against hers and jeered. "Me and you are going to have a time."

He held the knife with one hand and pulled the gown strap off Victoria's shoulder exposing her breast. "Oh, my . . . I'm going to take you out of here. If you make one sound, I'll gut you like a hog. Now, get up and let's go."

Victoria knew she had to distract him, so she could scream, hoping someone would hear her. "Can I please put my housecoat on?" she begged.

The man agreed and warned her again about not making any noise. Victoria lifted her robe from her bed and cautiously pulled it onto her shoulders. From behind, the man again clamped his hand over her mouth. "I'll warn you one last time, don't make a sound, or it will be your last. Do you understand me?"

Victoria nodded, letting him know she did understand. The man pushed her in front of him and said, "We're going out of the bedroom and down the stairs. Don't make me hurt you."

Frantic, Victoria mumbled through his fingers, "You won't get away with this."

"You speak boldly for someone that could die in an instant."

"You will be caught."

The man punched Victoria on her chin, dazing her. Putting her over his shoulder, he headed for the bedroom door. As he started through the door, Victoria grabbed the door's edge and kicked wildly. The man dropped her to avoid the clawing of his face and the pulling of his hair.

Amid the thunder, lightning and wind, a loud cry pierced Stephen's ear. Victoria took advantage of being dropped and finally had screamed. The man grabbed Victoria by her hair and pulled her down. She kicked against his knees and once again he released her. Victoria scurried to stand and move backward. A sudden slash of steel went through the air, just missing her face. She grabbed a picture frame and threw it at the him, catching him off guard. She rolled over the bed and ran out the door into the hallway and right into Stephen's arms. Stephen pushed her aside just as the man came charging through the door with the knife in his hand. He was swinging furiously at Stephen. Paul and Cordilia rushed out of their room at the end of the hallway to see what was going on. Philip, who was sleeping in the downstairs bedroom, hurried to the foot of the stairs.

The stranger knocked Stephen down. Victoria ran at the man with a vengeance. He wrestled with her at the top of the stairs as Paul rushed forward to aid Victoria. The man pulled Victoria in front of him as a shield, then threw her down the stairs. When Paul grabbed him, he vanished. Frantic, Stephen shouted, "Paul, where is he?"

"He disappeared while I was holding him. My God, Stephen, it was Telmar."

Philip shouted, "Stephen, you better get down here. I think Victoria is dead. Her neck is broken."

Cordilia gasped, "Oh God, no! no!"

From the flashes of lightning, Stephen could see Victoria's body lying lifeless in Philip's arms. Stephen moved in disbelief as he slowly made his way down the stairs. Paul lit a candle so they could see more clearly. Stephen knelt beside Philip and touched Victoria's neck, praying to find a pulse, but there was none. Dismayed, Stephen looked at Philip and cried, "Why?"

Ninety-Seven

Armor Bearers' Camp

A sudden blast of wind shot through the room, and a blinding flash of lightning illuminated their surroundings. Stephen lowered his head, and gripped with emotion, he held his hands over his face. When the wind ceased to blow and his eyes could focus again, Stephen found himself kneeling by a tree near the camp of the Armor Bearers.

Stephen heard music coming from the camp. He looked at the enormous bonfire and the warriors dancing and singing songs to the Most High."

Stephen wanted to mourn Victoria's death, but at this place and time, he could not allow anything to cloud his vision. He knew that God must have a purpose for her death, but what could it be? He also wondered about Cordilia, Paul and Philip, were they okay?

He watched and listened to the Armor Bearers for a few minutes. In his mind, Stephen knew there were many soldiers singing and dancing today who would surely die on the mountain. His thoughts were interrupted by a couple of welcome voices. "Rakar, it's sure good to see to you."

Stephen quickly stood and embraced Jim Lee and Dale Thomas. "I'm so glad to see my good friends. I can't even begin to tell you what all has taken place."

Jim Lee and Dale assured Stephen they knew everything, including Victoria's death. "Stephen," Dale said, "this is the last time I will address you as Stephen. You are here to walk in the destiny set before you. From now until after the battle, you will be addressed as General Rakar."

Stephen was surprised by his own response. "I accept that name. For the first time, I feel like Rakar. Right now, Stephen feels a million miles away, but Rakar has dominated my being." Stephen looked across the camp and sighed. "These warriors can dance and sing, but they are ill equipped for the last battle. Jim, I want you and Dale to take me to the mountain."

Jim hit his chest and nodded. "Yes, Rakar."

Dale called Stephen's name, stopping him from walking away. "Sir. I think it would be better for you to be in uniform at this time."

Stephen agreed. He lifted his hands toward heaven, closed his eyes and shouted, "Clothe me, Almighty God, with your armor!"

The ground rumbled and a surge of power shot through Stephen, energizing him with wisdom and clothing him with the mantel his mother had once worn. Stephen stood embellished in a white tunic that came just above his knees. Gold rope and tassels rested on his shoulders. Around his waist, a gold belt cradled an enormous sword. He slowly pulled the sword from his belt and marveled. The handle of the sword left him breathless. In it was a ruby that had been cut and smoothed into the shape of the cross. A gleaming red glow emanated from the gold handle. The wide blade was solid gold. The word TRUTH filled the middle of the blade. Stephen looked at the gold boots that were tied snuggly around the calves of his legs. Last was the gold helmet that fit soundly on Stephen's head. Jim Lee and Dale knelt to one knee and saluted. Jim Lee and Dale declared in unison, "General Rakar."

Stephen responded, "I may be a general, but what's a general without captains like you to stand beside me all the way. Now, let's go view the mountain."

Jim and Dale smiled. "Yes sir, General."

At once, the men were at the base of the mountain. Stephen observed the main strongholds that the enemy had set against the children of White Stone Kingdom, Emerald Kingdom and Highland Kingdom. The source of the stronghold went all the way back to the Garden of Fire. Stephen blew his breath out. "What are the people fighting with? Where are their swords?"

Jim Lee replied, "Sir, they have no swords. They have pledged their souls to the White Stone Kingdom, but that's basically it."

"Loyalty is a must, but if that's all you have, you'll die early in the battle," General Rakar said. "I need to meet with these soldiers. Today!"

"Yes, Rakar," Dale replied.

"Sir," Jim added, "who will we send to replace the warriors that are fighting? May I make a recommendation?"

Rakar nodded. "Please do."

"Why don't you visit them in the war zone? I think that will boost their spirits."

"You're right. We need horses. Is there a place nearby we can get some?"

"Yes, sir." Dale said.

In only minutes, Dale returned with three white horses.

Rakar observed the horses. "I don't think it's a good idea to ride into the military compound like peacocks. I want to go there to encourage the men and women that are struggling to stay afloat. My intentions are not to lord over the people, as the Pharisees do, and take their hope completely away. My strategy will always be to lift their heads to the One who can make the difference. Without the Most High God, we all lose."

Jim Lee earnestly agreed and brought three brown and white mares, "Are these suitable for you, sir?"

"Yes, these will serve the purpose. Dale, would you bring me a dark cloak?"

Puzzled, Dale asked, "Of course I will, but may I ask why?"

"The mantel I wear will shine by the glory of God and His truth, not by fine linen and gold belts." Rakar took the gold helmet from his head and handed it to Jim Lee. "Bring me a commoner's helmet. This is not the time to wear a gold helmet as a crown. Only One will wear the crown and it's not I. That honor belongs to King Rayon. All the finery has a way of making the poor feel inferior and producing pride in the one who wears it. We as leaders must remember what brought us to this place is the sin of pride: Queen Jewel, in all her grandeur, shined so brightly in her own eyes until she believed she could take the place of King Rayon. She fell and great was the fall. There is no room for that in the White Stone army. If we're not careful, we will be blinded by our own light."

Dale and Jim Lee were stunned at the general who stood before them. A transformation had truly taken place.

Ninety-Eight

Captain Adams

Rakar stopped at a small clearing of gray-barked beech trees on the side of a gentle knoll. Through the trees he had a clear field of vision across the opening and could detect any advancing troops. He saw a rider heading toward them. "Who is the rider?" Rakar asked.

"It's Captain Bill Adams," Dale said. "He is the commander of the troops here at the gorge."

Captain Adams dismounted and saluted the men. "I saw you coming, but I was a little thrown by your uniforms."

Jim Lee spoke up. "This is General Rakar."

Captain Adams tilted his head. "So, you are Rakar. I must say, I have heard a great deal about you from different ones. Welcome to the battle, sir." Captain Adams scratched his head. "If you don't mind my asking, where's your uniform?"

Rakar quickly explained his position on displaying his uniform at this time. "Tell me, Captain, when have these people eaten fresh bread and had a cool drink of water?" Rakar demanded.

Captain Adams laughed. "There's not exactly an eating establishment on every corner here."

Rakar frowned. "Do you find that question funny, Captain?"

The captain replied, "To be honest, considering where we are, yes, I do find a bit of humor in the question. I try to see that they have at least one ration a day."

Responding immediately, Rakar asked, "And what amount does a ration consist of?"

"One roll and a cup of water."

Rakar looked into the captain's eyes. "How many rations a day do *you* have?"

Insulted by the question, Captain Adams sarcastically snapped, "Sir, are you questioning my ability to run this post?"

"I don't recall asking anything about your ability. I asked how many rations a day do you make sure *you* have? Do you have rations once, twice, three times a day, or do you stuff your belly and let your troops starve?"

Through clinched teeth, Captain Adams replied, "You come out here like you know everything. You know nothing. I have been over these troops for years. I know what I am doing."

"If you knew what you were doing, these troops would not still be at the bottom level of the mountain."

Rakar watched the people struggling and had to fight the tears. He sternly ordered, "I want fresh troops brought in to take the place of those who have been fighting for a long time." Rakar faced the captain. "I want it done today! Do I make myself clear, Captain Adams?"

"You make yourself very clear! Let me ask you a question, General, where do I get these fresh troops?"

Rakar scanned the area and pointed to the tree line. "Who are the troops standing near the trees?"

"Those are the elite troops that aid me." Captain Adams responded.

Rakar solemnly came back, "I think those soldiers will work just fine."

"Sir, those troops are to be used only in an emergency."

Rakar frowned and shouted, "Wake up, Captain! This is an emergency. How many must die before you consider it an emergency? By the way, Captain, it wouldn't hurt you to join your men in the fight."

Captain Adams tightened his lips. "I'll tell the soldiers, but they are not going to like it."

Rakar put his face close to Captain Adams. "If you have a problem carrying out my orders, I will see that you are replaced."

Furious, the captain shouted, "You can't replace me. I take my orders from someone higher rank than you, Rakar."

"Captain Adams, Shemed is not higher rank than me. Jim Lee will replace your command today. You had better choose today whom you will serve. I want you to take those troops and relieve the soldiers that have served the longest. Clear?"

"Crystal clear!" Captain Adams shouted as he walked away.

Jim Lee and Dale stared at Rakar in wonderment. "Rakar," Jim said, "I'll take Mylo and set up headquarters and make sure your orders are carried out."

"Jim," Rakar whispered.

"Yes."

"From the moment Captain Adams dismounted, I knew he wasn't what he appeared. He was placed here along with his elite bunch by the enemy, to make sure the soldiers could get no farther than ground level of the mountain. The soldiers looked up to them and trusted them because of their rank. The fact that they are still fighting shows their desire to be free. I decree, by the help and grace of the Most High God, they will be free."

Ninety-Nine

The Closed Gate

That night, Rakar met with the soldiers. He made sure each one had fresh bread and cool water. Dale had brought coffee from the main camp and brewed it on site. There was a waterfall by the camp. Rakar made sure each one had a bath and fresh clothing. When fed and bathed, Dale called the meeting to order. Rakar stood at the opening of the cave and addressed the soldiers.

"Tonight, I want to open my heart to you. King Rayon of the White Stone Kingdom has sent me to the battle to instruct and care for you. In turn, the Most High God will guide me. I am nothing without Him. I don't know how to lead you to the pinnacle of the mountain except by God's wisdom. When I first saw the mountain, I was shocked by the warfare that was taking place. I thought the mountain would be my destiny. I was wrong. I realize, now, my destiny was the tremendous dark valley that was shown to me after entering the gate. There were countless people with their feet and hands bound. Many groped to find the way but were spiritually blind. Wailing, groans and expressions of sorrow in every possible form echoed through the valley. All were wounded and in desperate need of healing. They have suffered in the vast darkness so long, they had come to think pain and suffering was all there was to life. They had not seen the light for too long. Surrounded by hopelessness, they cried, and their cries for help have never left me. Many said they were brought daily to the gate called Beautiful. Daily the so-called priests and prophets from Gray Stone Kingdom passed by them as though they weren't there. I could see why the gate was called Beautiful. It was solid gold and embellished with every precious stone. The entrance was immense; however, boiling black smoke restrained the opening. Most felt the veil of the entrance had been stitched tightly together and God no longer heard their prayers. Queen Jewel used the deep magic to spin a smoke screen of deception so thick that most have come to believe the light would never shine again. The majority were too weak to fight any longer, but I bring good news to all of you here tonight. The light will shine again! The dark screen of deception will be cleared. White Stone Kingdom has brought forth true priests and prophets to lead and teach you. Queen Jewel and her deep magic are under our feet! We have had a giant battle before us, and as you know, it is now upon us."

General Rakar shouted, "Are you ready soldiers of the White Stone Kingdom to be free from the dark kingdom's lies?"

The people cheered. Rakar's heart melted at the response. "I want each one of you to start the victory tonight by praising The Most High God. Don't ask for anything tonight, just praise Him in your own way."

Some stood, others bowed, some raised their hands, and some lay with their faces toward the ground. Some sat in silence and some wept aloud. Rakar and Dale were on their knees with their hands lifted. The camp was teaming with praise. That night, the warriors of White Stone, Emerald Shores and Highland Kingdoms were renewed.

***

Upon hearing the worship, Captain Adams slipped away from his post and went into the forest. He went a short distance and shouted, "Shemed! Shemed!"

"What do you want?" Shemed growled. Before Captain Adams could answer, Shemed heard the praise that echoed through the forest. "What is this I hear?" he roared.

"It's the soldiers that you placed me over. General Rakar has relieved me of my duties and sent the elite and myself into the battlefield."

Shemed was furious. "You know what to do. You and your men are to take out as many as you can before their faith is revived. I will inform Jewel about what's going on. The last battle for this mountain will be fought soon. I will personally take Rakar out. Now, go before you're missed."

One Hundred

Not Focused

Rakar allowed the soldiers to sleep that night as he and Dale kept watch. Rakar climbed to the top of the cave and looked out over the exhausted warriors. The responsibility God had given him felt overwhelming. Stephen prayed through the night for the wisdom needed for the challenge ahead. Tears also fell for Victoria. He recalled her arrival at *Eden's Gate*. Gorgeous, yet the most arrogant woman he had ever met. Her wisdom about Eden and the Garden of Fire was astounding. He chuckled, remembering the many hysterical moments she had provided. He thought of Cordilia, Paul and Philip. Were they still at *Eden's Gate*? He wondered what his mom and dad would think if they could see him sitting on top of a cave, keeping watch for so many soldiers. For the first time, Stephen had a strong sense of belonging and knowledge of where his future would lie. A tap on the shoulder brought him back to the present.

"General Rakar?"

Standing, he answered, "Yes, I'm Rakar." A very, old man stood before him. His face had the look of one who had been in the battle for many years. In the moonlight, his white hair and full beard had a bluish tint. His shirt was ragged and swayed in the gentle breeze. Rakar could see that he was weak in body. He leaned to one side, upon a wooden walking stick.

"Who might you be?" Rakar asked.

The old man put both hands on his walking stick. "My name is Hopewell."

"That's an interesting name," Rakar said. "I don't believe I have ever heard it before. Why are you not resting with the other soldiers, Hopewell?"

"Lord be praised!" the older man declared as he, staggered back a step.

Rakar grabbed his arm to balance him. "Come, sit with me a moment," he said.

Hopewell chuckled and corrected Rakar. "You think I stagger because I am weak. Not so, young man. I stagger because of the glory of the Most High God. I've just come from the pinnacle of the mountain. While on the mountain, God told me that He has given you great wisdom and power, Rakar. There is enormous danger that comes with the kind of power you possess. You must never think that power is God's endorsement of you or the message you will preach to millions. The mantel God has covered you with is to testify of Him and Him alone. Don't ever look to yourself, Rakar. Keep your eyes on the Most High. You know the white linen uniform and the gold belt, boots and helmet were a test. God was proving you. You passed that test by using great wisdom. Even though that is your true uniform. King Rayon called you to this position ages ago. You earned the status because of your faithfulness to King Rayon and the White Stone Kingdom. King Rayon was entrusted to all the kingdoms, being the Most High's firstborn son. Keep your eyes alert, Rakar, the enemy is all around you. They've slipped in, even as you have watched this night."

Rakar sharp eyes scanned the area. "I've been watching. How did they slip in?"

Hopewell said, "You allowed your mind to drift to things you cannot control. Wondering what your mom and dad would think if they could see you here tonight. I'll tell you what they were thinking. They were screaming, 'Stephen, look to the East of you! The enemy has penetrated the camp. Look to the northern side, they're coming through in groves.' Victoria's death did have a purpose, and it wasn't for you to be killed because of daydreams. Cordilia, Paul and Philip, if they are at *Eden's Gate*, or not, does not make a difference. You're not there. You're here. Because of your daydreams, many will be wounded and some will die. Don't worry about Dale Thomas. He kept the South and West sides protected. Or it would *seem* he did. Learn from your mistakes, Rakar."

Hopewell vanished before Rakar could respond. Rakar called out for Dale Thomas.

Dale came running around the corner. "What is it, Rakar?"

Rakar told Dale about Hopewell and what he had said about the enemy penetrating the camp. "Send for the Armor Bearers to help in the attack that is upon us."

Dale mounted his horse and rode off. Rakar had Jim Lee sound the alarm and wake the soldiers. Before the soldiers could awaken, a bomb landed in the middle of the camp. Rakar heard the screams and moans come from the ones who were wounded. Before Rakar could come down from the cave, he heard the pounding hooves of many horses coming in the distance. He climbed to the top of the cave to survey the area. Rakar was left panting by the sight he saw coming over the knoll. At least two hundred horses, with riders, were approaching in a tight line. The riders rode under a black and white flag.

Rakar shouted, "Oh God, no!"

Instantly, arrows began flying through the camp. Many soldiers fell. Rakar took the sword from his belt and ran into the camp. A couple of bombs exploded nearby. When the smoke cleared, Rakar looked up to see the enemy advancing over the knoll into the camp. He ran about, exhausting himself, trying desperately to muster enough able troops to mount a decent defense. He thought, 'where are the Armor Bearers?' The soldiers grabbed swords, sticks, knives, or whatever they could find to engage the enemy. Rakar was fighting furiously, but he felt all would be in vain if the Armor Bearers didn't arrive soon. As soldiers were being killed or wounded all around him, the enemy seemed to have no losses. Rakar heard a whistle as an arrow flew past his head, then another and another. He fell to the ground to try to get a sense of where the arrows were coming from. To his dismay, Rakar saw Captain Adams and some of his elite soldiers, shooting arrows at their own soldiers. Rakar was stunned, but breathed a sigh of relief when he heard the trumpets and pounding horses' hooves of the Armor Bearers entering the North and the South of the camp. Captain Adams shot another arrow and hit the soldier beside Rakar. When the captain saw that Rakar had seen him, he turned and ran into a cave. Rakar motioned Jim Lee to come.

"Yes, sir!"

"Jim, Captain Adams and some of the elite troops, are shooting our soldiers. He ran into a cave on the mountain. I'm going after him."

Jim Lee grabbed Rakar's arm. "Do you want me to go with you?"

"No, stay here and help the soldiers."

"Sir," Jim Lee shouted.

"Yes."

"Be careful."

Rakar nodded and ran toward the mountain. He had to dodge a barrage of arrows to enter the cave.

One Hundred-One

The Enemy Gathers

Shemed summoned the leaders of the dark force to the gate called Beautiful. Telmar, Delilah, Iris and Captain Adams came instantly. Shemed was pacing like a caged animal. His long, white hair with a black streak in the middle was pulled back into a ponytail. His eyes were so black you couldn't tell if he even had pupils. His skin was a pasty white. He towered seven feet, all of which was solid muscle. His uniform consisted of a sleeveless, black, leather toga that laid about his thighs. A breastplate, made of silver, with a raised cobra, covered his chest. His head was adorned with a silver helmet, which served as a platform for a cobra with jeweled eyes and long sharp fangs that sat in a coiled striking position, towering over Shemed's brows. Black leather sandals were laced up to his knees. The straps stretched tightly against the muscles in his legs, leaving a web print in his dark, sweaty skin. The sword that hung from his side was so immense it carved a trail in the dirt as he walked. Two serpents twisted together, made up the handle of his great sword. Shemed came to a halt and furiously stabbed his sword into the ground. Wiping the sweat from his forehead he ordered, "Do you see this sword that I drove into the ground? I want each one of your swords along with mine, shoved through Rakar's despicable heart. Jewel has ordered us to make an end of him. Fast!"

Shemed paced back and forth until the end time warriors arrived. Shemed shouted, "We must protect Jewel and the deep magic at any cost. Rayon has released the white prophets to come against us. Haleb will lead them into the battle." Shemed shook his head and laughed aloud. "Rakar's appearance on the scene was the sign to us that the last battle has begun. He must be stopped. There is one person who will bring Haleb to his knees."

Shemed pulled his sword from the ground and held it high above his head and roared, "Queen Jewel!"

Dazzling displays of lightning ignited in front of the evil force. When it cleared, Queen Jewel, stood motionless before them with her arms folded and her eyes closed. Slowly, she lowered her arms and opened her mystical, oval green eyes. She raised her chin and moved slowly toward Telmar. Stopping before him, she seductively smiled. Without taking her eyes from Telmar, she said, "Why did you summon me, Shemed? Is there a problem?"

"Yes, my queen, there is."

Queen Jewel swiftly turned her attention to Shemed. "What male leader is about to meet his demise? It must be a man. If it were a woman, Telmar would handle the job for me. So, tell me, who is going down?"

Shemed shouted, "General Rakar!"

Queen Jewel egotistically laughed. "What a pleasure! I will handle this mission. He has never had an illusion like me before. When do you need the general disarmed?"

Shemed lifted his brows. "Today, my queen."

Queen Jewel's attention turned again to Telmar. She smiled and ran her finger down Telmar's cheek. "Consider it done."

Shemed and the leaders lowered their heads and shouted, "Glory to Queen Jewel and the Gray Stone Kingdom!"

Jewel waved her hand and disappeared.

Shemed whispered, "Tell the gate keeper no one is to enter the gate."

Captain Adams nodded. "Yes, Shemed."

"Delilah appeared among the group. She smiled at Shemed. "I got here as soon as I heard a battle is about to take place."

"How are things in Calvin Point?" Shemed asked.

"As they should be. Victoria's body will be burned to a crisp before the night is over."

"We better get back to the battle. Rakar is on his way."

One Hundred-Two

Meeting Queen Jewel

When Rakar stepped into the cave, it was the most intense darkness he had ever been in, other than the dark valley. Rakar's heart raced from fear. He took a few steps and turned to retreat, but he couldn't see where he was going. He stretched his hand forward to help find his way back to the opening of the cave, but there was no opening. He had gone only a few steps forward, turned and tried to back-track but still couldn't find the entrance. Sweat beaded on his forehead, and his mouth was so dry it hurt to breath in. "Oh, God," he prayed through trembling lips. Rakar could hear obnoxious breathing all around him. He raised his hands out in front of him, hoping to touch nothing but the entrance of the cave as he walked amid the darkness. He had taken only a few more steps when he felt someone touch him from behind. Rakar turned like lightning and shouted, "Who's there?" Then he felt someone touching him from the left and all around. Rakar ran so fast he could barely catch his breath. He stopped, leaned forward and held both knees. Slowly, he raised himself, put one hand on his chest and coughed. Rakar froze when laughter echoed through the darkness. Trying to see was useless.

"What's the matter, Rakar? Are you tired?" a deep voice from the darkness asked.

Rakar responded at once, "I'm tired of your games, Shemed. Are you afraid to show yourself?"

At once Rakar saw a dim light in the distance and began to move cautiously toward it. At the end of the darkness, a giant door gradually opened. Through the entrance, an enormous room was aglow with hundreds of candles. Rakar noticed right away a long, black table from the Middle Ages era. Around the table were twenty-four elaborate chairs having the appearance of thrones. The seats were covered with red satin padded cushions. The centerpiece on the table was a large, gold bowl with a stunning pedestal. The bowl was overflowing with fruit. At one end of the table, a crystal plate was filled with all Rakar's favorite foods, along with his favorite drinks and desserts. A black, wrought-iron chandelier hung from a towering ceiling with twenty-four large, red candles glowing brightly. The far end of the great room cratered a massive fireplace, which would hold half a log. Illustrious flags and tapestries garnished the walls of the room. Moving cautiously, Rakar's steps echoed like beating on an empty barrel with a stick. A large door opened at the right side of the fireplace. A lovely servant girl announced, "General Rakar, come and meet Queen Jewel."

One look at the radiant woman he was introduced to, gave Rakar the rationale for her name. She wore more jewelry than he had ever witnessed on one person. Her neck was layered with gold chains. Rubies, emeralds and diamonds filled her fingers. Rubies and emeralds framed her earlobes. Diamond combs assembled her auburn hair to the crown of her head. A gigantic emerald dangled from the gold chain that fit snuggly around her head and rested between her emerald green eyes. Gold bracelets adorned her wrists and forearms. A long, purple chiffon, sleeveless dress revealed her bountiful breasts. Her tiny waist was hugged by a wide gold chain. The elegant chiffon exposed her long shapely legs. Moving slowly toward Rakar, she extended her hand to him. Rakar held her hand and lowered his head. The candles sparkled like diamonds in the pupils of her exuberant eyes. Red full lips, painted eyes and the sensual smell of sweet perfume were fascinating. Rakar looked into her eyes, and her smile made visible her snow-white teeth.

Standing before him was the most enchanting woman Stephen had ever seen. Her eyes were riveting as she glared into his eyes.

"General Rakar, won't you please come and dine with me?" Queen Jewel asked as she pointed toward the end of the table. "I had my servants prepare your favorite foods."

Rakar looked at the table. "How did you know I would be here, and who told you about my favorite foods?"

"I know all about you, General Rakar. Now come eat, you must be famished."

When she took Rakar's hand, he followed without resistance. Her sophisticated beauty was stunning and evaporated all Rakar had heard about Jewel being the queen of the dark kingdom. She pulled him to his chair and he sat. Rakar was very hungry and thirsty. He picked up a fork and paused. Everything screamed for him to get away from Jewel immediately. He stood at once and threw the fork down.

"I didn't come here to eat. I came looking for Captain Bill Adams. What is this place and how is it in a cave on the side of the mountain?"

"You are so full of questions, Rakar. I'm a bit surprised you haven't asked who I am."

Rakar snarled. "I know who you are. You're a queen of something, but you're not *my* queen. King Rayon and the White Stone Kingdom are the ones I bow *my* knee too."

"Rakar, you and I are here because Rayon wants you here. I am a queen in Rayon's army. I want to assure you the only reason you couldn't find your way out of the cave was so you would end up here. If you could have found the exit, you would have never made it here to me. That's way I sealed the exit. Rayon said it was finally time for you to meet me."

Rakar fixed his stern eyes on Jewel. "And why is that, Jewel?"

Queen Jewel raised her head and moved to the fireplace. "Rakar, I serve under Haleb, one of the leaders of White Stone. You may have heard that Eri the Watcher was second under Haleb's command. Not true."

I don't trust you, Jewel. I don't believe you serve with Haleb or under King Rayon's command. My mother and father told me about you. You fell from White Stone. I saw you in Eden with Acor and Hannah."

Queen Jewel laughed aloud. "What a deception! Flesh man falls so easily for everything. I have dwelt in King Rayon's presence for eons. If you weren't supposed to meet me here, why would Rayon allow it?"

Rakar tilted his head. "I asked before and will ask again, 'Why would Rayon want me to meet you?'"

Jewel moved close to Rakar and spoke softly. "I've been ordered to warn you that everyone under your command is not as they appear."

"Then tell me, if you truly know who that would be?"

Jewel frowned. "Of course, I know who they are. How could I warn you, if I had no knowledge of who the enemy is?"

Tell me this, Jewel, why would Rayon bring me to you and not speak to me himself, or to one of my leaders?"

Queen Jewel turned her back to Rakar and stared at the amber flames in the fireplace. "If you believe that I wasn't sent here to bring you the warning, then you are free to leave." She waved her hand toward the door, and it opened at once.

Rakar didn't move. "I'm willing to hear what you have to say and then judge."

Jewel licked her lips and continued, "You're not going to like what I have to say."

"I'll be the judge of that, as well," Rakar said.

"Dale Thomas has been planted to destroy you, Stephen."

"That's a lie!" Rakar said without hesitation.

Jewel tightened her lips and snapped, "You're fast to judge without hearing me out."

Rakar's response was solid. "I know Dale Thomas. His spirit bears out that he is a true soldier of the Most High God."

"So, you are calling me a liar and I have barely spoken?"

"I've known Dale Thomas a lot longer than I have known you. I've seen him in action. I've seen him kill the enemy, and we have prayed to God together."

"Believe what you want, Rakar. Do you want me to tell you about your name?"

"What about my name?"

Jewel laughed aloud. "You're not General Rakar. You're Stephen Daniel Harris, the son of John and Rachel Harris. Your grandfather and grandmother sailed to the United States from Belfast, Ireland, on the, Queen Mary. I even know that you are still a virgin. Victoria was sent to seduce you in every sexual area. She was to lead you sexually into the places you have restricted yourself from. You passed the test, but came so close to giving in. I also know that Shemed told you that if you didn't kill Victoria, he would kill Leann Conners. Telmar killed Victoria. Must I go on, Stephen?"

Rakar snapped, "What do you want from me? I don't need you to warn me about Dale Thomas. I'll determine who he is. Now, if there is nothing further, I want to join my men."

Stephen Caught

Queen Jewel took a pear from the fruit bowl, licked her lips and took a bite. She licked the juice from her lips. "Hum, this taste so sweet." She placed it to Rakar's lips. "Taste it, Stephen."

Rakar allowed his eyes to meet hers. They held their stare for a moment without speaking. Her face was bathed in the flickering light of the candles. The red on her lips was so alluring. Still holding his stare into her eyes, Rakar bit into the pear. He knew in his heart he needed to look away, but he could not. Jewel put her hand behind his head and pulled his face closer. She pressed her full lips to Stephen's and passionately kissed him. "Stephen," she whispered. The lustful, breathy sound of his name on her lips made him shudder. He could feel his breath intensifying, and the urge to take her was overpowering.

Stephen whispered, "Oh, God . . . oh, God . . ."

Her breath was hot and rapid against his neck. *"Why don't I run? I need to run!"* Stephen thought. He could pull away from Leann and Victoria, but why couldn't he pull away from the sensual goddess before him. She took his hand and guided his fingertips to her lips. Stephen could barely breathe. *Why didn't I move her hand?* he thought. He could feel her fingers moving slowly up and down on his thigh. Again, she kissed him, but this time Stephen kissed back. He held her face in his hands and kissed her intensely. He was so caught up in the woman touching him, he had to remind himself at times to breathe. The thoughts racing through his head as he touched her soft skin were unlike anything he had ever experienced. Stephen trembled from fear and passion at the same time—so scared, yet paralyzed by her touch. Queen Jewel took the dark cape from Stephen's shoulders revealing the white uniform underneath. Kissing him eagerly, she removed the helmet and stroked his ebony hair. With her soft hands, she worked her way to the belt that held his sword, loosened his belt, and threw it aside. She took Stephen's hands and passionately whispered, "Come with me to the fire, Stephen."

Stephen followed Jewel like a lamb to the slaughter. He had lost sight of everything except the lust that burned like fire within him. A door opened at the side of the room that led the way to a large bedroom illuminated with candles. Deep purple, satin sheets and pillows adorned the round bed. Soft, white fur covered the floor. Queen Jewel guided Stephen to the bed and gently pushed him down. She removed Stephen's boots and the linen tunic he was wearing and threw it aside. She ran her fingertips across Steven's shoulders and whispered, "You are so beautiful, Stephen." With the clap of her hands, two servant girls appeared. She ordered them to run a hot bath with perfumed oils and soap, to bathe him and to bring him back to her quickly."

Stephen's will had fallen prey to the dark kingdom's deception. He settled into the hot water and closed his eyes, forgetting everything but the queen's beauty and touch. The servant girls bathed, dried and draped him with a royal blue silk robe. Upon entering the bedroom, Stephen's appetite peaked. Jewel had taken the diamond combs from her long, auburn hair that now lay loose down her back. The servants removed her robe, and she stood before him naked. His desire to run had vanished. Using the deep magic, Jewel pulled him to her, groaning out of control. Deep inside, the carnal passion that controlled Stephen was sheer ecstasy. He held Jewel snugly and trembled. Suddenly a pain shot through Stephen, triggering something from the depths of his soul. He felt dizzy. He closed his eyes as a deluge of exiled emotions thrust over him in a rushing torrent. He buried his face and tried to decree it away. He wanted to weep. Shaking out of control, Stephen tried to pull away from the enchantress that was touching him. Jewel put her arms around him and attempted to kiss him again.

This time Stephen fought back. "No, no!" he cried.

Jewel moaned, please, Stephen, one more time before you go. You were wonderful."

The realization of what he had done seized Stephen's soul. He had to forcibly push Jewel away. She sat on the bed and began to laugh out loud.

"You, weak fool," she snarled. Her voice was hideous and her beauty had faded. For a moment, the breath went out of Stephen's lungs, and he could only stare at the creature before him.

Her words pierced his heart. "You seem to have made a choice for the dark kingdom. I am so pleased, so pleased. I know you feel a bit sad now; however, wasn't it fun, General Rakar? You really are General Rakar, you know. It would appear that I have lied to you about your name. And it would definitely appear that you fell head over heels for it." Jewel laughed uncontrollably. "I'm such a naughty girl."

Stephen felt so numb that he could hardly discern what was real and what wasn't.

Jewel continued her rants as Stephen sat with his head lowered. "Answer me, Rakar, did you go to the Garden of Eden or not? If so, didn't you learn anything? Didn't you see how Acor was seduced?" Jewel stood and paraded around in front of the bed where he was sitting. "One kiss and you allowed me to take your mantel off. Another kiss and off came your helmet. A nibble on your earlobe, and your boots were removed. Alas, one touch to your thigh, and I took away your most crucial part of your armor, your sword. You stood before me naked. I marvel that you not only let me strip you of your armor, but even more that you could not wait to enter the forbidden fire. I heard your erotic moans and felt your untamed emotions. What is the Most High thinking of you now, General? You may as well ravish me again. Acor couldn't resist the seduction of the deep magic, so don't feel too sad, Rakar. You're not the only one. We all have those untamed characteristics. Rayon would deny his followers the excitement of the strange fire. I, on the other hand, encourage my followers to enter the fire as often as they like."

Rakar shook his head and whispered, "What have I done?"

Jewel put her face close to Rakar's. "You have satisfied the one thing you thought you had conquered, the lewdness of your weak flesh. I feel sorry for all White Stone's soldiers. Take Telmar. He was a servant of King Rayon until he met me and my mystical seduction. The deep magic can be very persuasive. However, you gave into it of your own desire. No matter, I will allow you to be a private in my army, and I will send for you often."

Enraged, Rakar stood, tightened his fists and screamed, "Shut up!"

Jewel chuckled. "Or what? You were so weak you didn't even put up resistance to slave girls bathing your luscious body."

Furious, Rakar shouted, "I said shut up!"

Jewel pouted and moaned. "You sure weren't talking to me like that a minute ago. Use a girl and then treat her like dirt. Men are all the same."

Rakar demanded, "I want out of here now!" He went to the door and tried to open it, but it wouldn't open. He turned and shouted, "Open the door!"

"I'll open the door . . . only because I have accomplished my mission. By the way, Rakar, you may look one last time at the weapon that brought you down so easily." Jewel pushed her shoulders back and rubbed her hands across her perfectly flat stomach. "When you need me, General, just call. I'll take you to the Garden of Fire anytime."

Stephen felt sick to his stomach. He stepped outside the door . . . not into the dense darkness as before, but onto a dirt road. The door slammed shut and vanished. Trees stood where the door had been. Stephen wandered aimlessly down the narrow, dirt road bordered with large pine and oak trees. Dust fogged the air with each step. The road was very dry, but the meadows were plush green. Where would the road lead? Was this place on the mountain? His insides felt as though they were going to explode. At this point, Stephen could care less if he died, or not.

One Hundred-Four

The Little Church

The dry, dusty road led to a small, country area. In the distance he saw a plank house with smoke spiraling from the chimney. The once white picket fence that encircled the yard of the house needed to be repaired. Stephen was so thirsty that he began walking toward the house, hoping to get a drink of water. He came to a small, opened gate and paused. Beside the house, a towering oak tree held a swing on one of the sturdy branches. The tree was filled with limbs that pointed in every direction. Abruptly, Stephen turned without entering the gate. Looking ahead, he saw on a small knoll before him a modest, white church that was in desperate need of a coat of paint. He stared at the church and wondered if it might be open. Curious to find out, he walked sluggishly up the hill and stopped at the plank porch. He felt too ashamed to even enter the door, yet the burning desire to enter could not be denied. Stephen started to put his foot on the bottom step but noticed the step was broken . . . like his heart. He wished there was some way to dull the pain and stop the voices from reminding him of what he had done. He moaned as he sat down on the edge of the porch. Sitting there, with his head lowered, he asked himself the question, *Why would I stay and listen to Jewel? I knew she was from the dark kingdom, yet I played right into her hands so easily? Was it her beguiling beauty, or was it something deep inside my own heart?*

He had fought with unyielding fervor to keep himself disciplined and pure. The mantel that was passed to him from his mother required that he have complete control over his body, mind and spirit. Until now, he had succeeded in remaining a virgin. His thought of hurting God was devastating, and how could he possibly face Leann? He had totally failed the test God had put before him.

Completely unaware of the time, Stephen had been sitting there until the sun had gone down. Exhausted, he thought of making his bed on the porch. Mounting guilt would not let him go inside the church. He stood to take his cape off to use for a pillow. Turning to face the church, Stephen's eyes widened as he noticed a faint light coming from the windows, and the door was now ajar. He looked around to see if he could see anyone. *Who turned the lights on, and who opened the door?* He had been sitting there all evening, and no one had approached or entered the church. Curious, Stephen decided to look inside. The second step that led to the porch cracked when he put his weight on it. Stephen gasped and leaped to the porch. Carefully pushing the door open, he called out, "Hello, is anyone here? Hello." He warily stepped inside the small dimly lit sanctuary. The floor and pews were made up of aged planks. Totally different than the churches he attended at Todd's Creek or Calvin's Point.

Again, Stephen called out, "Is anyone here?" Still no answer. He slowly closed the door and sat on the back pew. Flashes of many pulpits invaded his mind, which was a welcome change from the voice of his accuser. Raising his head, he saw something that was out of place in the humble surroundings. Above the common board pulpit was the most extraordinary stained-glass window he had ever seen. On the glass was depicted a soldier lying wounded beside a mountain stream. The colors were brilliant reds, blues, purples, greens, whites, and yellows. He sat for a while, staring at the painting on the window, and wondering how to ask God to forgive him.

Stephen closed his eyes and leaned his head back resting it on the back of the pew. He wanted to forget the mountain, General Rakar, Eden's Gate . . . all of it. All he wanted was for nothing else to happen to him, at least for a while. Regardless of what, it didn't matter. He was too broken at the present to deal with another thing.

He wanted to cry, scream, or beat the walls, but could not. What would his mom and dad think? Philip would have a fit. There was no telling what Cordilia and Paul would do if they could see him now. Leann was a godly woman, but would she never speak to him again if she knew of his grave sin? It wasn't just any woman he had fallen prey to, but Queen Jewel! She represented everything evil, and he knew it.

While staring at the wounded soldier lying beside the stream in the stained glass, Stephen began to softly quote scriptures. He had to fight against the opposing forces that would keep him in despair. Tears welled up in his eyes. Slowly, Stephen stood and walked to the altar. There, he knelt and wept aloud and called out to God. "Father, you know where I am. I'm lost, I'm scared, and I am so sorry. Please forgive me. Please forgive me."

Stephen sensed that someone was watching him. He quickly raised his head, only to see the old soldier Hopewell. Stephen whispered his name, "Hopewell."

Hopewell moved to Stephen. "What are you doing here, General Rakar? Get up and go back to the battle. Who is commanding your men?"

Stephen stood and stuttered, "You - you don't understand. I-I."

Hopewell frowned. "Did you ask the Most High to forgive you, or not?"

Stephen nodded yes.

"Then what's the problem? If you are forgiven, don't stay here and wallow in your self-pity. Get up and go on. Each moment you stay here is a wasted moment. Go back to the battle, General."

Hopewell disappeared before Stephen could say anything. Stephen wished he knew how to get back to the battle, but he didn't. Therefore, he decided to rest on the pew and pray God would help him find his way back to the battle. He folded his cape and lay down on the pew, hoping to get some rest.

One Hundred-Five

Rakar Wounded

Stephen felt sharp pains shooting through his arm and chest. He moaned fiercely and tried to turn, but the pain was too intense.

A low voice said, "Here, here, Rakar. Don't try to turn. Lay still until Mylo gets here."

Rakar blinked his eyes and groaned, "Is that you, Jim Lee?"

Jim patted Rakar's shoulder. "Yes, it is; you try to lay still buddy, Mylo is on her way."

"Where am I, Jim?" Rakar asked.

"You took arrow in your shoulder and have lost quite a bit of blood, but you're going to be okay." Jim said.

Tears welled up in Rakar's eyes, as he looked at Jim and whispered in a broken voice. "I didn't mean to do it. I don't know why I gave in to her. I knew better, Jim. I knew better."

"What are you talking about, Rakar? You gave into who?" Jim questioned.

Agitated Rakar said, "Queen Jewel. She was in the mountain." Rakar frantically scanned the area. "How did I get here, Jim?"

"Do you remember that you were going into the cave after Captain Adams? Just as you stepped inside, an arrow hit you. We brought you here and you have been unconscious until now."

Confused by his statement, Rakar asked, "How long has that been?"

"About twenty-four hours. Mylo has been on the other side of the mountain attending other wounded soldiers. That's what's taking so long."

"What about Queen Jewel and the little church with the stained-glass window?" Rakar asked.

Jim tightened his brows. "I don't know anything about Queen Jewel or a little church, but I do know you've been running a high fever and talking out of your head for a while now. I'll bring Mylo as soon as she arrives. Would you like a sip of water?"

Rakar tried to push himself up, but couldn't. Jim Lee again advised him to be still. "Rakar." Jim Lee said, "We've been praying for you. Our losses have been high. The enemy has continued to attack without ceasing."

At that moment, Mylo entered the cave. She immediately unzipped her pouch and took the red stone out. "Lord above, General Rakar. I don't like the circumstances that keeps bringing us together."

Rakar managed a grin. "Tell me, Mylo, where did you get the red stone?"

Mylo placed the stone over his face and moved it in a circle, then down his body. Rakar felt like hot coals were being poured over his frame. "How does that feel, Rakar?" Mylo asked as she put the stone away.

"I can't understand how that works." Rakar immediately set up as good as new. Only a scar remained. "You still didn't tell me where the stone came from."

"It came off the altar of the Most High God." Mylo replied sternly.

Stunned by the answer, Rakar asked, "The alter, how did you get it from the altar?"

"I earned it. I was entrusted to use it only for the kingdom of the Most High."

She patted his shoulder. "You take care and don't make me have to use it on you again, but if you need me, call."

The sounds of bombs exploding and gunfire echoed in the distance indicating there was no time to linger in the cave. "Jim Lee! Where is my sword?" Stephen asked.

He hurried to a green blanket and took the sword from underneath it. Rakar took hold of the handle and the ruby stone glowed, producing heat to Rakar's hand.

The ground began to rumble when a bomb hit close to the cave. Rakar heard the explosion then the chilling moans and cries for help. General Rakar rushed out of the cave and ran into a messenger. Breathlessly he uttered, "General Rakar, the northern side has been hit hard. The casualties are enormous."

Rakar put his cape on and asked the soldier to take him, and Jim Lee, to the northern entrance. As they hurried up the gorge, a cry sounded that sent coldness to their bones. People from all three kingdoms were in full retreat. The scene before them was utter chaos. The dark kingdom forces were driving the people from White Stone, Emerald Shores and Highland Kingdom's toward the narrow space that led into the dark valley.

Rakar shouted, "Jim Lee, sound the trumpet and send a soldier, find Dale Thomas and tell him to join us at the northern pass and bring reinforcements." After sounding the trumpet, many warriors came from the higher levels of the mountain to assist. General Rakar, Jim Lee and Mylo led the troops against the evil force with a vengeance. The first maneuver was to block the entrance to the dark valley to save King Rayon's people from a well-organized trap. After which they would surround the enemy force and destroy it. Some made their way through the narrow passage regardless of how aggressive the Armor Bearers were. Rakar swung his sword killing every enemy he fought.

Those that were not killed, began to retreat. The narrow opening of the gorge had been secured, or so Rakar thought. As the Armor Bearers moved forward from the narrow pass, General Rakar heard a distinct cry for help from behind him. He turned to view a hand coming from the darkness pulling a young boy into the trap. Rakar yelled and hurried to seize the boy, that was now at the entrance. Rakar took custody of the boy's waist and pulled him from the giant hand that held him. He pushed the boy to safety and groaned loudly when the hand grabbed hold of his arm and began pulling him into the thick darkness. Rakar swiftly administered a blow that severed the hand, but it was too late. He too had been jerked into the dark vacuum.

One Hundred-Six

Going through the Gate

$\mathcal{T}$hrough his spirit eyes, Rakar could see the immense valley filled with people. All of which were drawn into oblivion with lies and lovely illusions. Rakar made his way through the people. His ears were ringing with moans, groans, and cries for help. With every step he prayed, "Spirit of the Most High, be a light to my feet."

General Rakar saw the gate called Beautiful towering ahead of him. He was astounded to see Dale Thomas standing near the opening. "Dale, what are you doing here?"

"I was waiting for you. I knew you would come. Did you forget, I was the one that brought you here the first time?"

"I'm just glad you're here. We must do something to set the people free so they too can enter the gate they've been in darkness way to long."

Rakar moved to the center of the gate, raised his sword, and demanded, "In the name of . . ." Dale shouted, "NO RAKAR!"

Startled, Rakar turned to Dale who was holding his sword toward him. "Dale, what are you doing?"

"You are not going to open the gate, Rakar."

Rakar was stunned. "Why not? That's our mission as servants of the Most High God."

Dale's countenance and voice had changed. He shook his head and said in a deep pitch, "I am the keeper of this gate and no one is to enter. Most of all you, Rakar."

Distraught, Rakar shouted, "Oh my, God, not you, Dale. We prayed together and I saw you kill the enemy."

"No, Rakar. Some were sacrificed in order to draw bigger game. Like you."

A voice from behind Rakar shouted, "I told you Dale Thomas was not what he appeared, didn't I, General?"

Rakar gasped as Queen Jewel arrogantly come from the other side of the gate. Rakar looked at Dale and pleaded, "Dale, call out to King Rayon, he will set you free."

Dale laughed aloud. "I'm where I want to be, by choice. Queen Jewel is my master."

Rakar raised his sword and declared, "I am going to open that gate, Dale, in the name of the King Rayon. I'm going through, even if it means taking you out. I thought you were an Armor Bearer and my friend. Does Jim Lee know about this?"

"No one knows. They, like you, are too blind to see." He smirked.

"Let me correct you, Dale." Jewel inserted. "I knew and I told Rakar, but he was too busy wanting to enter the Garden of Fire to listen."

"I'm not sure I care for that, Jewel." A voice said. "I'm Telmar, the sex god of the dark kingdom. Were you trying to take my place, Rakar?" Telmar's black eyes gleamed. He pulled a gigantic sword from his belt and pointed it toward Rakar.

"I don't think Rakar understands that once you enter the strange fire, you can never go back again."

Rakar trembled when Pastor Reynolds came from the dense fog that blocked the entrance. "Pastor Reynolds!"

He laughed aloud and transformed before Rakar. "No, Rakar. I'm not your gutless Pastor Reynolds. Queen Jewel loves to use the pulpit for her work, therefore she ordered me to destroy the good pastor and preach the gospel in his place. Rakar, the congregation loved me."

"Shemed!" Rakar said breathlessly.

"Oh, Rakar knows who I am now, but sitting on the church pew, he was like everyone else." Shemed tauntingly said.

"You killed Pastor Reynolds?" Rakar asked.

Shemed pulled his sword and touched the end of the blade, causing blood to run down his finger. Licking the blood away, he said, "Yes, and for the same reason, I'm going to kill you. He knew too much. He was finding the truth about the mysteries of the ages. Those mysteries have been carefully hidden for eons and that's where they will stay. Your mother Rachel, and that dreadful Cordilia, thought that they could bring 'the truth' out and now you are endeavoring to do the same. Therefore, you too will die."

"Not today, Shemed!" A voice shouted.

Shemed swiftly looked to the right side of the cave. Haleb, moved slowly from the shadows and stood beside Rakar.

"Haleb!" Shemed gasped.

Immediately, another voice announced, "Surprise, Shemed! That dreaded Cordilia that you were just talking about is here to see that no harm comes to General Rakar." Cordilia took her place beside Haleb.

"Rehabiah! (Ree huh Bye uh) You she devil. I should have known." Shemed ranted.

"Where are your manners, Shemed? Calling my wife a devil. I may have to adjust your disposition." Paul stated as he took his place beside Cordilia.

Shemed growled, "Jathniel!"

At once, another voice declared, "I took the day off to have a good fight. I think I've come to the right place." Ian Jackson said, as he moved from the dark shadows, and took his place beside Rakar and the others.

Shemed raged, "Mikneiah! I hate you!"

"I know, Shemed." Ian mocked.

Another powerful voice declared, "I came because I am a lawman and somebody may need to be arrested." Sheriff Bolton jested as he to his place with Rakar.

Shemed shouted, "Ismachiah! I'll see you in hell."

Rakar was dumbfounded. He saw Cordilia and Paul, but in a different light than he could have imagined. Shemed had called each one by their angelic name. Rakar could hardly catch his breath. He knew about Haleb, Cordilia and Paul having an angelic name and his mom and dad, but Ian and Sheriff Bolton was a total surprise. They each wore the white linen uniform with gold trim. In raised lettering, 'Truth' filled the blades of their swords. With confidence, General Rakar untied the dark cape that hid his uniform and threw it to one side. Now was the right time for his rank to shine among the people and before the enemy.

Shemed and the evil force stood with their swords drawn. "I think you're standing on the wrong side, Haleb. Your perfect General Rakar has fallen from grace, to pleasure. He truly entered the forbidden tree in the Garden of Fire. Isn't that right, Rakar?"

"Your lies and illusions didn't bring me down. I did sin, by allowing you to play games with my mind. I should have rebuked it right away. I don't care what accusations you throw at me; I'm going through that gate. The people that fill the dark valley will be freed and will enter the gate called Beautiful. False priests and prophets will no longer prevent these souls from entering the Holy of Holies, where they can bask in the Shekinah glory of Most High God. The truth will set them free. They've never known why they're here, or what their destiny is, but that's about to change. As we speak, the true priests and prophets have been released to flood the earth with truth."

Queen Jewel roared, "Kill them!"

Instantly, swords were raised and cold steal clang together. Haleb was fighting with Telmar, Paul was fighting with one of Jewel's top generals, Amash. Cordilia grabbed Delilah as she entered the area. Ian fought with Queen Jewel, Sheriff Bolton with Dale Thomas and Rakar with Shemed.

One Hundred-Seven
Angelique

*A*ll of heaven was on full alert to witness the onslaught that would open the entrance of the gate called Beautiful. One stood alone, watching intensely. "Come on, Rakar, you can do it. Get him!" The voice called out. A touch on her shoulder caused her to jump. "Angelique."

She put her hand on her chest and sighed, "Yes." She paused, looked into the angel's eyes and froze.

"Is something wrong, Angelique?" He asked.

She slowly shook her head and laughed. "Eri! I knew I recognized your eyes. So, you were born Philip Dawson?"

Eri nodded. "Yes."

"I should have known. You were the one King Rayon sent to tell Rachel that she would have a son."

"Exactly."

"Stephen doesn't have a clue about you."

"No, he doesn't. Nor will he, until Rayon allows me to tell him. I was dispatched immediately after my visit to Rachel, I was sent into Cordilia's womb. I was to grow up with Stephen and watch after him."

Surprised, Angelique questioned, "Did Rachel and Cordilia know?"

"I was with Rachel when she died. She always thought that I reminded her of someone, but could never quite figure out who, like you. Before her last breath, I told her that I was Eri."

Angelique turned to watch Rakar in the fight. "Poor Stephen doesn't have a clue that he is one of the highest ranking angels in White Stone Kingdom?"

Eri looked toward Rakar and said, "He'll know when it's time. Angelique, would you like to join the fight?"

She quickly looked at Eri and said, "May I?"

Eri grinned and said, "You may join the fight, but first, King Rayon sent me to tell you that Rakar will be knocked down soon and he wants you to be there and send Shemed to hell."

Excited, Angelique pulled her sword, held it before her face. "It will be honored, Eri. Thank you."

Eri put his hand on her shoulder. "Go in the power of the Most High and be victorious."

She lowered her head and prayed, "Almighty Heavenly Father, empower me to glorify your name." Instantly, she was on her way to the raging battle.

Cordilia fought against Delilah with fury. Delilah and Telmar, using the deep magic, vanished. Dale Thomas and Captain Adam's managed to get away into the darkness. Haleb heard the rumble of enemy troops infiltrating the valley. He raised his sword and cried, "Father now!" Immediately, the true priests and prophets invaded the dark valley bringing light to untold numbers instantly. The screams and growls from the demonic force were deafening. As they retreated, hope was restored to those who had lost all hope. General Rakar was feeling exhausted from battling the seven foot tall Shemed. The two had the appearance of David and Goliath. Shemed knocked the sword from Rakar's hand. He dove to get it, but before he could stand, Shemed put his oversized foot on top of Rakar's chest. He raised his sword high and groaned loudly. "Today, you die, Rakar!"

Before he could bring his sword down, a voice yelled from inside the boiling black smoke that choked the entrance of the gate. "ASHBEL!" Like lightening, Shemed turned to witness Angelique moving through the smoke. Rakar lay there unsure of what was going on, but thankful. A moment later and Shemed would have taken his head. Shemed wiped the sweat from his brow and flung it into Rakar's face.

Looking as white as his hair, Shemed growled, "So, you have come to retaliate, Angelique?"

Rakar had heard the voice that came from the entrance of the gate, but saw no one. Shemed continued to hold his foot on Rakar's chest, while keeping his eyes on the gate. Thick, black smoke boiled from the entrance as Angelique pushed her way through. Rakar gasped, not from Shemed's huge foot but from the woman that evolved from the smoke. Angelique, pointed her sword at Shemed and demanded, "Remove your stinking foot from Rakar's chest or I'll decapitate you right now."

Shemed lifted his foot and turned to face Angelique, as though Rakar wasn't there. Rakar pushed himself up with his elbow, still in total shock from the awesome woman before him.

Shemed grunted, then raised his sword toward Angelique, "Do you remember the fun we had at the field of Baal, Angelique?"

"I wasn't sent here to remember anything. I was sent here, to send you to hell, and that I'll do."

Through gritted teeth Shemed roared, "I tremble at the audacity you display."

"It's so much more than audacity, Shemed. It's an order from King Rayon."

"We'll see who is the greater power."

Shemed and Angelique hit their swords together and pushed furiously toward each other. Angelique broke loose, kicked Shemed's knee, turned in a circle and slashed his arm. Shemed violently swung at Angelique. They hit their swords so hard together it was piercing Rakar's eardrums. Stephen scooted backward, not taking his eyes from the fight. He wanted to get his sword, but Shemed had kicked it against the entrance of the gate. Almost as soon as the fight started, Rakar heard a waling groan from Shemed. He dropped his sword and slowly fell to his knees. Blood gushed from his chest, arm and thigh. Angelic stood before him and announced, "In the name of King Rayon, I send you to your queen." With those words she raised her sword with both hands, bit her lower lip and swung the sword, taking Shemed's head from his shoulders. Shemed's head hit the ground flinging his helmet from his head.

One Hundred-Eight

Victoria Explains Eden

$\mathcal{R}$akar couldn't believe his eyes. Angelique looked at Rakar and smiled. "Praise be to our God and the White Stone Kingdom forever more, General Rakar."

Rakar breathlessly said, "Victoria?"

She extended her hand to pull Rakar to his feet. "In person."

He stammered, "I-th-thought-you were dead." Rayon took me from one dimension to another." She wiped the blood from the blade of her sword and said, "Now, I know why."

"Your angel name is Angelique?" Rakar asked.

"Yes. It has quite a flare to it, don't you think?"

"What was it about the name Ashbel that would make Shemed turn white as a sheet?" Rakar questioned.

"For eons, Shemed carried the title Ashbel. Which means (man of Baal.) Baal being the pagan god that demanded that the children were to be sacrificed on his altar of fire. While the people burned their young children, they would perform wild sex orgies in front of Baal's altar. Shemed's title Ashbel gave him the honored place of throwing the children, as they screamed for their mother's and father's, into the fire. He also lurked around the tree lines, taking young virgin girls and boys who dared to come to close to the forbidden field. He would bring them to the altar of Baal and there they brutalized in the name of Baal.

I was born to Adam and Eve at the beginning of the last earth age. Believe me, I know first-hand about the Garden of Eden. My mother had told me about the deception, and deep magic that was used in the Garden of Eden, how (the serpent) beguiled or, wholly seduced her. She also told me what it was like to know the purity of God. The pain of being driven from the garden, to the field, and having *Eden's Gate* closed. That's how I knew so much about the Garden.

I too, know about disobedience. All my brothers and sisters had been warned about a place in the field that was taboo. Mother told us about the demon god, Baal, and the wicked priest of the altar, Shemed.

At time's I would go for walks, hoping to hear something from the forbidden place. One day, my curiosity got the better of me. My walk took me just close enough to the field to hear music and laughter. Instead of running back to safety, I lingered. I moved closer and closer until I could clearly hear everything. I listened and wondered how it could possibly sound like so much fun if it was so bad. However, I knew I must get back before I was missed. I turned to go and standing behind me was the white haired seven-foot tall demon, Shemed. I tried to run, but he picked me up like a rag doll. His breath was appalling. His clothing consisted of a small loincloth. When he held me against his rough body that dripped with sweat, I literally threw-up. I was carried to the forbidden field, where I saw the colossal, stone statue of Baal. The smell of flesh burning is a stench that's indescribable. I know why sin is a stench in God's nostrils. A stench that horrifying, and sickening. It's hard to find words to describe the atrocities. As a young girl, and a virgin, the nudity and sexual acts taking place repelled me. Shemed put me on a rock, literally ripped my clothes off, and motioned the men and women to come. The gruesome things that they did to me . . ." Angelic lowered her head and continued. "I thought I would die in the field of Baal, but I didn't. When they were through with me, Shemed took me outside the field and tossed me to the ground like garbage. I remember very little after that, but there is one thing I will never forget. I called out to the Most High for help."

Angelique closed her eyes, as tears rolled down her cheeks. Rakar stood in awe as he listened to her words. A glow covered her countenance as she lifted her eyes toward heaven and shifted her conversation from Rakar to the Most High and uttered, "Father, I've never forgotten the warmth of your arms that day when you lifted me and brought me home. Throughout eternity, I will praise you for you love and mercy."

General Rakar gazed at Angelique without words. After a moment, she smiled at Rakar and asked, "What is it you want to ask? Your countenance screams that you have many questions. So, ask."

"Why were you sent to Eden's Gate?"

"Many reasons. One of which, was to help guide you to the truth about the seduction that took place Garden of Eden. To make sure you knew the other garden and the two trees of fire. The tree of fire that you could visit any time and be empowered with flame of the Most High. Or enter the forbidden flame that would in the end consume you. So, few know about the two gardens. Also, to add to your knowledge about the dimension where White Stone, Emerald Shores, and Highland Kingdoms are located. One of the best kept secrets of this age is King Rayon and the three heavens. Very few will ever find out about this dimension until much later. I was also sent to prove you. You had to know what it was like to be enticed as Eve, Acor, Tashmere, and many other children that fell prey to learn the knowledge of the forbidden fire. There the deep magic was used to lure them to the strange fire afterwards they were thrust into the dark kingdom, becoming slaves to Jewel's army. You had to experience Jewel's power that rendered you powerless. Because of your rank in White Stone your heart must to be pure. There are some things you still must work through before you preach to the world. The Most High has sent some powerful angels to war on your behalf. Haleb is one of the most powerful angels in White Stone's army. Not to mention, Cordilia, Paul, Ian, and Sheriff Bolton."

"Where is Philip? I know he has a part in my life, a big part, but he wasn't here. Why?"

Angelic lifted her brows and hinted, "You don't know who all was here."

Curious, Rakar asked, "Victoria! I mean, Angelique... what should I call you?"

Victoria chuckled. "Call me Victoria."

"Will you be back at Eden's Gate?"

"No, Stephen. I think I've finished my work here, unless my orders change. However, I will be here long enough to see you enter the Beautiful Gate."

Suddenly the earth rumbled as trumpets sounded long and loud. Rakar swiftly turned to witness the most humbling sight he had ever seen. Not one soul was left bound in the dark valley that was now illuminated with the light of truth. The Armor Bearer's marched before the true priests and prophets that had invaded the darkness sounding the trumpets and drums announcing that the battle had begun. The messengers were filled with the truth of God. They marched before the people that had been enslaved by deception. The truth had set them free. Haleb lead the Armor Bearer's that marched under the banner of White Stone, to the Beautiful Gate and halted the troops where General Rakar stood with Angelique.

Haleb held his sword in front of his face and announced, "General Rakar, all the souls have been loosed. You have been appointed the leader for the final battle. Take your place; it's time to lead the people through. Open the Beautiful Gate and guide these priests, prophets and warriors alike in the power of the Most High God."

Angelique handed Rakar his sword. She smiled and lowered her head. General Rakar took hold of the handle that blazed a brilliant red, bowed on his knees and cried aloud. "Almighty God! Creator of all dimensions, in your name, I take my place in the circle of life. I accept the destiny you have placed before.

Rakar faced the army of White Stone, Emerald Shores, and Highland Kingdoms and raised his sword. Looking across the courageous warriors that had fought in the battle from the beginning he trembled. They had all been badly wounded at one time, yet they had delivered so many. Rakar knew every wound the warriors had accrued for the glory of God would shine as gold throughout eternity. He trembled as he beheld the Ancient Ones that were called *The Angels of the Ages* that now circled the warriors.

Haleb stepped forward. "General Rakar, I see the wonderment in your eyes. Every warrior here is a chosen vessel. They have fought and stood true through every battle. I have witnessed many wonders since the creation, but none compares to true love. The wounds each soldier bares are lined with true love. Faithful leaders of God's people will display that love through obedience. A true leader will love unconditionally and will fight to see one soul set free. They serve whether they are paid here, or in eternity. It's not about money or status. It's about carrying on the work of the Most High and the White Stone Kingdom."

Rakar observed the chosen ones, carefully. Their eyes were alert like men and women that refused to recognize defeat. Rakar looked at Haleb, Mylo, Ian, Sheriff Bolton, Angelique and Jim Lee. Cowardice was not in any of them. Every line and scar spoke of generations of brave and gallant warriors. Rakar boldly turned and pointed his sword to the center of the smoke screen. Instantly, demons that blocked the gate had become visible. Doubt, oppression, depression, infirmities, poverty, low self-esteem, lust, hate, pride and many more made up the darkness. Rakar shouted, "For the Most High God and the White Stone Kingdom, I command every power of darkness that blocks the entrance of the Beautiful Gate, to be bound and return to the hell from whence you came!"

A hush fell as a drum roll rumbled. The Armor Bearer's gave a blast on the trumpets, Rakar raised his sword, the host shouted and marched toward the Beautiful Gate. When General Rakar's feet stepped through the entrance, the black smoke evaporated and he was left standing in the driveway just inside *Eden's Gate*.

One Hundred Nine

Back at Eden's Gate

Stephen frantically turned and whispered, "Oh, God! Where are the Armor Bearers?" He placed his hand over his mouth and closed his eyes.

"Stephen!" Someone called.

"Victoria? Victoria!" Stephen ran to the porch and sluggishly went up the steps. "Victoria." He whispered. He gently ran his fingers down her cheek. She slapped his hand and complained. "What are you doing? I just put my rouge on and you're streaking it. You have a phone call and by the way, I'm not your secretary."

Elated, Stephen grabbed Victoria and embraced her. "You're not dead! You're here. You said you didn't think you would be back at *Eden's Gate*, but you're here. I love you, Victoria and I am so proud of you!" Tears ran down Stephen cheeks.

"Stephen, what's wrong with you?" She pushed him away and grumbled, "This dress just came from the cleaners and now look at it. You wrinkled it. Have you been drinking too much coffee?"

He took Victoria by her shoulders and asked, "Where is Cordilia, Paul and Philip?"

Victoria frowned and pushed him away. "Glory be, are you doing drugs, Stephen? You know they left for home the day after the trial. You hugged them and told them good bye. They told you they would be back in a few weeks. Don't you remember that?"

Stephen asked, "Victoria, how long have the Dawson's been gone?"

Victoria tilted her head and frowned. "Good heavens, it was yesterday. Where have you been, Stephen?"

Without answering, he asked, "Victoria, where's Ian?"

"He received a call from home. There was an emergency and he needed a few days off. No, I don't know what the emergency was. By the way, are you still going to Todd's Creek soon?"

Stephen frowned and asked, "Todd's Creek? What are you talking about?"

"Stephen, I think you're borderline crazy. I don't have time for this. I must finish packing. Charles will be here to pick me up in twenty minutes. By the way, Leann is on the phone."

Victoria swiftly turned and went into the house. Stephen ran after her. "Victoria!"

She stopped at the foot of the stairs. "Yes!"

"Why are you packing?"

"What kind of a question is that? You know my time at *Eden's Gate* has ended. I've done very well. I get all of Grandmother Stanton's fortune. She thinks you and *Eden's Gate* did wonders for me."

Victoria held Stephen's chin in her hand and shook it. "Wait until you read my magazine article about you, Calvin's Point, Ian Jackson and the charming Sheriff Bolton. It's going to run in three monthly issues. The whole world is going to know about you and *Eden's Gate*."

Stephen felt numb. Everything that had taken place burned in his soul. Victoria hurried up the stairs and Stephen hurried to the telephone. He explained to Leann what had been happening and promised to see her later.

In only a few minutes, Stephen saw the white limousine coming up the long driveway. He went outside and waited to greet Brenda Stanton. Charles got out and shouted, "Howdy, Mr. Harris! I pray you're doing well this beautiful day."

"Yes, Charles, I'm doing fine."

Charles quickly opened the car door for Mrs. Stanton. He took her hand and helped her out. Charles excused himself and hurried inside to get Victoria's luggage. Mrs. Stanton took Stephen's hands and said, "I want to thank you, personally, for what you have done for Victoria. I knew *Eden's Gate* would do wonders for her and of course I was right. You'll find that I deposited a little something extra with the $25,000.00 I promised."

Stephen shook his head. "I don't want your money, Mrs. Stanton. It's been a pleasure to accommodate Victoria. At first it was rocky, but nothing I couldn't handle."

"Let me look at you Stephen. What is this new found excitement I detect in your voice?"

"I don't know how to explain it, but when I can, I will let you know."

Charles and Victoria made their way to the car with her vast amount of luggage. Victoria looked elegant in snug fitting, sleeveless, black silk dress with a high turtleneck. A long white silk scarf with black roses draped her neck. A wide brimmed black hat with a white silk band shadowed her brow. Black and white patent leather pumps with thin ankle straps framed her long narrow feet. Her enticing perfume filled the air. Long teardrop, pearl earrings dangled from her earlobes. Ruby red lipstick colored her full lips and her long blonde hair shimmered in the sunlight. What a vision!

Brenda Stanton got into the car. Victoria smiled and closed the car door without joining her grandmother in the car. Brenda quickly rolled the window down. "I'm only teasing you, Grandmother."

"I would hope so, Victoria. I'm not trying to eavesdrop, it just very stuffy in the car."

Stephen slightly grinned at Victoria and took her hands. "It's been a pleasure to have you as my guest at *Eden's Gate*. Some of the time, anyway."

Victoria nodded. "Thank you, Stephen, for everything. There are some great things ahead for you. You have my number, call me in New York anytime. I'm going to miss this place and the people. Including Ian, but don't tell him I said that."

Victoria and Stephen embraced. "You're always welcome at *Eden's Gate*." Stephen whispered.

"Even after you're married?" Victoria teased.

"Anytime."

"We had better be going, Miss Victoria." Charles said as he opened her door.

Victoria quickly hugged Stephen and whispered, "With God, all things are possible, General Rakar. Don't forget Angelique told you that."

She hurriedly got into the car before Stephen could respond. The white stretch limousine exited Eden's Gate.

One Hundred Ten

The Gate Opens

That night after Stephen had prayed, he went to bed but couldn't sleep. His mind was on overload. The house felt so empty. He missed Victoria, Cordilia, Paul and Philip. The alarm clock on the night stand said it was midnight in bright red numbers. Stephen wanted to clear his mind, so he put his robe on and made his way to the porch swing that repeatedly proved to be a place of solace, like his dad told him.

The beauty of the full moon illuminated the night. A meager gust of wind stirred a sweet smell from the large magnolia tree that stood at the side of the house. Stephen couldn't remember when he had seen so many stars in the sky at one time. He pushed himself back and forth and recalled the events at the Beautiful Gate. Over and over, Stephen envisioned himself going through that gate leading the people. Looking at the sky he wondered what his near future would hold? Stephen knew Leann would help fill a big part of his future, however, the part of his future that burned like fire in his soul, no man could satisfy. The one thing he had known, since he was a little boy, was finally maturing. He would one day preach the gospel around the world. Knowing the magnitude of responsibility being entrusted to him was at times frightening. He also knew the call on his life would bring immense opposition from the dark kingdom.

He smiled remembering, King Rayon, and the ancient book, titled, Angels of the Ages. Stevens vision of the mighty warrior eagle Raptor, and the White Stallion, as they entered the arena at the Garden of Eden. Stephen lifted his hands toward heaven as he remembered the magnificent *Angels of the Ages* as they entered the theater in their white linen robes. Each one held their towering posture straight; their eyes were clear and bright and their steps were filled with commitment. Stephen messaged his temples trying to make since of it all. Sitting on his porch at Calvin's Point, it all seemed like a fairy tale, was it a dream? As he pushed back and forth the poem, he had heard earlier took total control of his spirit. Even though he had only heard the poem once, he repeated it word for word.

Through the garden gate.
Are riches yet unknown.
Through the garden gate
Is the pathway to the throne.

What treasures there await me?
What glory will I behold?
What mysteries there will unfold for me?
The half has not been told.

So I journey on though most times,
Rough be the road;
The Spirit from the garden
Will not seem to let me go.

"Enter in, enter in,"
 Are the words He spoke to me,
"And the glory of the throne room,
 Your eyes will surely see."

Stephen looked to the sky and closed his eyes, and again he asked, "Father, is this all a dream? It seems so real, but is it?"

When Stephen opened his eyes, he gasped and leaned back in the swing. Standing at the gate was the ancient warrior, Hopewell. Stephen's eyes widened when he saw Hopewell was holding the ancient manuscript Angels of the Ages in his arms. The volume that held the ancient names of the warriors that had fought and stayed faithful to the Most High God from the beginning. Hopewell nodded and raised the book toward the sky and disappeared into the night. Stephen secured the house and went up the stairs to his room and firm bed hoping for some very peaceful sleep. He had barely closed his eyes when the sound of pouring rain, thunder claps and sheets of lighting shook the house. He got up and set on the edge of the bed, his body dripping with sweat. How could this be? Stephen questioned. An hour earlier the sky was clear, the full moon lite up the sky and millions of stars twinkled. He had checked the weather earlier and there was no call for rain for another week. Stephen walked to the window and pulled the curtain back. Lightning was so vast the sky was bright from the glow. He looked toward the front gate. A streak of lightning shot from the sky and landed the top of the gate. As the storm began to pass. Stephen closed the curtain and snuggled back into bed. As he drifted off to sleep, unbeknown to Stephen the gate began to open.

The End